The
Wicked Girls

The Wicked Girls

ALEX MARWOOD

PENGUIN BOOKS

PENGUIN BOOKS
Published by the Penguin Group
Penguin Group (USA) Inc., 375 Hudson Street,
New York, New York 10014, USA

USA I Canada I UK I Ireland I Australia I New Zealand I India I South Africa I China
Penguin Books Ltd, Registered Offices: 80 Strand, London WC2R 0RL, England

First published in Great Britain by Sphere, an imprint of Little, Brown Book Group 2012
Published in Penguin Books 2013

ISBN 978-1-62490-660-2

Printed in the United States of America

Set in Sabon LT Std

For William Mackesy

Prologue

1986

There's a blanket, but from the aroma that rises from its folds, she guesses it's never been washed. The cells are overheated and, despite the fact that Jade balled it up and pushed it into the corner of the room when they first brought her in here, the stink of stale piss and unwashed skin is hard to ignore. Officer Magill picks it up and holds it out towards her, wadded in her hand. 'You're going to have to wear this,' she says. 'Over your head. Apparently they're not allowed to see your face.'

It's hardly necessary. Jade's face was all over the papers months ago, and will be all over them again tomorrow. She looks at the blanket, repelled. Officer Magill's eyes narrow.

'You know what, Jade?' she says. 'You're welcome to go out there uncovered if you want. They're all dying to see you, believe me. It's no skin off my nose.'

They've seen me already, thinks Jade. Over and over. In the papers, on the news. That's why they make us queue up for those school mugshots every year. It's not for our families. It's so there's always a picture to sell to the papers. So they have something to hang a headline on. THE WORLD PRAYS. FIND OUR ANGEL. *Or, in my case,* ANGELIC FACE OF EVIL.

Through the open door, she can hear Bel screaming. Still screaming. She started when the verdict came in, and it's been hours since then. Jade has been able to hear only silence

1

through the thick cell walls. No sound gets through: not the baying crowd, not the hurried feet passing by in the throes of preparation. Occasionally, the metallic slick of the eyehole cover being pushed back, or the sonic boom of another heavy door slamming shut; otherwise, stone-built silence, the sound of her own breath, the sound of her racing heart. When Officer Magill opened the door, the noise was overwhelming, even here in the basement: the feral, chanting voices of strangers wanting Justice. The crowd wants her. Her and Bel. This much she knows.

Magill holds the blanket out again. This time, Jade takes it. They'll make her wear it one way or another, willing or not. Their hands brush, and Magill snatches hers away as though the child's skin is coated with poison.

Bel sounds like an animal, shrieking in a snare.

She'd chew her own arm off if it helped her get away, thinks Jade. It's worse for her than it is for me. She's not lived her life in trouble, like I have.

Officer Magill waits, her mouth downturned. 'How do you feel, Jade?'

For a moment Jade thinks that she's asking out of concern, but a glance at that face shows her otherwise. Jade gazes at her, wide-eyed. I feel small, she thinks. I feel small and alone and scared and confused. I know they're shouting for me, but I don't understand why they hate me so much. We didn't mean it. We never meant it to happen.

'Not good, is it?' asks Magill eventually, not requiring a reply. 'Doesn't feel great, does it?'

Bel's voice, the sound of struggle in the hallway: 'Nonononono! Please! Please! I can't! I want my mum! Mummeee! I can't! Don't take me out there! Nononono dooon't!'

Jade looks back at Officer Magill. Her face is like a Halloween mask, all swooping lines in black and red. She glares with all the loathing of the voices of the mob outside. Jade is guilty. No one has to act as though they presume her innocent now.

That's it, that's us: not 'the suspects', not 'the children in custody'. We're The Girls Who Killed Chloe. We are the Devil now.

Magill glances over her shoulder to see if any of her superiors are listening, then lowers her voice.

'Serves you bloody well right, you little bitch,' she hisses. 'If it was up to me they'd bring back the death penalty.'

fallen over. Martin pushes himself off the bed and goes to the window. Cracks open the curtain and looks out. Eight young women, in various stages of inebriation. The bride – shortie veil and L-plates – is on the ground, felled by six-inch heels and a portly backside. She flumps about on the pavement in her tubular mini-skirt, stomach flopping over waistband and tits overspilling her *décolletage*, while two of her friends haul at a pale and dimpled arm. The other friends are scattered across the pavement, pointing and staggering as they howl with laughter. One of them – hot pants, giant hoop earrings and a horizontal-striped boob tube – is pestering men for a light as they weave their way past the flailing bride.

Boob Tube strikes gold. A stag group – the town is overrun with them every weekend, the sort of stags who can't afford, or who lack the passports or the probationary permission, to spread sangria vomit over warm Spanish concrete – pause, light her up, fall into conversation. Well, mutual shouting. No one communicates under Martin's window at anything less than a roar, ears destroyed by thumping basslines, sense of other people destroyed by the alcohol and ecstasy and cocaine that seem to cost less than a packet of smokes these days. And you don't have to go outside to take them.

The bride finally regains her feet. She is limping, or pretending to, and uses the shoulder of a stag for support. Martin watches as the man's hand creeps down over the tube skirt, inches its way in from behind. The bride cackles, slaps him off half-heartedly and bats her lashes encouragingly. The hand goes back. They set off up the street, heading towards the nightclub quarter.

Boob Tube lags back, leaning against a shop window, talking to the man with the lighter. She sways from side to side, doesn't seem to notice as her friends disappear round the corner. She tugs at her top, pulling the droop from squashed bosoms, and flicks lacquered hair out of her eyes. Smiles at the man coquettishly, pushes lightly at his upper arm. So goes the business of modern mating. You don't even need to buy a girl a drink any more. Just lend her your lighter and she's yours for the taking.

Dropping the curtain, Martin shambles back into the darkened room, depression seeping into his pores. He doesn't understand the world. Sometimes he feels like they pick the road outside his flat just to taunt him. To remind him of the fun he's not having; of the fact that these spangled, dancing creatures would scutter over to the other side of the pavement if he tried to join in. Whitmouth is a disappointment to him. He thought, once his mother died and he was able to choose his destiny, that the world would be his oyster, life would roll his way at last, but instead he finds himself observing other people's fun as though he's watching it on television.

I thought it was Fairyland, he thinks, as he switches on the unshaded ceiling light. When I was a kid. When we used to come down here from Bromwich. It was families, then: cream teas, and the helter-skelter on the pier the tallest building for miles. That was why I came back here: all those good times, all those memories, all that hope. Now I hardly dare to look in shop doorways as I pass them, in case I see Linzi-Dawn's knees hitched up and Keifer's low-slung jeans humping away between them, and me excluded, never wanted, always looking in.

She still hasn't replied. Martin's skin prickles as he stares at the blank display. Who does she think she is?

Throwing the phone down on the bed, he turns on the television, watches the bad news scroll out on the BBC. Dammit, Jackie. You have no right to treat me like this. If you were going to turn out like the rest of them, why did you pretend to be something else?

Another shriek in the street. Martin presses the volume control, turns it up to full. The rage of rejection crawls beneath his skin; invisible, unscratchable. All she needs to do is text him back. He doesn't want to go out, but if she refuses to respond he's going to have to. As his mother was always assuring him, persistence is the most important quality in life. And he knows that he is the most persistent of all.

Chapter Two

Amber Gordon clears out the lost-property cupboard once a week. It's her favourite job of all. She likes the neatness of it, the tying up of loose ends, even if the loose end is simply deciding that, if someone's not come back in nine months, they never will. She enjoys the curiosity, the quiet sense of snooping on other people's lives as she marvels at the things – dentures, diamond earrings, diaries – that they either didn't notice were lost or didn't think worth coming back for. But most of all, she enjoys the gift-giving. For the Funnland cleaners, Sunday night brings the chance of an early Christmas.

It's a good haul tonight. Among the forgotten umbrellas, the plastic bags of souvenir rock, the *A Present from Whitmouth* keyrings, lie moments of pure gold. A gaudy gilt charm bracelet, hearts and cupids jangling among shards of semi-precious stones. An MP3 player: a cheap thing, none of the touch-screen bells and whistles, but working, and already loaded with tunes. A jumbo bag of Haribo. And an international-call card, still in its wrapper and unactivated. Amber smiles when she sees it. She knows who would benefit from a good long call home. Thanks, fun-seeking stranger, whoever you were, she thinks. You may not know it, but you'll have made one St Lucian very happy tonight.

She checks her watch, sees that she's already late for tea break. Locks the cupboard back up, drops the gifts into her shoulder bag and hurries across the floodlit concourse to the café.

Moses is smoking again. It's something of a sport with him. He knows that she knows – now that everywhere is non-smoking, a single whiff of tobacco indoors stands out like lipstick on a collar – and that she knows that it's him who's doing it. And yet he likes to test it anyway, to bend the rules and see what will happen. They've reached an unspoken truce on the matter. Amber feels that there are battles worth fighting and battles that are a waste of breath, and this is one of the latter.

And anyway, he's a good worker. By the time the café staff arrive in the morning, their territory will gleam with hygiene and the scent of chemical lemon.

She sees him jump and drop his butt into the open Coke can in front of him when she pushes the door open, suppresses a smile as he assumes a look of injured innocence and, at the same time, pretends not to have noticed her. Amber pointedly meets his eye, as she always does, and gives him the knowing smile she always gives him. Life is full of small complicities, and she's found that being boss involves even more than before.

Amber misses very little that goes on in Funnland. The room is full of people whose small stuff she resolutely doesn't sweat. Jackie Jacobs, and the fact that all work grinds to a halt when her phone rings, but who keeps up morale with the stream of innuendo that pours from her mouth between times. The fact that Blessed Ongom is first into and last out of the café every night but works half as hard again as any of her colleagues in the hours either side. And Moses, of course, who has the stomach of a robot and can be relied on to clean up customer deposits that reduce weaker colleagues to tears.

The room is crowded. Their communal tea break is a ritual that none of these night workers would miss for their lives; not even the new ones, not even the ones whose English is so sketchy they have to communicate with smiling and sign language. A night spent scraping off the evidence of other people's fun is a wearisome thing, Amber knows that. If a sit-down and a handful of sell-by-yesterday doughnuts make the whole thing bearable, she sees no point in token whip-cracking. As long as everything's done by shift's-end at six in the morning, she doesn't question how her staff timetable themselves. It's not as if Suzanne Oddie or any of the rest of the board are going to be down with stopwatches and clipboards when they could be tucked up under their 500-thread-count Egyptian cotton sheets. This is the great advantage of unsocial hours: as long as the job's done, no one cares who's doing it or how it gets there.

Moses' face falls and his dark eyes fill with doubt as Amber alters her course to approach his table. He thinks I'm going to tell him off at last, she realises. Even though we've known each other for years, the fact that I've been promoted makes him – makes all of them – look at me now with a touch of suspicion. She smiles, and sees the wariness deepen. Forces herself to laugh, though she feels a tiny bit hurt. 'It's OK, Moses,' she calls re-assuringly. 'I've got something for you.'

She reaches his table, takes the card from the bag and holds it out. 'Lost-property night,' she says. 'It's got about twenty quid on it, I think. I thought you might want to call your gran.'

The suspicion falls away, is replaced by deep, warm pleasure. Moses' gran, back in Castries, has been ill lately; isn't expected to last much longer. Amber knows he'll never find the cash to fly back for the funeral, but at least a final phone call might help ease the loss. 'Thank you, Amber,' he says, and beams a wide white smile at her. 'Thanks. I appreciate it.'

Amber tuts, tosses her hair. 'It's nothing,' she says. 'No skin off my nose,' and walks on. She knows, and everyone else does too, that this is not entirely true. Her predecessor in the job treated lost property as a personal bonus. But she couldn't do that. She's never earned this much in her life, and she'd feel ugly, keeping these treats from a group of people whose lives are lived on minimum wage. These aren't just her employees, they're her neighbours. Her friends. If she kept herself apart at work, they'd soon keep themselves apart on the high street. She gives the bracelet to Julie Kirklees, a skinny eighteen-year-old whose Goth eye-paint, she often suspects, hides black eyes, and walks on to the counter.

She pours herself a cup of stewed tea from the urn and adds two sugars. Eyes the display fridge and the domed plates on top. There are precious few perks to this job, but an almost limitless supply of leftover junk food is one of them. Amber suspects that some of her staff live on little other than half-stale hamburger buns, lukewarm frankfurters, sausage rolls, cold chips; tinned tomato soup and apple turnovers their only vegetable input.

She's not hungry, really. Just wants to stretch out the interval between doing the accounts and starting on the single cleaning duty she reserves for herself because she can't trust anyone to do it well enough. Her eye skims over the plates of scones, the giant, softening chocolate-chip cookies. Blessed holds forth behind her, her voice filled with refined African distaste.

'I don't know,' she is saying, 'what they are thinking. And their friends … are they animals, these people?'

Amber selects a ham salad sandwich with yesterday's sell-by. It will be sludgy in the centre, the crusts like cardboard, but there's not much that's savoury on offer and she's not in the mood for sweet.

'What's that, Blessed?' she asks, turning to their table.

Jackie drains her coffee mug. 'Blessed's found another turd,' she announces.

'What?' Amber sits down and starts to unwrap her sandwich. 'On the waltzer?'

Blessed nods, pulls a face. 'Right in the middle of the seat. I don't understand how they manage it. I mean, they must have to take their trousers down to squat.'

Jackie's face goes dreamy. 'I wonder if they do it when it's moving?'

'I'm sorry, Blessed,' says Amber. 'Are you OK dealing with it? Do you need me to ...?'

'No,' says Blessed. 'Fortunately, Moses has dealt with it already. But thank you. I appreciate the offer.'

'Thank God for Moses,' says Jackie. By her elbow, her phone leaps suddenly into life, skitters across the table.

'Good God,' says Tadeusz, springing suddenly awake from his small-hours reverie. 'I don't believe you. Two-thirty in the morning? Who gets calls at two-thirty in the morning? Woman, you're insatiable!'

Jackie kisses her teeth. 'You wish,' she says. Picks up the handset and frowns. 'Oh, fuck sake.'

Amber takes a bite of her sandwich. Warm, soggy, somehow comforting. 'What's up?'

Jackie slides the phone over to her. Tadeusz reads the text on the display over her shoulder. *Where are you? You have no right to do this. call me!*

'Someone's keen,' he says.

'Fucking nuts, more like,' Jackie says.

Tadeusz stares at her with renewed respect. 'You've got a stalker?'

She looks up from the screen sharply. 'Does that raise my value in the market, Tad?'

Tadeusz shrugs. His own, lean, slightly lupine appearance has accustomed him to easy attractions, clingy extractions. Blessed looks concerned. 'Who is this man?'

'Just ... Stupid little arsehole. I went on two dates with him.'

And the rest, thinks Amber uncharitably. But she says nothing, slides the phone back across the table. She learned long ago not to be a judger. Out loud, at least.

'You don't reply, do you?' asks Blessed. 'You shouldn't respond, Jackie.'

Jackie shakes her head. 'Not any more, no. I was stupid and humoured him for a bit at the beginning, but no, not now.

Weaselly little wanker. I only went on the second date 'cause I felt sorry for him that he couldn't get it up the first time.'

'Jackie!' Blessed protests. She hates talk like this. And yet it's always at Jackie's table that she sits. 'Because you shouldn't. Respond. You must be careful. Women get killed, you know. You know that. You need to be careful.'

'Oh, hardly,' says Jackie. 'He's not a bleeding serial killer. He's just a sad little wanker.'

'You shouldn't joke about this,' says Blessed. 'That's two girls this year already in Whitmouth, just off the strip. And you don't know anything about this man. Not really.'

'I wasn't joking, Blessed. Sorry.'

Blessed shakes her head. 'Well, don't. I don't understand how people can be so casual about it.'

''Cause they weren't from here,' says Tadeusz. 'Simple as that.'

'That's terrible,' says Blessed. 'If you think that.'

'But it's true,' says Tadeusz. 'No one from around here knew either of those girls, so it doesn't count.'

'But they're still *people*,' says Blessed.

'Yes, they are,' says Jackie. 'But they're not *our* people. If it was *our* people we'd be too scared to go out. Thank God it's outsiders, that's what I say.'

Blessed shakes her head, sorrowful. 'How cold you are, Jackie.'

'Realistic,' corrects Jackie.

'How long has this been going on, anyway?' asks Blessed. 'This man ...'

Jackie sighs and puts the phone down. 'Christ. For ever. What is it, Amber? About six months?'

'I have no idea,' says Amber. 'Why would I know?'

She could swear she sees Jackie pout. 'Well, he's *your* friend.'

It's news to her. 'You what?'

'Martin. Bagshawe.'

The name's faintly familiar, but she can't attach it to a face. Shakes her head and feels herself frown. 'Who?'

'Vic's birthday.'

13

'Vic's birthday? That was months ago.'

'Yuh-*huuh*.'

Amber shakes her head again. She doesn't remember that much about Vic's birthday. Especially not what other people got up to.

'I know. Told you,' says Jackie. 'Can't shake the grimy little weasel off. Where the hell did Vic get a nutter like that for a friend?'

Amber casts her mind back. A Saturday night, the Cross Keys. Not so much a party as a telling-your-mates-where-you'll-be. Vic on fine form, his arm slung round her shoulder all night, drinking Jack and Coke and not saying a word when she got in her third glass of dry white. A good night, a fun night. And vaguely, from the corner of her memory, she remembers Jackie, late in the evening, wrapped round some bloke, a diminutive figure in, as far as she remembers, an anorak. An anorak on a Saturday night. Jackie must've had the Heineken goggles on to have copped off with that.

'Don't blame Vic, Jacks. You can't exactly tell someone to go away in the Cross Keys, can you? He's just some bloke who goes in there.'

'No,' says Jackie. 'He said Vic was …'

Amber can't quite suppress a smirk. 'And it didn't occur to you to ask Vic?'

'Well, if somebody'd *warned* me …'

'If you'd *asked*, we might've been able to. I don't suppose Vic even knows what his name is. He's just one of those weird little pub people you can't shake off.'

'You see,' says Blessed, 'that's what I mean. You need to be careful. You can't just … pick people up in pubs.'

Jackie shoots her a look. 'Yeah. Church isn't my scene, Blessed. Thanks all the same. It's the way it is. Christ, I only talked to him in the first place because I felt sorry for him.'

'You're all heart, Jackie,' says Tadeusz.

'Yeah, well,' says Jackie, 'we can't all be jammy slags like Amber. Not all of us have a lovely warm Vic to come home to.'

'You should tell the police,' says Blessed. 'Seriously. If the man is harassing you.'

Jackie laughs. 'Yeah. Right.'

'No, you should. If it worries you, you should ask for help.'

Amber is often amazed that, of all the people she knows, the one who shows unshakeable faith in the authorities should be a woman who spent the first two thirds of her life in Uganda. Blessed has emerged from sub-Saharan hell with a moral framework that puts her neighbours to shame. She remembers her final gift, and reaches into her bag. Leans towards Blessed and lowers her voice as the others carry on talking. 'I found this in the lost property,' she says. Holds out the MP3 reverently.

'What is that?' asks Blessed. 'It certainly isn't something I've lost.'

'It's an MP3 player,' says Amber. 'I thought Benedick might like it. I'm sorry it's not an iPod, but it does the same thing.'

'Really?' Blessed looks gobsmacked. 'But this must be worth a lot of money, I would think.'

Again Amber finds herself shrugging off her own generosity. She knows how tight Blessed finds life as a single mother, knows that her son lacks a lot of the gadgets his peers take for granted. 'Probably not. I don't know. But it's got some music on it already, look. To start him off, anyway.'

'I ...' Blessed looks up at her with tear-filled eyes. 'I don't know what to say,' she says.

'Then don't say anything,' says Amber. 'Just take it.'

'Why don't you just change your phone?' Tadeusz picks up Jackie's handset and starts scrolling through the menu.

'Doh,' says Jackie. 'Because I can't afford to?'

'Ah,' says Tadeusz. They all understand about not affording stuff. You don't work nights cleaning up other people's leavings if you have a choice about it. He presses Reply, starts keying in letters.

'What are you doing?' The alarm in Blessed's voice is palpable. 'Tadeusz! Don't!'

Tadeusz continues to type.

'I said, don't reply. If you reply you give him hope that they have a relationship. She must ignore him. It's the only way.'

'It's OK.' Tadeusz glances up, shoots her a small smile.

'Give it back, Tadeusz,' says Jackie.

He hits Send. Hands the phone back.

'Shit,' says Jackie. 'What have you done?'

She stabs at the buttons, scrolls through to her Sent box. Opens the message and starts to laugh.

'What is it? What does it say?' asks Blessed.

'"Your message could not be sent because the number is disconnected." Genius. You're a genius.'

Tadeusz pushes back from the table and folds his arms, gratified.

The phone vibrates again. Jackie reads the text out. '"Testing".' She starts to key.

Amber checks her watch. It's knocking three. There's a lot to get through before dawn. 'Come on, guys,' she says. Stands up to show she means business. 'Time's getting on. We need to get back to work or we'll be here all night.'

All round them, the staff are taking her cue and beginning to move. By the window, Moses ostentatiously rolls a cigarette to smoke in the open air. They push themselves to their feet. Tadeusz is on café duty tonight. He takes the others' mugs and ambles off to the kitchen bins.

'Right,' says Jackie. 'No rest for the wicked.'

Chapter Three

The girl is dead. She doesn't need to go near her to see that. Chinless, sightless, rag-doll dead. Wearing a striped tank top and a tube skirt; both have gathered around her waist, puppy-fat breasts and white thighs reflected in the mirrors, back, back, back to infinity.

Amber is not looking directly at the body. She's nowhere near, in fact. She's cleaned the mirror maze so often that she knows its tricks and turns, the way a figure at the far end of the building can seem, when you enter, to be standing right in front of you.

Or – in the case of the dead girl – half lying, her head and shoulders pressed against the wall.

Amber grips the door frame, struggles to breathe. Oh shit, she thinks. Why did I have to find her?

She can't be more than seventeen. The mottled face – the mouth half open as though she is trying, one more time, to take a breath – still has traces of unformed childhood around the jaw. Blonde hair, blown and flicked up. Giant hoop earrings. Eyes made huge by half a pot of electric-blue eyeshadow, glitter gel spangling the naked *décolletage*. Platform boots, improbable in the angles they form with the mirrored floor.

She's been at Stardust, thinks Amber. Saturday. It's Seventies night at Stardust.

She feels sick. Glances behind her through the open door and sees that the concourse is empty. As though all her colleagues have dropped off the edge of the world.

She steps inside and closes the door to block out the light. Doesn't want anyone else to see. Not yet. Not while shock has ripped her mask away.

Thank God I'm wearing rubber gloves, she thinks nonsensically. She has cleaned the place every night for the past three years and, however careful she is, her fingerprints will be all over it. Let alone the prints of half the visitors who've passed through since this time last night. They try to keep the smudges down by handing out disposable plastic gloves on the door, but you can't actually force someone to wear them; can't police the interior 24/7.

Innfinnityland is the only attraction Amber cleans herself, since her promotion. The place makes everyone uneasy, as though they are afraid that they will get lost and never find their way back, or that the mirrors themselves are infected with ghosts. Too many times the work, which needs to be autistically methodical, has been rushed and skimped, and smears have remained; and in a place like this, a single smear becomes an infinite number, the original hard to track down if you're not working your way through, fingertip by fingertip, glass by glass. She decided long ago that it was easiest simply to do it herself. Wishes fervently now that she hadn't.

The girl has green eyes, like Amber's own. Her handbag – mock-croc – has fallen open and scattered poignant remnants of plans made, hopes cherished. A lipstick, a bottle of JLo, a pink phone with a metallic charm shaped like a stiletto court shoe ... breezy statements of identity, turned tawdry beneath their owner's glassy stare.

There is no blood. Just the impression of squeezing fingers livid on her neck. This is the third one this year, Amber thinks. It can't be a coincidence. Two is coincidence; three is ... oh, you poor child.

Amber is cold to the bone, though the night is warm. She

edges her way forward slowly, like an old person, one shaking hand supporting her against the mirrors as she moves. As she advances, new reflections cross her sight line: a million corpses strewn across a hall of infinite size.

Then suddenly, herself. Face white, eyes large, mouth a thin line. Standing above the body like Lady Macbeth.

What were you going to do? Touch her?

The thought freezes her to the spot. She's not been thinking. Shock has turned her into a creature of instinct, an automaton. Has made her forgetful.

What are you doing? You can't be involved. You can't. Anonymous. You're meant to be anonymous. Get involved, they'll work it out. Who you are. And once they know who you are …

She feels panic start up inside. The edgy tingle, the queasy itch. Familiar, never far from the surface. She needs to decide quickly.

I can't be the one to find her.

She begins to back away. Feels her way back to the entrance.

The dead girl gazes at infinity. Damn you, Amber thinks, suddenly angry. Why did you have to get yourself killed here? What are you even doing here, anyway? It's been closed for hours. The park's been closed for hours.

She catches her own thoughts and lets out a barking, ironic laugh. 'Shit,' she says out loud. 'Oh God, what am I meant to do?'

Go and find help. Do what anyone would do, Amber. Go out there and act the way you feel: shocked and scared. No one's going to ask questions. There's someone killing girls in this town, but it doesn't mean they'll recognise who *you* are.

But they'll take your photo. You know what the press are like. Anything to fill their pages; details to make up for lack of facts. You'll be all over the papers as the woman who found the body.

I can't do this.

Someone tries the entrance door, the sudden noise of the handle turning uselessly making her jump. She hears Jackie and

Moses: Jackie chattering and flirting, Moses responding in monosyllables, but the smile clear in his voice.

'She's always in here,' says Jackie. 'After tea break. Amber? You in there? The door's locked!'

Amber holds her breath, afraid that even the sound of her exhalation will call to them. Oh God, what do I do? I've got to get out of here.

'C'mon,' says Jackie. 'Let's try the back. Maybe she's taking a break.'

'Sure,' says Moses.

That's it, there's no escape now. She hears their footsteps recede down the steps as they walk off towards the entrance to the service alley. Two minutes before they get here, maybe. She can't get away, can't undo the moment of discovery.

She straightens up, steps over the girl's marionette legs and hurries to the emergency exit hidden behind the black curtain beyond. Best they find her out on the steps, out in the fresh air, throwing up.

9 a.m.

Her parents' bedroom door is open, and the cheesy tang of unwashed skin and bedcovers hangs over the landing like marsh gas. Her mother's not up yet: she can see her formless mass pooled beneath grey blankets. She hovers in the doorway, tries her voice:

'Mum?'

Her mother doesn't answer. But she sees slight movement in the ham-hock arm that pins the blankets down, and knows she's awake.

'Mum?'

Lorraine Walker takes one of her grunting breaths and turns on her back; stranded, like an upturned turtle. She turns a blank, defeated face and looks at her daughter. 'What?'

The voice is damp, sweaty, indistinct; she's not got her teeth in yet. It's a hot day already, though it's not yet ten o'clock, and Lorraine's twenty-five stones will be suffocating her beneath the covers. Jade can see that she's got her dress-up nightie on: knee-length flower print in brushed nylon, big enough to cover an armchair. Her skin is white against it, her elbows poking out between mounds of blubber.

'There's nothing for breakfast.'

'Chrissake.' *Mrs Walker heaves herself upright. Jade looks at her mother's molten face. She isn't involved enough to feel disgust.* 'Ask your dad.'

Yeah, right. That'll work.

Jade turns away and descends the staircase. Zig zags along the downstairs corridor. Ever since she can remember, her home life has consisted of picking her way from one place to another. Her father fancies himself a scrap-metal merchant, but really he's a hoarder of crap other people have thrown away; and a lot of it has made it into the house because he's afraid someone else will covet his collection of hubcaps and hinges, rust and rubber, as much as he does.

In the kitchen she tries, half-heartedly, to find something to kill her hunger. But there's nothing on the shelves. Six empty cereal boxes, the plastic wrapper that once held a Wonderloaf, a pint and a half of milk that has solidified and separated.

It could be evening before someone notices and does something. He mother, despite her bulk, seems capable of lasting all day without anything passing her lips. Both her parents keep themselves going on a diet of Nescafé and Old Holborn, with the odd rabbit for variety when the snares work. I suppose she can live off her reserves for a while, Jade thinks – the furthest down the road to judgement she ever goes.

She can hear the old man swearing and hammering out in the yard. I'm not going anywhere near him when he's in that mood. I'll get a broken lip, and I'll still be hungry.

She spots her father's jacket hanging over the back of a chair. The summer really must have heated up if he's not wearing it. She never sees him without it; can often tell when he's coming without hearing him, from the combined aromas of tobacco, sweat and pig shit woven into the fibres. She glances into the yard to make sure he's really as far away as he sounds, then tip-toes over and puts a hand in a pocket. His tobacco tin, some bits of formless metal, a penknife. And – yes! – her fingers close over the reassuring, joyful warmth of a twenty-pence piece. Twenty p. He probably won't even remember he had it. That's enough for a Kit Kat, at least. Or a Mars Bar even. It's not much, but if she eats it slowly, it should get her through the day.

Chapter Four

'Because I said so,' says Jim.

That one's not going to work for much longer, thinks Kirsty. Another fourteen months and she's officially a teenager.

'"Because I said so"? Seriously?' sneers Sophie. 'Can't you do better than that?'

The toaster pops up. Kirsty puts another couple of slices in, spreads olive-oil margarine on the done ones. Ooh, she thinks, I wish we had one of those four-slice jobs. I must have spent three weeks waiting for toast over the course of this marriage.

Jim puts the *Tribune* down and slides his spectacles to the top of his head. He's recently accepted that his hairline is never going to magically move forwards, and has adopted one of those ultra-short cuts. Kirsty likes it. It's a bit metrosexual, and has brought back his cheekbones; makes him look leaner and more intense. I like the fact that I still fancy my husband after thirteen years, she thinks, and smiles to herself as she brings the toast to the table. But he's going to have to grow it in soon, if he's ever going to get to second-interview stage. No one wears their hair like that in the world of finance.

'Because,' says Jim, 'it looks awful, that's why. Little girls with pierced ears look awful, and I'm not having you go to upper school wearing earrings.'

'But why?' she whines again. Adds: 'I'm not a little girl.'

'Because,' says Jim.

'But Mum got her ears pierced when she was a baby!' protests Sophie.

Jim shoots Kirsty a look. Too much information, it says. What did you want to tell her that for?

'Your mother is a wonderful woman,' he says. 'But trust me. She's who she is *despite* her upbringing, not because of it. You'd like to end up in care too, would you?'

The toast pops up again. Kirsty turns back. Yeah, it was the earrings, she thinks. That's what did it.

Luke tears his eyes from his Nintendo. He only ever looks up from his screen when he sees an opportunity for mischief. 'Are we snobs?' he asks.

'No,' Jim says firmly. 'Why do you ask?'

'Well ...' He scratches his head. Oh God, has he got nits again? wonders Kirsty. I'm going to have to shave his head to match his dad's. 'Lots of things.'

'Like?'

Luke prods at his toast. 'We eat bread with bits in,' he says.

'So does the entire population of Eastern Europe,' replies Jim.

'And we never go to McDonald's,' says Luke reproachfully.

'I don't want you to end up with diabetes and hurty hips. And anyway, we're economising. Use your knife, Luke. Don't just chew your way round the edges like that.'

Sophie examines her reflection in the back of a spoon, flips her hair at it. Adolescence is inches away.

'Eat your toast, Sophie,' Kirsty says. 'What do you want? Marmite or marmalade?'

'Nutella.'

Kirsty and Jim's eyes meet over their children's heads.

'I *know*,' groans Sophie. 'We're *economising*. How long are we going to be economising *for*?'

There's a tiny silence, then Jim answers: 'Until I get a job. Come on, you guys. It's time we got out of here.'

The ritual response: 'Uuuh, Dad!'

Jim stands up. 'Do you want a lift or not? Seriously. I'm not in the mood for any nonsense today. I've got a lot to do.'

'Nonsense'? You would have said 'bollocks' when we first met, reflects Kirsty. Parenthood has turned us into pussycats.

'I'm not finished,' protests Sophie.

Jim pauses briefly. 'Well, you can eat it in the car, or walk. Your choice.'

'I don't see why I have to go to stupid summer camp anyway,' grumbles Sophie. 'Holidays are meant to be holidays, aren't they?'

'Yes,' says Jim. 'But sadly there's a rest of the world that has to go on while you're not at school.'

'We thought it would be more fun than staying in your room all day,' says Kirsty.

'Mum used to keep us company in the holidays,' Sophie says. 'I don't see why *you* can't. It's not like you've got—'

She catches her mother's eye, sees the warning in it and stops her sentence. Gets up from the table and scuffs her way over to her trainers in her navy-blue socks with her big toes sticking out. Socks, thinks Kirsty. They grow out of everything. I'll need to stop in at Primark. And maybe it's a good thing she doesn't like summer camp, because if things don't improve, it'll be the last one she goes to. We'll be farming her out to a sweatshop this time next year.

She glances at Jim and sees, to her relief, that he's brushed Sophie's tactlessness off. She can never be sure, these days. Sometimes a careless word, some assumption that he'll be available, that he has nothing better to do, will send him into a spiral of self-doubt that will kibosh the job hunt for days. He's being so good about it, she thinks, but it's hard for all of us, and sometimes he forgets that. It scares me to death, being the only one bringing in money, but I can't talk to him about it. Every time I do, it sounds like a reproach.

Jim tucks his folder into his briefcase and comes over to kiss her goodbye. He's still treating job-hunting like a job, thank the

Lord. It's when he takes to his pyjamas that she feels she'll really need to worry.

'Sorry,' he says, gesturing at the uncleared table. 'I'll do it when I get in.'

She feels herself quail at the humbleness. They're both uncomfortable with the way he's taken over the bulk of the domestic duties, even though it's the reasonable thing to do. 'It's OK,' she replies. 'I don't have to leave till eleven anyway.'

He shrugs the bag up on to his shoulder. 'What's on the list today?'

'Press conference. Some new political movement. Authoritarian UKIP or something.'

'Sounds like a laugh.'

'Fish in a barrel,' she says.

Jim laughs. 'When in doubt, be facetious, eh?'

'First law of journalism.'

Another tiny, awkward pause. She avoids enquiring as to his plans for the day. Since his redundancy, the fact that all his days follow a similar pattern of poring over the job ads, drinking coffee and doing afternoon housework is a subject that makes them both wince. Kirsty knows how she would feel herself if she were in his position. She loves work, defines herself by it. Just the thought of no longer doing it fills her with a deep, aching melancholy.

'What are they called?'

'The New Moral Army.'

He laughs. Picks up his tea and drains it. 'Oh, good Lord. Kids, come *on*!'

'It's going to be a short day today, I reckon,' she says. 'I won't have to reach for a joke at all. Just type up the speech.'

'I've never heard of them.'

'No. They're new. That bloke Dara Gibson making his move.'

'What? The charity bloke?'

Kirsty nods. Dara Gibson, a self-made billionaire, has made a

26

splash lately with a series of high-profile contributions to cancer, animals, ecology and miserable kids. All the emotive causes, none of the donations anonymous.

'Hunh,' he says. 'Might have guessed he had an agenda.'

'Everybody's got an agenda of one sort or another.'

Chapter Five

A nice young constable gives Amber a lift home in a squad car, drops her off shortly before eleven. She feels wiped out, dirty and dry; but the sight of her own front door raises her spirits, as it always does. The door itself makes her happy. Just looking at it. It was the first thing they bought after they moved up to ownership: a proper, solid-wood, panelled front door to replace the wired-glass horror of council days. It represents so much, for her, this door: solidity, independence, her gradual rise in the world. Every day – even a day like today – she finds herself stroking its royal-blue gloss paint with affection before she puts the key in the lock.

Amber hopes Vic'll be awake and is disappointed to find the house silent as she opens the door and breathes in the scent of the pot-pourri on the hall table. She glances into the living room, runs an automatic eye around it. Quiet and dark and neat: the sofa throws in place, the glass-and-wicker coffee table empty save for the couple of coasters that have their home there, papers put neatly away in the magazine rack. Rug hoovered, pictures straight, TV off at the wall, not just on standby. Everything is as it should be. All that's missing is Vic. 'Hello?' she calls.

From the back of the house, faintly, a chorus of yips. The dogs are still out in the garden. They've probably been out there all night again. It's not that he does it deliberately; it's just that the dogs aren't figures in his emotional landscape. They're *her* dogs, not his, and Vic has a talent for simply editing out things that don't engage him.

Amber is bone-weary. She plants her bag on the hall floor and walks through the kitchen – hard-saved-for IKEA cabinets, a vase of flowers on the gateleg table, yellow walls that fetch the sun inside even when it's overcast – to open the back door.

The day is already warm, but Mary-Kate and Ashley shiver among the pelargoniums like the pedigree princesses they are. She bends and scoops them up in her arms: surprised again, as she is every time she does it, by the fact that they really don't seem to weigh any more than the butterflies their breed is named after. Delicate, curious noses, fur soft as thistledown. She squeezes them close to her cheeks and is rewarded by great bursting wriggles of love.

She feeds them, makes a mug of tea and goes up to give it to Vic. She needs him. Needs to know the world is still the same.

He's still asleep. Vic's working day on the rides at Funnland starts at three, ends at eleven, and he often goes out to wind down afterwards – just like an office worker, only six hours later. Their lives are turned upside down from the rest of the world's, and from each other's. Occasionally they'll see each other as her shift begins, but sometimes the only words they'll exchange in a week will be on the phone, or as she gets into bed. It's the price they pay for the life they've made. And it's a good life, she assures herself. I would never have dared to think I'd have a life like this.

Mary-Kate and Ashley follow on her heels, shuffle about the carpet, sniff Vic's discarded clothes in the half-light through the thin curtains. Amber stands at the foot of the bed for a moment, the mug warming her fingers, and studies the familiar features. Wonders, again, what a man like that is doing with her. At forty-three he's still handsome, his dark hair still full, the fine lines that are beginning to creep across his weather-tanned skin just making him look wiser, not more tired as her own are doing to her. You'd never tell we were seven years apart, she thinks. What's he doing with me, when he could have anyone?

She puts the mug down on his bedside table. Steps out of her sensible work shoes, sheds her jacket on to the chair. Catches the musky scent of her own armpits. Feeling another rush of weariness, she remembers the girl's purple face, the burst capillaries, and wants to weep.

Vic stirs and opens his eyes. Takes a moment to focus. 'Oh, hi,' he says. 'What time is it?'

She checks her watch. 'Ten past eleven.'

'Oh.' He disentangles a weight-toned arm – an arm that filled her with lust back when they were getting together; that made her weak as he wrapped her into it – from the bedclothes and runs his fingers through his hair. The sleep-tangles fall instantly away. That's Vic: a single grooming gesture and he's ready to face the world.

'You're late,' he says, and there's an edge of reproof to the statement.

'There's a mug of tea.' She waves her hand at it, sits down on the bed and rubs at her tired calves. 'Didn't you get my texts?'

'Texts?'

'I've been texting you all night. I tried calling too.'

'Yeah? Oh.' He picks his phone up from the bedside chest of drawers, holds it out so she can see the blank display. 'Sorry. I switched it off. I was tired.'

She feels a twinge of resentment, squashes it down. He doesn't suspect that anything is wrong. You can't blame him for that.

'Christ,' he says, 'you smell a bit ripe.'

'Sorry,' she says, and bursts into tears.

Vic lurches forward and pinches the back of her neck between thumb and palm, like a masseur. 'Hey,' he says. 'Hey, I was just saying, Amber. It's OK. It's no big deal.'

Her tears dry as suddenly as they've come on. She finds that this is often the way with her emotions and that, though she's good at controlling them, tears are rarely far from the surface.

She loosens his grip, stands up and eases herself out of her trousers, rubs the place where his hand's just been. Feels guilty. Stop it. Stop it, Amber. It's not his fault. Be nice.

Suddenly, she doesn't want to tell him. Doesn't want to tell him because she doesn't know how she wants him to react. Doesn't know if she could bear sympathy, doesn't know if she could bear not to get it. The last time Amber saw a murdered body, there were days of pretending, of hugging it close to herself, of hiding. A bit of her wants to try it again with Vic: to see if the outcome will be different this time. Stupid thought. The police are swarming all over Funnland, the park is closed. She could keep it to herself for no longer than it took him to go in for his shift.

'Something happened,' she tells him; keeps her voice even, controlled, as though she's discussing a surprise electric bill. She keeps her back turned, doesn't trust her face.

Vic sits forward. 'What?'

Amber folds up the trousers, lays them on the chair. 'At work. Tonight. I ... oh God, Vic, there's been another girl killed. At work.'

'What?' he says again. 'Where?'

'Innfinnity.'

'Innfinnity?' She hears him hear the word, take in the implication of what she's just said. Amber's the only one who ever goes to the mirrors at night. It doesn't take long for him to understand that she's the one who found her.

'Babe,' he says. 'Oh, babe. You must have been so afraid. You should have called me. You should have let me know.'

She's annoyed. Turns and glares. 'I did. I called and texted. I already told you. All night. Turn it on. You'll see.' They don't have a house phone, just pay-as-you-go mobiles.

He picks the phone up again, switches it on. 'Amber. I'm so sorry.'

She sits on the edge of the bed as the phone lets out a series of incoming-message beeps. Rubs her neck again. Vic kneels up behind her and bats her hand away. Starts to knead the muscles: powerful, working-man's hands squeezing, pressing; strong fingers straying upwards, brushing the line of her jaw. She has another brief flash of the swollen face, the bruised lips parted to show young white teeth. Shivers and closes her eyes. He presses the heel of his hand to her spine, pulls back on her shoulder. She feels a tiny skeletal clunk somewhere deep down and sighs with relief. When I was young, I had no one to do this for me. I thought back pain was just part of the human condition. Thank God for Vic. Thank God for him.

'What was it like?' he asks. 'Who was she?'

'Some poor little girl. Can't have been more than twenty. All dressed up for a night out. Oh God, Vic, it was awful.'

'But how? What happened?'

Amber sighs. 'I don't know. If I knew that, I'd either be psychic or a policewoman, wouldn't I?'

The hands fall abruptly still. 'You know what I mean, Amber.' He sounds offended.

'Sorry,' she says, hastily. 'I didn't mean to be rude. It's just been ... a long night ...'

He forgives her, thank God, and the hands start their work again. It's only a day since their last disagreement, and she can't bear to start again. Vic has so many good qualities, but he can hold a grudge for weeks, the chill of his vexation filling the house with silence. She had been half afraid throughout her shift that their stupid spat might have kicked another episode off, until her discovery drove it from her head. It's probably, she reflects, why he had the phone off. But I'm not going to push things by asking. Not when he's being so nice.

'So what was it like?' he asks again, abruptly. 'I don't suppose you've ever seen anything like that, have you?'

She turns and looks at him. She doesn't know what she had been expecting, but his look of sharp enjoyment surprises her. He covers it quickly with concern, but she's seen it now, and it feels ugly. It's not a real thing to you, she thinks, any of it. Not the girl under the pier, not the one they found in among the bins in Mare Street Mews, not this. In fact, now there've been three of them, and only a fool wouldn't be asking if it's the same person doing it, you're probably just feeling a bit more excited – like Whitmouth's finally on the map. It's the same thing that keeps people reading the papers every day: if it's not *your* family, if it's not one of *your* friends, a murder is little more than a night out at the cinema; something to discuss gleefully at the pub.

The girl's face flashes through her mind again, pop-eyed and black-tongued, cobweb veins on livid cheeks. Death, so abnormal yet so familiar: the shock, the cavernous emptiness behind those reddened eyes; it's what it always looks like. Nobody dies and looks like they'd been expecting it.

'It was …' She has to think about her words. Strives to recall her emotions, to separate her response to the scene in front of her from her panic on her own behalf. 'I don't know. It's weird. It was like I was in a bubble. Watching myself. In a weird way, I felt like I wasn't really there.'

Vic leans back and opens the drawer in his bedside table. He fishes out his Ventolin inhaler. Takes a puff. 'Bet you were scared, though,' he says, his voice small from holding his breath. 'Was there a moment when you thought they'd think you'd done it?'

'Vic!' She's scandalised. 'My God!'

'Sorry,' he says. Breathes out.

7 p.m.

'We can't go home like this.'

They face each other in the field, waist-deep in cow parsley. The sun is low, but still bright, and they cut smeared and dingy figures now they're out in the open. Bel looks down at her hands, and sees that her nails are cracked and black from digging. Looks back up at Jade. She's filthy. Earth and lichen, scraps of leaf and twig, scratches from thorns and bark on her arms and shins.

'My mum'll kill me,' says Jade.

'It's OK,' says Bel. 'Just put it all straight in the washing machine. She'll just put stuff on top. She won't even notice.'

Jade is appalled. There is no washing machine in the Walker household. She's always thought of them as things you found in launderettes. That Bel would assume they had one underlines the gaping chasm of difference between them. Jade's mother does the family wash by hand, soaking everything in a heap in the bath on Monday night, then squeezing and scrubbing it wheezily through before pegging it all out on the network of lines she's rigged up across the yard on Tuesday. It's just another thing that makes Jade stand out at school: that all her clothes, hand-me-downs from older siblings, are grey and threadbare compared with her peers'. Everyone knows that the Walkers are dirty and have no self-respect; someone makes sure to tell her so every day.

'I can't, she ...' Even now she is unwilling, in front of this girl with her cut-glass accent and her Levi's jeans, to admit the whole truth. She doesn't have friends, but she knows instinctively that this new, shining person would vanish from her life in an instant if she discovered the full extent of where she comes from. She still hasn't realised that their brief friendship is already over. 'She'll kill me,' she finishes lamely. 'Look at me.'

'Come on,' says Bel. 'We've got to get clean.'

They pick their way back along the sheep path to the stream. The meadow is splashed bright yellow with islands of dandelion and ragwort. They are silent, now, and don't dare look at each other. Their hateful task has robbed them of the chatter of the early hours. The only words they can find are practical, brief. They scramble along the bank to the pool. It seemed deeper when they were floundering about, fighting for footholds, but the water is deep enough to reach their thighs, and runs clear, the mud they kicked up all settled. Neither mentions what they're doing, but each girl looks about her surreptitiously for Chloe's blood, for any signs of what has happened here.

'Come on,' says Bel again. She strips off her top, her jeans, and dumps them into the water. Jade hangs back. 'Come on, Jade,' she urges.

'Then they'll be wet,' says Jade doubtfully.

'We'll squeeze them out. And it's still hot. They'll be dry in no time. And anyway, we can say we fell into the river. No one knows where we've been all day. Come on!'

Jade strips off her top and skirt. Her knees are green from kneeling in the woods. She wades reluctantly down into the water and stands there, shivering despite the heat, hugging the clothes to her chest. Bel snatches them away, throws them into the water. 'Scrub,' she orders. 'Come on. Just get on with it.'

Bel drops to her knees, water up to her chest, and rubs vigorously at the dirt on her arms and shoulders, the sweat in her armpits. Dips her head beneath the surface and re-emerges, dripping and swiping the grime from her face. Gestures to Jade to follow suit.

I can't, thinks Jade. That's where she ... Where her face ...

'I can't swim,' she says.

'Don't need to. Come on.'

Bel lunges suddenly forward and grabs her by the arm. Stares hard into her eyes. 'Jade. Don't go soft on me now. If you don't do this, if you go home looking like that ...'

She avoids completing the sentence. Doesn't need to. Knows that Jade is filling the words in for her. They'll know. They'll realise. Already they're distancing themselves from what they've done. Trying to separate the actions they're taking now from the reason why they need to take them.

Jade kneels and plunges beneath the water, like a Baptist.

She opens her eyes below the surface, sees that the water is once again thick with kicked-up mud. It's dark down here. Quiet. This is what she saw, she thinks. This is how it was, her last moments.

Chloe's face looms at her through the gloom. She kicks back in panic, struggles upward, bursts out into air. She flounders through the water to the bank. Half crawls, half runs to the top. Stands there shuddering in her underpants.

They reach the gate. Each girl is dripping, clammy in her damp clothes.

'We'll split up,' says Bel.

She's much calmer than me, thinks Jade. She seems to know what to do. If it was just me, I'd have made so many mistakes by now. They'd all know already. That it was me.

'I'll go back through the village,' says Bel. 'To mine. They can't know we were together. Do you understand?'

Jade gulps, and nods. 'Yes.'

'They can't know we were together, ever,' says Bel. 'You know that, don't you? We can't see each other again. If we see each other, we just pretend we don't know each other. OK?'

'Yes,' says Jade.

'Do you understand?' asks Bel again. 'Not ever. Do you understand?'

Jade nods again. 'Yes. I understand.'

'Good,' says Bel.

She turns away and starts across the meadow, towards the west end of the village. The sun is beginning to set, and she casts a long shadow.

Chapter Six

Stan's already rolled a cigarette while the press conference was wrapping up, and lights it as they step into the car park. 'Good God,' he says. 'What sort of morons put on a lunchtime bloody press conference and don't even lay on any bloody sandwiches? You've got to do sandwiches if you want a good write-up. Everybody knows journalists need sandwiches. I could have been in the pub.'

Stan is old-school. Very old-school. He comes from the days when journalism was largely conducted in bars, and somehow he continues to live his life as though those days still existed. By modern Fleet Street standards he is a dinosaur, still doing his research by telephone and attendance rather than news feeds and a couple of hits on Google. But he sucks you in when you see him and reminds you what attracted you to the job in the first place.

He plonks himself on a wall that holds in a bunch of evergreens and a collection of discarded fag butts and soft-drinks cans. Kirsty grins and settles down next to him.

'Yeah. That was pretty much a waste of time, wasn't it?'

A rich Guinness growl emerges from his throat. 'Still,' he says, 'at least it got me away from Sleaford.'

'You've been up in Sleaford?'

'Yes. Even the name sounds like something you find on your shoe, doesn't it? I had to volunteer to cover this just to get out of there. What I want to know is why they can't start murdering people in places you'd actually want to go to. Seriously. How about the seaside, for a change? Just bloody selfish, I call it.'

'Child F and Child M?'

Stan nods. Another week, another outbreak of schoolchild violence: two twelve-year-olds bullying another till he jumped off a railway platform into the path of an oncoming train. The whole thing recorded on CCTV, so there was no doubt as to the identity of the guilty parties.

'Of course,' says Stan, 'if they hadn't got rid of the staff on that station, they wouldn't have needed the CCTV and someone might've stopped it. Shit. What a world we live in. Price of everything, value of nothing. There seem to be bottomless funds for wheelie-bin Nazis, but God forbid you'd want to protect someone's kids from a pair of bullying scumbags.'

Her heart jolts. She's always thought of Stan as relatively liberal. For a crime reporter.

'Seriously?' She says. 'Bullying scumbags?'

Stan sighs. 'Yeah, I know. But that's the trouble, isn't it? Poor little shits didn't stand much chance of being anything else. The usual shower of useless parents, absent dads, third-generation doleys. I went and doorstepped Child F's mum. Exactly what you'd expect. Still in bed at one o'clock and a bunch of kids doing wheelies on the pavement outside among the dumped fridges. And do you know what she said?'

Kirsty shakes her head.

Stan adopts a Universal Northern Accent. '"Nowt to do wi' me,"' he says. '"He's out o'control, that one."'

'Yes, but …' she begins timidly. She never knows how to argue this subject.

'Yeah, I know,' Stan sighs again. But it would be so nice if just occasionally people would try not acting up to their stereotypes, wouldn't it? And at least F's mum was honest. Know what the other one said?'

His voice goes high and sappy as he imitates Child M's

mother. '"I love my kids. I don't care what he's done, I love him anyway."'

Kirsty remembers her own mum, glimpsed on a TV screen before someone hurriedly switched it off: flower-patterned polyester tent-blouse, fresh-bought for court, and trousers straining around the apron of stomach lying on her thighs, her hair scraped greasily back off a defiant face. Same thing, same phrase exactly; and after that, silence. Not a visit, not a birthday card. Love and presence, as Kirsty discovered, are not the same thing.

'If she'd loved her kid,' he says, 'she'd have done something to teach him right from wrong.'

The hotel's plate-glass door opens and several representatives of the New Moral Army exit, the placards that have recently decorated the conference suite under their arms. Kirsty grins. 'You sound like you're about to sign up for that lot.'

Stan laughs. 'Yeah, I do, don't I? Anyway. How many words have you got to scrape off the bottom of the barrel about this lot, then?'

'About six hundred. News feature. You?'

'Same. But for Features.'

'Lucky sod.' Features tend to allow more leeway in terms of letting their writers express opinions, draw analogies, recall similarities between the story at hand and ones from the past. Which, in the case of a story like this, can be a blessing. The launch she's driven an hour to attend lasted fifteen minutes, and consisted of a speech of Cameronesque moral blandness followed by a Q&A of New Labour evasiveness. She's going to be hard pushed to extract a couple of hundred quotable words from her digital recorder, and her shorthand pad is mostly filled with desperate descriptive squiggles about the set-dressing. 'Have you got any more idea about what they stand for than you did when you went in?'

Stan shakes his head. 'The world's going to pot and Something Must Be Done? Something like that.'

'Mmm,' says Kirsty. 'That's what I thought too. And what is the Something?'

'Don't ask me,' he says. 'This Gibson bloke made his money from "What would Jesus do?" merchandising, didn't he? Key-rings and flip-flops and that?'

'Yes.'

'Well, I should think he'd do whatever Jesus would do, then, wouldn't he?'

'Good point.'

'Though I think Jesus would have started by providing sandwiches. What have you got lined up for the rest of the week?'

Kirsty shrugs uncomfortably. The silly season is not the best time to be a freelance journalist in a world that feeds itself by recycling the news wires. Especially not one with a redundant husband and half the staff of News International still morbidly freelance. 'Nothing much. I'm pushing to go in for shifts, but they're not biting.'

'I know what you mean. My patch has got so big I'm buying a van to kip in. I hardly ever get home these days.'

They eye the young followers of Dara Gibson. Dark suits, tidy haircuts. They certainly look businesslike.

'What we need is a nice juicy serial killer,' says Stan. 'Or an industrial disaster. Something that'll get us over the holiday slump.'

'Mmm,' agrees Kirsty. 'Only not too glamorous, or they'll be sending people down from London to steal our jobs.'

Someone from London walks past: Sigourney Mallory, from the *Independent*, talking on her mobile and ignoring them. The two stringers eye her with suspicion. 'What's she doing here?' asks Kirsty.

'Dunno,' says Stan. 'Slumming it. She's not been outside the Circle Line in years.'

The conference has been unusually well attended for an event of such little importance. People launch political pressure groups every day of the week. If the NMA had made their pitch once

Parliament had come back and news had restarted, they'd have got a two-inch 'News in Brief' if they were lucky.

'D'you think they're Scientologists, maybe?' asks Stan. 'They certainly *look* like Scientologists.'

Kirsty shakes her head. 'Too much Jesus talk, not enough conspiracy theory. No. It's just a rich man's vanity project, isn't it? Nothing to see here. Move along.'

'Right,' says Stan. 'I saw a pub on the ring road that said it did food. You coming?'

Kirsty jumps down from the wall, hoicks her bag on to her shoulder. It's already two o'clock, and she has a five o'clock deadline. 'No,' she says. 'Got to get home and file.'

'Christ,' says Stan. 'File from the pub like a normal person.'

Her phone goes off in her pocket. She gets it out and looks at the display. Withheld. It'll be the *Tribune*, or the bank, one or the other. One offering money, one asking for it. It's not likely to be work, she thinks. They know I'm on a deadline, and anyway, it's not commissioning time of day; it'll just be starting to get frantic. The daily tides of newspapers wash the editors to the phones to dole out pieces between morning conference and the first rush of copy; after that they'll just be calling to shout at you for filing late. It's the bank, she thinks. It must be. Oh shit, I can't talk to them. Not when I've got to have my brain together. She lets it ring out, puts it back in her pocket, feels the buzz of the incoming message a few seconds later.

'Come on,' wheedles Stan. 'A quick drink and a sausage-an'-chips will set you up a treat. I'll lend you my dongle.'

'You know how to get to a girl, Stan,' she says. 'No, look, I've got to get the kids' tea on once I've filed. I can't be sitting there on the lager with you all afternoon.'

Stan tuts. 'I dunno. Journalists aren't what they used to be, are they?'

His phone too starts up in the pocket of his mouldy old parka. He gets it out, doesn't even bother to look at it, answers. 'Stanley Marshall?'

He puts his computer bag down on the tarmac, listens intently. Then: 'Fuck me. Where did you say? In the hall of bleeding mirrors? Someone's got a sense of humour.'

Kirsty gazes round the car park as she waits for him to finish, sees that all her colleagues are glued to their phones, nodding animatedly, scribbling stuff on the back of their hands. Shit, she thinks, that *was* work, wasn't it? There's some sort of big story kicked off, and I went and sent it to voicemail.

'Yeah,' says Stan. 'Yeah, sure. I'm in Kent anyway. Yes, with the car. Don't worry. New Moral Arsewipes? Yeah. Sure. I can probably be down there in couple of hours. Fine. Yes. I'll call when I'm *in situ*.'

He's already picking his bag up as he hangs up, pulling a pack of Drum from his jacket. Looks down at Kirsty as he drops his phone back into his pocket. 'If that was the *Trib*, you'd better call 'em back pronto,' he says. 'You don't want this going to anyone else.'

'What's up?' she asks, her heart sinking and leaping all at the same time.

'Well, looks like this lot are off the news agenda, that's for sure. A murder. Down in Whitmouth. Third this year, and it looks like there were two more with the same MO last season.'

'Whoa,' says Kirsty.

'Yup,' says Stan, with a happy chuckle. 'Looks like I've got what I wished for. We're off to the seaside!'

Chapter Seven

'Living the dream,' says Jackie, and cracks open her tinny.

'You're easily pleased.' Amber throws her a grin.

'Well, come on,' says Jackie. 'Who would want to be anybody else right now, right at this moment in time?'

'Jackie!' says Blessed pointedly.

Jackie frowns at her, then glances at Amber and remembers. 'Oh, sorry,' she says. 'I didn't mean it like that. I just meant – you know. Whitmouth. On a sunny day.'

Amber can't suppress a smile as she looks down the beach. Half a mile of brown shingle overshadowed by a silent rollercoaster, a run-down pier, a couple of dozen bright-decked fast-food stalls strung along the edge of the pavement, canvas awnings flapping in the Channel wind, a towel and a plastic beer cooler.

'You have a point,' she replies.

'This is why I live here,' says Jackie.

'Me too,' replies Amber. It was the sea that first brought her here. But the sea's not the only reason she stays. There are better bits of sea, she knows, and better towns, and probably better neighbours than this group of hers who've come down here together, but Whitmouth, with its lack of glamour and its contempt for aspiration, with its ceaselessly changing, unobservant crowds, makes her feel safe. She felt when she got here that she could put down roots, but still feels a tiny thrill of surprise every time she realises she's actually managed it.

'So how *are* you, Amber?' asks Jackie, her voice syrupy with unaccustomed sympathy. 'Are you holding up all right?'

You know what? thinks Amber. I'm shit, thank you very much. I found a murdered body thirty-six hours ago and I keep seeing it when I'm trying to get to sleep. 'I think I prefer it when you're being a hard-faced cow, Jackie,' she says. 'At least it's sincere.'

Jackie lets out a cackle.

'It's true, though,' says Blessed, who is sitting on a cushion she's brought down specially, and knitting a jumper to protect her precious son from the bitter winds of winter. 'It's not really appropriate, is it? For us to be taking advantage of the situation like this.'

'Oh, Blessed,' says Jackie, 'what were we going to do? None of us killed the girl, and none of us knew her. It's not our fault that we're not allowed to go to work, is it?'

Blessed takes a sip of her ginger beer. Picks up the tongs and pokes at the coals of the barbecue. 'I think this is ready,' she announces. 'No, I know what you mean, Jackie. But a party ... is this the appropriate response?'

Maria Murphy rubs sun cream into her skin as though she were on the Costa Brava, and watches her boys frolic on the shingle. 'It's not really a party, is it, Blessed? It's just, like, everyone who lives here actually getting to use the beach for a change, isn't it? It's not like anyone *planned* it. Oh God, he's going to send that ball into the sea, I swear he is.'

They follow the direction of her gaze. The men from the estate are playing a scuffly, laughing game of six-a-side, sliding about on the shingle, breakwaters for goals. Funnland's backbone, unexpectedly at leisure, rioting like schoolkids on a snow-day. It was Jackie's idea in the first place, though it was Vic who told Amber about it, and who persuaded her that staying locked in the house wasn't going to bring the girl back, or make Amber's part in it go away. And she's glad he did. He's right, of course. Nothing will undo what she's seen, but life has to go on. She doesn't spend enough time with her colleagues as friends, these days, and it sometimes feels as though a clear glass barrier has dropped between them since she took her management position.

'It's true, though,' says Amber. 'Staying indoors isn't going to change anything, is it? Lying in a darkened room crying isn't going to make me unfind her.'

'That's the spirit,' says Maria. 'I wish I could have a bit of whatever you're always on.'

'Ray of sunshine, that's me,' says Amber, and beams.

Maria sits up sharply and glares at her eldest son. 'Jordan!' she shouts. 'If that ball goes in the sea, you're going in to get it!'

Jordan Murphy glances over his shoulder with all the insolence of fourteen. His brothers – matching no. 3 cuts and a real diamond earring in each left ear – are romping in the sea with other boys off the estate, fighting for primacy over the old inner tube from a juggernaut.

Jackie narrows her eyes. 'Hah. Who wants to see *his* skinny little bod? I'm holding out for Moses or Vic. In fact,' she drains her tinny and throws it carelessly on to the pebbles, 'if I thought your Vic was going to get his top off, I'd kick the ball in myself.'

'Steady,' says Amber.

'Oh, come on,' says Blessed. 'Even I would be happy to see your husband go into the sea. You have to admit that he's quite beautiful.'

Amber laughs uncomfortably. She knows their intention is harmless, but people referring to Vic's good looks – and invoking the marriage they never had – has always made her feel like she's dancing on the edge of a precipice. I know he loves me, she thinks. I don't need a piece of paper to tell me that. And I know I'm just paranoid. Vic's as loyal as the day is long. But I wish other women wouldn't keep reminding me how many of them would be in the queue if there was ever a chance. 'He's not just a pretty face, you know,' she says. 'There's more to him than that.'

'Yeah, but he *is* a pretty face,' says Jackie. 'And Jesus, the arms on him.'

'Arse?' asks Maria. 'Jacks, did you really just talk about Amber's bloke's arse? You're awful. You just don't know when to stop, do you?'

'Arms,' protests Jackie. 'I said arms!'

'Yer, right,' says Maria. 'C'mon. We should start cooking, if we're going to.'

Amber gets up on her haunches, and the dogs, lying on a corner of the rug, prick up their ears. She shushes them down and flips the top of the cooler. She's been to Lidl; she's the only one who has a car. And besides, she wants to do something for them all. The loss of wages will hit them hard in a couple of days, and she feels strangely responsible. As though she didn't just find the girl, but planted her there.

'OK. Burgers, chicken, sausages. Blessed, there's rolls in that placcy bag over there.'

'Amber Gordon, I love you. What would we do without you?' says Jackie.

'Find someone else to twist round your little finger, I should think,' Amber replies. But she feels warm and pleased. Glad she made the effort. She separates out the burgers and lays them on the grill of the nearest barbecue. They're fatty. A cloud of cheap-meat smoke rises from the coals.

Maria waves a hand in front of her face and lights a cigarette. 'Oi oi,' she says, looking up the beach towards the pier, 'you've got company, Jacks.'

They turn to look, and see Martin Bagshawe standing by a waste-bin, watching them.

'Dear God,' Maria frowns at him, watches him catch her stare and look away, 'does he never take that anorak off?'

'Not as far as I know,' says Jackie. 'Never seen him without it.'

Even when you were fucking in the Cross Keys car park? wonders Amber. Slaps her own wrist.

'He still calling you?' she asks.

Jackie nods. 'Yup. Creepy little fuck. I wish he'd just – *go away*.'

'We could get the boys to have a word,' says Maria, 'if you want.'

'No worries,' says Jackie. 'Looks like your steely glare's done the job anyway.'

Martin turns away, trudges off towards the manky dark bit under the pier. There are steps on the other side, leading up on to the boardwalk, and an exit on to the Corniche. Doesn't want to walk past us, thinks Amber. Afraid we'll say something. And he's probably right too. Behind them, Moses executes a sliding tackle on Vic, shingle showering out on either side. The women roll, as one, to their knees. 'Whoa!' shouts Jackie. 'Oh my *Gaad*!' yells Maria. Amber leaps to her feet. 'Are you OK? Baby?'

The two men sit up, look at the women with surprise, pull each other upright and barrel away towards the far goal.

'Don't you want to play, Ben?' Amber turns back to Blessed's fourteen-year-old son, who leans silently against the breakwater, reading a biology textbook. Benedick glances up, shakes his head and goes back to the page. He's a serious, slightly pudgy child. Amber suspects that the weight of his mother's hopes for him hang heavy on his shoulders. He's got the MP3 player plugged into his ears; he shrugs without taking the earphones out to hear what she's said, and carries on reading. I hope he'll be OK, thinks Amber. I hope he gets to be happy.

'How's he getting on at school?' she asks his mother, flipping the burgers as she speaks.

'OK,' replies Blessed. 'He's high in his class,' she adds proudly.

'That's good. He's clever.'

'He'll be a doctor one day,' says Blessed firmly.

'I'm sure.'

'And he's good with computers.'

'Is he?' She's not surprised. Benedick is just the sort of solitary child you'd expect to spend his free hours indoors. 'Likes the internet, does he?'

'Yes,' says Blessed. 'I suppose it's a good thing we don't have it at home, or I'd never see him.'

'You don't have the internet? I thought they all used it for their homework these days.'

'He goes to the library for that. They have computers there.'

'You don't have a *computer*?'

Blessed shakes her head. 'He had one, but something called the motherboard died. That's what they said. Anyway, something that can't be mended, and only one week after the guarantee ran out.'

'Oh, Blessed,' says Amber, 'that's a bummer.'

'I'm saving for a new one,' says Blessed. 'Maybe for Christmas. They're so expensive.'

'Oh, wow,' says Amber. 'I didn't know. Why didn't you tell me?'

Blessed shrugs. Takes up her knitting again.

'Well, it'll keep him off the porn sites anyway,' says Maria. 'My Jordan's a bugger for those. I can't go into his room most nights, I'm so scared of what I'll find.'

Behind her, Jason Murphy punts the ball as it flies towards the goal. It's a wild shot, and hard. The women watch as it flies high and wide over the beach and bounces on the surface of the water.

'Aah,' says Jackie, and opens another can. 'Showtime.'

Chapter Eight

Kirsty looks up at the rusting network of struts and pillars that supports the walkway from the turnstile on the seafront to the pier's end. It's dark here, dank and smelly – not just the brine-and-fish tang of rotting seaweed, but the fug of generations caught short, of picnics half eaten and discarded, of a leaking something pooling beneath the rocks.

It's not the nicest town she's ever been in. But in terms of why she's been sent here, that's no bad thing. Her job is to find fifteen hundred words of the sort of Sunday feature that makes readers feel better about their own lives. To skim over the rides and the ices and the bright animal-shaped inflatables, the exquisite pleasure of chips hot and salty from the packet in a stiff sea breeze, the joyous shock of Channel water on naked skin, and show instead the mile upon mile of grey post-war prefabs blotched back into the marshland around the estuary, the crumbling plastic fast-food shopfronts, the stressed lives of a largely itinerant population whose employment prospects are seasonal, the Georgian façades peering out between plastic and neon. To make Balham look balmy in comparison. No town where a killer is on the loose is allowed to be a nice town: it's an unwritten law. If things like this happened in nice towns – the places where people buy Sunday papers and read them – then who would be safe?

And yet, she can't help liking it. Despite the run-down, ill-stocked shops. Despite the pallor of skins that should be brown from seaside living, the fact that there's not a colour that occurs in nature to be seen on the Corniche. Despite the tears on the faces of Hannah Hardy's hungover friends when they discovered why she'd never made her way back to their static caravan last night, despite the fact that everyone here who is over fifteen looks closer to forty, there's a gaudy, gutsy bravery to Whitmouth that she finds surprisingly charming. Part of her, despite the grim nature of the work that brought her here, feels like it's on holiday. She likes Whitmouth and she thinks she likes its people.

Like the big group fifty feet from where she stands: one of those working-class parties where the women sit together while the men play a rough, elbowing game of football with frequent breaks to drink fizzy lager from the can and pass a fat, rough-rolled joint between them. The sort of gathering, she reflects, that I would have been grateful to be included in, once upon a time. Maybe that's the reason I like it here. In another life, I would have thought it was heaven.

And yet here she stands at the spot where Nicole Ponsonby, this summer season's first victim, was found. Nicole was lying, quite peacefully, face-up, with one arm thrown back behind her head. She would have looked for all the world like another teenage sun worshipper, were it not for the fact that she was lying on a heap of rags and bottles in the deep shade of the breakwater, and that her face was blue.

That was 13 June. Nicole had been in Whitmouth for four days at the time she met her death. She'd last been seen stumbling off from the Sticky Wicket pub, a skinful of snakebite and a lovebite on her neck, in search of chips. She was from Lancashire. She was nineteen years old and had left school the previous year with A levels in catering sciences and business studies. She had wanted to go into the hotel trade, and had been working as a receptionist at the Jurys Inn in Manchester for the previous three months. The trip to Whitmouth had partly been a scouting expedition to see if she couldn't move a bit further up the food chain in one of the hotels along the Kent coast. She didn't have a boyfriend, hadn't had one since the sixth form.

She had come here as a child two or three times, with her parents, Susan and Grahame, and her two brothers, Jake and Mark. A nice, clean, respectable girl the vast majority of the time – not out of control habitually, but cutting loose with her mates the way teenagers do. No one had noticed her between her leaving the pub and turning up strangled twelve hours later. Of course they hadn't: she was unremarkable, and the streets were crowded.

As Kirsty stands thinking about the girl and the circumstances of her death, a man in an anorak – he's got the look of a stoat or a ferret, she thinks, all pointy teeth and beady little eyes – pauses as he passes her.

'Can I help you?' he asks. His voice is flat, nasal, toneless.

'No. Thank you,' she says, trying to sound kind and friendly, but clear. Then, 'Well, yes, actually, as you ask. Are you from around here?'

'Yes,' he replies with an edge of annoyance, as though the answer is so obvious a child could see it.

'Oh, good. I've been having trouble finding anyone who isn't a tourist.' This is a minor lie. Truth is, the locals she's found have shown admirable loyalty to their home patch and she's alarmingly short of attributable scared-to-go-out, quaking-in-bed quotations that will make the people of Cheltenham grateful for their property prices. If she can't get some soon, she's going to have to make them up. 'Do you mind if I ask you how you feel about all this? These murders? As a local resident?'

The suspicion dials up. 'Why do you want to know?'

Kirsty adjusts. Turns the transparent charm up a notch. 'Yes. Sorry. I should have introduced myself.' She offers him a hand to shake, though the thought of touching his greyish skin makes her feel uncomfortable. 'Kirsty Lindsay. The *Sunday Tribune*. I'm writing an article about—'

'I know what you're writing about,' he says, and he puffs with pride as he says it. You get this sometimes. Though most people are nervous around journalists, afraid of letting out too much information about themselves, unsure of where a question will lead, there's always the odd one who sees an approach as evidence that they are important, and that the journalist has seen it where their neighbours have not.

'Sure. OK, yes, of course you do,' she says. 'So I was wondering—'

'I'll tell you what I think,' he says. 'I think the lot of you should go away. No one wants you around here.'

'Oh, look,' protests Kirsty. 'We've got to report the news.'

'Yes,' he says, 'if you call it reporting. I know what you'll do. You won't ask anyone who actually *knows*. That's not what you want, is it? You just want to bring your London sneering down to the provinces. We'd be fine if you'd all just go away and leave us alone.'

'I—' She looks at the tufty hairs on his carelessly shaved cheeks, the tight lips set in stubbornness, the unreasoning knee-jerk dislike in the eyes, and knows her answer. She's not going to get anything useful out of this guy. Just the sort of formless disapproval that blames the media rather than the man who's actually killing people. 'OK,' she says, 'thanks anyway.'

'You can't quote me,' he says. 'I didn't give you permission to quote me.'

'I don't have your name anyway,' she says. Walks away up the beach before he can prolong the encounter. Feels, nonetheless, his eyes bore into her back as she skirts between the barbecue and the perimeter fence of Funnland, a festoon of yellow police tape marking out the hole in the short run of wire fence behind a bucket-and-spade stall. From this side, the amusement park's concrete fortifications make it look a bit like a prison camp. The front wall, on the blowy road everyone jokingly calls 'the Corniche', is bright with hoardings and coloured lights.

Besides the big party, a few knots of young people talk and doze away their hangovers, and play Frisbee in T-shirts and long shorts. A camera team wanders among them, recording vox pops. Kirsty wonders how the lure of appearing on television can overcome the horror of doing so without make-up or preparation.

'Yeah, of course I'm scared,' says a young woman as she passes, 'but what am I supposed to do? I only get a week's holiday. I've got to have fun, innit?'

'So are you going to come to Whitmouth again?' asks the reporter.

'Probably not,' she replies. 'It's a bit pants, really. The booze is dead expensive and, did you know?, that amusement park' – she gestures at the hulking wall of Funnland, where the police are spending their second day sweeping every inch between the fence and the death site with camelhair brushes – 'has been closed ever since we got here. And in high season too!'

She visits the Antalya Kebab House, where the second victim, Keisha Brown, was last seen. The owner is Turkish, voluble and unfriendly. 'So why are you suddenly interested?' he asks. 'You know what? This happened twice last year as well. There were two girls last year, and they were just as dead then, and you didn't give a toss. Not one reporter, not one newspaper, apart from the *Whitmouth Guardian*, nobody from the telly *then*. They were invisible then. Might as well never have existed. But *now* … you've got some *glamour* now. You're all looking for your Hannibal Lecter and now it matters, isn't it?'

'Fair point,' she says. There are two murders every day in the UK. Only a third of them make much more than a downpage NiB in the papers. You've got to have a stand-out quality, or a determined family, for your death to get past the news editors. 'But I'm here now. At least it's a chance to put that right now, eh?'

'You gonna buy something?' he asks gruffly, glaring with deep dark eyes.

'What's good?'

'Everything's good.'

'I'll have a doner and a Coke, please.'

'Chips?' he barks.

'No,' she begins, then hurriedly assents. No point in blowing her chances for the price of a bag of chips. 'And a receipt, please.'

She waits a couple of beats as he turns to the fryer and plunges the basket into the oil. 'So do you remember her?'

He has his back turned. She can see his reflection in the mirrored wall behind the grill, napkin-scrawled, sellotaped-on specials framing his black hair. He's fifty-something, and looks older. Everyone looks older around here.

Stop it, she thinks. You've turned into the worst sort of bourgeois snob while you weren't looking. Just because you write for an audience doesn't mean you have to share their views.

He shrugs. 'Not really. Yes, sort of. But only because of what happened. I wouldn't have remembered anything about her except for the fact that I found her body in among my dustbins. *Then* I remember her. Sort of.'

'Was she with people? Alone?'

'I don't know. A lot of the time it's hard to tell, especially on a Saturday. Sometimes they're alone when they come in and not when they leave. They're like animals on Saturday night. You'd think, what with them being on holiday, Saturday wouldn't be such a big deal, but you'd be surprised. They still get dressed up, get drunker, stay out later. Don't know how to queue, don't know how to wait. Must've been twenty, thirty, hanging around, inside, dropping stuff on the pavement. Chips, chips, chips. Twenty alcopops and then they think chips will put them right. I've got CCTV. Something kicks off every Saturday. CCTV saves me hours giving statements.'

'So she's on it?'

He nods. 'Yeah. Like I say, nothing remarkable. She comes in, she gets her chips, she talks to some boys while she waits. She liked vinegar. Must've used up half a bottle. Fanta. She drank Fanta.'

'And the boys?'

'I don't know. Ask the police. They must've told you anyway. It wasn't them. They were too drunk to stand up, most of them, let alone strangle someone. Except by accident maybe. So she gets her chips, she leaves, I carry on serving. We're open till four on Saturday. I can turn two hundred kilos of chips on a good night, high season. We're the only shop that's open when the clubs let out, and most of them would sell their aunties for a bag of chips.'

'So then?' she prompts.

'Half-four I'm taking out the trash, waiting for the oil to cool down enough to drain the fryer, and ...' He shrugs again. As an obituary, it's not much.

'It must have been awful,' she says sympathetically.

'Yeah ...' He starts to wrap her kebab in paper. 'It's not something you see every day. You want chilli sauce?'

'Thanks.'

'Thanks no or thanks yes?'

'Thanks yes. Thanks.'

'Open or closed?'

'Closed, please.' It's only going to go into the first bin she passes when she gets out of sight.

He slaps the bundle down on the counter.

'Twelve pound fifty.'

'Twelve *fifty*?' she squeaks.

'Twelve fifty,' he says firmly. 'And a receipt.'

Kirsty suppresses an eye-roll and hands over the money. The press aren't the only people for whom serial murder represents a business opportunity.

She can't get into Funnland. A notice on the staff gate, where a handful of cold-looking hacks and snappers huddles among piles of cellophane-wrapped carnations, says that it will reopen tomorrow. She's worked with one of the photographers a few times before, and wanders over. 'Anything much?' she asks. 'Seen Stan Marshall?'

He shakes his head. 'I should think he's in the pub. Nothing much here. Managing director, that Suzanne Oddie, and some other suits.'

'Anything to say?'

'Blah blah unprecedented, blah blah sympathies to family, blah blah cooperating with the police to the fullest extent, blah blah reassure our customers. There's a press release.'

Jeremy from the *Express* hands it to her. There's not much. Park open again asap, Innfinnityland closed, probably to be demolished. Heartfelt sympathy. She takes a picture with her phone. She'll read it off the jpeg later.

'What are you doing here anyway? I thought Dave Park was here for the *Trib*.'

'He is. He's Mr Hard News. I've got the colour feature. Town in torment. Lock up your daughters. Price of beer. You know.'

'Ah, the Sunday stuffies,' says a hack from the *Mirror*. 'Nothing new to say, just more of it.'

'Still,' says the snapper, 'nice work if you can get it.'

'Someone's got to use the five-syllable words,' she says. 'To give the rest of you something to sneer at. So what do we know? Anything new on the vic?'

She quails faintly inside as she says it. The vic – a life reduced to flippancy.

'Nothing new. The mum and dad are doing an appeal this arvo in the town hall.'

'Is that where everybody else is?'

The man from the *Mirror* tuts. 'Don't be stupid. It's not till four. They're all in the White Horse, up on Dock Street.'

'News-gathering,' says the photographer, and winks.

Chapter Nine

Amber's in the kitchen, on the phone in pursuit of a computer for Benedick, when someone starts pressing the doorbell. Urgently and insistently, over and over, a couple of seconds between each peal. Whoever it is, they want in, now.

'I wonder who that is?' she says, cutting the call.

Vic looks up from the *Sun*. 'Well, I'll guess it's either a waif or a stray. Stray, probably, by the sound of the ring. Waifs don't ring that hard.'

'Ha,' she says, and runs for the door.

A figure stands with its back to her, the hood of an Adidas top pulled up over its head, gym bag over its shoulder, scanning the cars and concrete bollards of Tennyson Way as though expecting someone to appear.

'Can I help you?' Amber asks. The figure turns. It's Jackie Jacobs, looking just awful. Below the top she wears what look like pyjama bottoms and a pair of the shuffle-along flip-flops Romina used to wear. Her face, devoid of make-up, is lined and grey, with deep vertical runnels on her upper lip.

'I didn't know where else to come,' she says. 'I'm sorry.'

'Oh my God,' says Amber. 'Come in.'

She stands back to let Jackie pass, and follows her indoors. Vic sees her from his seat at the kitchen table and shoots to his feet. 'What's up, Jacks?'

Jackie pushes her hood back. Her hair is greasy, unbrushed.

Amber finds it hard to believe that this is the same exuberant creature she shared the beach with yesterday. 'He's just standing outside my flat and he won't go away,' she says, and bursts into tears.

Amber doesn't need to ask who she's talking about. 'Oh my God,' she says again.

'He's just ... there. All the time. He just sits outside the flat. Or he's ... you know. Like yesterday. Down at the beach, or down at the supermarket, or wherever I am. I feel like I'm going mad.'

'You're not.' Amber takes the bag, drops it on the stairs. It's clear they've got a house-guest. Amber Gordon's Home for Fallen Women, Vic calls it. When he's feeling nice. Sometimes, depending on the guest, he calls it the Whitmouth Dog Sanctuary. 'I can understand why you feel that way, but you're not. You haven't spoken to him, have you?'

'No,' says Vic. 'You're supposed to ignore them.'

'I've tried,' says Jackie. 'But what am I supposed to do? If someone's there every day, when you go to the shops, waiting outside work, ringing on the doorbell, leaving messages, leaving ... *daisies* on your doorstep ... *you* try ignoring it.'

'Oh God, Jackie. You always make a joke of things. I didn't realise it was this serious.'

They follow Vic back into the kitchen. He goes to fill the kettle. The Whitmouth solution to all troubles, a nice cup of tea and a biscuit. And God knows, for most troubles it works a treat.

'I know. Yes,' says Jackie. 'I guess maybe I didn't either. I thought he'd get the message or something. Get bored. But since you ... The body. That poor girl. One minute she's alive and the next some bloke's just ... Maybe it's freaked me out more than I thought it had. But it's worse now. I can't ... I really can't be there any more, Amber. He just stands there and stands there, and it doesn't seem to make any difference what I do. I've no idea when he sleeps, 'cause it feels like he's there twenty-four/seven.'

'It's OK,' says Amber. 'You can stay here. As long as you like. Till we work out what to do.'

She glances up at Vic. He's standing by the sink, his face inexpressive. If he has any feelings on the subject, he's not sharing.

Jackie goes pink about the nose and takes a pack of blue Camels from the pocket of her jacket. Searches around for a lighter. Vic clears his throat.

'I'm sorry, Jackie,' he says, 'd'you mind taking it out to the garden?'

She looks surprised, as though no one has ever suggested such a thing before, but picks up the pack and starts to get up from the table.

'I'll get you an ashtray,' says Vic.

She looks unexpectedly grateful. 'Thanks,' she says.

Amber follows her out on to the patio, Mary-Kate and Ashley tip-tapping quietly at their heels. She's proud of her little patch of ground. The salty estuarine soil makes it fairly useless for growing things, but she's filled it with pots and baskets of busy Lizzies and geraniums and verbena, and the little garden is bright and welcoming. The chairs are tipped up against rain, their cushions in the shed. She pulls them out, brushes water off their coated-wire seats. 'Sorry,' she says.

'What? Oh, no. Don't be stupid. It's your house.'

Vic appears with the ashtray, puts it on the table, smiles and retreats indoors.

Jackie lights up. Amber can see the nicotine bliss cross her face, remembers it well. She gave up for Vic, but she still misses it, every day. 'God, you have an ashtray. Most people don't do that, and then they give your stubs *looks*, like they're nuclear waste or something. Even when they're in the bin with the potato peelings.'

'Yeah, we'd never do that,' says Amber.

'No,' says Jackie, 'Vic's got the manners of a priest.'

'Well, I wouldn't go *that* far,' says Amber, but quietly she thinks, yes, that's how the world would sum up our relationship, probably: *polite*. Vic has great manners. It was like getting into a big warm bath, meeting Vic: having doors held open and appreciation shown, knowing that a dish eaten from would quickly be cleared and cleaned. After all those years, she'd been quite afraid of men, of their drives and stubbornness; thought them bullies, only interested in personal gratification.

And then there was Vic. Hands always clean despite the running repairs that form a large part of his duties on the Funnland rides. A please and a thank-you and a protective arm ushering her through the crowds. She remembers noticing him, the way he'd give a helping hand to customers as they tottered on and off the rides; how he'd always have a smile and a laugh for anyone who wanted one; how he could appease the most swaggering yob in search of aggro. Whitmouth relationships aren't long relationships, on the whole, but it's six years they've been together now, and if politeness is the price you pay for longevity, then thank God for good manners. All those years, when she longed to fetch up in a place of calm – she still finds it difficult to believe it's happened.

'You don't realise how lucky you are. I'd give anything to have a bloke like that,' says Jackie, and looks tearful again.

Amber reaches out and rubs her forearm, feels awkward doing it. She's never really learned the touchy-feely habit; hasn't thought of Jackie as an intimate. 'Don't, Jackie,' she says. 'It's all right. You'll be all right.'

Jackie stares at her cigarette, her face working. Mary-Kate comes and stands on her back legs, front paws resting on Amber's thigh. Automatically she takes her hand from the arm and chucks her dog behind the ear.

'It's not *fair*,' Jackie bursts out. 'It's just not bloody *fair*. I *never* catch a break.'

Vic appears in the doorway, calm as ever. He's carrying Jackie's bag. 'I'll put this in the spare room, Jackie,' he says. 'OK?'

Amber knows that the gesture is more about his aversion to

mess than about hospitality. Vic likes everything to have a place. The bag will have been bugging him since she arrived. Jackie interprets it differently and sees it as a gesture of welcome. She tears up again. 'God, you guys. I don't know what I'd do ... Honestly. I swear, half this town would've fallen apart without you.'

'Oh, come on, Jackie,' says Amber uncomfortably.

'She's right, you know,' says Vic, from the door. 'Salt of the earth, our Amber. D'you know what she's been doing all morning?'

'No,' says Jackie, with little enthusiasm. She's never that interested in other people, especially when a drama of her own is under way.

'Calling everyone on the estate to see if they've got a spare computer for Benedick Ongom. She's been on the phone all morning, haven't you, darling? I had to get my own bacon sandwich.'

He moderates the complaint with a bright and winning smile, but Amber hears it anyway.

'Yes,' he continues. 'She's amazing, really. Sometimes I can't help wondering if she's got a guilty conscience. If she's making up for something she did in a past life, or something.'

Jackie laughs. Amber, blushing, hurries the subject away from herself. 'So tell me what happened? I'm still not sure I get it.'

'It just – I don't know why he's doing it. You know? I don't get it.'

'No,' she says. 'Well, I don't suppose you would. He's obviously not right, is he? Anyway, I thought Tadeusz had seen him off. With that text.'

Jackie shakes her head. 'I think it's made him worse. He's angry now. I can feel it coming off him. He just seems to be out there the whole time. And it's going to be worse when I go back to work. Going out at night, all by myself.'

'That's OK. I can give you a lift,' says Amber, calmly adding another item to her list. There's room in the car. She's only shuttling Blessed at the moment.

'But it's not just that, it is? I'm not sleeping, either. I feel like I'm going to wake up and find him standing over me or something. Seriously. He's just there, all the time. I feel like I'm going mad ...'

Vic watches them through the kitchen window: the two blond heads bent together, the curl of smoke rising off Jackie's cigarette. They've forgotten all about him. Out of sight, out of mind, he thinks. Women. The minute you're not talking, you might as well not exist. He studies them quietly, his face blank. He feels dog-tired. He used to feel exhilarated for days at a time, during high season, but the thrill gets shorter-lived year on year. Eight different resorts he's worked over the years, but nowadays Whitmouth seems to tire rather than thrill. It's my age, he thinks, catching up with me. I'm getting too old for this. I need to find an easier way to live. I don't think I'll have the energy for much longer. It really takes it out of me.

Jackie's left her tea mug on the table, a swill of tannin on the bone-china inside. He picks it up and takes it to the sink. Scrubs methodically, thoroughly, as he listens to the murmur of the women's voices. Wipes round the sink, polishes the chrome dry and puts the cup on the folded tea-towel on the drainer.

Out in the garden, Jackie's phone starts to ring.

'Don't answer it,' Amber says. 'Leave it.'

Jackie regards the phone as though it's a turd she's found in her handbag. 'I wasn't planning to.'

The phone rings out. Jackie lights another cigarette. Amber suppresses an eye-roll.

'I'll get Vic to make up the spare bed,' she tells Jackie.

'God, he's so great,' says Jackie. 'How did you manage to find him?'

Her phone rings again.

Chapter Ten

I'm a lousy wife. He's really hacked off with me and I don't blame him. Oh God, I can't wait for this evening to be over. What the hell made me behave so stupidly? I don't suppose I was even legal to drive when I got into the car this afternoon.

Kirsty uses the cover of being in the kitchen to down a pint of water and slam three ibuprofen down with it. She feels like she's been turned inside out, and her guilty conscience makes it worse. It's like a frenzy, she thinks. Not the drink in itself, but the company of journalists. You can't have a dozen hacks spend an evening together without everyone getting so blotto they can barely stand up; it's never happened.

She drains the glass and refills it. Opens the fridge and gets out the gravadlax, the bags of salad. The sort of food they've not been allowing themselves for months. But exigency has driven her through the aisles of Waitrose like a WAG with a Man U pay cheque. The whole family will be living on beans and rice for the rest of the week to pay for this dinner, but none of the people in the dining room is going to know that. Nothing breeds success like success, and if Jim's going to get a job, they must persuade these money people that he doesn't need one. The good side plates are laid out on the countertop, checked for chips, and all she needs to do is fill them, decoratively, while their guests drink Sophie's shoe fund in Sémillon-Chardonnay.

She feels an urge to vomit and swallows it down. Flaming

shooters. At your age. At *any* age. What on earth possessed you?

Because it was fun. Because I love the company of journalists. Because I love their casual, competitive intelligence, their ranty partisan opinions, the way they compete to reduce everything on earth to a five-word headline, their cynical search for the perfect pejorative. Because I'm tired of being good, and I'm tired of being patient, because I've been living it small for months now and I just needed to kick over the traces, and because I got caught early for my round in the White Horse and wanted to get my money's worth back. Because you can't describe what a town where people come to go on benders is like unless you've gone on one there yourself. Because, despite the heartless carapace we all carry around with us, spending a day digging up the detail on the deaths of five young girls is depressing enough to drive anyone to the bottle. And because I just bloody forgot about this dinner party.

The door bangs back and Jim enters, the sociable-host smile dropping from his face as he crosses the threshold. He lets the door swing to before he speaks. 'Fuck's sake, Kirsty,' he mutters. 'What've you been doing?'

Her skin feels raw under the thick layer of make-up she's slathered on to hide her pallor. 'Sorry,' she says. 'Had to take a painkiller.'

Jim's jaw is set like concrete as he snatches up the salad bags. 'Christ,' he says. 'I'll do it. You open the salmon.'

He turns his back and rips open the packets. Pea-shoots, watercress and rocket, the TV-chef dream combo. A small earthenware jug of dressing he made this afternoon waits by the salad bowl. He dumps the leaves in, sloshes on the dressing and starts tossing. Miserably, Kirsty finds the kitchen scissors and begins cutting open the salmon. Her hands are shaking, visibly.

'Sorry, Jim,' she says for the eighteenth time, laying the slices of fish as neatly as she can on to the plates. 'I'm really sorry. I didn't mean to.'

He's so angry he can't even look at her as he dishes the salad out next to the fish. 'I really don't think sorry's good enough right now. You *knew* how important tonight was. You're just ... *selfish*. I can't think of another word for it. Just bloody *selfish*.'

'Yes,' she says, penitently. 'I know. It was. I am. And I'm really, really sorry.'

Miserably, she cuts open a sachet of the mustard sauce that came in the packet. Squeezes it over a portion of fish.

'*NO!*' He grabs her wrist and his cry is loud enough to be heard through the door. The murmur of voices dies down for a moment. Someone giggles.

'What?'

'Don't use the *packet* stuff, you idiot. I made some.' He flourishes a beaker of identical yellow glop that's been sitting by the sink.

'Oh shit, sorry.'

He shakes his head again, suppressing his rage with difficulty. 'Look, just get out of the way. I'll do it. I can't believe you'd do this to me. These are people who eat in restaurants all the time. Like they're not going to notice the sauce came out of a packet.'

'Sorry,' says her autopilot. She feels so wretched she's amazed she's still on her feet. All she wants to do is curl up in front of the telly and doze until bedtime. I will never drink again, she thinks, for the 763rd time in her life.

Jim doles out the sauce, turns and hands her two plates. 'Here. Take these through. You can have the bought one. I'll bring it through last. And for God's sake pull yourself together.'

Kirsty gulps. Together, they go back to their guests.

'Here's mud in your eye,' says Lionel Baker, and she flinches: even in her fragile state, golf-club phrases make her skin crawl.

'Cheers,' she says, and raises her untouched glass. Puts it to her lips but doesn't take a sip. Partly because she fears her liver will explode if a drop of alcohol goes into her body, but mostly because Jim's eyes bore into her like a laser every time her hand strays towards the stem.

Sue Baker giggles and clinks her glass. 'Such a funny phrase,' she says. Sue's the real deal: a woman who chose to Make a Lovely Home the moment she landed herself a stockbroker, and hasn't had an original thought since she decided to have ornamental cabbages as the table centrepieces at her wedding. I must be nice, thinks Kirsty. If Jim's going to tap these people up for a job, they need to remember what good hosts we are. Lionel's ten years older than Jim, ten inches larger about the waist and ten times more pleased with himself. But he's also been a partner at Marshall & Straum for years, and they all know he's recruiting again now that the worst of the shitstorm is over. Jim and Gerard Lucas-Jones, the other husband at the table, were on his team when he got promoted. Everyone is pretending that they're old friends.

Sue puts her glass down and picks up her knife and fork. 'How lovely,' she says, with a patronising edge. 'I haven't had gravadlax in years. Did you cure it yourself?'

Of course you haven't, thinks Kirsty viciously. Gravadlax is *so* 1980s, darling. I'm sorry they were out of black-cod sashimi by the time I got to Waitrose.

'Afraid not,' says Jim. 'Kirsty's been away, working. I made the sauce, though.'

She smiles quietly. Jim takes pride in being 'good' in the house; always has done. But it's not the right image for a Master of the Universe, he remembers. 'It's one of the great things about working from home,' he adds hastily. 'Two hours' commute clawed back every day.'

'And all of it spent cooking,' jokes Kirsty experimentally.

'Well,' says Jim meanly, 'it's better than drinking myself into a stupor, eh?'

Everyone laughs, the barb floating over their heads. '*Lucky* old you,' says Lionel Baker, sounding exactly like his wife. 'I long for more time at home, of course. But tell me.' He turns to Kirsty, and she can see that his enquiry isn't steeped in approval.

Lionel's a dinosaur. Working wives are not his cup of tea. 'Away *working*? How *grand*. Do a lot of *travelling*, do you?'

'Not travel, exactly,' she replies, trying to work out how to play things down so the job that's keeping them all afloat sounds like an indulgent husband's tolerance of the little lady's hobby. 'But, you know, a few overnighters here and there.'

She can see him placing her as a travelling saleswoman; wouldn't mind, particularly, except that sales is probably not the top job for a wifey. Jim intervenes. 'Kirsty's a stringer,' he says, 'for the *Tribune*.'

'What's a stringer?' asks Penny Lucas-Jones. She teaches French and Italian at a girls' boarding school outside Salisbury. It fits in well with childcare.

'A journalist,' Jim tells her. 'She covers a patch of the south-east so the staffers don't have to leave London.'

'A hack!' says Lionel. 'Well, *well*! Doorstepping celebrities, eh? Hacking phones?'

'No,' says Jim. 'They have specialists for phone hacking.'

'Mostly crime,' Kirsty says. 'And, you know – London people visiting the provinces.'

The joke falls flat. He's taken me literally, she thinks. Of course he has. Prising him out of Belgravia was like pulling hens' teeth, and now I'm blowing it. She feels another wave of nausea break over her, gulps it back. I bet I'm green, she thinks. Which at least will cover the yellow of liver damage.

'How exciting!' says Gerard Lucas-Jones. 'We read the *Tribune*, funnily enough. Well, Penny does. I'm more of an *FT* man myself.'

'I've not noticed you in there,' says Sue. 'Do you get published often?'

'She got two pieces in this week, actually,' Jim says. 'She had a full page today, and she's got *two* on Sunday.'

'Clever girl!' says Lionel, drawing out the 'i' in girl so it lasts two seconds.

Sue has the grace to look faintly embarrassed. 'What about?' she asks.

'Oh, this rather sad-sack bunch of moral rearmament nutjobs

who launched this week. But it was a bit of a damp squib, to be honest. And the other one's on Whitmouth. The Whitmouth murders. I'm still writing that.'

'Ah, yes,' says Lionel. 'Prostitutes, isn't it?'

Mustn't argue, she thinks. We're here for Jim's career. And frankly, I don't have the spit for it anyway. I got most of my bile out last night. 'No,' she replies, 'just girls on holiday. Teenagers having fun, you know?'

Her mind conjures up an image of Nicole Ponsonby's sister on the Whitmouth Police station steps, behind a bank of microphones, weeping. Begging for someone, somewhere, to dob the killer in. The families always think the pain will go away if the killer is caught; that they'll get some kind of closure. Like drowning sailors, they grasp at any straw of hope, anything that suggests that they won't be feeling like this for ever. Kirsty's seen them so often now, struggling to get words out, propping each other up on tottering legs. Knows that the weeping never ends, not really.

'A bit of a shithole, isn't it, Whitmouth?' Lionel asks, and crams half of his starter in his mouth in one go.

'I suppose so. Depends on what you like, really. I think it has a – I don't know, a sleazy charm.'

'Went to Southend once,' he says. 'Someone's idea of an ironic stag weekend. Now *there*'s a shithole. As bad as that?'

She thinks. She's done a fair amount of time in Southend. It's a fruitful venue, if you're on the crime circuit. 'Yes,' she says. 'But pebbles, like Bognor.'

'Oh, *Bognor*,' he says, as though he need say no more.

The conversation hits a lull. Kirsty looks down at her plate, struggles to find a new topic. Struggles not to vomit. She can feel Jim burning to start in on vacancies, but it's too early. They need to wait till the crème brûlée is on the table. Business can never be discussed directly until you're eating crème brûlée. She can feel herself getting hot, just from the contact of the wine with her lips. Thinks she might be about to break into a sweat.

*

The pinger goes off in the kitchen: time to take the meat out and put on the mange-tout. She excuses herself and goes through.

Taking the pork loin from the oven, she puts it on the dish to rest, then goes to the freezer and finds a packet of peas to press against her forehead. She's closer to forty than thirty, but she still finds formal entertaining a strain. And that's without a professional lady of the house like Sue Baker at her table. Kirsty has seen her eyes drift over their sitting room, their dining room, seeking out signs of non-conformity or dirt.

Come on, Kirsty. There's something you're meant to do. What is it?

She presses the peas against the back of her neck and checks the kitchen for signs of disarray. Sue's the sort of person who will insist on helping clear, the better to snoop. Notes, lists, photos, clamped to the fridge door with Sistine Chapel magnets. A cork pinboard sporting the kids' schedules: Sophie piano, Tues 5; Luke football, Weds 6; swimming, Sat 9. Sophie has arranged the leftover push-pins in the shape of a heart – her favourite image at the moment, apart from Justin Bieber. They've cleared the usual packets of breakfast cereal and thrown-down schoolbags from the work surfaces; now, just a bottle of excellent claret (two school uniforms' worth at Tesco), open and breathing, stands below the newly scrubbed spice rack, the dishwasher humming beneath. A normal middle-class kitchen, she thinks, tarted up to impress the Lucas-Joneses. My mum would say I was a snob because there aren't any chickens under the table.

She remembers what else she needs to do. Fills a pan from the kettle, puts it on the stove. God knows what she'd say about me serving mange-tout, she thinks.

Back in the dining room, the conversation has moved on. 'I just don't see,' Lionel is saying, 'why they should get anonymity. That's this society all over, isn't it? Everything skewed in favour of the perpetrator, not a thought for the victim. Have you been covering this?' He turns to Kirsty as she takes her seat again.

'Sorry,' she says. 'Lost track.'

'Child F and Child M.'

'Oh. No. Sleaford's off my patch, I'm afraid. I've got a friend who has. He's been finding it very depressing.'

'Well, I was just saying. It's disgusting.'

'Yes ...' she says, vaguely. 'Awful. That poor child.'

'No, not just that. The way the establishment's swung into gear to protect the little' – he pauses; he's obviously been about to say 'shits' '– sods that did it.'

'Well, the whole thing's *sub judice*,' says Jim. 'You'd want them to get a fair trial, wouldn't you?'

Lionel snorts. 'Fair trial? It's on *film*, for heaven's sake.'

Kirsty feels the blush creep up her cheeks. She always finds conversation of this sort difficult; feels exposed, endangered. A small, paranoid part of her wonders if the subject's been raised because someone knows more about her than they're letting on. 'And they've got siblings,' she protests. 'Surely you don't think the other kids deserve to get mob justice for what their brothers did?'

Lionel snorts again. 'It's that sort of woolly liberal sentimentality that leads to situations like this in the first place.'

She can see Jim's woolly liberal hackles rising. Don't, she thinks. Please don't. You can't get into an argument. Can't piss him off, let him think you don't admire every pearl that drops from his mouth. Not when we've gone to all this effort.

'More wine, anyone?' she says hurriedly. The two women assent volubly, praise the choice of grape, fuss over their husbands' glasses: they too have read that there's about to be dissent and join forces to keep things nice. Lionel's having none of it. Kirsty wonders if he's enjoying himself; if he knows why he's been asked here and is taking full advantage of the company's powerlessness to contradict.

'The fact is,' he says, 'for the good of society as a whole we should identify the murderous little monsters and lock them up, and do it *before* they kill someone else's child. We don't seem to care about the victims any more. It's all about the criminal. Poor little crim, let's make excuses. And yes, actually – the public ought to be protected from them. And their vicious little siblings.'

The words burst out before she can stop them. She feels as though her heart's about to burst from her chest. 'But they're *twelve years old*!'

'Exactly!' he replies. 'Just goes to show. It starts young. You can't just go, "Yeah, poor little kiddies", because someone else's poor little kiddie has ended up dead.'

'But their brothers and sisters haven't done anything!'

'Yet,' he says. Stares her in the eye. '*Yet*,' he repeats.

There's a moment's silence. I must stop, she thinks. I'm close to going off on one here.

Sue is obviously having similar thoughts. She hurriedly polishes off her last sliver of salmon. 'Well, I must say, that was a real treat!' she says brightly. 'I must remember gravadlax.'

'Here,' says Jim grimly, standing up, 'let me take that for you.'

She follows him into the kitchen with the other plates. He's tipping the mange-tout into the boiling water. There's a high-pitched whine in the centre of her head, boring through her brain like an awl. She grabs another glass of water, downs it, prays hopelessly for relief. I will never drink again, she promises silently once more.

'What can I do?' she asks.

'Not get so pissed you can't function the next day,' he mutters.

'Oh God, Jim, I've apologised. I'm sorry. I'm doing my best.'

'Yeah, well,' he says, 'it's not just about today though, is it?'

'That's not fair. That's *so* unfair, Jim!'

'Not from where I'm standing,' he says.

'Please let's not do this now.' The water has stirred something up in her stomach. She feels it lurch, feels her gullet spasm. Oh shit, she thinks. I swear I'll never drink again. Never. I swear.

'We've got to talk about your drinking,' he says.

'Oh, look! As if *you've* never had a hangover!'

Jim slams the mange-tout into the colander. 'You knew how much it mattered that we did well tonight,' he says. 'Are you *trying* to sabotage me?'

Kirsty gags. Slaps a hand over her mouth and flees the room. Hears his muttered 'Oh God' as she goes.

She makes it to the downstairs loo with a second to spare. Retches over the bowl and drops to her knees as an explosion of old drink, water, this morning's sausage sandwich and tonight's starter pumps out of her body. She must have stopped digesting at some point in the small hours. She starts feeling better the moment it's all expelled. Fortunately, she learned the knack of silent vomiting soon after she joined the *Mercury*. It's one that's stood her in good stead.

She stays leaning on the seat for a minute, waiting for the sweating fit to die down. She feels weak and tired now, but the giddiness is receding. God, I'm a lousy wife, she thinks again. And he's right. I need to stop with the drink. It's a really childish way of dealing with stress.

She gets up and checks herself in the mirror. Her eye make-up has smudged slightly, but the colour is rapidly returning to her face. She rinses her mouth out using the mouthwash that lives behind the curtain, fills the air with the aerosol scent of freesias. Puts on a new layer of lipstick, smacks her lips together. OK, she thinks. That's better. I can face the world.

She goes back to the kitchen, finds it empty, the pork and its dish gone from the work surfaces, the vegetables dished out and waiting. She grabs them up and goes into the dining room, smiling brightly.

'I'll tell you what, Kirsty,' says Penny, once everyone's served and settled, 'I was wondering if I could ask a favour.'

'Fire away,' says Kirsty. Favours done by her must put Jim in pole position for favours in return. 'What can I do?'

'Well, we like to have people come and give careers talks at the school. What do you think? Would you think about coming in and talking about journalism at some point?'

'I ...' she says doubtfully. She's not comfortable on stages, in front of crowds.

'I know you're busy,' says Penny. 'But we'd give you plenty of notice. Everything needs plenty of notice now, because it takes months for the CRB checks to go through.'

Instantly she's blushing and stammering. She's on a lifetime licence. A disclosure form won't reveal who she is, but it will certainly show that she's got a record. And Jim knows nothing. Not about her past, not about the reality of her present.

Penny smiles. 'I know. It's ridiculous, isn't it? Lots of people feel offended, but honestly, it's just another piece of bureaucratic form-filling.'

'Another job-creation scheme,' says Jim.

Lionel takes a drink. 'That's exactly the sort of thing I'm talking about,' he says. 'It's all upside-down nowadays. The government squandering millions of pounds of our money making out that innocent people like you are suspects when we all know where the problem actually lies.'

'Well, you don't *actually* know for sure,' jokes Jim. 'My wife could have a long criminal history, for all you know.'

Lionel gives him the patient look of someone with no sense of humour. 'I'm just saying,' he says slowly, 'that the apple doesn't fall far from the tree.'

Kirsty rises to the bait. Grabs the chance to take the focus away from school visits.

'Seriously? You'd just chuck them on the scrapheap?'

'Well, let's face it. You can pretty much predict which kids are going to turn out feral, just from looking at their parents.'

'Wow,' she says. '*Wow.*'

'Come on,' he says. 'You can't deny it. I bet you've got apartheid at your own school gates. Don't try and pretend you haven't.'

'I ...' she says.

'It's hardly a new phenomenon. Generation after generation like that. Where there's a fat slattern mother feeding her kids McDonald's and shouting at the school staff, you can guarantee there's a fat slattern grandmother necking cider and fighting with the neighbours.'

'Gosh,' Kirsty says again. Remembers her maternal grandmother's neat cottage: ceramic dancing ladies lined up on the windowsill, not a speck of dust anywhere. She probably thinks – thought? Kirsty has no idea, even, which members of her family are still alive – that the problem stemmed from her daughter having taken up with a gyppo. She certainly wouldn't have seen that there was a connection between her respectable chapel-going rigidity and the unwashed, thieving grandchildren who swarmed off Ben Walker's pig farm. 'So you're saying it's genetic, then?'

'Well, you can't deny it runs in families.'

Kirsty suddenly remembers that there's mustard in the kitchen; excuses herself to go and fetch it. She can't hear any more for the time being.

11 a.m.

'No! Out!'

Bel looks up, expecting to see that a dog has wandered into the shop. A girl her own age stands in the doorway. Shorter than she is, with a pinched look of resentment on her face.

Mrs Stroud comes out from behind the counter and advances on her, waving one hand ceilingwards. 'Out!' she barks.

'Oh, come on,' says the girl. 'I only wanted a Kit Kat.'

'I'll bet you did,' says Mrs Stroud. 'Out!'

The girl is plump, in a malnourished sort of way. A faded red polka-dot ra-ra skirt, frills above the knees, and an overtight striped halter top. Pierced ears, from which dangle a pair of low-carat gold hoops. Her brown hair, slightly greasy, has been given a rough kitchen-scissor cut at chin level. Bel carries on selecting her pick-'n'-mix as the scene unfolds. Tries not to look like she's watching, but doesn't manage well.

'No, look.' The girl opens her palm to show a twenty-pence piece. Certainly enough for a Kit Kat, and probably a few Fruit Salads as well. 'I've got money.'

'Oh yes?' The woman has reached the door and is holding it open. 'And where did you nick that from?'

The girl looks livid.

'Come on. Out. You know there's no Walkers allowed in here.'

Ah. Bel understands now. She's a Walker. She's not actually seen one close-up before, apart from the straggle-haired, enormously fat mother who occasionally pushes an empty pram up to the bus stop. But the whole village knows who the Walkers are.

'Ah, c'mon!' The girl tries again.

'No! Out!'

The Walker girl turns on her heel and trudges from the shop.

75

Mrs Stroud slams the door behind her hard enough that the bell clangs for three full seconds. Then she squeezes back in behind the counter, perches on her stool and returns to leafing through a subscription copy of True Life Stories that's not been collected yet.

'How's your mum and dad?' she asks suddenly.

'Stepfather,' corrects Bel.

'Whatever,' says Mrs Stroud. She's a shrewish woman, even without the irritation of a Walker in her shop. She likes to describe the place as 'the heart of the village'. Which means that it's the place where most of the local malice and rumour is collected and disseminated. And she knows that, as the owner of the only shop in the village, she has an audience that needs to keep on her good side and tolerate her mark-ups and nasty tongue, for convenience's sake.

'In Malaysia,' says Bel.

'Malaysia, eh? What's that then? A holiday?'

Bel grunts.

'So, what? Taken your sister, have they?'

Bel sighs. 'Yes,' she replies. 'Half-sister,' she adds.

'I'm surprised they didn't take you then?' The question is pointed, sharp. How she loves an opportunity to get a dig in at a child.

Bel feels a twinge of irritation. 'Yeah, well,' she says. 'I don't suppose they did it with you in mind.'

Mrs Stroud takes offence. Offence is her default position. 'Well!' she says. 'No need to speak like that!'

Bel says nothing. Mrs Stroud licks the tip of her tongue and flips a couple of pages, noisily.

'I can ban you just as easily as I can ban a Walker,' she bursts out. 'Don't think just because you come from the manor that that'll make a difference.'

Her back turned, Bel rolls her eyes. She turns back to face the shop and gives the old bat a broad smile. 'Sorry, Mrs Stroud,' she says, her voice full of oil and honey.

'I should think so,' says Mrs Stroud. 'I can't believe your father would like to hear you talking to a grown-up like that.'

'Stepfather,' says Bel.

'Whatever,' says Mrs Stroud. Leans her chin on her hand and glares at her magazine.

Bel looks at her aslant. Turns her back and shifts her bag across the shelf to cover her hand movements. She picks up a Curly Wurly and balances it on the pick-'n'-mix pot. Then quickly, surreptitiously, she snatches up a four-finger Kit Kat and drops it into the depths of her bag.

'How much are the Flying Saucers?' she asks, casually.

'Two p,' says Mrs Stroud, not looking up.

Two p? They're a penny each over in the shop at Great Barrow. God, Mrs Stroud knows how to rip every last penny out of people too young to drive a car. Bel selects one in each colour and drops them into the pot, then goes up to the counter to make her purchases. The Kit Kat seems to be generating heat through the walls of her bag. She has the money to pay for it, but that's not the point.

Out in the silent village day – too early for teenagers, the grown-ups at work or fiddling away being house proud – she finds the Walker girl sitting on the Bench, glumly drumming her heels on thin air. She sits down next to her.

'Hi,' she says.

The girl ignores her.

Bel feels around in her bag – not much in there apart from a copy of Jackie and her purse – until her fingers close on the stolen Kit Kat. She pulls it out, offers it.

'What?' asks the girl.

'I got you this.'

The girl looks suspicious. Glares at Bel.

'What for?'

'Whatever. D'you want it or not?'

'How much?' she asks doubtfully.

'Don't be stupid.'

77

'I've got money,' she says, aggressively. 'I'm not a bloody charity case.'

'Yeah,' says Bel, 'but I didn't pay for it, you see.'

The girl looks stunned. Then admiring. Then curious.

'Silly cow,' says Bel.

The girl laughs. 'Yeah,' she says. 'Silly cow.'

She takes the chocolate, finds a trench beneath the wrapper and runs a thumbnail down it. Snaps off a finger. 'D'you want some?' she asks, unenthusiastically. Offering stuff to someone else comes uneasily to her. She doesn't get much chance to practise.

'No thanks,' says Bel airily, and shows her paper bag of sweets. 'I'm fine.'

The girl is relieved, but doesn't say it. The two sit quietly for a while in blazing sunshine, savouring the twin pleasures of sugar and summer holidays.

'I'm Jade,' says the girl, eventually.

'I'm Bel,' says Bel.

Chapter Eleven

Martin tries Jackie again. He's been ringing all day, and all evening, ever since she vanished in that minicab. Knows she'll answer eventually; and if she doesn't, he'll go back up there and wait for her to come home.

He fills in a couple of hours by googling Kirsty Lindsay, the journalist who tried to chat him up on the beach. A bit of him had expected to find that she was just pretending to be a journalist – he's never heard of her and thought she seemed pretty unprofessional, the way she just started talking to him like that, without identifying herself – but to his surprise he finds that she does exist; that she has scores of bylines, in fact.

He trawls through the Google hits to learn the nature of the beast while he waits for Jackie to answer. He knows that her phone is working again, because he dialled it once when he was following her down Fore Street, heard it ring in her pocket and saw her pull it out and check the display. It's only a matter of time before she responds, he thinks. All women want a man who's loyal. They say so all the time. Well, if she wants loyal, he'll show her loyal. No matter how long it takes. The phone rings out, again and again. He wonders if she knows that her voicemail has been deactivated.

He wonders about journalists as he reads. About their intrusive nosiness, their assumptions, the way they damn entire groups with a single sentence. The hacking scandal was just the tip of the iceberg, really. Lindsay doesn't seem much worse, or much better, than the rest of them. She doesn't seem to have any specialist knowledge, or cover any particular subjects, other than that most of what she writes about happens in the south-east. But she's certainly got opinions. Plenty of those.

He rings Jackie. He waited, after she left in the minicab, until it got dark, until all the lights were on in her block and the doors firmly locked, and then he left. He doesn't give up easily, but he's not a fool. She's gone away for the night. Has she got a new man? Replaced him that easily, that casually? No. It can't be that. He's seen enough of her life to know that she's not been dating.

He sits with the phone between his knees and glances at the clock radio: 10.45 – news over, *Question Time* in full swing. He'll ring her once more, then he'll watch to the end of that and try her again. She has to answer eventually.

He carries on reading Lindsay's bylines as *Question Time* plays in the background. She's very patchy, he notices. Sometimes she seems capable of doing her job and just reporting actual news, but a good half of the time she inserts herself, shows her partisan attitudes, even makes jokes. It's those articles, he notices, that seem to carry her picture at the top.

'Unprofessional,' he mutters as he mouses and clicks. The way she digs and exposes and thinks it's OK to be flippant about her subjects. Maybe I ought to take up journalism. Maybe I should start by doing an exposé on *her*.

Jackie's still not answering. He puts the phone on to Speaker and Automatic Redial and continues his search for Kirsty Lindsay. She doesn't have a Wikipedia page. Doesn't seem to show up at all much before 1999. Degree from the Open University, 1998, then a slow trickle of bylines from a local paper in the Midlands. He starts searching backwards. Tries Facebook, Myspace, Friends Reunited, Genes Reunited. She has no presence on any of them. Doesn't get a mention attached to any school, any reunions, any relatives; clearly never won a prize, never distinguished herself in any way, and no one has been looking for her.

Suddenly he realises that a voice is coming from the handset. She's picked up. He snatches it up and puts it to his ear. 'Hello?'

A woman's voice, cold and hard; suspicious. 'Who is this?'

'Who is *this*?' he asks.

'Who did you want to speak to?'

'Jackie. Jackie Jacobs,' he says. 'Have I dialled the wrong number?'

A fractional pause. 'Who's calling?'

'Martin,' he says.

'Martin who?'

'Martin Bagshawe.'

He hears her breathe. The voice is faintly familiar. It's some-one he's met before, someone he knows. Not well, but he doesn't know anyone well, really.

'OK, Martin,' she says, 'I need you to listen to me very care-fully and pay attention to what I say.'

A surge of adrenalin makes him dizzy. She's dead. Something's happened to her.

'Is Jackie OK?' he asks. 'What's happened?'

'She's fine,' she says sharply. 'And Martin, in answer to your question, *you're* what's happened.'

Her voice changes, as though she's reading a pre-prepared speech off a piece of paper. 'Listen, Martin, you need to under-stand. Jackie is not your girlfriend. She's not your friend. In fact, she finds your behaviour aggressive and frightening.'

'I—' he begins to protest, but she ploughs on, ignoring him.

'Martin, I want you to listen very carefully. Jackie wants noth-ing to do with you. What you've been doing, all this following and watching, it's harassment. It's not a show of devotion and it won't persuade her to change her mind. You need to stop it. Now.'

Who is this woman? He knows the voice; it's maddeningly familiar. Now he hears his own breath, coming fast.

'I don't know who you are …' he begins.

'It doesn't matter who I am. All you need to know is that

Jackie is in a place of safety and she wants you to leave her alone.'

'Place of safety . . . ? What are you—'

'You heard me, Martin. And I'm telling you now, you'd be well advised to listen to what I'm saying. You need to leave Jackie alone. You need to stop.'

'If Jackie wants that,' he snaps, abruptly angry, 'she can tell me herself. Who are you? Who are you to tell her what to do?'

'No,' says the woman. 'She's not coming to the phone. I'm going to hang up now, Martin. And when I do, you're not to call this number again. You're not to call, or send any other type of message, to this number. You are not to come to her house, not to come to her place of work, not to follow her in the street. Do you understand? Because if you do, we will be calling the police. Do you get that?'

He can barely articulate. His lips are cold and numb, his throat constricted. 'Yes,' he mumbles. Whoever this woman is, she's not going to listen to reason. She's got to Jackie and she's going to destroy everything, twist it till it looks ugly, deformed. He won't argue with her. People like that – it's not worth wasting your breath.

The line goes dead. He dials again. It goes straight to the plummy robot woman, who tells him that the mailbox has been deactivated.

His hands are shaking.

Chapter Twelve

He's a cocky young sod. Kirsty can tell by the swagger, by the imperious curl of the lip, by the way he wears his hat slightly off-centre, as if to make a point. By the fact that he's got his nightstick out as he patrols up and down the line and slaps it against his palm, rhythmically, as he eyes the women with an expression somewhere between a sneer and a leer. There's a few of them in every town. He reminds her of her brother Darren: his air of sex with a predatory edge. A nasty young man, but he might well be useful.

She can't wait to be done with this piece. She wants to get home and sort things out with Jim. And she still has the remains of her two-day hangover. She wants to be at the dining-room table that doubles as her office, back in Farnham, with a cup of proper coffee and the laptop open and her husband mollified. She will be, soon. Just needs to mingle, like the rest of the press pack, with the first trippers back into Funnland, and she's out of here. She has fifteen hundred words to file by lunchtime tomorrow and needs to get writing.

The queue edges forward. She's amused to see that a lot of her colleagues are also mingling undeclared among the civilians in the hope of picking up some juicy, usable quotes without having to seek permission, studiously ignoring each other though they will all be buying each other drinks in a couple of hours. Stan shambles up the street, looking as hungover as she feels. The landlord of the White Horse will probably be able to take the rest of the summer off. Few drinkers are as free-spending as a journalist on expenses.

He walks past the straggly queue and straight up to her.

'Sorry about that,' he says loudly, for the benefit of the people behind. 'Took ages to find a parking space.'

He slots himself in beside her, lowers his voice. 'Of course, it's less about the queue than the company.'

'Is that you being roguish?' she asks.

He slide his specs down his nose, twinkles at her over them. 'I wouldn't know how.'

He offers her an Extra Strong Mint and they shuffle along companionably.

'Get back to your room all right the other night?' she asks.

'I should be asking *you* that,' he says. 'You were so many sheets to the wind I thought you might go flapping off across the Channel. And how *was* your room, after you dodged the Ripper?'

'Thanks for that, Mr Pot. It was great. It had a sink in the corner for throwing up in. But tell you what, I'm in such bad odour at home, I should be wearing a hazard label. I completely forgot we were having some City cheeses over to dinner to try and oil them up for a job for Jim.'

'Oops.'

'I was so hungover, I actually threw up.'

'Not at the table, I hope?' asks Stan.

She laughs.

'We'll make a pro of you yet, my girl.'

'Anyway,' she says, 'I don't think you can call him a ripper, can you? Strangler, surely?'

His face takes on a contemplative look. 'The Whitmouth Strangler. It doesn't have much of a ring to it, does it?'

'The Seaside Strangler?'

'Nice. Like it. I found what looked like some dried snot on my bedspread. Which wasn't very conducive to a good night's sleep.'

'Bed-bug numbers are up globally, you know.'

'For God's sake. I'm getting that camper van. I hardly ever go home as it is.'

'Then you could go to the seaside every day,' she says.

'Ah, wouldn't that be lovely? I must say, I'm enjoying this little interlude.'

'Me too,' she says. 'It's like being on holiday. Are you going on the rollercoaster?'

'Wouldn't miss it for the world. You?'

'Still feeling a bit frail,' she says. 'I might have to give it a miss.'

'Amateur,' says Stan, and shakes his head. 'How's your piece shaping up?'

Kirsty shrugs. 'Oh, you know. You can find whatever your editor wants you to find. Jack's after Third Circle of Hell stuff. So that's what I'm giving him.'

'That's why I joined the press,' says Stan. 'The relentless quest for balance. Jack does so love to sneer at the proles, doesn't he?'

'That's a bit harsh. Have you seen what the *Guardian*'s been saying?'

'Well it *is* the *Guardian*. It's either that or they'll have to find a reason why Israel's to blame,' he says. 'So how was the press conference?'

'Oh God. I didn't go. I was sort of expecting *you* would.'

'Ah. Oh well. It'll all be on AP anyway. You home tonight?'

She nods. 'As long as he hasn't changed the locks. I'm on the motorway the second I'm done here. Can't bloody wait.'

She catches the look on the face of the woman behind her, that peculiarly British suspicion of snobbery, and corrects herself in a louder voice. 'I hate these overnighters,' she tells Stan, while looking the woman in the eye. 'Doesn't matter where. I just miss my family so much, you know?'

Stan nods. 'Yes. I remember the days when I had one of those to miss.'

*

Jim calls just as the gates to Funnland open.

'Hey,' she says. 'How are you?'

'More to the point, how are you?' he asks. 'You didn't say goodbye before you went.'

'Mmm,' she says. 'I wasn't entirely sure of my welcome.'

'Yeah,' says Jim. 'You *are* an arse, you know.'

She feels a rush of relief. If he's back to administering direct insults, it means he's over the hump. 'Accepted and understood,' she tells him.

'Save it for the judge,' he says. 'Are you still coming home today?'

'Trust me,' she says, 'I've only had a bottle and a half of Chardonnay. I can drive it blindfold.'

They laugh. The queue edges closer to the gate and she tucks the phone into her chin to look for her wallet. The nasty young security guard has moved up to stand by the kiosk and smirks at people as they pass, as though he's got a dirty secret on each of them.

'OK. I'll see you later. Oh, and Kirsty?'

'What?'

'I missed you saying goodbye this morning. Don't do it again, eh?'

The words wrap her like a warm blanket. 'OK,' she says. 'I'll remember not to repeat the error.'

Who wants to ride dodgems at half-ten in the morning? There's actually a queue for them, though perhaps that's more a reflection of the fact that half the rides and stalls aren't open yet than of any particular desire for whiplash. There's a startlingly handsome man in charge: dark-haired, with a panther-like grace. He's clean, unpierced, no signs of the inking you'd usually expect on the arms of someone in his trade. Kirsty wonders idly how someone so good-looking ended up working here, rather than for, say, Models One, and passes by.

Most of the other hacks make a beeline for the offices, in the hope that Suzanne Oddie will be on the premises. Kirsty hangs back as Stan wanders over to the café, sees him sit down watchfully at one of the fixed tables outside. He always looks like he's not working, but he's the one who actually comes up with the goods. Plays on the fact that the young all believe that men revert to childlike innocence the minute their hair turns grey; gets the waitresses gossiping in a way she can never manage.

Another security guard has been posted outside the entrance to Innfinnityland, where the body was found. He's arguing with the hack from the *Star*, arms folded firmly across his chest, head working slowly and firmly from side to side. Of course he is. The attraction is closed, 'out of respect'. The forensic team have departed, but no one's going to get in for the money shot.

Except Kirsty.

She finds the cocky guard from the front gate drinking a can of Fanta behind the teacup ride. Now *here's* a man with ink on his body. He's not gone as far as LOVE and HATE knuckles, but a smidge of spiderweb sticks out of the back of his starched blue collar.

She stops beside him. 'Hi,' she says.

He lowers the can and looks at her. He looks a bit like a whippet, except that no whippet has mean little watery blue eyes like that.

'Bet you're all glad to be back at work,' she says.

He looks her up and down once more, then realisation dawns. 'Oh, right, you're a journalist,' he says.

'Yes.' She sticks out a hand. 'Kirsty Lindsay,' she says.

He shakes it, weakly, just like she'd expected.

'And you are?'

'Jason,' he says, uncertainly.

'Hi, Jason,' she says, and gets out her wallet. 'I'll bet you've got the keys to everything here, haven't you?'

*

She meets him at the back of the café; he doesn't want to risk being seen walking across the grounds beside her. There's a door by the disabled bogs that leads through to the storage alley. The alley runs between the perimeter fence and the backs of a series of stalls and sideshows: old-fashioned hoop-la, a shooting gallery, Dr Wicked's House of Giggles, the NASA Experience, The House of Horrors, Innfinnityland.

At first glance, the alleyway looks as though it's strewn with dead bodies. Dead, naked bodies. Kirsty feels a shudder of horror run through her before she realises that they're just rejects from the waxworks, chucked out carelessly to rot in the daylight.

Jason emerges from between the shooting gallery and the ghost ride. He looks both shifty and pleased with himself in equal measure. Getting one over on the bosses, she thinks, is as important to him as the twenty quid which is burning a hole in his pocket. He beckons with a jerk of the head, and starts walking towards the back of Innfinnityland. She hurries to catch up. Now that she's out the back here, where no one's bothered with paint jobs and carved fascias, she sees that the attractions are housed in shabby Portakabins: bits of insulation tumbling out where cladding has come loose, spaghetti-knots of thick black wiring leading from the junction box against the fence.

'Five minutes,' he says. 'That's all you get.'

'That's all I need,' she says. She wants to grab a couple of rough photos, drink in a bit of atmosphere, that's all. It won't take long. She can make up anything she can't remember. After all, no one's going to be going in and correcting her.

'And I've got nothing to do with it,' he says. 'I'll come and get you, but if there's anyone there, I'm here to throw you out, OK?'

'Of course. Thank you for this.'

He grunts. Stops at the foot of a set of metal steps. 'OK,' he says. 'It's up here.'

She brushes past, puts her hand on the tubular banister. Jason starts to hurry away.

She's halfway up when the door at the top of the steps opens. She freezes. Nowhere to go. She's caught in the act. A woman emerges. She's tall, and dyed blond: short, practical hair, skin that's seen better days, rubber gloves and a pail full of cleaning materials hanging from her arm, a large black mole on the edge of her smile line. She stops, looks puzzled.

'Can I help you?'

'I was just . . .' Kirsty hunts for an excuse. Arse. That's twenty quid wasted.

'This building's closed,' says the woman. 'What are you doing back here anyway? You shouldn't be here.'

'I just . . .' Kirsty says again, then thinks, what the hell. I'm here now. What're they going to do? Arrest me? She puts on her most persuasive, friendly, conspiratorial face. 'I just wanted to get a look inside,' she tells her. 'I don't suppose you could . . .? Just for a moment?'

The woman looks at her as though she's crawled out from under something. She's familiar, thinks Kirsty. Why's she familiar? She gives her a nice open smile. Wonders if she's got another twenty in her wallet. 'Go on,' she says. 'Just for a minute.'

A frown. The woman shouts, down the alleyway, at the guard's hurrying back. 'Jason! We've got a stray here!'

Kirsty sees Jason turn reluctantly back towards them. She has seconds to make her final pitch.

'Come on,' she says, 'be a darling. I'm not going to do any harm.'

'Jesus,' says the woman. 'You people disgust me. Seriously. Don't you realise? There was a girl *dead* in here. Not some – dummy in a movie. A girl. A sweet, breathing, laughing teenage girl. She was alive, and now she's dead, and people's lives are *devastated*—'

Her voice cuts off halfway through the sentence and Kirsty hears a gasp, as though someone's punched her in the solar plexus.

She looks up at the woman's face and sees that it has gone white, the eyes bulging, the jaw dropped back to show snaggled teeth.

'What?' she asks.

'No,' says the woman. 'No, no, no. Shit, no. No. You can't be here. You can't. Shit. You've got to go.' She clutches on to the top of the railing as though the strength has gone from her legs. 'Oh Christ,' she says, and she's almost weeping. 'Oh my God, Christ, please no. Jade, go. You've got to go, *now*.'

Chapter Thirteen

Amber understands now what they mean when they talk of a rush of blood to the head. She feels a pressure inside her skull that makes her fear that it will crack, like an eggshell. She feels her heart, thump-thump-thump, feels the strength leave her limbs, sees darkness creep in around the edge of her vision. This can't be happening. It can't. Sixty million people in the country; what are the odds she'd just ... be here.

Jade, now that she's heard Amber speak her name, looks as though the same physical phenomena are afflicting her. She sways, shroud-white, on the bottom step. Stares up at Amber as though she's seen a ghost. In a way, she has. They've both been dead and buried for decades now. Annabel Oldacre and Jade Walker, to all intents and purposes, ceased to exist when they vanished into the system. It wasn't safe for them to keep their names in detention, even when they were still theoretically presumed innocent. They might never have had visitors themselves, but their fellow hoodlums did, and even back then there was good money to be made from the News of the Screws for tales from the inside. Especially tales of Wicked Girls and their Wicked Ways.

Jason Murphy, Maria's little jackal of a husband, is approaching, slowly and unwillingly.

'Bel,' says Jade.

Amber shivers. She hasn't heard the name as a form of address in decades. She is no longer that girl. Everything about her is changed. Only continuity can keep you the same, and she has been Amber Gordon for almost as long as she can remember.

'Please,' Amber says again. 'You've got to go.'

Jesus, she thinks. She looks ten years younger than me. She feels a surge of resentment towards this woman. Hair well cut – not showy, but fall-into-place neat, subtly highlighted, shiny; skin unlined; clothes not flashy-expensive but clearly not from market stalls either. Her black leather boots are classy, though. You don't get that sort of firm-yet-yielding leather in Primark. Incarceration's treated you well, then, she thinks.

She glances up. Jason Murphy is a few feet away now, lurking in that vulpine way of his. Has he seen that something's going on? Something more than he'd expect? She has always suspected that Jason's studied indifference to the world hides a sharp eye for a situation – as long as that situation provides an opportunity for himself.

She pulls herself together. 'This area's off limits,' she says sternly. 'Even if – even if the situation was different, you'd still not be allowed back here. Staff only.'

Jade's still not found her voice. Amber looks up the alleyway, nods at Jason. 'I don't know how she got back here,' she says to him, 'and I'm not going to ask. Just get her out of here.'

Jason steps forward and takes hold of Jade's arm. She jumps, as though she's been ambushed, whirls her arm from his grip as though it burns.

'Come on,' says Jason. 'No point arguing.'

She turns back, looks at Amber, wide-eyed. 'Bel,' she says again.

Amber pretends to ignore her. The name, each time she hears it, makes her jolt inside. Stop it. *Stop it.* Do you want them to find out? Do you? Do you want the crowds on your doorstep, the shit through your letterbox?

She turns away and goes back through the door.

*

Once she's safely inside, Amber allows her legs to buckle. She slumps against the mirrored wall, slides down it to the floor, stares at her grey-white reflection. Her hands and feet are cold.

'Ah, well,' says Jason, letting go of Kirsty's arm the moment he knows they're not overlooked. 'Tough luck.'

He's preparing to put up a fight if she asks for her money back, but she seems strangely distracted, following him like a zombie. He doesn't really understand what he's just seen, but knows that this was something more than her simply getting caught. He could swear he saw something pass between the two women; even that they recognised each other. Maybe he's wrong. This woman's small and slight, and would be no match for Amber Gordon: maybe she just got scared at the sight of her.

Most people would, he thinks, and chuckles inwardly. The woman had a face so grim on her just now that you could have cast her in *Lord of the Rings* without make-up, even if she didn't have that great knobble on her upper lip. God knows what Vic Cantrell sees in her. It must be some sort of mother thing, because it sure as shit isn't sex. Not after the nights he and Vic have had, prowling the nightclubs on the strip, fucking and fingering the slags on holiday. I must ask him one day, he thinks, if she knows what he gets up to when she's at work. Maybe she lets him. Maybe she thinks it's the only way she'll get to keep him.

The journalist's silence is disconcerting. She's gone a strange shade of grey, and clutches the strap of her bag like a security blanket.

'It's OK,' he reassures her as they emerge into the park. 'She's not going to tell. She won't even remember which one you were.'

She gulps. Looks at him with huge eyes, as though she's only just noticed that he's there. Stumbles away towards the café.

He notices that Vic is watching them as he rides on the back of a bumper car, holding on casually with one hand. He's seen them emerge from the alleyway, and looks amused. Jason grins at him and flashes the universal hip-spaced-hands and crotch-thrust gesture at her retreating back. Vic laughs, gives him the thumbs-up. Jumps acrobatically on to the back of a new car to give the girls a thrill.

She wants strong coffee. Her hands are shaking and, despite what the health bores say, she finds that caffeine calms her. But of course the coffee in Funnland hasn't seen a bean in eighteen factory processes. She fills the cup up with creamer, empties three sachets of sugar on top and carries it out to a bench. Checking her watch, she is surprised to see that only fifteen minutes have passed since she spoke to Jim.

The park has filled up. The kiddie rides are up and running now, and the first nappy change is taking place on the wooden table next to her. She realises that she's still shaking. She takes the lid off the coffee, sips, scalds her mouth. She'd forgotten how much hotter instant is than the real thing. Wonders at the changes in her life since she last saw Bel Oldacre: that she has become an espresso-drinking, pesto-eating member of the balsamic classes. Back home – back in the time she thinks of as 'before' – a meal was Budgen tea and white toast with jam; potatoes and spaghetti hoops; and, occasionally, a glut of pig meat when her dad took the shotgun down to the corrugated-iron Nissen huts that functioned as sties. A place like this would have seemed like an unattainable heaven to her, somewhere to see on the telly and dream of visiting.

Was that really Bel? Was it? How can this have happened? Under the weatherbeaten skin, the brassy cropped hair, the stained polyester overall? My God. She looks the way I was meant to look.

Kirsty doesn't think she would have recognised her had she not been recognised herself. Though she's surprised no one thought to remove that blemish – so recognisable, so discussed – from Bel's face when they were setting up her new identity. She supposes that more of the child she once was must still be recognisable in her own face, mole or no mole, than she realises; and the thought frightens her. Bel, up till now, has remained eleven in her mind. She barely remembers her, if truth be told; is more familiar with her features from those bloody school photos, the ones that get pulled from the archive whenever there's an anniversary, whenever another child earns the sobriquet 'unspeakable'. They only knew each other for the inside of a day. And afterwards, standing silently side by side in the dock, barely glancing at each other except for when one or the other of them was testifying. It wasn't like they were best friends. Or even habitual ones.

But here they are, their names inextricably linked in the minds of the world. And banned by law from ever seeing each other again, as long as they live. Venables and Thompson; Mary Bell; Walker and Oldacre – back in the days before Child Protection took them out of public circulation, child murderers' names were as well known – better, often – as the names of their victims. If she quoted their names at a dinner party, the majority of the guests would nod knowingly. Chloe Francis? They'd probably need prompting.

Her mouth is as dry as the desert. She screws her eyes up and forces more scalding liquid between her lips, holding it on her tongue and breathing in, hard, to cool it.

It's a condition of your licence, Kirsty, she says to herself. No one around you even knows there's such a thing as a probation order in your name, but it's there nonetheless. For the rest of your life. You are not to see, or speak to, or have contact with each other ever again. Like you'd ever want to.

Oh, but I do, shrieks a small, angry voice inside. I do. More than anything. More than anything on earth. She's the only one who knows. The only one who knows how it feels. The only other *me* in the world. Twenty-five years I've been holding this in, living with my guilt, mastering the art of dissimulation. Twenty-five years with no family, lying to the friends I've made, lying to Jim, lying to my children. How would they look at me,

95

if they knew? He's a forgiving man. But could he still love me, if he knew he'd married The Most Hated Child in Britain?

Bel Oldacre. Kirsty doesn't even know her new name.

It's raining by the time Amber works up the guts to leave. She's hidden away for hours: first in the empty mirror maze, then in her office, among the files and the boxes of J Cloths, until the afternoon shift is over; scared to come out, scared to show her face in the park. Outside, the rumble of the rollercoaster, the screams of its passengers; inside, the silent scream in her ears. Then, as an English summer storm sets in, the sounds die down and the music, ride by ride, is switched off. It's not worth wasting the power, as the crowds drop as the rain gets up. Any punters who want to stay are given a refund, or offered free entry another day. Most of them don't even think to ask; just rush their wailing kids off to the weather-proofed arcades on the Corniche.

Still, she is afraid. She scuttles from her office towards the staff gate as though she expects Jade to be lurking in the shadows; pulls her fleece tight round her breasts and wraps her scarf – everyone who lives in Whitmouth carries a scarf with them wherever they go, even at the height of summer – round her head to hide her face. Crazy, she knows: even if Jade had been hanging around, she would have been cleared out with the rest of the stragglers an hour ago. But still, she is afraid.

Jason Murphy is sheltering in the hut, eating a cheese-and-onion pasty with his feet up on the desk. He looks at her, all insolence in his navy sweater, peaked cap shoved to the back of his head, as she swipes her card across the reader, clocking out.

'All right?' he says.

She feels a surge of annoyance. She knows perfectly well how Jade Walker found her way to the mirror maze. And the fact that he knows that something else has happened has given him some edge, some stupid sense of power. He smirks as he watches her.

'No,' she says, turning to him, 'I'm not all right, actually, Jason.'

That look, that ugly sense of entitlement, the refusal to accept that 'respect' is a two-way street. Jason wants respect all the time: she's seen him squaring up to neighbours, to kids, to random men in the street, demanding it. She's never seen him do anything to earn it.

'If you ever do anything like that again,' she says, 'I'm going to put you on report.' She's not his direct boss, but she's management, and has authority of sorts over everyone who isn't. And she's damned if she's going to let him forget it.

'Do what?' he says – whines – though he knows what she's talking about.

'You know what,' she says. 'You're here to provide security, not take beer money off anyone who wants to give it you. There's computers here, Jason, and cash, and it's your job to see they don't get stolen.'

'She got past me,' he says sulkily.

She waits two beats, giving him the gimlet eye. 'Don't give me that,' she says. 'If I ever find out you've been up to that sort of trick again, I'll be reporting you, do you get me?'

He tries to give her the eye back. Fails. Amber perfected the art of outstaring the enemy at the Blackdown Hills detention centre. It was necessary for survival then, and it's a skill she has never allowed to fade.

'And get your feet off that desk,' she says.

Slowly, sulkily, he drops one foot, then the other, to the ground. Links his fingers over his vulnerable crotch.

Amber says nothing more. Lets herself out of the street door and closes it behind her.

'Skanky cow,' mutters Jason, putting his feet back up on the desktop and picking up the remains of his pasty. 'Skanky cow,' he repeats, and rips off a mouthful with his teeth.

Out on the Corniche the rain is horizontal; there's barely a body to be seen. Amber swings right, hurrying for the bus stop.

A voice calls her name. Her old name. She freezes.

'Bel!' it calls again.

Jade Walker emerges from the doorway of The Best Fish and Chips on the South Coast, walks towards her. She must've been waiting for her to come out. Shit.

Amber hurries forward again. Pretends she doesn't hear.

Jade raises her voice. 'Bel! Please!'

She swings round, catches a blast of rain-shards full in the face. It blinds her for a second. When her vision clears she sees that Jade is still there, blinking at her, hair rat-tailed on to healthy pink cheeks.

Amber has to stop her. Has to shut her up. The woman has lost her mind, isn't thinking things through at all. She needs to shock her into understanding. She races towards her, raging; sees her recoil and feels pleasure in making her do so. Jade's smaller than she is. Bearing down, she knows she could take her out with a single fist.

She grabs her upper arm, clamps down on the muscle like a vice, digging in her fingertips to make it hurt.

'Go away!' she hisses. 'Do you hear me? Don't call me that. Don't follow me. Just *fuck off*. We have nothing to say to each other.'

'Bel . . . '

Amber shakes her head, side to side, over and over like an angry dog. Hears her voice rise to a shriek to combat the wind. 'No!' she shouts. 'I don't know that name. That's not my name. Just – *shut up!* Shut *up!* You know we're not meant to see each other. You *know!* Are you mad? Go away!'

She throws the woman's arm away like a chicken bone. Pushes her for good measure. Jade stumbles back a pace, stands staring at her with what looks like despair. Good. Bloody *good*.

She forces her voice back under her control. She can't afford this level of agitation. Even here, on this empty boulevard, eyes will be watching. She can't let anyone see. Right outside work, for God's sake. What is she *thinking*?

'I'm not Bel,' she says. 'I haven't been Bel for years, you know that. Just like you. What are you *doing*?'

'I didn't mean ...' begins Jade. 'I – if I'd known I'd've—'

'Well, what are you doing now? You should have gone. What do you think they'd do if they ...? Shit. Just go. Don't follow me. Just fuck off back wherever you've come from.'

She turns on her heel and walks towards the bus stop. There's a bus due in three minutes and she's damned if she's going to miss it.

She is jittering by the time she enters the shelter – anger, fear, shock, all turned to adrenalin. Her breath rasps in her throat and she has to sit down, hard, on the graffitied bench. There's no one here, thank God – no one who knows her, anyway, just a couple of kids wrapped in teenage lust in the corner. They glance up briefly, his hand inside the front zip of her jacket, then turn back, indifferent.

Amber breathes. Holds her hands out, palms down, watches them tremble. I can't do this, she thinks. It's too much. I can't lose this life. Not because of a stupid coincidence. No one's going to believe we just met by accident. It would never happen. Shit. Am I going to have to move on again? What's she doing here, anyway? What the hell is she doing here?

She sees the bus approach, pushes herself up and goes outside to hail it. It pulls in: crowded. The smell of damp hair and Persil bursts out as the doors open.

She feels a hand grip her arm. 'I don't—' says Jade. 'I'm not ... look.'

She presses something into Amber's hand. Amber looks down. It's an old cigarette packet; a telephone number is scrawled on it in black biro.

'I just ...' says Jade; looks her in the eye.

Amber shakes the hand off her arm and mounts the steps of the bus.

Chapter Fourteen

Busy, busy, busy. It's what she's always done when she's wanted to avoid thinking: she finds something to *do* instead. It's why the house stands out from its neighbours, a little oasis of mainte-nance and tidiness in a world where redundant washing machines suffice as garden ornaments. Washed windows, bright white nets, sills and woodwork freshly painted, hanging baskets colourful from spring to winter. Vic says it attracts attention, that standing out in a place like this is not a good thing, but she finds it hard to stop. On the days when she can't get to sleep, she'll be out there taking a busman's holiday with a scrubbing brush on the path and the front step, pulling out the furniture to hoover behind it, walking the area round the front of the house with rubber gloves and a bin liner, collecting Greggs sausage-roll bags.

There are a couple more flapping on the pavement in front of the gate. Amber stands in the rain and struggles with the urge to clear them up. In the end she concedes defeat, pulls the plastic bag she habitually carries from her handbag, and sets about picking up, rain on her back, hair plastered to her face.

Next-door's front door opens and Shaunagh Betts comes out, her toddler Tiffany strapped into her pushchair. 'Ooh, Amber,' Shaunagh says, 'putting us all to shame again.'

Amber straightens up, forces a smile on to her face. 'Well,' she says, 'someone's got to do it.'

She sees Shaunagh take offence, realises too late that the comment has been taken as criticism, not self-effacement.

'Yes, well,' huffs Shaunagh. 'I'm sorry we don't all have *time*.'

'No, no . . .' Amber begins, but mother and child have already started off up the road. Amber sighs and goes into her safe house.

The back door is open and Jackie is huddled in the garden. Amber has a moment of stupid panic when she catches sight of her silhouette. She had briefly forgotten that she had a houseguest at all. Mary-Kate and Ashley have come indoors and are cuddled up together on the living-room sofa; they look up guiltily when she enters. Thank God I've got home before Vic, she thinks, scooting them back to their basket. He's finding it hard enough having an interloper in the house without seeing that as well.

Fortunately, Jackie's not an observant sort. Doesn't notice Amber's fraught state, just raises a hand in greeting. 'You're wet,' she says.

'So are you,' says Amber. 'For God's sake come into the kitchen.'

'No, you're all right,' says Jackie. 'I'll wait till I've finished this.'

'It's OK,' says Amber. 'Vic's not back for hours yet.'

'Yeah?' She looks grateful. 'OK.'

She comes in, stands dripping on the doormat, cigarette in hand. There's a damp towel hanging over the back of a chair. She's obviously been coming in and out all morning. Amber hands it to her. She rubs unenthusiastically at her hair. The kitchen steams up, smells of tobacco and unwashed fleece.

'How was your morning?' asks Amber.

Jackie shrugs. 'OK. Bit boring. I watched *Trisha* and *Jeremy Kyle*.'

'Might as well have just stood at the window and saved the leccy.'

Jackie laughs. 'So is work back on tonight then?'

Amber nods.

'Thank God for that,' says Jackie. 'It's bad enough not being able to go home without being skint on top.'

'Yeah, I can imagine,' says Amber, who's paid for every meal Jackie's eaten since she got here, apart from the bag of chips she bought yesterday and left, unwrapped and half eaten, on the kitchen table.

At teatime she takes Jackie's keys and walks the dogs up to her flat to get her a few changes of clothes. She's been wearing the tracksuit she arrived in for two days and, now that it's damp, that fact is impossible to ignore. And a walk is a good way to avoid thinking, anyway. There's always stuff to see and do on the Wordsworth; always enough external input to keep her thoughts at bay.

The scarlet plastic lettering that marks Jackie's block out from the identical grey structures around it has long since come loose. 1 3–19– -OLE-IDGE –ESCEN- , it reads. An old mattress, stained with salt air and a thousand nocturnal incidents, leans against the wall by the dustbins. Everyone knows that if they don't pay the bulky refuse fee, the council will come and fetch things away eventually anyway. By the end of each six-month waiting period, the estate's pavements are strewn with legless beds, springless sofas and scorched coffee tables; teenagers gathering on them the way they used to on the Bench back in Long Barrow.

The lift isn't working. She plods up the three storeys to Flat 191.

The place smells stale, though Jackie's only been gone three days. Tobacco, old food and the same faint must that always rises off her fleece in the warm, all mixed in with the synthetic waft of a plug-in air freshener in the hall. A bin bag of dirty laundry sits inside the front door, waiting, top gaping open, to go to the launderette. Amber twists up the top and knots it. She might as well take it down, as she'll pass the shop on her way home. She goes into the living room. An ashtray the size of a paddling pool overflows in the middle of an MDF coffee table. A couple of plates, traces of ketchup and grease dried on, lie crusted beside it with a pint glass that has clearly held beer, flecks of hardened froth up the interior walls.

In the kitchen, a couple of pans in the sink, an old ready-meal carton on the yellowish Formica. She's no great housekeeper, Jackie, but she's not filthy either. And you can't judge someone by how they keep their house in moments of crisis. Amber's seen enough interiors, in the bedsit life she led after they tipped her out of Blackdown, to know that Jackie has many rungs to slide down the ladder of self-worth. She chucks the carton and quickly washes up the pans and the plates, leaves them on the drainer to dry.

The bedroom is dim, the forty-watt-equivalent overhead bulb too weak to illuminate it properly. Amber throws open the curtains. Glances out and sees, with a jolt, the rainproofed figure of Martin Bagshawe standing beside the overgrown forsythia opposite. He must have arrived after she did; she certainly didn't spot him as she was going in. Maybe he saw her coming and hid? No. Don't be paranoid. He doesn't know it was you on the phone.

For a moment their eyes meet. She ducks back into the room. Yes, but he knows now, she thinks.

She looks around at Jackie's possessions, feeling guilty, as though she's stealing, or reading her diary. A tumble of bed-clothes, a half-empty water glass, a copy of *heat*, a bedside lamp in the style of Tiffany. Not much furniture: the bed, a bedside table, the built-in cupboard. She studies the hanging clothes, and is surprised to see that Jackie owns half a dozen pretty dresses: optimistic cotton with spaghetti straps and generous skirts. She's so used to seeing her in work gear, or in her ubiquitous denim mini-skirt, she's never thought she might have other moods. She scoops a couple into the red suitcase that lives beneath the bed, adds two pairs of jeans from the pile beneath the radiator, a couple of pairs of elastic-waisted trousers, some T-shirts. Snatches up the collection of cleansers and creams on the bathroom shelf, notices the toothbrush still in its mug. Adds it to the case, and doesn't ask herself how Jackie's been cleaning her teeth over the time she's been staying. Maybe she just hasn't, she thinks, fleetingly. God, I hope she just hasn't.

He's still there, in the drizzle. She studiously avoids his gaze, hurries past as though she's not registered his presence at all. She can feel his eyes boring into her back as she strides up the road towards the launderette, bin bag in one hand, suitcase dragging behind her, the dogs' leads hitched over her arm, but he says nothing.

5 p.m.

'What do we do? What do we do?'

'Shut up. Shut up. Let me think.'

They stare at the body.

'She's stopped bleeding.'

'I know.'

'That's good, isn't it? She's not bleeding. Maybe she's . . .'

'No,' says Bel. 'I don't think so.'

Jade looks down at her hands, as if she's never seen them before. As if they've suddenly been attached to her by magic. She wipes one – mud, blood, river weed – on her skirt, then sees that she's just made it worse.

'Fuck,' she says.

It looks like someone's stolen the scarecrow from the top field and dumped it at the water's edge. Floppy, dirty, torn.

'Chloe?' says Bel, tentatively, though she knows it's no use. She pokes at her with a toe.

'Oh shit,' says Jade, 'I'm going to be in so much trouble.'

Bel's head snaps up. 'Shut up. Just shut up. Who cares about you? Who cares? Look at her.'

Jade looks again, then bends down and lifts a floppy arm by the wrist, watches it drop like dough into the mud when she lets go.

'Chloe?' She echoes Bel, as though the name were an incantation, as though it will restore life if they say it often enough. There's a big gash in her scalp. It has barely bled. Don't, don't, don't, she thinks. People don't just die like this. Not when we hardly did anything. My nana took six months to die, up in the back bedroom; we could hear it every step of the way. How could she die so quickly? 'Chloe?' she says again.

The anger has drained from Bel's face, leaving her as pale as ashes beneath her suntan. Jade notices the smattering of freckles across her nose; that ugly mole standing out like an ink blot. She goes to try the hand again. Bel grabs her wrist.

'Don't.'

'We have to see,' says Jade. 'We can't just leave her.'

Chloe lies like a rag doll, her legs still in the water. Bel feels as though she's wallowing beneath the surface. Jade's voice comes to her distantly, through the sound of rolling waves. She looks again at the small body, its face pressed into the riverbank where they turned it in a last despairing hope that the water would somehow drain out. 'Let's turn her over,' she says.

It's worse when they can see her face. They know she's really dead now. There's mud, got into her eyes. They lie open, unblinking, staring at the sun through a film of dirty brown. The face is a mosaic of mud and gravel, of leaves and tiny petals; a string of duckweed tangled in hair that itself resembles weeds and string.

Oh God, her eyes, thinks Jade. I will remember this. I won't forget this, the way her eyes look, for the rest of my life.

Chapter Fifteen

He is giddy with outrage, white-hot in the head and unsteady on his feet. His brain seethes as he strides down London Road from the Wordsworth to the centre of town, his vision so impaired by the tunnelling effect of adrenalin that twice he lurches on the pavement and feels the scrape of his nylon sleeve against the plate-glass windows of sleeping shops. Amber Gordon. That fucking bitch Amber Gordon. Who does she think she is? And she pretended she didn't even know me.

It's all clear to him now, clear as day. Amber Gordon is the reason why Jackie has cut him off. She's Jackie's boss, he remembers that. And she's Vic Cantrell's – *something*. Because there's no way that hard-faced bitch could fool anyone that a man like Vic is interested in her for anything other than what he can get from her. You just have to look at her standing next to him – the cheap dye job, the leather jacket that must be twenty years old, that fucking mole in the middle of her face – to know that they're a mismatch.

But Jackie? He understands now; at least partially. Jackie's weak, she's greedy, she's a coward – but the power behind the throne is Amber fucking Gordon.

His blood has turned to ice. He elbows his way through the queue outside DanceAttack, barely hears the cries of protest that follow in his wake. I hate her, he thinks. She's not worthy. I don't know why I ever thought she was.

The girls are out in force tonight: another Whitmouth party night. Blond and black and neon-red, their hair is piled up, hauled straight, built out and supplemented. They swish improbable nylon tresses into his face as he passes, clutch Primark purses to diamanté belly buttons, slip credit cards deep into their padded bras for safekeeping. And as usual he is invisible. All these girls, looking for excitement, and not one of them so much as glances at him.

Who is she? Who the fuck is she? Who the fuck does she think she is?

He despises her, now he knows. She's not his chance at salvation: she's a weak, greedy slag. I don't know why I ever thought that she was different, he thinks. I need my head examining.

She has to pay, he thinks, though he's not sure which 'she' he's thinking of. I have to make her pay.

He's too wound up, his muscles aching with adrenalin, to go home, to lock himself inside those enclosing walls and pace the cluttered floor while the party goes on outside. He feels isolated enough on a normal night; on a night like this he feels like it will drive him mad. He's uncomfortably aware that his rage has given him a flabby, half-hearted erection. It throbs awkwardly against the front of his trousers as he walks, anorak-pocketed hands crossed in front of him to hide it from the people who are no more looking at him than they are wondering what their mothers would say if they saw them now. His temples pump with frustration, with rejection, with rage. He can't go home. The walls won't let him breathe.

He checks the contents of his pocket, finds fifteen pounds and a handful of change. Not enough for any of the nightclubs – even Stardust is twelve pounds to get into these days, and a glass of Coke alone costs three. I'll get some chips, he thinks, and take them up on the war memorial. It's quiet on Mare Street at this time of night. Maybe if I'm there long enough, the noise will have died down a bit by the time I get home. And if Tanqueray

Tina is up in her usual spot, I might be able to parlay something out of my tenner.

At the death-burger van he buys a saveloy, its brazen tumescence mocking the half-formed thing inside his Y-fronts, to go with his chips, snatches up a chip fork, a little devil's prong of plywood, and a handful of napkins and hurries off across the Corniche.

Mare Street, as he had expected, is almost silent, the sounds of the crowds behind him quickly fading away to film-soundtrack level. Now the centre of town has been pedestrianised, the road leads effectively nowhere, and no one much comes up here once the shops have closed. He idles his way along the pavement, feeling the heat of his food emanate through its polystyrene tray, and turns the corner into Fore Street, suddenly longing for the salt-and-stodge mouth-feel of fried potato. He stops by the old horse trough and pulls open an edge of the bag. He won't unwrap it fully now; hates the sight of people eating while they walk. He just needs to get it open enough to access a morsel or two.

Someone coughs, up ahead.

Tina stands half in the shadows at the mouth of an alleyway: mini-skirt, denim jacket garnished with studs and fringing, white stacked heels, no tights. She carries an oversized black bag, the sort of bag you'd expect to find on a mother. He can't imagine that a bag like that could house any load other than baby wipes and half-chewed rusks. But there it is, hanging off the shoulder of an alky grandmother looking for trade.

'Hello, love,' she says. 'Haven't seen you up here for a bit.'

Martin feels a rush of irritation at the familiarity. It doesn't matter that he's been forced to use her services before; he feels affronted that she should treat him like a regular. But he tucks his chip fork back into his palm and goes to meet her.

'Aah,' she says. 'You brought me some chips.'

He doesn't reply; clutches the bundle of food closer to his chest.

'You after some fun tonight, then?' she says.

Martin looks at her. Thinning scarlet hair scraped back into a high ponytail, thyroid eyes and lines like gouges on her forehead. He can smell the gin fumes rising off her, even from four feet away. And yet. The insistent, angry pulsing in his crotch is still there, and he fears he'll never have peace till it's gone.

She steps towards him, reaches out a hand and lays it over the bulge. 'Ooh,' she says. 'Looks like you are. Give us a chip. I'm ravishing.'

'Not opening them yet,' he says.

'Whatever. So what's it going to be, then, Mart?'

How does she know my name? I've never told her. I'm sure I've never told her. He feels his anger rising again, deep and itchy. It's a network of witches. They know fucking *everything*.

He shakes his head, tries to walk on. But she tightens the grip on his crotch, squeezes in a way that both enrages and engorges. 'Come on, honey. You don't want to waste it. I can make that better, quick-time.'

Oh God. Those fingers, with their chipped scarlet nails, an inch long and sharpened for fighting, are frightening, but the thought of them pumping up and down around his cock, of the pull and squeeze and professional twists of someone else's hand, is too much to bear. 'I don't have much money,' he says.

The grip loosens. She steps back.

'How much?'

'Thirteen quid.'

'Thirteen quid?'

He nods feverishly. Knows that even to someone as far gone as this, thirteen quid is a pitifully low offer.

'Never mind,' he says. Starts to walk on, though his cock seems to have taken on a life of its own now. There won't be anyone up at the war memorial. Needs must, he can relieve himself quickly up there, use the napkins for clean-up.

He gets five paces along the pavement when he hears her 'Oi!'.

Stops and turns and sees that she's got her hand on her hip and has hoisted the bag further up her shoulder like someone who means business. 'Thirteen quid and some chips,' she says, 'but you don't get no French for that.'

Martin follows her up the alleyway.

She leads him deep into the dark – further than he thinks is necessary to hide them from casual eyes – and steps in behind a dumpster. Smiling, he deposits the chips on the lid, steps forward wolfishly and leans a hand, still gripping the chip fork, on the wall behind her shoulder.

'Come on then,' she says, and yanks at his buttons.

Martin doesn't want to look at her, doesn't want to see that raddled face, the inch of roots on the hair that's bent towards him. He looks up, stares at the patch of grey night sky between the gables, and feels her hand delve into his pants, the grab of flesh on tender skin. Yeah, he thinks as she hauls his member into the damp night air, spits on her palm and starts to work it. Thirteen quid well spent. I don't need Jackie Jacobs. What made me think I wanted her and her—

A flashback. A car park, Jackie tugging at him like this woman's doing, frustration mounting, a tipsy swearword falling from her lips.

His cock goes soft.

'What?' says the woman. 'Come on, lover. I'm not going to spend all night.'

Martin feels his cheeks begin to burn. It's gone. There's no more feeling in it than if it was someone else's. The woman yanks at his flaccid organ like it's a cow's udder, pulls harder, gives the head a couple of backhanders and gives up. Lets out a laugh.

'Better luck next time,' she says. 'Quickest thirteen quid I've ever earned.'

He's outraged. 'You what?'

'I'm not bloody staying here all night,' she says.

'You don't think I'm going to pay you for that?' He's hot with wasted ardour, with humiliation. Walks backwards, tucking the useless appendage back inside his damp pants.

'Course you are.' Her voice starts to rise. 'I done what you wanted. Not my fault you can't bloody keep it up.'

'Course I couldn't,' he grumbles. His fingers have turned to thumbs, fumble at his buttons like they're anaesthetised, the chip fork hampering his efforts. He's angry again, disappointed. Had needed the relief of quick, dirty ejaculate and is livid with frustration. 'I saw your fucking face, didn't I?'

He turns and starts to walk away towards Fore Street.

'Oi!' she shouts again.

'Fuck off,' he says over his shoulder. 'You got your chips, didn't you?'

There's a moment's silence, then the woman lets out another squawk of rage. 'Oi!'

Unsteady footsteps clatter up the alley behind him. Martin whirls to face her, raises a fist, chip fork sticking out from gripping palm, towards her face. She halts, abruptly. Stares at him in alarm for a moment, then sees the weapon he's wielding and bursts out laughing. 'Oh, you sorry little fuck,' she says.

His erection is back. He can feel adrenalin like speed in his blood.

'Don't laugh at me,' he threatens. 'Don't you fucking laugh at me, or I'll—'

'You'll what?' Wide-eyed with mirth, she motions at his fist. 'You'll stab me with a chip fork?'

Martin looks over at his raised hand, sees his plywood weapon. Thinks vaguely, as though the thought were coming from far away, yeah, what the fuck?

He punches it into her neck.

He steps back, shocked at his own strength. Tenses in preparation for a fight, because he knows one will be coming now.

The woman slaps her hand to her neck like she's been stung by a wasp, feels the plywood handle protruding from her flesh.

Looks astonished, then outraged, then blackly furious. 'You little fuck!' she says. 'You bloody little fuck.'

She feels her way round the handle, grips it between thumb and finger and pulls it out. Brandishes it at him, lips drawn back over yellow teeth. 'You little fuck!' she shrieks again. And then she notices the blood that spurts across the pavement, that hits the wall, and understands the truth.

'Oh fuck,' she says, and clamps a hand over the wound. It's a stupid wound, a tiny double puncture, but the skin is ragged and her carotid ripped. Her hand is immediately slippery with blood; it gushes out from between her fingers, pours down her neck. Quickly, blackly, soaks the stonewashed denim on her shoulder.

'What have you done?'

Martin stands there and watches. This wasn't what he'd expected, but now it's happened, he feels a rush of startling pleasure; a sense of power he's never felt before. Look at her. Look at the silly bitch, she's all over blood. I did that. I did that to her.

'Fuck, help me,' she says, and puts the other hand up; pleads with her eyes, understands that no help is going to come. 'Jesus. Oh Jesus.'

She takes a step towards him, and he sees it turn into a stagger. She can't be bleeding out yet, he thinks. It must be panic. She's scared. Yes. The fucking bitch is scared. I did that. Me. She's scared because of something I did.

'You've got to call an ambulance,' she says. 'I'm really hurt.'

He's cold all over, but his cock is magnificently, triumphantly hard. He shrugs indifferently. 'Got no phone,' he says, and walks away.

Chapter Sixteen

She's never unlearned the habit of hope. Ever since she can remember, Amber has woken with the same thought: today will be a good day. She learned the practice in her stepfather's house, clung fast to it at Blackdown. Has marked her life out in small milestones of happiness – the dogs, Vic, her home and its improvements, birthday parties, small gestures of friendship – and refuses to dwell on negatives.

She lies on her back, arms spread across the empty bed, and stares at the daylight leaking past the curtains on to the bedroom ceiling. Day workers are beginning to come home; she can hear engines and car doors and bellowed greetings out on Tennyson Way. The bed is hot, the room frowsty. She throws off the covers and lies there, cooling off. The sun has obviously come out while she's been asleep. She's missed another summer day. But thank you, thank you, for giving me summer. It's going to be OK, I can feel it in my bones. I worry too much, that's the problem. Nothing bad can happen, I've come too far.

Amber gets up, takes a shower and washes last night's work out of her hair. The water, lukewarm, wakes her up a little. She can hear faint sounds of movement downstairs. Vic is still home – it must be his day off – but she doesn't hear the sound of voices and guesses Jackie has gone out.

Rubbing her hair with a towel, she checks the clock by the bed. Five p.m. Several hours to work-time. For once, it's worth putting on home clothes. She digs through the wardrobe and chooses a sundress, gaily printed with a pattern of birds and tropical foliage. Slips it over her head, feels the pleasure of dressing pretty for once, and goes down to find her common-law husband.

He's sitting at the kitchen table, all the windows and the back door thrown wide. Her bag sits before him, open. He holds something loosely in his hand. She greets him brightly. He merely looks at her, silently, in return. Amber feels the smile slip from her face. The day goes dark.

'What's wrong?' she asks.

He opens his hand and shows her. 'So what else have you been lying to me about?' he asks. His voice is cold, reptilian. She blanches. The Other Vic is back.

He's holding the cigarette packet Jade pushed into her hand yesterday. She'd shoved it into her handbag and forgotten about it. She stares at it like a rabbit caught in headlights. 'No, Vic, I ... They're not mine,' she stumbles.

He raises his eyebrows, then drops them so his eyes are hooded. 'Liar!' he says accusingly. 'Didn't I tell you? Don't lie to me. I told you, Amber. I will always find you out.'

'Vic ...' Lying is his big bugbear, his pet hate. He's always said it: lying is the biggest betrayal of all. 'Vic, I'm not lying to you.'

'Or what?' he asks. 'You think I'm stupid then? Don't take me for a mug, Amber.'

'I'm not. I—'

'The whole place stinks of fag smoke. Did you think I wouldn't notice?'

'That's Jackie. C'mon. You *know* she smokes like a chimney. I'm sorry. It was raining and I let her smoke in the kitchen.'

'Yeah,' says Vic. 'Good try.'

'No,' she says, knowing she's fighting a losing battle. Once he's got the bit between his teeth, there's no stopping him. He'll twist and twist her words until whatever she says sounds like lying. He'll do it once a month or so, and leave her wrong-footed, shaking. And yet, every time he does it, she tries to protest, tries to assure him he's wrong, keeps hoping that one day the outcome will be different, the way she did as a child. It's like some ritual dance they have to perform with the dark of the moon. He'll apologise afterwards, beg forgiveness, but the intervening days will be a cold, baleful hell of accusing looks and silent judgement. 'No, you've got it all wrong. I swear, Vic.'

'If you'd just tell me the truth, it'd be a different matter,' he says, ignoring her. 'That's the thing I don't understand. Why you have to lie about things when you know what it does to me.'

She's aware that a big fat lie is coming from his own mouth. Come on, she thinks. You don't really think that. If I came to you and said, 'Hey, Vic, I've decided to go against your wishes and take up smoking again,' you'd never just say, 'Oh, OK, babe, that's fine as long as you've told me.' You know I only gave up because you made me; because the sulks and the barbed remarks about my body smell and the refusal to kiss me wore me down. And the stupid thing is that I know, deep down, that you don't really care either way. That the reason smoking was an issue was nothing to do with any of those things, or with fear about my health or yours, it was all of it about control. All about imposing your will on mine and watching yourself win.

'I'm not lying,' she repeats. She snatches the pack from his hand, turns it over to find Jade's phone number. 'Look. That's why I've got it. See?'

She realises her error the instant the words leave her mouth. Wonders if she will ever learn. He's got her now, can segue straight into new accusations.

He takes the pack from her. 'What's this?'

'A phone number,' she says hesitantly, wishing she could backtrack. 'You know how people write phone numbers on fag packets.'

'People?' A small smirk plays at the edge of his mouth. 'And what *people* would that be, then, Amber? You didn't tell me about any *people*.'

Christ, she thinks. Now I *do* have to lie.

She knows she sounds as guilty as he's making her feel as she fishes around for the right words. Vic is turning the pack over and over in his hands as she speaks.

'Just ... this chick I used to know,' she says, and sees his eyes flick up to read her guarded expression. 'Like ... You know ... Ages ago.'

'Chick,' he says.

Don't. Don't rise to it. You know how, when he's in this mood, he will interpret any sort of excuse, any sort of explanation, as protesting-too-much. 'Yes, *chick*,' she says, trying to make it sound firm and hearing the defensiveness in her tone. 'Chick from Liverpool. She used to live two doors down from me.'

He says nothing.

'She was at Funnland,' she says. 'I bumped into her. Vic ...'

He shakes his head, slowly, emphasising his disbelief. 'Yeah, right.'

'What?'

'OK. So you bump into some *chick* and you don't tell me about it?'

'Jeez. You don't tell me every detail of *your* day, do you?'

'I would if it was something like this.'

'I'm sorry,' she lies. 'I forgot about it. It's not as big a deal as you're making it out to be.'

Of course she'd not forgotten. Not the shock of meeting Jade, not the unpleasantness of trying to shake her off. But a scrap of cardboard in the bottom of a loaded handbag? Yes. Maybe the forgetting has some Freudian element to it, is an unconscious way of avoiding dealing with the evidence of the encounter, but she certainly had forgotten, until she saw the pack in Vic's hand.

'OK,' he says. 'What's her name then? This *chick*?'

Amber panics. She can't use the real name; has probably used it, out loud at least, less in the past twenty-five years than any member of her generation except Jade herself. She flails internally, tries to think of an alternative, finds that every female name she has ever known has fled her head. 'Jade,' she says.

She sees a flicker behind the unwavering smile. Some strong reaction, suppressed so she can't read it. The name has some resonance for him. What it is, she doesn't know.

'Yeah, not fast enough, Amber. You took much too long making that up.'

'No,' she says. 'Jade. I just couldn't remember her surname. She just ... lived down the road, you know— I don't know if I ever even knew it. I swear to you, Vic, I'm telling the truth.'

'Well,' says Vic, and picks up the phone. 'There's only one way to find out.'

He dials. There's silence in the kitchen. Vic smiles at her coldly as the ringtone kicks in. He puts the handset on Speakerphone and waits, staring her out like a crouching panther. Christ, she thinks. What am I doing here? Do I even like this man? Sometimes I feel like I don't even *know* him.

A man's voice, on the other end of the line. 'Hello?'

Vic's head jerks; a tiny movement of huge significance. 'Who's that?' he asks.

'Jim,' says the man.

'Jim,' repeats Vic, and raises a cynical eyebrow at her.

'Who's that?' asks Jim.

'Vic,' says Vic. 'Sorry, *Jim*, I was looking for *Jade*.'

The man at the other end of the line sounds calm, casual, unfazed. Her bloke doesn't know either, thinks Amber. Her whole life's as big a lie as mine is. 'No, sorry, mate. I think you've got the wrong number. No Jade here.'

'Oh,' says Vic, 'OK. Thanks, *Jim*.' He emphasises the syllable for Amber's benefit.

''S'OK,' says Jim, and hangs up.

Vic puts the phone down on the table. '*Jim*,' he says.

She leaves it for ten minutes, then follows him upstairs. He's locked himself into the bathroom; she can hear the sound of running water. She taps at the door and listens. No answer. 'Vic?' she calls timidly. Hears the water being turned up harder.

In the bedroom, a shirt lies on the bed; one of his going-out shirts. Her heart sinks. He always does this when he's angry. Goes out after work without a word and, often, doesn't come back all night. She's felt this mood building for days now. Jackie's presence – her discarded towels, her unwashed tea mugs, the brimming ashtray in the garden – has been increasingly irksome to him. She regrets having asked her to stay. It doesn't help that Jackie, at close quarters, has proved to be one of those self-absorbed individuals who never notice much beyond their own boundaries. She talks incessantly, every thought that enters her head falling instantly from her lips: lists the source and cost of every purchase she makes, counts calories – her own and other people's – out loud, rehearses the detail of every slight, every snub, every overlooking that fills her life.

He's using this as an excuse, she thinks. Really, this is about resenting the fact that I imposed a guest on him without consulting him, and about the fact that I'm too weak to ask her to leave. But raising a subject like that would require that we actually talk, and Vic will do anything to avoid having to do that. He would always rather make his point by withdrawing his presence.

She hears the bathroom door open, turns to see him emerge, topless, his muscles rippling above his jeans. He's shaved, and gelled his hair. Rubs at the back of his neck with a towel. A clean one, she notices. He's got it out of the airing cupboard specially. He brushes past her and enters the bedroom; throws the towel pointedly into a corner.

'Vic,' she says.

He ignores her. Goes to the bed and picks up the shirt.

'Are you going out?'

He pops open the mother-of-pearl buttons one by one, still refusing to look at her. I ironed that damn shirt, she thinks. 'Yes.'

'Vic.' She doesn't know what to say. Wants to persuade him to change his mind, knows the desire is pointless.

His back still turned, he slides his arms into the sleeves and begins to button the shirt up. She can see from the set of his shoulders that he is angry and cherishing his anger. Which is worse? she wonders. A man like Vic, who expresses anger with silence and isolation, or one who, like most of the men around here, expresses it loudly, often physically. Sometimes, as she tip-toes around him, sick with misery and wondering where he goes when he takes off, she wonders if a brief, flailing burst of rage wouldn't be better.

'Please,' she says. 'Can't we talk?'

He turns his profile to her, his mouth downturned. 'Nothing to talk about,' he says. 'I don't want to hear any more lies. I'm done listening to you.'

'I'm not lying!' she protests for the thousandth time. 'Vic! Why won't you believe me?'

He whirls and strikes, like a cobra. She recoils, tries to get away, but he grabs her arm, grips like a vice and pushes his face close to hers. His eyes have narrowed to slits, and glitter like dia-monds. She can smell the mint on his breath where he's brushed his teeth. He's planning to score tonight, she thinks. To get back at me. Does he think I don't know? Or is it the other way round? Does he do it to see how far he can push me before I crack?

'Don't you dare speak to me!' he hisses. 'I know all about you, Amber. You liar. You bloody, filthy little liar! You've been lying to me all along, haven't you? I know what you're like. I know what you're all like. I thought you were different, but you're not, are you? You're just another fucking – *slag* –' he lets go of her arm, walks abruptly away, 'like all the rest of them. A lying' – he carries on buttoning his shirt, the words coming out calm and matter-of-fact, now that this brief burst of temper is over – 'fuck-ing – slag.'

He pushes her on to the landing. She props herself against the banister, shocked. He marches past, stone-faced. Moments later, she hears the front door slam.

11.30 a.m.

'You got any scars?' asks Jade. The roundabout is slowing down, and she's not sure she can be bothered to hop off and push any more. It's funny how boring roundabouts get; she never gets bored on the swings.

'Scars? Yes.'

'Me too,' says Jade. She rolls up her top and shows a line of livid ragged dots running across her ribcage. 'Barbed wire,' she informs Bel. 'When I was three.'

'Cool!' says Bel. 'How?'

'Fell over,' says Jade.

'Did you have to have stitches?'

Jade shakes her head. 'My dad said it was my own stupid fault.'

'Mmm,' says Bel, following the logic.

'I'll never learn if I don't see the consequences,' says Jade. 'Go on then. Show us.'

Bel considers, then rolls up her sleeve. Shows the scar down the inside of her upper arm. 'Operation,' she says, 'where I broke it. I've got a metal pin in there. I set off bomb detectors in airports. It was all sticking out through my skin and everything.'

'Nice!' says Jade. 'How'd you do that, then?'

The roundabout reaches a standstill. Bel considers her story. 'Fell downstairs,' she says casually, 'when I was four.' Doesn't add any detail. Some things you don't tell to just anybody; she's long since learned that.

Jade pulls off her sandal to display a slit between her big toe and the next one along. It intrudes a good half-inch into her foot, a ropy red scar delineating the edges.

'Crikey!' Bel is impressed. 'How did you get that?'

Jade tuts. 'Me and Shane was playing chicken with Darren's hunting knife and I didn't get out of the way. My dad says I don't have the sense I was born with.'

'Did you go to hospital with that one, then?'

'Are you kidding? They'd have the SS on us in no time, a Walker coming in with a knife wound.'

'What's the SS?' asks Bel.

'Social Services. People that come and take the kiddies away,' explains Jade. 'They don't approve of people like us. I'm on the At Risk register,' she adds proudly. ''Cause of Shane. 'Cause he fell off the garage roof when Mum wasn't looking and that's why he's like he is.'

'Really?' Bel's thrilled.

'Stupid,' says Jade. 'Could've happened to anybody. Got any more?'

'I've got no toenail,' says Bel, kicking off her shoe.

Jade studies her big toe admiringly. 'Woah,' she says.

Bel feels rather proud. She was too small when it happened for her to have any memory of it, and the lack of it makes her nervous in crowds, when she thinks people might be careless where they step – but to impress a Walker is an achievement. She wonders whether to show the scar on her scalp and decides not to. She's already learned that there's such a thing as too much information; and besides, it, too, didn't merit a hospital visit.

'D'you want to go on the swings?'

'Sure.' They jump off the roundabout and walk across the grass. 'They're crap now, these swings,' says Jade. 'They've gone and put stops on them so you can't go too high. Steph says you used to be able to go all the way over the top.'

'Who's Steph?'

Jade rolls her eyes as though it's the stupidest question in the world. 'My sister. She lives over at Carterton now.'

'Where's Carterton?'

Jade shakes her head again. This girl really does ask some

stupid stuff. 'Miles away,' she says, 'but she's got a Ford Cortina. Only, her boyfriend won't let her drive it without him there, so she has to wait to come over. She says the swings used to be on rings, so if you swung and swung, you could loop the loop.'

'Wow. I bet that was fun,' lies Bel.

'Yeah, and they used to have competitions. See which of them could jump the furthest by letting go at the top of the swing. She says she used to be able to get all the way to the sandpit. Only then Debbie Francis went and landed on the see-saw and knocked her front teeth out, and then the council came along and fixed it so's you can't go higher than halfway now.'

She pauses as she selects her swing, climbs on board the yellow one. 'Debbie Francis spoiled it for everybody,' she announces.

Bel chooses the red swing, settles on to the seat. Kicks her feet up in front of her and starts to fly. 'So how many brothers and sisters have you got?' she asks.

'Six,' announces Jade self-importantly. 'Shane, Eddie, Tamara, Steph, Darren, Gary.'

'Are you Catholics?'

'No,' says Jade suspiciously, as though the question has been designed to catch her out. 'We're Christians. You can't say we ain't. We go church every Christmas.'

'No, no,' says Bel. 'I didn't mean that. I meant ... Never mind.'

'I'm the youngest,' says Jade, proudly. 'My mum says I'm her afterthought.'

Bel kicks higher. She can see over the hedge at the top of her arc, and notices a group of teenagers walking up the lane towards them. They've got a littlie in tow; keep stopping to yell at her to keep up. 'Well, I'm a bastard,' she announces.

Jade frowns at her reprovingly. 'Who says that?'

Bel shrugs. 'Everyone. It's a fact.'

'You shu'n't let people call you things like that,' Jade says. 'My dad says, if someone wants to disrespect you, you bloody well show them what disrespect means.'

'No,' says Bel. 'Really. I'm a bastard. A proper one. My mum had me without being married.'

Jade is scandalised. 'You're joking me! You know what you're saying, don't you? You just said your mum was a slag!'

'No I didn't,' says Bel.

'Yes you did! Oh my God! You did!'

'She was nineteen years old and she made a mistake.' Bel parrots the summary of her own existence.

'So that kid, your sister. Is she a bastard too?'

'Half-sister,' corrects Bel. 'No. She's a real *daughter*.'

'And your dad's not your dad?'

'Course not. My so-called "real" father runs a bar in Thailand. I've got two bastard half-sisters, but no one seems to mind that.'

'Have you met 'em?'

'Don't be stupid. I've not even met him. Lucinda calls them Nong and Pong.'

'Who's Lucinda?'

'My mother.'

'Wooah,' says Jade. 'My mum'd slap me all ways to Sunday if I tried calling her Lorraine.'

'Lucinda would kill me if I called her Mummy,' says Bel. 'She says I make her feel old enough as it is.'

The teenagers have reached the gate. There are seven of them, all dressed in uniform. Both boys and girls sport huge hair and eyeliner. Great streaks of blusher slash across cheekbones, headbands encircle foreheads and gobs of panstick cover the volcanic surfaces of their faces. The boys wear grandad shirts tucked into jeans so tight they probably threaten their future fertility, and the girls have layered the entire contents of their wardrobes, one on top of the other, in imitation of Madonna. It's actually inside-out dressing, thinks Bel. Bra on top of vest on top of T-shirt.

'Oh shit,' says Jade. 'It's Darren.'

Bel looks up, interested. Even she has heard of Darren Walker. He's sixteen and something of a local celebrity. And not in a good way. Since Darren was expelled from Chipping Norton

Comprehensive at fifteen, six months before he was legally able to leave without help, he's been circulating between the Bench, the war memorial and the playground, with, as rumour has it, only the occasional hiatus for a bit of house-breaking in the villages down the road to finance his fags and cider. In village terms, he's the equivalent of a gangland warlord and, as a mystery winner in the genetic lottery, is blessed with the sort of strong-but-silent good looks that result in regular catfights in the village-hall toilets. Despite his family's reputation for smells and parasites, Darren's been through half the girls in his school year and half of the year above.

Bel drinks in the Adam Ant bone structure, the mop of fine chestnut hair, the long, lean, hard body, and wonders how this god-like being can be related to the pug-faced girl beside her. As someone who's never had much luck on the popularity front, Bel's already lining Jade up in her head as a potential Best Friend. But even so, she has to admit that the girl looks like she's been carved out of lard. Darren's got his arm slung loosely round the shoulders of Debbie Francis, the girl who once head-butted a see-saw, and Bel feels a surge of envy at the sight of it. Then he sneers, and her temporary illusion falls away.

'Off!' he says.

Jade grips the chain of the swing and glares at him. 'Fuck off, Darren.'

'Wooo-OOOO-oooo!' go the acolytes.

'We've brought Chloe up to go on the swings,' says Debbie.

Jade shrugs. 'Plenty of swings to go round.'

'Yes, but,' says Darren proprietorially, 'we want that one.'

As if for the first time, he notices Bel. Turns his honeyed gaze upon her and looks her up and down. She blushes furiously, stares rigidly at the church spire in the distance. 'Who's your friend?'

'Nuffin to do wi' you, Darren Walker!' shouts Jade.

'I know who that is.' A boy with a pair of George Michael dangly pirate earrings steps forward and stares at her, arms

folded. He's been cultivating a sparse, soft beard, and Bel recognises him as Tony Dolland, the son of the man who owns the garage. Her stepfather has been locked in a legal battle with his father over a planning application for the last two years. They have to drive to Chippy to get petrol now. 'That's Annabel Scaramanga.'

'No it's not,' she says. 'My name's not Scaramanga. It's Oldacre. I'm Annabel Oldacre.'

The woooo rises again, blots out the sun. The little girl is hanging back, looking at Bel with astonishment, as though she's just opened her mouth and spoken German.

'Well, hoity-toity!' yells Debbie. 'Say "air"!'

'Air,' says Bel, suspiciously.

'Say "hair"!' shouts Tony.

The swing slows beneath her. She's finding it hard to keep up the impetus while she waits to work out what's going on. 'Hair,' she says.

'Say "lair"!' calls someone else.

The word comes out quietly. Her mouth seems to be furring up.

'Now say 'em all together,' says Darren, approaching.

'No,' says Bel.

'All right then. Get off that swing.'

'No,' says Jade. 'Fuck off, Darren.'

He jumps forward, grabs Jade's seat on the upswing, brings it to a violent, sudden halt. Jade loses her grip on the chain, tips backwards and crashes, legs in the air, on to the dusty earth beneath. She lies stunned, gasping for breath.

'I told you,' says Darren.

'Fuck you, Darren,' she chokes. Her heart wants to burst through her ribcage.

'I'd get up if I was you. You don't want to get a bash on the head to go with the one on your arse. C'mon, Chloe!' He turns to the little girl. She's about five. Her baby face peers out from the hood of her pink nylon anorak, which she's tied firmly

126

beneath her chin despite the warmth of the day. She's flushed with heat, and hangs back behind Debbie, staring at Jade with anxious eyes.

'Go on,' says Debbie.

'Don't want to,' says Chloe.

'Don't worry about her,' says Darren. 'She does what I tell her.'

He prods at Jade with a toe. 'Go on. Can't you see you're scaring her?'

Jade sits up and glares murderously at the child, rubbing her upper arm where she's caught it on a stone. Chloe understands the meaning of the look, and ducks further behind her sister.

'Stop showing off, Darren,' says Jade. 'Nobody's impressed.'

'Come on, Jade,' says Bel. 'Let's just go.'

Her voice sparks another chorus of 'woo-oo's from the older kids. She ignores them with a look of imperious contempt.

Jade is boiling with rage and humiliation, but she's not stupid.

'C'mon, Chloe!' says Darren again. The kid comes unwillingly towards him, propelled by her sister. Debbie's wearing a tight striped sleeveless T-shirt, a bibbed gymslip and the legs of a pair of cut-up footless tights on her arms. A studded leather jacket hangs self-consciously over her shoulders. She's scraped her hair back into a ponytail and glued false eyelashes over her own stubby blond ones. She bats them at Darren. Crucifix earrings jiggle against her cheeks.

'You shouldn't be selfish,' she says piously to Jade. 'She's littler than you.'

She picks Chloe up and deposits her on Jade's still-warm seat. Starts to push.

'I'm hungry,' says Chloe.

'Oh, for God's sake. I've taken you to the swings, haven't I?' snaps Debbie.

Chapter Seventeen

'No, sorry, mate. I think you've got the wrong number. No Jade here,' says Jim.

Kirsty feels her hands slip on the wheel, hurriedly compensates as the car jerks to the left.

'Mum!' Sophie protests from the back. Her orange juice has gone all over her tennis gear.

''S'OK,' says Jim, and hangs up.

'Sorry,' says Kirsty. 'Sorry. Don't know what happened there. I just slipped.'

'I'm all wet now,' whines Sophie.

'Never mind,' says Jim. 'It'll be dry by Monday.'

Casual. I must act casually. 'Who was that?' Kirsty enquires. Changes down to third as they approach the roundabout.

'Wrong number,' says Jim. 'Wanted someone called Jade.'

'Oh,' she says.

'What's for tea?' asks Sophie.

'I don't know,' she says vaguely. 'Fish fingers?'

Jade. A man who wanted Jade. Not her. Not Bel: a man. Jesus. Is someone on to me? Or was it just coincidence? Oh God, has the *Mail on Sunday* finally tracked me down?

'Fish fingers!' protests Sophie. 'But it's Saturday!'

'So what?'

'Other people get a takeaway on Saturdays! Chinese or something.'

'Yeah,' says Jim, 'other people don't get tennis lessons and piano lessons. It's an either-or choice here, Sophie. We're not rich. People like us don't get both.'

'Hunh,' grunts Sophie.

'I'm doing a roast tomorrow,' says Kirsty encouragingly. 'Chicken and all the trimmings. Stop kicking the back of my seat, Sophie.'

'But I'm a vegetarian!' she cries.

'Really?' Jim turns around. 'When did this happen?'

'You don't listen to a *word* I say.'

'Of course we do, Sophie,' he teases. 'Every single word. No wonder you don't want fish fingers. What do you think, darling?' He turns to Kirsty. 'Can we whip her up a nice salad?'

'Of course we can,' says Kirsty. 'We've got lots of salad in the garden just waiting to be eaten. I'm so sorry, Sophie. If you'd *told* us, we'd've been picking it for you every day.'

Sophie groans. 'Not *that* sort of vegetarian. Not a *salad* vegetarian.'

Jim catches Kirsty's eye. 'Ah. A chocolatarian.'

Sophie glares out of the window. 'I don't like fish fingers.'

What if we get home, and there's photographers on the door-step? What will I do? It will kill them. Not just the revelation: the lie. He'll find out he's been living with a stranger all these years. He'll think that if I could lie to him about something so huge, I could lie to him about anything. He'll end up wondering if I ever loved him at all.

'No skin off my nose, sweetie,' she says. 'How about a lettuce sandwich?'

'A lettuce sandwich isn't dinner!' she protests.

'You'll be eating a lot of lettuce if you're going to be a vegetarian. Might as well get used to it.'

'And broad beans,' adds Jim. 'Don't forget those.'

Luke's standing outside the rugby club when they draw up, his boots dangling by their laces over his shoulders. 'I wish he wouldn't do that,' says Jim. 'He goes through a pair of laces a week.'

He reaches over and beeps the horn. Luke jumps, turns and waves. He comes running over, grinning, and hops into the car.

'How was it?' asks Kirsty.

'Awesome,' he replies. 'I scored a try. And Mr Jones says I might be able to try out for the first team in a year.'

'Fantastic!' she says. 'Luke! Sit on the bin liner, darling. You're going to get mud all over.'

'Oh, sorry,' he says, and settles into his seat. Sophie looks at him the way all little girls look at muddy little brothers.

'What's for tea?' he asks.

'Well, we were going to have fish fingers, but your sister wants a salad,' says Jim. 'She's turned vegetarian.'

Luke howls with disgust. 'You're kidding! I can't eat salad. I've been playing *rugby*.'

Jim shrugs. 'Well, it's not up to me. Perhaps you can negotiate.'

Kirsty puts the car into gear and pulls into the road. Luke frowns at Sophie.

'All right,' she says. 'I'll eat fish, OK? I'll be a fishatarian, if it makes you happy.'

'Pescatarian,' says Jim.

'Whatever,' says Sophie, and folds her arms.

It must have been Bel, Kirsty thinks. Is it that her voice is so deep he thought she was a bloke? It didn't sound like it. But – I don't know. Please, please, please, God, let it have been Bel. Let it not have been someone else, someone with another agenda altogether.

'But I'm not eating any stinking chicken,' says Sophie.

'Fine,' says Jim. 'But don't think that means you can double up on roast potatoes.'

Chapter Eighteen

Blessed loves Whitmouth in the hours around dawn; partly because it's cool and the air is clean, but mostly because dawn means that the long night's work is approaching its end and the moment when she can lay her tired bones in her warm soft bed for a few hours is approaching. Tonight she's scrubbed and polished every seat on the roller coaster trains, swept down what she still thinks of as its station-stop and given every touchable surface a going-over with a spray-bottle of antibacterial cleanser and half a dozen J Cloths. She's cleaned the perspex windows that allow queuers to see what's going on in the rest of the park as they inch their way up the stairs. She's wiped off the hair gel and Sta-Sof-Fro that greases every pillar at head height.

Now she's in the roped-off area under the tracks, sweeping up the wrappers and coins and condoms and other small treasures that have fallen from unsuspecting pockets as the train looped the loop. It's sticky down here, as surprising numbers of people still take drinks containers on the ride despite the warnings not to. You can always tell them later, in the park, because they are the ones with a sugar-dressing on their hair and a faint look of sheepishness about them. By season's end the area below the tracks will need to be washed down with a power hose, but there's little point in doing so before then, as generally only the cleaners come here. Blessed always saves this chore for last of all, so that she can see what's there by pale grey daylight. It's a popular job, this – goes to the senior cleaner and was passed down to her when Amber moved up to management – because it's amazing what people fail to notice they've lost until after they've left the park. There's usually a tenner in change down here; and sunglasses and prescription glasses and small items of jewellery; tubes of sweets and bunches of keys (which always go to Lost Property); and, sometimes, a wallet. Their owners probably think they've been pickpocketed, which is why they never return to claim them. As a Christian, Blessed used to have qualms about removing the cash before she handed the wallets in, but she knows that if she doesn't take the opportunity, Jason Murphy or one of the other guards will, and then it'll go on drink or drugs or some other form of frittering if it's them. The proceeds of her own dishonesty go straight into Benedick's med-school fund. She thinks of her 'victims' as benefactors.

Tonight has produced relatively thin pickings. Yesterday was overcast, so sunglasses (which she can sell for fifty pence a pair to the second-hand shop on Fore Street) have stayed firmly in bags, and jackets have covered the loosest pockets. But she's found £3.60 in change (almost half an hour at minimum wage, after all) and three packs of chewing-gum, which Ben will like. And a hairpiece: a foot-long clip-on ponytail in golden synthetic blond. She's about to drop it in the bin liner, marvelling at its owner's obliviousness, when she thinks, No, it's in good condition. I'll see if Jackie wants it before I throw it away. We waste far too much in this world.

She stretches her back and checks her watch. Five-twenty: nearly clocking-off time. She'll stay till her contracted five-thirty before she punches her card. No one gets any prizes for doing their job efficiently at Funnland; they're paid by the hour and that's that. And besides, she likes to get a lift from Amber if she can, and Amber is always the last to leave. She decides to go and look for Jackie. Picks up her bin liner and ambles in the direction of the dumpsters.

*

132

Jackie's on the phone. Five-thirty in the morning, and she's still found someone to talk to. She's finishing up in the coconut shy, not that there's ever much to do other than check that the coconuts haven't cracked open to reveal their concrete interiors, and to dust the prizes so it's not too obvious how rarely they get won. She stands in her novelty rubber gloves with the frilled lace cuffs, back to the park, and doesn't see Blessed approach.

'That's right, babe,' she says. 'Till it's sore.'

Blessed hesitates. This sounds as though it might be a personal conversation. Not that Jackie keeps many of her thoughts personal. 'And then when you think you're all wrung out, I'll suck my finger and—'

Blessed hurriedly coughs. Jackie jumps, and looks guiltily over her shoulder. Breaks into a grin when she sees Blessed and holds up the rubber-clad finger that's just been the subject of her conversation. 'Gotta go, babe. Yeah, later. I'll be waiting.'

She hangs up. 'Hey.'

'Hello,' says Blessed. 'How are you today?'

'Better now it's home-time,' says Jackie. 'Is Amber ready yet?'

'I don't know. I'm sure she'll come and find us. I brought you this.' She fishes the ponytail out of her plastic bag. 'Someone lost it. I thought it might suit you.'

Jackie lets herself out through the hatch, comes and looks, a frown on her face. 'Second-hand hair?'

Blessed feels herself blush. Knows she's done another of those cultural misreadings that have tripped up many budding friendships since she got here. Not that she has any burning desire for intimacy with Jackie. Rather, she feels she might start keeping Benedick away from her, now he's reached adolescence. 'It doesn't look as though it's been used,' she stammers. 'I think whoever owned it must have put it on new yesterday.'

Jackie seems reluctant even to touch it. Under her critical gaze, Blessed sees that it is a poor thing; that to someone used to the cheap and plentiful luxuries of a wealthy country, second-hand hair is barely less disgusting than a second-hand toothbrush. 'Yeah, you're all right, Blessed,' she says. 'Thanks anyway.'

Blessed shoves the ponytail into the bin liner, tries not to show her embarrassment. If she'd been in Jackie's position, she would have accepted the gift with a show of pleasure, even if she had every intention of putting it in the next bin she passed. She feels a twinge of nostalgia for the manners she was raised with.

'So are you ready to go?' she asks.

Jackie nods. 'I should coco. I'm knackered.'

'Me too. It's a long night.' They start to walk towards the dumpsters, bin liners bouncing off their calves. 'So what plans do you have for the rest of the day?'

'Sleep as long as I can,' says Jackie, 'then Morrisons, I guess. I've got nothing in the house.'

'You're back home, then?'

Jackie nods. 'Yes. Went back today.'

'Oh good,' says Blessed. 'I am glad to hear that.'

'It was getting awkward.'

'I can imagine. No one likes to outstay their welcome.'

'I don't like living by other people's rules,' says Jackie. 'People all over my business, you know?'

Blessed raises an eyebrow. A part of her is glad to remember that Jackie has a hard time being grateful for anything. That it's not just her own gifts that come up lacking. 'So you think your ... problem has passed?' she asks, with gentle irony. Amber told her last night about her conversation with Martin Bagshawe and she's interested to know who will get the credit.

'Yeah,' says Jackie. 'I think he's got the message. In the end you've got to be firm, ain't you? Stand up for yourself.'

Blessed allows herself a small grin; turns her head away to hide it.

Amber is already waiting in the changing rooms, whirling her keys round her index finger like a child's toy. She looks tired and grey, her eyes red at the edges, but no one looks their best at this time of day. 'Ready?' she asks. Her voice sounds like it's coming from a distance. Blessed is always intrigued by the way voices sound so different in the early morning, as though their owner's attachment to life has faded with the smallness of the hour. It's not long past peak death time in hospitals, she reflects. We're probably all half out of our bodies, around dawn. The room is full of silent wraiths who were the life and soul of the cafeteria four hours ago. The three women gather their belongings from their lockers and swipe themselves out on to the seafront.

It's going to be a beautiful day. Jackie looks up at the clear blue sky as they walk past the front of the park, and grins. 'That's me down at the beach, then,' she says. 'Might as well not go home, really. All I'm going to do is sleep in the sun, anyway.'

'Seriously?' asks Amber.

'Naah,' says Jackie. 'Just joking.'

Amber shakes her head. 'You should know better than to make jokes at this time of day, Jackie.'

Jackie shakes a cigarette out of her jacket pocket and lights it. 'Yeah,' she says.

'How can you smoke?' asks Blessed. 'Doesn't it make you sick?'

'Well, it might do if I'd just got up,' replies Jackie, and releases a stream of smoke into the sparkling air. 'But I suppose, given I'm coming out of work, that this is the equivalent of five in the afternoon for me. What glamours have you got lined up for the day, Blessed?'

'The usual,' she replies. She will get Benedick up, check that he's done his homework, feed him and send him to school. It's only a year or so since she stopped walking him there, a ritual that caused increasing discord between them as he plunged into adolescence. Then she'll sleep for a few hours, get up, shower and go to work her afternoon shift at Londis. It's only a four-hour shift, which allows her to spend the evening with her son before Amber picks her up at quarter-to ten.

Jackie takes another suck on her smoke. 'I don't know how you can work all them hours. Don't you ever have any fun?'

'The trouble with this country,' says Blessed, 'is that no one has any idea of work.'

'Trouble with the Third World,' replies Jackie, 'is that you're all suckers.'

'Thank you, Jackie,' says Blessed. 'I will try to remember. But there are two of us, and only one is allowed to work. It won't be so many years until Benedick is a doctor, and then he can support me.'

Amber stops short on the pavement and slaps her forehead. 'Shit,' she says.

'What?'

'Sorry, Blessed. I forgot. I meant to give it to you at tea break. It's in my office. I'd forget my head if it weren't screwed on.'

'You're going to have to slow down,' says Blessed. 'I'm a few feet behind.'

'The computer. I managed to get hold of a computer for Ben. Maria Murphy, believe it or not. They've bought Jared a Wii and he doesn't need his old laptop any more.'

Blessed feels herself light up. 'Really? You did that for me?'

'I told you I was going to try.' Amber smiles proudly. She really does look tired, thinks Blessed. Like she hasn't slept. But praise Jesus, I prayed for a miracle and Amber Gordon has brought it to us.

'You are an angel,' she says. Life has rendered her dry-eyed and patient, but she feels the welling of tears in her throat. 'I swear to God. He will be grateful. I know he will. But no more grateful than I am.'

Amber shakes her head. 'It's OK. It's nothing. Just a couple of phone calls. Look. I'll go and get it now, and you can give it to him when he gets up.'

She pulls her keys from her pocket, throws them to Jackie. 'Let yourselves into the car,' she says. 'I won't be a minute.'

*

They walk on in silence, Blessed rich with her blessings, Jackie full of her deprivation. Amber's managerial position doesn't extend to a space in the staff car park, so she always leaves the car at the Koh-Z-Nook, the Anglo-Thai tea rooms on the far side of the pier. They're only open from breakfast through to six, so there's always room in there, and it's safer than leaving it out all night on the club strip. It's a boring little walk, all concrete and shutters, but once they get past the high locked gates of the pier there's a lovely view of the sea.

'That's nice,' says Jackie.

'So nice,' says Blessed.

'Why doesn't anyone ever do anything like that for me?' Jackie complains. 'I haven't got a computer neither.'

Because you wouldn't know how to use it? thinks Blessed. 'You could try giving it up to Jesus,' she suggests.

Jackie snorts like a horse. 'I've been asking Jesus to let me win the lottery for years,' she says. 'Maybe I'm just not the sort who gets their prayers answered.'

'It doesn't really work like that. You need to ask him for a solution. To help you help yourself. I asked every day, and he has sent me Amber. You never know what form your solution will take, but it is unlikely to come in the form of winning the lottery.'

Jackie shoots her an evil look. Blessed bounces it off. She's used to the resentment of the unsaved, and nothing can puncture her happiness this morning. The question of the computer has weighed heavily on her shoulders. To be relieved of it is a miracle indeed.

She breathes deep of the morning air and smiles at the sky. This far down, the street is peaceful, the wash of the sea placid on the stones beyond the pier. There's a nightingale in the botanical gardens; the town is so quiet that its song rings out, clear and true, caressing the back of her neck and stroking her cheeks. She pauses to listen. Jackie takes a couple of paces, then stops impatiently to look at her.

'What?'

'Listen,' says Blessed.

Jackie frowns and cranes. Blessed sees her hear nothing, decide that it's the quiet she's meant to be listening for. 'Yeah,' she says. 'Very nice,' and stomps on.

Blessed hangs back and listens for a moment longer, glad of the chance to do so without interruption. The bird sings with all the joy of summer. Thank you, God, for bringing me to Whitmouth. It wasn't what I imagined when I started my journey, but I am glad it was here that I came.

She sees Jackie turn the corner into the Koh-Z-Nook's car park, hears the sound of a scuffle and a bellowed swearword. Gives up on her reverie and shuffles forward as fast as her flip-flops will take her.

Jackie sits on the ground, rubbing her knee and glaring at a shoe lying on the tarmac. It's a peep-toe wedge, lime-green, the ankle strap snapped clean through. 'Fucking fuck,' she says.

'Are you OK? What happened?'

She looks at the palm of her hand, brushes pieces of grit from her mount of Luna. 'Fucking fell over that fucking shoe.'

'Oh dear. Are you hurt?'

'Yes,' she snaps, then: 'Not much. No fucking thanks to the fucking moron who just dumped that there. Fuck sake. Why can't they just bloody pick up after theirselves?'

Blessed offers her a hand. Jackie stands and rubs her elbow, muttering. 'Bloody accident waiting to happen. I'll fucking brain them if I ever find out who it was.'

'Come on,' says Blessed. 'Let's get you to the car.'

She offers an arm to her colleague, who limps dramatically as they cross the car park. The Panda is tucked neatly into the far corner, in the shade of a scrappy hedge. It's not until they get round the back of the car that they see that the owner of the shoe has been tucked as neatly away behind it, bare feet poking under the driver's door, her battered face peering sightlessly out from a halo of gorse and sea-spurge.

Chapter Nineteen

Amber comes down the steps of the police station to find that there's already a knot of onlookers on the pavement outside. News travels fast in Whitmouth. The car is taped off in the Koh-Z-Nook's car park, jailed as an accessory after the fact. Blessed and Jackie, as the ones who actually found the body, are going to be in the station for a while longer. She's going to have to take the bus home. She sets off to walk up to the Funnland stop.

It's nearly ten, and the Corniche is full of strollers and mobility scooters: the morning demographic. Dodging around them, Amber doesn't hear her name being called until she's nearly at Klondike Junction. She looks around, confused, then spots Vic, arms brown and shapely in a white T-shirt, leaning against a minicab parked up in the layby fifty yards back. He waves. Her heart leaps. She crosses the road and walks back to him.

'What are you doing here?'

He wraps an elbow round her neck, kisses her cheek. 'I heard.'

'You heard?'

'Jackie called me. I came down to see if you were all right.'

'Thank God you did. I was dreading the bus.'

'C'mon.' He opens the car door. 'I'll take you home.'

*

She sinks into the back seat and closes her eyes. She doesn't recognise the driver and is slightly surprised, as most of them live on the estate. Vic gets in next to her and closes the door. 'Back to Tennyson Way, please, mate,' he says.

She feels the engine rev, and the car moves forward. Knows he's watching her and opens her eyes to look. He's smiling. 'How are you doing?'

She sighs. 'Oh, you know.'

'Not really,' he says. 'That's why I asked.'

Amber closes her eyes again and lets her head drop back against the headrest.

'You must be starting to think someone's got it in for you,' he says.

Her eyes fly open again. 'Vic! My God! What a thing to say!'

He shrugs his shoulders, all blue-eyed innocence. 'I was just saying. You must've thought it yourself, Amber.'

The driver is watching her in the rear-view, a glint of amusement in his eye. Amber clams up and turns her face away. Vic slips a hand round the back of her neck and strokes her hairline. She shrugs him off, stares out of the window.

'Don't be like that, babe,' he says. 'I came to pick you up, didn't I?'

Mary-Kate and Ashley come bounding out the second she opens the door, and the fact that he's let them in tells her more about his mood when he got home than anything he's said so far. They circle round and round on tiny paws, gazing at her with all the rapturous joy of the innocent. Amber scoops them up and rains kisses on their heads. She's never felt such pure and simple affection as she feels for these loving little beings. Wishes that human relationships were as simple.

She goes through to feed them, notices that the washing machine is on and nearing the end of its spin cycle. Fastidious as ever, she thinks. Nothing stays in the laundry basket for long in this house.

'D'you want a cuppa?' he asks.

She shakes her head. 'I'm dead beat, Vic. I'm going to have a wash and a lie-down.'

'OK. I'll just get this lot hung out,' he says. 'It's good drying weather.'

She's brushing her teeth when he comes in and stands behind her, looks at her in the mirror. She looks back, relieved that, despite everything, the row is clearly over. And then he touches the small of her back and she sees that Other Vic is not quite gone yet.

His arms slip round her and he folds her into a bear hug, presses her crotch against the basin. Shit, she thinks. He's still here. This is not her Vic, this man with the manically cheerful grin, the sudden physical gestures. He does sometimes come home in moods like this, but she's never learned to accept them. He won't let her go. She doesn't feel as though she's being hugged, she feels pinioned.

'Hey, Amber,' he says quietly. She can feel his breath on her neck, feel his torso pressed against hers. He kisses her throat, just above her collarbone, and she has to struggle with the urge to push him off. He was so angry yesterday. She should be grateful that the mood has passed so quickly. She forces herself to relax, to raise a hand and caress his face. She can feel the beginnings of a hardening in his crotch. Oh shit, she thinks. Asks herself why she thinks it. It's been weeks since he's touched her like this, and God knows she's longed for it to happen. She should be grateful. Should be glad.

'How was your night?' she asks, by way of distracting him. 'I didn't ask. I'm sorry.'

'Oh, babe,' he mumbles, and turns her to face him. He's fully hard now beneath his jeans. He grinds his groin against hers. She feels a stir in response, but it feels nasty, dirty. 'It was OK. I went to a bar. Had a few drinks. Calmed down. I'm sorry. Really, I'm sorry. I wouldn't want to hurt my girl, you know that.'

'You believe me?' she asks.

Vic pulls his head back, looks down into her face with a

141

strange, detached good humour. Starts to manoeuvre her towards the landing. She goes unwillingly, more to avoid new disagreements than from any desire to participate. 'It doesn't matter if I believe you.'

'Oh, Vic,' she says, 'if you can't trust me, then what's the point?'

'Trust's not the point,' says Vic. 'It's whether I forgive you that's the point. And I forgive you.'

He thrusts a knee between her thighs, pushes her against the landing wall. Puts a hand round one of her buttocks and humps himself against her, like a dog.

I don't want this, she thinks. I want to talk. I don't understand men. The way they can just ignore everything when their hormones are leading the way. I can't just ...

She can feel his hands working their way up, tugging at her trousers.

'Vic ...' she says. 'I've had a shitty night. I'm all sweaty. And I'm tired.'

He's not looking at her any more. Has his jaw dug into her neck. 'I'll sort you out,' he says. 'I'll make you sweat some more before we're done.'

'I ...'

He's got the trousers down to the tops of her thighs. Shit, she thinks, he's going to do it anyway. Whether I like it or not.

The bear hug's back, and he's picking her up bodily, hauling her into the bedroom. 'That's it,' he croons. 'That's right.'

Shit, she thinks, just go with it. Just get it done with and, maybe after, he'll let you talk. Lucky Jackie's not coming back any more, she thinks. Lucky she's not going to walk in and see this. God knows what she'd think, after this morning.

By the bed, he puts a foot behind her ankle and pushes her so that she tumbles backwards beneath him. Hoicks down her pants and grips her pubis proprietorially. 'Yeah,' he says. 'That's it. You know you want it.' With the other hand he unbuttons his jeans and pulls his cock out. It's thick, engorged, purple.

He climbs on top and begins to thrust.

Chapter Twenty

Her name is Stacey Plummer, and she is a veterinary nurse. Was. At twenty-five she is older than the other victims, and the post-mortem shows that she was stone-cold sober, to boot. At midnight on Saturday she tired of the company of her friends, who were intent on drinking the bar at the Hope and Anchor dry before hitting a nightclub, and set out to walk home to their B&B. Her body was found six hours later, in a beach-café car park, by yet another cleaner from Funnland on her way home from her night shift. Those women must be really starting to hate their jobs.

It takes almost two days to identify her, mostly because her friends were so hungover that they didn't leave their room other than to eat their full English, and assumed that she'd gone home in protest. And partly because the killer has stepped up his game. Stacey's face has been beaten so badly that her gamine features have been almost obliterated.

The other victim is a different type of person altogether, though the occurrence of two murders so close together has kicked off a frenzy of fear and speculation. Tina Bentham, a forty-five-year-old grandmother of four, an alcoholic and occasional prostitute. Found by council bin men on Monday afternoon in a gore-soaked alleyway off Fore Street, her body undamaged apart from a couple of old, probably unrelated, bruises, and a ragged double-puncture wound to the neck that has ruptured her carotid artery, causing her to bleed to death. The victims, and the manner of their deaths, are so different that the police – and, even more, the press – are beginning to speculate as to whether there's a single killer at all.

Kirsty arrives on Tuesday afternoon, before Stacey's name is released to the press. She doesn't want to be within a hundred miles of Bel, but Dave Park has gone up to Sleaford, where Child F and Child M are due at the magistrates' court, and work is work is work. I'll keep my head down, she thinks. It's not that small a town; I'll probably never bump into her, especially if I stay away from the theme park. She wishes fiercely that she'd never handed over her number. Doesn't know what temporary madness possessed her.

The town is buzzing, despite the images on the news-stands. The cash registers in the pubs and cafés ring red-hot as the press corps huddle behind their windows, getting news off each other between the ritual announcements. The sea thunders up the pebbles, washing evidence and bathers in its wake. Police tape turns quickly to streamers which whiplash over the promenade, catching the unwary with paper-cut edges. The streets are crowded with health-and-safety officers handing out *Keep Yourself Safe* leaflets, with feminist groups and opportunist politicians and churches and police liaisons and council tourism officers reassuring holidaymakers. Travelling burger vans park up on the double yellows on the seafront on the safety-in-numbers assumption. Hotel rooms are full and cafés are running out of bacon butties. Through the steamy atmosphere of the penny arcade, frustrated sunbathers huddle over slot machines, watching their what-the-hell money drain away at a pound a minute. Funnland, with its high walls and patches of shelter, is doing a roaring trade. There's nothing, it seems, like a serial killer to foster a tourist boom.

Kirsty can't find parking anywhere near the front and ends up leaving the car at the Voyagers Rest (no apostrophe; she wishes she were less sensitive to these things). With a scarf wrapped across her face she trudges a mile through the pedestrian maze of shopping streets to the sea.

There's a queue outside Funnland, just as though it were another normal day. She looks at the people shuffling up the line and wonders if Bel is inside.

Amber studies Suzanne Oddie's skin. It's shiny and brown and taut, and holds no clue as to her age. And yet somehow she looks every year of it. That's the thing with plastic surgery and all the rest of the stuff rich women spend so much on, thinks Amber. It's not really about making you look younger. It's to make you look more expensive.

Suzanne is looking at the books, frowning over a pair of tortoiseshell-rimmed designer spectacles. She wears a suit that Amber recognises as Chanel. Beneath the desk, a pink-soled stiletto heel drums back and forth. She has three rings on her left hand – one engagement, one wedding, one eternity, the stones the size of corn kernels – and a tourmaline knuckleduster on the right. Amber feels dowdy and poor in front of her. Of course, she is meant to, today. Today, Suzanne is power-dressing to make the pecking order clear.

'*Eighteen* tampon-disposal units? Seriously?'

'You need one in every cubicle,' says Amber.

'Why can't we just have them out in the washroom? And leave bags on the cisterns?'

Amber shrugs. 'Up to you. I'd've said it was a false economy. What with the plumbing, and the cleaners resigning. I think you're overestimating the average punter's sense of communal responsibility.'

'Mmm,' says Suzanne; looks suspicious that a cleaner should be using such long words. Drums her nails again on the desk. Then she looks up, sharply. 'Well, we need to make economies somewhere, Amber.'

Why? She wants to shout. Why? Thanks to the murder, and its I'd-forgotten-about-Whitmouth effect, we're having the best season in living memory. There's queues thirty minutes long just to get in through the front gate. 'Really?' she asks, faintly.

'Yes. We're in a recession, you know.'

Ah, she thinks, yes. The recession. 'But we're doing well here,' she argues, aware that she's wasting her breath. 'Just judging by the amount of rubbish we're carting out, numbers must be well up.'

Suzanne doesn't look at her. Has she always avoided my eye like this? wonders Amber. Was I just so keen to please that I didn't notice? Suzanne flips the page as she speaks. 'Yes, well, but these murders are upward blips in a general downward trend. We can't rely on them for ever.'

Amber's eye pop. She's not seen the murders from the business perspective. 'No, I suppose we can't,' she says.

'Especially with Innfinnityland out of action,' continues Suzanne. 'A total waste of an asset. We're going to have to invest capital in finding another use for the space.'

Yes, thinks Amber. That Strangler's one selfish bastard. She waits while Suzanne rattles her fingernails a bit more, wonders what's coming next.

'Twenty-six cleaners,' she says eventually. 'It's a lot.'

'Most of them on minimum wage,' Amber points out.

'That's still ...' she turns to the calculator, taps away, 'twenty-three-grand-odd a month. That's a lot to be paying for cleaning.'

'It's a lot of cleaning,' Amber replies. 'Coke and ice-cream aren't the easiest things to get off.'

'Still,' says Suzanne. 'We're not *made* of money.' She fingers the strand of pearls around her neck, looks at Amber patronisingly. 'You're discovering the down side of management, I'm afraid,' she says. 'Sometimes you have to make the tough calls. That's what we pay you for.'

Not enough, Amber thinks. 'Can I just ... get it straight what it is you're after here, Suzanne?'

She smiles, tight-lipped. 'Oh,' she says. 'I'd say twenty per cent?'

Amber feels like she's going to have a heart attack. 'Twenty per cent? Off the wage bill?'

'Oh, no,' says Suzanne airily. 'Wherever you want to find it.'

Her mind's racing. 'You mean, off the whole budget?'

Suzanne Oddie meets her eye icily. 'Yes, Amber. That's what I mean.'

Dear God. She wants me to lose a hundred thousand pounds off a budget that's already creaking at the seams. I'm using the cheapest everything. There isn't anywhere to get any of this stuff cheaper, unless I go to China myself and bring it back on foot.

'Suzanne ...' she begins.

The smile again. 'Yes?'

'I ... that's a lot to ask out of the blue.'

'Oh, it's OK,' says Suzanne. 'I'm not asking you to do it by tomorrow. It's over the whole year.'

'Yes, but ... twenty per cent?'

Suzanne looks down at her pad. 'And how much is it we pay you, again?'

She feels a blush. She's not counted her own salary into the mix. 'Twenty-two thousand five hundred.'

'Hmmm.' Suzanne makes a note.

Martin feels strong, powerful, confident. Feels the way he's always thought he should. It's as though Saturday night has taken a big syringe full of self-esteem and shot it directly into his veins. He rarely leaves the house before noon, but today he's been striding the streets of Whitmouth since nine o'clock, ear-wigging the shuffling crowds, listening to the talk on the streets and bathing in his glory. I exist now, he thinks. I really exist. They're all wondering who I am.

He strolls up Mare Street, past the scene of his triumph, and feels the swell of pride as he sees the yellow tape flapping in the wind. Lets himself indulge in a moment's sensual memory – the whore staggering from side to side, hand hopelessly clutching the gouting wound. He had to jump back a few times to avoid getting gore on his new trainers. I need to be more careful, he thinks. That's not the way to do it, not if I don't want to get caught. I need to learn a thing or two from that other guy. Try something less messy next time.

But he doesn't think the next time will need to come for a while. This is the best he's ever felt. My God, he thinks. I haven't even thought about Jackie Jacobs in a couple of hours. She's nothing to me now. She doesn't deserve me. Not now I'm Someone. I deserve better than her. Her and her prison guard Amber Gordon. They can't keep me down any more.

As he's thinking it, someone brushes his sleeve as they hurry past, apologises, and he looks up. It's that journalist who chatted him up on the beach: Kirsty Lindsay, flashing him a smile as she hurries on towards the front. Wow, he thinks. I've been so caught up in my triumph that I completely forgot to look up what she wrote on Sunday. He makes a mental note to check the *Tribune* website when he gets in, but decides to follow her for a while first. She won't be able to brush him off the way she did before. When she notices him, she'll see he's Someone too.

She's dressed down for the day in jeans and a mac, but he sees that there's a nice body under the clothes. She's not spectacular, not flashy like the mayfly beauties who totter past him on the strip at night; but she has the sort of solid, womanly good looks, the evidence of self-respect, that a Someone should be aiming at. She's talking on the phone, has an oversized computer bag hanging off her shoulder, clamped to her body by her other arm, and looks younger than he remembers from their brief meeting. He waits till she's got a few feet further on, then falls into step behind.

Whoever's at the other end of the phone isn't happy with her. 'I know, darling, and I've told you I'm sorry,' she says. 'It's not like I'm here for a fun day out. I can think of a lot of places I'd rather be.'

She stops, and he almost runs into the back of her. He quickly diverts to read the small ads in the window of the newsagent's. He doesn't really need to bother with the pretence, as she's too absorbed in her call to notice what's going on around her. I should warn her, really, he thinks. To pay attention. People get pickpocketed all the time because they're not paying attention. Maybe that would be the way to get her talking. She'd be grateful ...

'Yeah, yeah, I know, Jim,' she says. Her voice is less posh than he remembers; he's surprised by that. 'And again, I'm sorry. What? Yeah, I know. Blimey. Like women haven't been complaining about *that* for centuries.'

He's beginning to be concerned about the tone of her voice when she lets out a laugh. 'I told you not to call me when I'm at work,' she says.

'Yeah, yeah,' she says. 'Nag, nag, nag, bitch, bitch, bitch. Here I am working my arse off to keep you in the style you want to be accustomed to and all you do is complain. You don't even keep the house clean.'

Martin doesn't really understand what's going on. It doesn't sound like a happy marriage. She'd never talk like that to me, he thinks. You've got to have respect in a relationship, or it will never work.

She laughs again. 'Yeah, not a chance. I wish I could, but there's no point. I'd just have to come back tomorrow, and I've got copy to file this afternoon. What? Yeah. Pissing down, and the sort of wind that tears your knickers off. Yup. Yes, I *am*, you dirty sod. The Voyagers Rest. The *Trib* really know how to treat a girl, don't they? Still. No. Not yet. Tomorrow, probably. Yeah. I'll give you a call later. Yes. I promise. *Promise.* Yes.'

She hangs up, drops the phone into her bag. Walks on, then turns abruptly into Londis. He follows her in and watches her buy an egg sandwich and a bottle of sparkling water.

*

Amber's head is so full she feels it will burst. Meetings with Suzanne Oddie always leave her feeling wrong-footed, ill-educated and unimportant, but today's has left her terrified.

They'll hate me. All of them. The ones I sack and the ones who will have to take on the extra work for no extra pay. And who do I sack? Who? There's no way to reframe this; no way to make the outcome a good one.

A little voice says: Jackie. She pushes it down. Being a selfish house guest doesn't mean she deserves to lose her job.

Shit, she thinks. Shit, shit, shit, shit, shit.

She sees Vic, working the waltzer. A couple of girls in the queue have obviously noticed him, are nudging each other and passing comment the way girls always do. She feels a sharp ache in her lower back, is suddenly aware again of the bruises on her thighs, as though the sight of him has set the pain off. I hope he comes back soon, the Real Vic; I can't take much more love from the Other One.

Vic sees her, and a smile flickers across his face. He's feeling right on top again; he's got the old adrenalin surge. Feels like it will last for days this time, like it did in the old days. Yeah, he thinks at the departing back. But I'll be home tonight anyway, won't I? When I feel like it.

He spots the girls in the queue, gives them a treat with his sparkling eyes. Sees them look at each other and burst into a fit of giggles. It's so easy, isn't it? he thinks. Just so damn easy. Women, they're just there for the taking. A flash of your arms and a Bacardi and Coke, and you can do anything you want. That's why I stay with her. She's not a pushover. A woman with a bit of self-respect, that's what I like. That and the other.

Not so much self-respect yesterday, he thinks.

The girls come round again; they're pretending not to look, simpering into each other's eyes. He knows the routine. Three more circuits and they're all his.

He steps over to the nearest gondola, sets it spinning, raises shrieks of fear-filled pleasure from the tarts inside. The graze on his knuckles is beginning to scab over, and splits slightly when he grips the seat-back. He quite likes the feeling. It makes him feel alive. He spins the gondola again and listens to them scream.

Amber doesn't want to stay in the park. Feels as though everyone – though only a couple of cleaners are on duty, emptying bins and rushing over to the rides when the Tannoy calls for an emergency mop-up – knows about what Suzanne's just said in their private meeting. She goes back to her office and collects her bag and coat, leaving her umbrella behind. There's no point, on a day like today; it'll have gone inside-out before she's got as far as the rock shop.

The Corniche is virtually deserted, though it resonates with the delicious scent of frying onions from the burger vans. Amber walks towards the bus stop, feeling miserable. Everything aches, partly from tiredness, partly from Vic, partly because (she's noticed) bad news always shows up first in her shoulders.

She walks on, eyes a knot of people gathered by the town hall, shouting questions. Press, she guesses. In the middle she recognises a couple of local councillors, hair brushed and business suits on specially for the occasion. She realises with a frisson that one of the journalists – close to the outside of the crowd, Martin Bagshawe standing near by seemingly hanging on her every word – is Jade Walker. Christ, she thinks. I've got to get out of here. She steps up her pace.

Kirsty's got her MP3 out. ' ... So what you're saying, in effect, is that they asked for it?'

The leader of Whitmouth Council glances at his head of PR and goes into denial mode. 'I would never suggest any such thing,' he replies. 'You're putting words in my mouth.'

Martin Bagshawe hangs back, strains to hear what they're saying, but finds it hard over the sounds of the seafront. Hears her say 'asked for it' and thinks: My God, she's fearless. And he remembers Tina and her taunting, and thinks, Yeah, but she's not wrong, is she?

'Not really,' she says.

'I was just saying that there has to be an element of personal responsibility involved,' says the councillor. 'It's not the same thing at all.'

'Personal responsibility not to get randomly murdered?'

He smiles uneasily, wishing he'd never got into this corner. 'You wouldn't walk barefoot across a minefield, would you?'

'If I knew there was a single landmine somewhere in several thousand square miles and I needed to get home, I'd probably take a punt on it, yes,' she says. 'Are you saying that men are helpless victims of their own urges, then?'

'No. Of course not. But the fact is that there is *a* man who seems to be just that at large in this town,' he says, 'and like it or not, our young women – our visitors – need to take this into consideration. We do have a problem, with a minority of our visitors, of overindulgence in alcohol, and alcohol makes people careless. We're simply begging these young women to keep themselves safe, that's all. We don't want any more deaths in our lovely family resort.'

She's vaguely aware that someone is earwigging them, glances up to see a small, ratty man in an anorak, pretending to read. He's familiar, but it takes her a moment to place him. Oh yes, the bloke from the beach. One of those weirdos who pop up wherever there's news, gawking and looming and trying to get on camera. He gives her a ghastly smile, the sort of smile that suggests that he's not had much practice at doing it. 'It's time *somebody* said it was wrong,' the weirdo tells them. 'There's thousands of decent people in this town, but you'd never know it from the way the *press* go on.' He pauses, seems to find something wrong with what he's said. '*Most* of them,' he adds. 'Most of the press. Not all of them.'

The councillor takes the opportunity to slide away from an awkward conversation, glad-hands the little man as though he's a visiting dignitary. She wonders whether it's worth persisting. But there's a press conference in twenty minutes down at the police station, and she should head there, in case there's actually any news.

She glances over at the far pavement and catches sight of Bel, hurrying away. Christ, she thinks. That's the last thing I need. Please don't let her have seen me.

' . . . dressed like tarts, howling under my window,' the man is saying. He casts a look so full of longing at Kirsty that the skin on her back crawls. The councilman puts a calculated hand on his upper arm, just above the elbow, the way a kindly vicar would do.

'And we want you to know that we hear your concerns,' he says.

Kirsty takes the opportunity to turn away while the hand is still there. The last thing she wants is to get sucked into another discussion with the bloke from the beach. She feels twisted with tension. Bel looks like she's heading for the seashore. I'll go the other way, she thinks. I can take a detour to get to the police station. She pops the MP3 into her bag, throws Rat Man a grin and a propitiatory little wave, and turns back to the far pavement.

Amber takes refuge in the shadows between the whelk stall and the bucket-and-spade stall, and watches which way Jade goes. Watches her hunch against the wind and turn up her collar to shield her face from the horizontal rain. She turns up the alley by the Cross Keys, heading for Fore Street.

Crazy, she thinks. What am I doing, hiding? This is *my* home. *My* town.

But she wonders. Every day she's thought of this woman, if only in passing. A single day's acquaintance, and they have been constant companions ever since, though it looks like their outcomes have been different. Jade looks like she's thrived, she thinks; as if rehabilitation has been as good for her as it was bad for me.

She can taste bitterness in her mouth. Feels as though life's been unfair, *knows* it's been unfair: somehow, Jade has been rewarded where she has been punished. Look at her, she thinks. Walking about in broad daylight, her head held high, while I'm scurrying through the shadows. Does she even think about me? The way I think about her? Half love, half rage, the friend I never got to have, the source of everything rotten in my life?

She realises that there are tears on her face, mingling with the rain. Stops in her tracks and grips at the strap of her bag while a wave of grief breaks over her, shocks her with its power. I was a child. And everything – everything – got snatched away in one wicked afternoon.

She dashes the back of her hand across her eyes and strides back to the Corniche. *She*'s the interloper, not me. And if she's going to invade my territory, she can answer some questions.

Martin tries to look unfazed, though inside he is squirming with embarrassment. I can't believe I said that, about the press. She'll think I think she's like the rest of them now, even though I tried to get across that I'd said it wrong. I've blown it, and I didn't even manage to talk to her properly. I'll have to keep trying. She'll want to listen to me once she sees who I am.

He shakes off the councillor's clinging hand, and walks on towards town without bothering to say goodbye.

Kirsty hurries inland, checking her watch. Ten to three. The press conference begins in ten minutes. She needs to get up there, to where the crowds are beginning to gather, to get through the cordon with her credentials and find herself a spot where she can record what's said. It won't be easy, in weather like this, and taking notes in the rain is the Devil's own business. And that's when you've got a working brain.

She stops by a shop selling brightly coloured plastic beach toys, stares at fluorescent windmills as they rattle in the breeze. Maybe I should buy one for Sophie. Yeah, because what's missing from Sophie's life is a windmill on a stick. Get a grip, Kirsty. You're here to do a job. You can't let your concentration slip. You're only as good as your current job, you know that. Doesn't matter how much you've done before: one cock-up and you're dropped, that's how the world of freelance works especially with half the staff of the *News of the World* wandering the streets looking for work. She'll be avoiding you as much as you're avoiding her; the stakes are equally high for both of you.

A tap on her shoulder. She turns. Bel has stepped back a pace, is regarding her with the same mix of fear, curiosity and disgust that she feels herself.

'Amber,' says Bel. 'That's my name. Who I am. Amber Gordon.'

Kirsty takes a moment to find her voice, and is amazed by how steady it is when it finally comes.

'Kirsty,' she says. 'I'm Kirsty.'

Noon

Jade is being Madonna. Everyone's being Madonna this summer, though the older girls are finding bits of lace and fingerless gloves in dressing-up boxes to look the part more convincingly. Jade's had to make do with wrapping a cotton scarf they've found, damp and slightly grubby, tied to the lychgate of the church, round her head, and hitching up her ra-ra skirt to show a greater expanse of thigh. She stands on the church wall and gyrates, flinging her hands above her head and clutching them together to flex her chest muscles.

'Like a vir-gin – pooh!' she pants, for the dance is energetic and her stamina spud-fed. She runs her hands up and down her body suggestively. 'Fucked for the very first time.'

'Touched,' says Bel. 'It's "touched".'

'You don't really believe that, do you?' asks Jade. 'Luh-ike a vur-ur-ur-ur-gin, uh-when yuh heartbeat's nuh-nuh-nuh necks to mine.'

She wobbles, saves herself with a whirl of the arms. Kicks out one hip then the other, like a burlesque dancer. 'Wuh-hoooo-uh-uh-uh-woah-o-uh-woah-oh, woah-oh,' she sings. Bel thinks for a minute, then climbs up beside her, strikes a pose.

'No, no,' says Jade. 'Not like that. You've got to give it welly with the hips. Like you're on a gondola.'

Bel's not allowed to watch Top of the Pops, *so she's not seen the video. In fact she only knows the song from listening, transistor radio pressed to her ear on bottom volume, to the chart show on Radio Luxembourg after bedtime on a Sunday night. But she imagines what it would be like to be on a wobbly boat on an Italian canal, and thrusts her hips out as though trying to keep her balance. 'That's it,' puffs Jade, and they both giggle.*

The church door clunks open, and one of the Good Women of the Flower Committee, as Bel's stepfather Michael calls them, steps out, carrying a pair of green-encrusted glass vases. She wears a Puffa jacket and tartan trousers, and her grey hair is clamped down by a silk scarf printed with snaffle bits and spurs. She tips the dregs from the vases into the church's side-drain, straightens up and addresses Jade and Bel.

'What are you girls up to?'

'Nuffink!' Jade employs her default response.

'It doesn't look like nothing to me.' Her voice, adjusted to disciplining dogs in the open air, roars across the graveyard like a hurricane. 'What are you doing on that wall? I hope you're not damaging it.'

'No, we're not,' says Bel in her plummiest tones. 'We're just dancing.'

'Well, you can go and dance somewhere else. If that wall falls down, we'll be expecting your parents to pay for it.'

Jade looks down at the century-old cross-stones beneath her feet. 'We'll take that chance,' she tells her. 'Don't think it's going to fall down for a bit.'

'Don't be cheeky!' bawls the woman. 'I know who you are, Jade Walker. Don't think the whole village hasn't got its eye on you!'

'Yes, sir, no, sir, three bags full, sir,' says Jade, and Bel sniggers. Girls in her world don't talk to grown-ups like this. And if they do, they get sent to their rooms. Or, in her case, the cellar.

The woman tuts and heads back into the porch. Casts a parting shot over her shoulder. 'I'm very busy or I'd be sorting you out right now, young lady,' she says. 'As it is, I'm going to finish these flowers, and by the time I come out I expect you to be gone.'

'Or what? You'll call the vicar?' asks Jade.

'Hunh,' says the woman, and slams the church door.

'Silly cow,' says Jade. Crosses her wrists above her head and circles her hips suggestively. 'Yuh so fine, and yuh mine.'

Bel copies the stance, joins in singing in her fine contralto. 'Ibbe yoz, tuh the enduv tiy-yime—'

'Woah,' says a male voice. 'It's an itty-bitty titty committee.'

Bel starts, wobbles, clutches Jade's arm for support. They hold balance for a couple of seconds then plummet together into the graveyard. Bel catches her thigh on a tilted gravestone as she falls, breaks the skin.

'Ow!' She looks down at the blood beginning to seep through the pink cotton of her shorts. Jade struggles to her feet and stands, arms akimbo, on a mossy box-tomb.

'Piss off, Shane,' she says.

Bel looks up. The eldest of the Walker boys stands on the pavement, a cut-price Martin Kemp in leather jacket and swooped-back hair, grinning blankly.

'Who's yer little buddy, Jade?' he says.

'Piss off, Shane,' she says again.

Bel stares at him long and hard. She's never had a chance to study him close up before; the general village policy is to scurry past when he appears, eyes averted. Shane, at nineteen, has a string of convictions for burglary and car theft: lacking his brother Darren's street smarts and driving skills, he keeps getting caught. He's only avoided prison because of his famously low IQ, but everyone predicts he'll end up there sooner or later.

'Think you're the Human League, do you?' he asks. His jaw seems to dangle from his skull as though its fixings have never been properly tightened, so that his lips have a wet, loose look to them.

Jade pulls a tuft of grass and earth out from by her foot, lobs it at him. 'I said piss off, Shane!'

'Going down the Bench anyway. Oh, and Jade?'

'What?'

'You been nicking again? Only our dad's after your hide.'

'Oh, fuck,' says Jade, and sits down hard in the grass. Bel's never met anyone who swears with such casual calm before, as though the words were simple adjectives. She's impressed and unnerved at the same time by it. If she let the sort of words slip from her mouth that Jade uses without seeming to even register them, she'd be locked up for days. She gazes at her admiringly, her hand still clamped on her leg.

'I hate this bloody village.'

'Me too,' says Bel.

'Does it hurt?' asks Jade.

'Bit.'

'Let's have a look.'

Bel lifts her hand away and shows her. There's a graze the size of a fist on her thigh, a bruise already forming. Pinpricks of blood seep into the wound, filling out, closing up.

'Fuck,' says Jade admiringly.

'It doesn't hurt. Not really,' Bel says proudly.

Jade shoots darts of poison at Shane's swaggering back. 'Bastard,' she says. Then: 'You ought to wash that.'

'Oh, it'll stop,' says Bel.

'It was only twenty p,' says Jade. 'How could he notice twenty p?'

'Grown-ups,' says Bel authoritatively, 'notice everything.'

Well, if it's me they do, she thinks. If it's Miranda they don't notice a thing. Or if they do, they find a way to blame it on me anyway.

She gets to her feet and hobbles over to the wall. 'What's your dad going to do?' she enquires.

Jade shrugs. 'God knows. But I'd better keep out of his way for a bit.'

'He's not going to hit you, is he?'

Jade acts scandalised, the way she's been trained. 'Of course not! Who do you think we are?'

Yes, thinks Bel. Best not to talk about it. Not till I know her better.

'I'm going to get a bollocking,' says Jade. 'Best not go back for a while. Maybe I can put the money back and he'll think he made a mistake.'

'Yeah,' says Bel. 'Good plan.'

Jade sighs. 'Bloody Kit Kat's not going to get me through to teatime though,' she says.

'That's OK,' says Bel. 'You can come back to mine.'

Jade raises her eyebrows, unused to invitations. She's certainly never issued one herself, even if she had anyone to ask. 'Won't your mum and dad mind?'

'Stepfather. They're on holiday,' says Bel with affected insouciance. 'In Malaysia.'

'What, and they didn't take you?'

'No. They've taken Miranda. But I was naughty so they left me behind.'

'So they've left you all by yourself?'

Bel waggles her head. 'Don't be stupid. Romina's there. But she does what I tell her.'

Chapter Twenty-one

It's dark inside the café. It takes a moment for her eyes to adjust and make out Amber, sitting on a sofa in a corner at the back, her features half hidden behind a pair of gigantic sunglasses, despite the gloom. She's not sure what she should do next, now that she's finally spotted her. What *do* you do in a situation like this? Smile and wave?

As she approaches and the other woman's features fall into focus, she see that Amber's face is solemn, slightly defiant, slightly frightened. She vacillates between staring hard at Kirsty and looking anywhere *but* at her as Kirsty winds towards her. She feels the way I feel, thinks Kirsty. She doesn't know what to do or why she's here, any more than I do.

She arrives, standing awkwardly in front of Amber, who stays in her cushioned seat as though she's been nailed there.

'Hi,' she says. What now? Do they shake hands? Kiss?

They do neither. She puts her bag on the Bali Teak coffee table and slides into the vacant end of Amber's sofa. It's a Chesterfield: old leather, the worn spots covered by a length of woven *ikat*. A five-dish candelabrum, stalactites of melted wax depending gracefully from elaborate ironwork arms, sits unlit on the table before them.

They stare at each other. Kirsty is struck, again, by how old Amber looks, how strained. She sits and fiddles with the cigarette packet Kirsty scrawled her number on, turning it over and over between her fingers and drinking her in expressionlessly. I wish she'd take those damn glasses off, thinks Kirsty.

'I'm going to get a coffee,' she says. 'Do you want anything?'

Amber jerks her chin towards the counter. 'I've got a tea coming,' she says.

Kirsty subsides. 'OK.'

They look away from each other to cover the silence. Kirsty takes in her surroundings. It's the sort of boho bar she thought she'd left behind when she left London, a place that would be right at home in Brighton: stripped brickwork, painted floorboards, velvet drapes, sunburst clocks, Moroccan mirrors, gold-painted wall sconces. There are twenty tables altogether, each surrounded by a collection of second-hand sofas and antique bucket chairs, mugs and cups and plates and glasses mismatched beautifully in junk-shop chic, a buzz of laid-back relaxation she's not found in this town, where pursuing the next thrill is the order of the day. The artists have started colonising Whitmouth. I guess Whitstable's got too expensive. Give it a few years and a couple of gay bars, and this town will be following the rest of the coast up in the world.

Over by the steamed-up window, she sees the stringer from the *Mirror*, coffee and a roasted-pepper-and-mozzarella ciabatta by his elbow, typing frantically into his laptop. Her own deadline is seven o'clock and she has no idea how she's going to meet it. She barely remembers a word from the press conference. He doesn't see her, and she hopes it carries on that way.

Amber studies her silently, her mouth downturned. 'We shouldn't be doing this,' she says.

Kirsty turns back to look at her. 'No. It's stupid. We're stupid.'

'If they ever found out ...'

Kirsty knows what she's saying. They're violating their licence, deliberately and clearly. If someone saw them now, it would be the end, for both of them. They've stepped over the line and there's no way they could claim coincidence. 'It's once, Amber,' she says. 'Just once. And after this we're done. They won't find out. It's not like we're tagged or anything.'

'How often do you have to report in now?' asks Amber.

'Once a month. Or if I change address, which I never do. If I go on holiday. Abroad. You know.'

'How does that work? How do you fit it round your ...' She gestures at the netbook, the notebook and the mobile phone she's put on the table.

'I'm freelance. Really I can say I'm anywhere, anytime, and no one would know any different.'

'Useful,' says Amber.

'Mmm.' She's not sure how to respond. 'How about you?'

Amber shrugs. 'I work nights.'

'Mmm,' says Kirsty again, and cranes round to find a waitress.

'I wouldn't even know how to get a passport,' says Amber.

'It's not that difficult,' begins Kirsty. 'You need your birth certificate and your deed poll ...'

She sees that it was a rhetorical statement, clams up. She's so used, through parenthood, through work, to being the person with the information, the one who offers advice, that she's forgotten that it's not always being solicited. Amber's lips are pursed and she's looking away again, over Kirsty's shoulder.

'Sorry,' says Kirsty.

'It's OK,' says Amber. They both fall silent again, studying each other's features. Putting them together with the children they both once knew.

'So you look as though life's treated you OK,' Amber says pointedly.

What do you say to that? To someone for whom life has clearly not done the same? 'Yes. Can't complain'?

'Yes,' she says meekly. Vertical lines run down Amber's upper lip, as though her mouth is pursed a lot. Two more deep verticals divide her eyebrows. Kirsty is getting marionette lines and horizontals across her forehead, light crow's feet at the sides of her

163

eyes: the lines of interest and smiling, and none of them as deep, or as firmly etched, as Amber's. Amber's blond hair crackles on her scalp like seagrass. Her hands, wrists, neck, ears are devoid of ornamentation, other than a dull, practical watch on a waterproof band. Kirsty feels uncomfortably overdecorated, conscious of her engagement ring, which cost, by tradition, an entire month of Jim's salary; of the fact that her necklace and earrings are not only matching, but are set with real emeralds, even if they are small ones.

Amber's nails are cut short, the cuticles dry and ragged against work-roughened skin. Kirsty, though she spends too much time at a keyboard to maintain a manicure, nonetheless keeps hers shaped, and protected with a coat of Hard as Nails, the skin regularly fed from the tube of cream she keeps in her bag. Nothing speaks more about the contrast in our lives, she thinks.

'So you're a journalist, then?'

'Yes.'

'You could barely read when I knew you.'

Kirsty blushes, feeling ashamed at the memory. Remembering posh Bel Oldacre back on a summer's day and feeling ashamed again. 'Well, you know – I was lucky at Exmouth ... I wasn't allowed to just hide at the back of the class and fulfil expectations ...'

Amber goes pale, sits back. She seems – scandalised. Angry. Wow, thinks Kirsty. I've hit a nerve.

'Exmouth? They sent you to Exmouth?'

Everyone in juvenile facilities knows about the other ones; the big ones, at least. They are discussed – constantly, fearfully, enviously – as inmates come and go, are transferred and given licence. Kirsty knows how lucky she was, being sent to Exmouth. Knows every day, is reminded every time she has to do a story on any related subject, how lucky she was. 'Uh ... yes,' she says carefully, still feeling out the land.

'Do you know where they sent me?' asks Amber. The words are more accusation than question.

'No,' says Kirsty. 'No, of course I don't, Amber. You know I don't.'

'Blackdown Hills,' she says.

'Jesus.' Once again, she's stuck for words. Feels sick with shock.

'Heard of it then?' Amber glares, the accusatory tone back again. 'It's closed down now, of course.'

'Yes,' she replies. 'Of course. I covered the closure.'

'Yeah,' says Amber bitterly. 'And I've heard of Exmouth too.'

Kirsty shakes her head, feels a strange urge to apologise, as though her own escape from the world of lock-down and pin-down and short, sharp shock is the source of Amber's misfortune. But Blackdown Hills ... they used to use Blackdown Hills as a threat, at Exmouth. It was where they sent you if they thought you were never coming out.

'Yes. God knows. Luck of the draw, I guess,' she says, uselessly.

'Yes,' says Amber, 'I *guess*.'

Amber looks at Kirsty and feels a stab of heartache. Of course I thought you'd got the same punishment as me, she thinks. Of course I did. And now look at us. We're the diametrical opposite of what anyone would have said would happen if they'd seen us that first day, sitting on the Bench. I feel like a lab rat in a bloody psych experiment.

Kirsty is looking down and away, her cheeks touched with pink. She looks ashamed, as though Amber's fate is her fault. They're both lost for words, both briefly adrift in memory.

'So have you got kids?' Amber changes the subject abruptly. She doesn't know why this is the first question that comes into her head, but it is.

'Yes,' says Kirsty. 'Two. Luke and Sophie. She's eleven, he's eight.'

Instinctively she starts to reach for her bag to find the photos she keeps in her wallet, changes her mind, puts her hands back on the table.

'Good for you,' says Amber dully.

'You?' asks Kirsty, timidly. Please let her have *something* good. I don't know if I can bear the guilt.

Amber shakes her head. 'No. No, nothing like that.'

Kirsty wonders, as she always does when this issue comes up, how she is supposed to respond. Is she supposed to commiserate? Gloss over it? Spout one of those lucky-old-you palliatives parents often seem to feel obliged to come up with, which everyone knows are insincere?

'Would you have liked that?' she asks. 'To have had children?'

'Of course,' replies Amber, and meets her eyes. 'But there you go. Luck of the draw again, eh?'

'I'm – I'm sorry,' says Kirsty, and looks ashamed again.

'We've got two dogs,' says Amber. 'Well, me mostly. I don't think he gives two hoots either way. Mary-Kate and Ashley. Papillons.'

Kirsty laughs. 'Good names.'

'I know. It's a bit mean, but ... ' Her expression softens suddenly, and her face takes on a glow. She looks pretty, for a moment. Younger. Kind. 'It's not the same, of course, but it's – I love them. Stupid amounts.'

'They're great, animals,' says Kirsty inconsequentially.

'Have you got any?'

'A cat. The thickest cat in the world. He just sits there, mostly.'

'What's he called?'

'Barney.'

'Right,' says Amber, and Kirsty can't tell what she's drawn from the name. By God, she's unreadable, she thinks. Apart from that flash of anger, I'm getting just about nothing from her. A normal person would be spilling tells all over the place. I know I am.

The waitress arrives, bearing Amber's tea. It comes in an earthenware mug the size of a dog-bowl. 'There you go,' she says. 'Nice and hot.'

Amber takes it, barely thanks her.

'Can I get a latte?' asks Kirsty.

'Sure.'

'Ta,' says Kirsty. Her first latte in Whitmouth. It comes as a relief.

'Back in a tick,' says the waitress. Kirsty turns back to Amber, sees that the unreadable has become eye-rollingly amused.

'Yeah,' she says. 'We *do* do latte in Whitmouth,' she says pointedly. Tears the tops off four sachets of sugar and dumps them into her mug. Sees Kirsty looking and gives a small, mirthless laugh.

'Habit,' she says. 'All the energy of a biscuit, and it's free.' She eyes Kirsty as she stirs her tea. 'So you live in London, I suppose?'

Kirsty lets out a small laugh. 'No. Why would you think that?'

'Oh, you know. Lattes and that.'

Kirsty hears her own false-sounding laugh again, wishes fervently that she didn't always do that when she's nervous. 'No. Farnham.'

'Surrey? Nice.'

'Yeah,' says Kirsty, and experiences a jolt of annoyance. She's putting me into a box. Now she knows I drew the long straw at the beginning, nothing I've done is going to be anything other than luck, to her. 'Well, we had to work hard to get there, but yes.'

'I'm sure,' says Amber, the unpleasant edge back in her voice. 'And what does he do, your husband?'

Kirsty had never thought that Jim's disaster might ever stand as validation of herself. Grabs it anyway and waves it in front of her former friend like a badge of honour. 'He doesn't, at the moment. The recession's got us. It's been a year. I don't know where the time went. We're ... well, I'm doing everything I can, you know?'

Amber softens slightly. 'Oh,' she says. 'I'm sorry. That's tough.'

Yes, thinks Kirsty. It is. It *is* tough. It's scary and fretful, juggling the debts, robbing Peter to pay Paul, sacrificing everything to avoid the bank that sacked him getting wind that we can't actually cover the mortgage we hold with them as a consequence. But, yeah, it's middle-class tough. I know that. No pressure groups weeping for us.

She knows she needs to ask some questions; that this might be the only opportunity she ever gets. Doesn't know where to start. 'And you? You mentioned someone?'

'Yes,' says Amber. 'You – your husband, I guess – spoke to him the other day. Vic. We live together. Six years now.'

'Good ... I ... good,' she says lamely, aware as she says it how condescending the comment must sound. 'How did you meet?'

'Work. We work together. Well, not together, but he works at Funnland too. You?'

'Oh,' says Kirsty, 'the usual. Mutual friends. We just ... you know. Talked to each other a few times at parties, and ... you know.'

Parties, thinks Amber. Another thing I've missed out on. At least the sort of parties you're talking about: ones where people mix over the taramasalata and ask each other to dance. Why do I feel like she's rubbing my nose in it?

'So does he know?' she asks. 'Your husband? About you?'

'Jim?' Kirsty feels the prickle of hair on her arms at the thought. 'God, no. Not a thing. I couldn't. I wouldn't know how ...'

Amber's tone turns harsh, interrogatory. 'So what do you tell him? What's your cover story?'

'I ... bad parents. Care system. Don't want to go back there. You know.'

'And he accepts it?'

'He ... At first I think he used to have a fantasy that he could bring about some sort of miracle reunion, you know? But he gave up a long time ago. I think he just accepts it now. Just thinks of it as being what makes me *me*. That I don't want to go back there and I don't want to be reminded.'

'I'll bet you don't,' says Amber.

Kirsty gulps. This isn't going well, she knows. Though she'd had few expectations that it would. 'What about your ... Vic? Does he know?'

'He doesn't ask,' says Amber. 'I guess maybe that's why I'm with him. He never asks. Not about anything, really. He's the most uncurious person I've ever met.'

*In*curious, says Kirsty's mental editor. She slaps him down. But God, that sounds so – empty.

Amber sees the thought cross her face. 'Oh, don't feel sorry for *me*,' she snaps. 'I don't need your pity. It's how I like it, trust me.'

Kirsty feels herself blush, looks down. The waitress returns with her coffee. 'I put some chocolate on top,' she tells her. 'I hope that's OK.'

'Thanks,' says Kirsty, who's more of a cinnamon girl.

She stirs the drink, peeps at Amber. 'I'm sorry, Amber.'

A frown: suspicious, defensive. 'Sorry? What about?'

'No,' says Kirsty hastily. 'I didn't mean it like that. I didn't. I was trying to apologise if I'd offended you. And because I ... I didn't know about Blackdown Hills. I didn't know that had happened to you.'

'Yeah? And if you'd known, what would you have done about it? Come galloping to the rescue?'

'You know I ... Oh, God. I just didn't know, that's all. And I'm sorry.'

The defensive look is still on Amber's face. I'm handling this so badly, thinks Kirsty. Jim would do it so much better. He'd know how to talk to her. I wish I could ask him.

Amber is shaking her head repetitively. 'Yeah, well. I'm not the tragedy you seem to think I am, Jade. As it goes. It may not be *Farnham*, but I'm doing OK. For your information, we've bought *our* house, too. I'm not a charity case. I don't need your pity, thanks all the same.'

Kirsty is ashamed, wrong-footed; squirms at the tone. She's angry with *me*? I didn't do it. I didn't send her to Blackdown. 'Yes! Sorry. God, I'm doing this all wrong. I know I am. I didn't mean to …' She dries up. Stirs her coffee again, miserably, while Amber studies the flock wallpaper from behind her stupid sunglasses. Kirsty catches sight of a figure in the window: Rat Man, from before. He's leaning his arm along the glass to shade his eyes, and peering in. Funny little man. Something of a pest around here, I'll bet. She turns her gaze back.

'You know what I think?' ask Amber.

Kirsty doesn't really want to know. But she owes it to her. 'No,' she says.

'I think you got Exmouth and therapy and education because you were the kid who got led astray,' she says. Challenges her to contradict the statement. 'In the end, that was what it was.'

'Amber, I had to work for it!' she protests. 'They didn't just hand me university on a plate. I did it on my own.'

Amber's eyes narrow as she interrupts. 'Yeah, but we all know why you got the chance to do that, don't we?'

'Why?' asks Kirsty, miserably.

Amber fiddles with her teaspoon and glares at her. 'Because I was evil, and you were misguided. It was what they said in the papers, after all. There's nothing like a cut-glass accent on a kid to make her an evil bitch, is there?'

The words come out in a rush, the flow stopping suddenly, as though she's run out of breath.

'Oh God, Bel,' says Kirsty. She doesn't want to believe it. A kid's a kid. Surely that's true, isn't it? 'I'm so sorry. I'm sorry. I'm sure it was just a lottery thing. It has to have been.'

Amber looks away again, her face inscrutable behind her dark glasses. 'Yeah, well,' she says. 'Don't think you can just come in here and get my forgiveness. It's not absolution time, Jade. Just so you know. I don't think it's OK that you got helped and I got punished. Whatever the rest of the world thinks. I was no more responsible for what we did than you were. And now I know, a bit of me's going to hate you till the day I die.'

Chapter Twenty-two

Amber stands no chance of snatching sleep before her shift begins, so she comes in to work early. She feels restless, uncertain, and wants to be among people, because people are the best way to stop you thinking. Amber never comes to Funnland as a visitor, and finds herself suddenly keen to experience the pump-pump-pump of music, the hyped-up laughter of strangers, the breathless whirl of light and movement, without thinking about the junction boxes and the pistons, the pulleys and the cranes and the smoke and mirrors that bring it all to life.

She comes in through the back gate. Jason Murphy is off, she notices; a thin, solemn black man she doesn't recognise watches her as she swipes her card and opens her locker. She nods at him and receives a neutral nod – neither friendly nor unfriendly, nor curious nor bored – in return. She dumps her bag, but keeps her jacket on, emptying her keys and cash into the buttoned breast pocket.

She can hear the strains of 'We Are Family' coming from the waltzer, 'Blue Suede Shoes' from the Terror Zone, 'Echo Beach' from the Splash Zone; her ear has become so attuned to the repetitive assault to the senses that she can hear each song individually, knows that each will be followed by 'I Feel for You', 'Rock Around the Clock' and 'Once in a Lifetime'. Somewhere out there, she knows that Vic and his mate Dave are doing their Sister Sledge dance together, their little bit of showbiz, all manly shoulder-leaning and jazz hands; a little bit of theatre that makes the punters laugh and feel like they've witnessed a moment of joyous improvisation. Improvisation that, if they hung around the same spot long enough, they would get to see at eleven minutes past the hour, every hour. In seventeen minutes' time the students at the roller coaster queue will 'spontaneously' become Take That, patting their chests and pointing to their crotches with choreographed abandon.

Automatically, she runs her eye over the punch cards in the rack. Funnland still has a punch-card system, as well as the swipe-keys, so that Suzanne Oddie can tell if any of the staff have been sneaking in for a bit of fun without paying. Few cards have been punched yet: just the early-evening skeleton crew who circle the compound, emptying bins and picking up litter with long-handled tongs. Amber had to fight long and hard to get the tongs: before she did it, the cleaning was an onerous cycle of stoop and stand, stoop and stand, absenteeism through back strain a serious problem. She notices that Jackie has punched in already; wonders why her laziest colleague is suddenly keen. Starts worrying, again, about what she's going to do about the budget.

Shit, she thinks. I'm not going to get a minute's peace. If I'm not thinking about what happened this afternoon, I'm going to be worrying about that. I don't see how I'm going to do it. Could I cut back everyone's hours, so no one has to go? Christ. And then it would be unfair on everyone.

She realises that she's been standing here for a full minute, staring at her locker door as though in a fugue, and that the security guard is staring at her, this time with curiosity in his gaze. Pull yourself, together, Amber. Come on.

She shakes her head impatiently and heads out into the park.

The rain has died off and the park smells of damp and doughnuts. Over the babel, beyond the howls from the rollercoaster, Amber can dimly hear the crash and drag of the sea. She walks and pauses, only half aware of the surging crowd, and considers her options. She has been in Whitmouth for years, but has never ridden its famous roller coaster. She was too poor to afford the entrance fee when she first arrived here, and lately familiarity has rendered her almost immune to its existence, beyond the need to scrape and scrub its surfaces clear of chewing-gum.

She shakes her head, like a horse under attack by a fly. It's not work-time yet. She refuses to allow herself to think about work until her shift begins. It's intruded enough on her day already and, as days go, anyone would say that it had been a bad one. It was a mistake, facing Jade, thinking she was ever going to get a resolution; she knows that. She sets out to the head of the queue.

The roller coaster is always staffed by teenagers and early-twenty-somethings, a crew employed on the basis of their looks. It's Funnland's most prominent attraction, and policy dictates that the showpiece ride should have the showpiece staff. They even dress differently from the rest of the park staff: jewel-like in wasp-yellow Bermuda shorts and skin-tight scarlet T-shirts with the ride's EXXPLODE!! logo scrawled across the front. She knows them all, of course. Two are the offspring of her own staff and one, a girl called Helen, lives four doors down on Tennyson Way, and is on her way to Manchester Uni and the big wide world in the autumn.

Helen's on the gate now. Undoes the staff barrier and lets Amber through. 'Hi, Mrs Gordon,' she says. 'How are you?'

'Good, thanks,' lies Amber.

'Is there something up?' asks Helen with polite concern. Amber is always amused, the way this girl talks to adults as though they were teachers, in an era when even teachers don't get talked to like teachers. 'Do we need to suspend?'

'No, no,' says Amber. 'Nothing like that. It just suddenly hit me that I've been working here six years and I've never once ridden this thing.'

'Ooh,' says Helen, and laughs. 'Ooh, how funny. I rode it about six times a day, the first week I was here.'

'Yes. Of course, I'm not here when it's working, most of the time.'

'No,' says Helen. 'I guess not. Anyway. Let's sort that out.'

She waves a hand at the front boarding gate, where four people – the winners of the queuing system – stand proudly awaiting the next train. 'Get yourself in the line for car one and you can get on the ride after next.'

Amber quails slightly at the thought of being at the front. Her natural comfort zone would be better served by having some other cars, rather than clear air, in front of her. But she knows she's being honoured, and concedes. As she takes her place, she is rewarded with the silent, baleful scrutiny the British reserve for queue jumpers.

The train pulls in and the queuers close ranks, as though they expect her to push in. Amber stands back to preserve their blood pressure, turns away and surveys the park.

On the far side of the concourse, the staff gate opens and a knot of people steps through. She recognises one of them as Suzanne Oddie, and sees that she is surrounded by the deep blue and health-and-safety yellow of what can only be police uniforms. She doesn't think much of it. There have been police in and out of the park since the murder, and there's the odd copper in here every day, even in the quiet times. She moves to the front of the gate as a new wave of riders is let through from the main queue, sees a sea of disappointed faces as they catch sight of her standing there. There's hardly ever just one single seat taken on a row. People like to ride in pairs: courage in numbers.

What's Jade doing now? she wonders. Did she find our little tea as disturbing as I did? My God. I had no idea. All this time I'd thought she'd be like me: trained by fear, squashed by shame, ducking out of harm's way, keeping her head down. And now I know that everything was different for her, I'll never be able to forget it. I've let the genie out of the bottle. It won't go back.

It's not fair. It's not bloody *fair*.

A train thunders overhead and her skin tingles with the change of air pressure. It's been designed that way so that the screams from above will raise adrenalin levels. With three trains on the circuit, you hear this twice while you're queuing, and, whatever your rational brain tells you, your lizard brain is primed, by the time the safety bars clamp down, to believe that it faces danger. For Amber, accustomed to waiting in the dark for the sound of approaching footsteps, to striving never to attract attention, it's a disturbing sound. She wants to turn tail and flee. But her train is rumbling to a stop and the passengers behind her are bunching to board, and she knows it's too late. As the riders before her detrain on to the far platform, she steps with wobbly ankles into the pod and takes her seat.

Shit, what am I doing? she asks herself. This is a crazy, stupid thing. It's more like punishment than pleasure. But maybe that's exactly why I'm doing it. I feel bad, so now I'm beating myself up. I'm doing what I was trained to do. After all, in a place like Blackdown Hills, the best they hoped for was that we'd own the blame and learn to take our punishment.

The harness comes down, clunks into place. Pin-down. The people next to her breathe, laugh and throw each other antici-pation-filled looks. Amber grips the padded shoulder bars and closes her eyes. Gulps. I hate things like this. That's the real reason I never go on them. Every other reason is just an excuse. Over and over in my life, I've felt like I was falling out of control. There's no way I'd volunteer to feel like that for fun.

'Hold tight, here we go,' bellows the automated announcer, and the wheels lock into place on the track. Oh shit, thinks Amber. There's nothing I can do to stop it now.

She remembers her first night at Blackdown Hills. Still scream-ing after the sentence, her throat hoarse but her voice carrying on unbidden. The shower, half cold, the ache of medicated soap, the empty, falling blackness. My mum. She wasn't even there in court. They hate me. I am their disgrace. She remembers black night through the bars on the windows, the falling silence as she walked, late and damp and frightened, into the mess hall for the first time. Hard, speculating eyes turning to check out the notorious newcomer. Officer Hills pushing her forward by an arm, no sympathy in her demeanour.

They reach the crest of the first climb. There is nothing between her and the track, clear air before the plunge. The train creeps forward, gathers momentum and clunks violently to a halt, throwing her forward against the restraints. She is hanging face-down, a hundred feet of drop before her. She feels her stomach lurch. The woman next to her starts to cackle nervously.

Lying awake. It was at Blackdown Hills that she learned not to sleep. After lights-out was the feral time, when girl gangs stalked the corridors and misfits wept with fear. Bel Oldacre, awake in the dark, ready to claw her way through the walls as, night after night, she listened to the click and scritch of metal as people tried the lock on her barricaded door. Sometimes a muffled cry or the sound of a chase invaded the darkness. They knew who she was. Of course they did. How many twelve-year-olds who talked like the Queen were there in the country's institutions?

I can't go back there. It would kill me.

The train lets go. Her heart bounces off her spine and the woman next door lets out a howl of joy and terror. The drizzle hanging in the air is a million pinpricks. She realises that she has bared her teeth in fear. The track disappears in front of her; all she sees is emptiness and, impossibly far away but looming at ever-increasing velocity, the million stones of Whitmouth beach.

Amber screams.

She's green and weak by the time they trundle into the station. Every limb turned to jelly. Her companions are laughing, savouring the endorphins, shouting brilliant-amazing-fuck-let's-go-again at each other. And all she feels is sick and feeble. If anyone were to tell her that she had to go round once more, she would die, there on the spot, she knows it.

She wonders once again what Jade is doing. She had a deadline to meet, she knows that, but it's approaching dusk now, so she must have filed, if she managed it. Is she thinking about me? Or has she just forgotten? Written it off as one of those things, and gone back to her ordered life? Her hands are shaking. Gradually, her hearing lets in more than the sound of the blood pumping in her ears, and she registers the opening strains of 'Could It Be Magic'. It must be half-eight already.

If I sit down and have a coffee, she thinks, maybe I can find someone I know to chat to; reassure myself with the familiar. At least I won't feel like this, trying to stay upright on legs that don't want to hold me.

The crowd has cleared from the platform now, and she's the only person left. She feels her way along the wall until she finds the stairs and staggers down, gripping tightly on to the rail.

Her route to the café takes her past the shooting arcade, the ghost train, the kids' merry-go-round – still occupied, despite the hour – and the dodgems. She half expects to see Vic there, then remembers that he and Dave have swapped on to the waltzer tonight, for a change. Instead she runs into Suzanne Oddie, frowning as best she can through her botox as she peers around in search of someone. Standing a pace behind her are three police constables and another whose uniform places him higher up the food chain.

'Ah!' says Suzanne, spotting Amber. 'You'll know.'

Amber recognises the senior policeman. He was the one who came with her and Jackie – accompanied them, she thinks in police-speak, and smiles for the first time today – down to the station the night she found Hannah Hardy. He smiles and greets her by name. Suzanne looks surprised, then suspicious, then ploughs on.

'Ms Gordon knows everyone,' she says.

'Yes,' he replies, 'I'd noticed.'

'Is there anyone in particular you were looking for?' asks Amber.

'Yes,' says Suzanne. 'Victor Cantrell. He's meant to work on the dodgems. Would you recognise him?'

Amber feels once more as though she is falling.

3.30 p.m.

Jade crawls through the hole in the hedge and lands up in a patch of stinging nettles. Swears loudly, because she knows that Chloe will find a way to roll in them, however much she tries to beat them out of the way. She's beginning to really, really hate this kid. She's a walking damage magnet. And every time she falls over, that squealing wail starts up: a noise as annoying and invasive as a police siren, reverberating in her skull like a dentist's drill. And now it's going to be stinging nettles.

'I told you we should've gone along the road,' she snarls.

'No you didn't,' snaps Bel. 'It was you that said it was quicker this way. I asked if there was a footpath!'

It's the dog days of summer and the ground is hard. All three of them are bruised and scratched from falls and climbs and brambles, and now Jade's hands and knees are coming up in a white, leaky rash where she's crawled on the nettles. Her mouth is parched; she can feel the dryness creeping down her throat, feels like her eyelids are lined with sandpaper. Her temper is rising to match Bel's. Their brains boil with heat and resentment.

'Come on,' she snaps back. 'Mind. There's nettles.'

Bel pushes Chloe forward. They've learned, over the last hour, that she has to go in the middle everywhere. She's too young and stupid to lead the way, and if they both go first she hangs back until someone has to crawl or climb or push their way back to get her. I'm never having children, Bel thinks. Not if there's a chance they'll turn out like this one. She looks at the purple face – the cheeks streaked, the chin a spongy mass of tears – and feels a surge of contempt. The kid reminds her of Miranda – spoiled, useless, favoured Miranda – and the contempt turns to rage. They always blame me. Every time anything goes wrong, they blame me. It's not fair.

'Don't be so bloody pathetic,' she says. 'Go on.'

Chloe lost a shoe somewhere back in the mud at Proctor's Pond, and her white socks are filthy. She squats and looks at the hole in the hedge, and starts to whimper again. Then she gets down on hands and knees and begins, slowly, to crawl. God, thinks Bel, she's got a bum the size of an elephant. How can someone that small have such a big bum?

Experimentally, she gives the bum a shove with her foot. Chloe pops through the hole like a champagne cork; lands flat out, face down, in the nettle bed. There's silence for a moment, as she takes in her situation, then the howling starts up. 'Waaah. Waaaaaaaah. Wah-oooooooow!'

Jade puts her hands over her ears. I can't stand this, she thinks. How come nobody ever puts a gag on her?

'Shut up, shut up, shut up!'

Chloe's face, hands and thighs are covered in welts. She stares down at her palms and starts to scream. They must be able to hear this all the way over at Banbury. Jade feels her eardrums begin to rattle. Grabs the child by the arm and hauls her upright. 'Shut up,' she shrieks, 'or I'll give you something to cry about!'

Jade's the youngest in her family. Has spent many happy hours in the charge of resentful elder siblings, has never had to take charge of a younger one. She does what Tamara and Steph and Gary have all done to her many times to deal with tantrums: she whacks her across the cheek.

Chloe shuts up, double quick.

'I'll put a bloody gag on you if you start that again,' Jade threatens. She doesn't really understand why she's in such a temper. Doesn't know about dehydration and overheating and blood sugar; just knows that Chloe is a burden she never asked for and doesn't want. 'We'll find some dock leaves,' she tells her. 'They'll sort it out.'

'I want to go home!' wails Chloe. 'I want my mum!'

Bel crawls through the hole and stands up. This afternoon seems to be going on for ever.

Chapter Twenty-three

Kirsty learned years ago that work is the great solace. In fact it was Chris, her counsellor at Exmouth, who introduced her to the concept. For a year she had felt as though her head was full of wasps: repetitive thoughts blocking everything else out. They found out quickly that she was barely literate, that what time she had spent at school had been wasted by the expectations of her teachers. At eleven, she had never learned to concentrate. Now, whenever she tried, pictures of Chloe would burst into her head: pictures of her mum, her brothers, the crowd outside the crown court; and she would be angry, tearful, hopeless.

Then one day she'd spent a whole hour with Chris, reading slowly through, of all the mad unteacherly choices, a chapter of James Herbert's *The Rats*. For an hour, someone else's peril was at the forefront of her mind. She wanted to read on and find out what would happen next. So, through graphic descriptions of people being chewed alive, she learned the solace of reading, and from that she slowly learned the solace of learning, and then of writing, and then of asking questions and hearing answers and making something of those answers. And one day she discovered that she had become a success story – the child who was rescued. And she's never forgotten.

After she left Bel in the café, she had two hours to turn her copy round and, as ever, the rush of delivery, the fix that keeps her coming back, was fierce. Every day it's the same: the eleven o'clock post-conference call, the moment of panic as she realises the extent of the task ahead, the scramble to find out as much as humanly possible and translate it into a thought-through, shaped and crafted story, the rush of damn-I'm-good that catches her by surprise every time she presses Send and her words fly through the ether to end up on strangers' breakfast tables. There is no time to think of anything else.

And tonight she hits her deadline just as she always does. She's filing for the home-news pages of the daily paper today; tomorrow and the next day it's more of the same; and another feature for the Sunday. People love salacious detail, says the editor, and the *Trib*'s sales figures bear it out.

Within three minutes of sending, and calling in to say she's sent, and cracking open the quarter-bottle of Soave she's found in her mini-bar, she is in tears. She sits heavily on the orange candlewick bedspread and lets the tears flow, mouth open as if to catch them as they pour down her cheeks. She wishes she hadn't agreed to meet Amber, has always coped with the past by simply not allowing it in. Kirsty can go for days – weeks, sometimes, even – without thinking about it. By living in the present, by planning for the future, she had thought that she had come to terms with history.

She wishes she'd had more time to prepare. A million questions circulate in her mind now that she is no longer in the presence of the person she can fire them at. In some ways, that day feels more like a film she once saw than a drama in which she took an active part. It seems so distant, so unrelated to the person she feels herself to be, that, though it plays out in her mind often, it has the glossy Technicolor unreality of events once seen on a cinema screen.

She wonders if Amber feels the same, or if those awful events still hit her with the sick, giddy panic that still occasionally rips Kirsty from her sleep, when her guard is down. She wants to know how Amber copes with lying, day by day, to the people she loves the most. Most of all she wants to know if Amber is afraid, as she is afraid. And if she is, which fear assails her the most: the violence of strangers or the destruction of those she loves.

The thought of Jim, and of the children, wrenches out more tears. Jim's kindness, his confusion when he encounters deceit or malice, is both his great strength and his great weakness. The thought of his hurt, of the loss to the children, if they ever found out that they had been loving someone who didn't exist, leaves her gasping for breath. He thinks she's a good person damaged by life. She knows, deep down, that she is – must be – rotten to the core, and that the one thing she must do is protect them all from the ugly truth.

She cries until she is weary, her shoulders aching, the skin beneath her eyes red-raw. And when she's calmer, when she thinks the danger that she might simply spill the truth in a destructive attempt at shriving has passed, she calls her husband.

'Hey,' he says. 'Where do we keep the spare batteries?'

'Top left drawer in the garage,' she says. 'What's run out?'

'Someone forgot to switch his Duelling Monster Truck off again.'

She feels tired and distant, but comforted by the commonplaces of life going on without her. 'He's got to stop doing that.'

'Yeah,' says Jim. 'He's not going to, though, is he, while he's got no incentive.'

'What do you think?'

'Make him pay for his own?'

'Out of his pocket money?'

'It's what it's meant to be for.'

'Mmm.' She thinks. 'He doesn't really get enough pocket money for battery-buying.'

'Tough,' says Jim. 'Sorry. How else is he going to learn?'

It feels good to talk about something so mundane. Even the fact that they're avoiding the elephant in the corner – the endless, terrifying outward trickle of their savings – is somehow comforting.

Her nose is blocked and she's breathing through her mouth.

182

She doesn't want to give the game away by blowing her nose, but her experimental sniff alerts him anyway. 'Are you OK?' he asks.

'Yeah,' she says. 'Just tired. And missing you.'

'Oh, darl.' She can picture him, lying out on their big corner sofa, heels up on the backrest now she's not there to protest. He's probably got his specs off by this time of night, his eyes big and vulnerable without them. 'I hate it when you go away.'

Now he knows about them, she sees no point in hiding her tears any more. Indulges in a huge honking blow into a wodge of bog paper.

'Eww,' she hears him say, 'thanks for sharing,' and she giggles despite herself. How can one person be so able to make you feel better? What a responsibility to heap on someone else's shoulders.

'What's your room like?' he asks. 'I want to imagine you there.'

'Bit early for that, isn't it?' she teases.

She hears the smile across the ether. 'Give me an image to take into the bath with me.'

'Well,' she looks around, tries to find something to describe. She stays in enough of these salesmen's hotels to know that they all look alike.

'I've got a four-poster tonight,' she informs him – an old, old game they've played since they met – 'with naked ladies on the posts.'

'My favourite type,' he says solemnly. 'Does it have curtains?'

'Of course,' she says. 'Red velvet ones with gold fringing.'

'Sophisticated,' says Jim.

'Sexxy,' she says, emphasising the 'x'. 'The floor is gold as well. Real gold, I think.'

'Must be cold.'

'Underfloor heating. Ooh. And I've got a platinum ice bucket.'

'Classy,' he says. 'Is there room service?'

'No,' she says. 'But there's a bistro.'

'A *bistro*?' She hears him sit up. 'Baby, I'm dumping the kids and coming straight there. Why didn't you say you had a *bistro*?'

'It's open from twelve a.m. to nine a.m.,' she reads from the information card. 'And serves a variety of mouthwatering mains and light snacks. Lasagne is their speciality, apparently.'

'Bugger,' says Jim. 'I wish you'd said ...'

'I didn't know, Jim,' she says. 'You know the *Trib*. Always springing surprises on you.'

'So did you file?' he asks.

'Yeah, I filed,' she says.

'And what's the latest?'

'Nothing you won't see on the news tonight. A poor old bat of a clapped-out prozzy, and the poor girl's still not got a name. No bag, no phone, no wallet, no friends who've noticed she's gone yet.'

He pauses as he thinks about this. 'Ah, I see,' he says, gently. The fear of dying unnoticed has always plagued her. 'Awful,' he says. 'Sorry, Kirst. You must hate this job sometimes.'

'It's OK,' she says, mournfully. 'It goes with the territory, doesn't it?'

'I guess. I miss you, you know.'

'Me too.'

'You still home the day after tomorrow?'

'Please God,' she says. 'How are you all doing? Kids eaten yet?'

'Yeah.'

'What did they have?'

'Bread and gruel. Why don't you just jump in the car and come home?'

Kirsty sighs. The thought of home, of a warm bath and a back-rub, is almost unbearably attractive. 'I can't,' she says. 'I'm sorry, darling. It'd be nearly midnight by the time I got there, and there's a press conference at eight tomorrow morning.'

Press conference. A couple of Plod standing on the station steps, mechanically reading out a statement and then replying,

'I'm afraid we can't comment on that for the time being' in response to every question. 'And if I don't make myself go out digging tonight, I'll just have to add it on to the end of the trip. I'll make it up to you,' she says. 'At the weekend.'

'Hmm,' he says. 'Shall I send the brats on a sleepover?'

'Why not? Either that or we can just lock 'em in the cellar till we're done.'

The Soave seems to have gone already, though she doesn't remember it going down. Weak, watery stuff, made for girls, not pros. She rolls off the bed and checks the fridge. A half-bottle of chilled Beaujolais and some vodka miniatures. She checks the card, and sees that the wine is £11.25. Holy cow. She'd have picked something up at Londis when she was in there, but she'd promised herself that tonight was going to be a dry night, after the other day. Hadn't been planning on spending the afternoon with someone she once committed a murder with, of course. She shrugs and cracks the screw-top, pours half the bottle into her toothmug. I'll think about my drinking tomorrow. No one's going to begrudge me a glass or two tonight.

'Hey,' he says, 'I was wondering ...'

'Uh-huh?' The wine is sour and thin. She's never liked Beaujolais. Really has to want a drink to want to drink it. Takes another gulp and screws her face up as she swallows. I know what he'd say if he was here in the room. Sometimes, this stay-ing-away thing's a blessing.

'I was wondering maybe if I oughtn't to be retraining. I don't know how much longer I can fool myself that I'm going to get back into what I used to do. And we can't carry on like this for ever.'

She thinks. 'It's a thought, I guess. No luck today then?'

'No. Nothing.'

They're silent for a moment, then, 'I hate this,' he says. 'I hate being a useless appendage. I never thought I'd be on the scrapheap at forty-two. It wasn't the plan.'

'Oh, Jim. You're not. You're not either of those things. I

wouldn't know what to do without you. You know that, don't you?'

She hears him sigh.

'We'll get through this,' she assures him, and refills her glass. 'It's not for ever. There's more to come, I promise you.'

She's got beeps. Takes the phone away from her head and sees that it's a withheld number. 'I think that's work,' she tells him. 'I'd better go.'

'OK,' he says. 'Call me back later?'

'I'll try, darling. We'll talk about this when I get home, OK?'

'OK,' he says, small-voiced.

'I love you,' she says, automatically.

'Love you back,' he replies automatically. They don't even think about what they're saying any more, when they say it.

She sends him away, picks up the line. 'Kirsty Lindsay?'

'What time do you go to bed?' Stan asks.

She doesn't even blink at the overfamiliarity; knows he's talking about her paper's initial print deadline. 'First edition's about eleven-thirty,' she says. 'Why?'

'FYI,' he says, 'the name's Stacey Plummer. The girl. And the cops have taken some man in for questioning.'

'What for?' She's alert, back on the job, the wine draining from her brain as though someone's pulled a plug. 'Do you know? What did you hear?'

'Something to do with fingerprints in the mirror maze. Ones that shouldn't have been there. Employee at Funnland, apparently, but not to do with that bit of it.'

'Ah, shit.' She subsides. 'There must be hundreds of prints in that room. It's a public space, for God's sake.'

'Apparently not,' says Stan. 'They have someone standing on the door handing out plastic gloves. Obvious, really. I'd never thought about it; the place would be covered in handprints in minutes if they didn't. So, no, actually. It's got fewer prints than your average surgical suite. Just the odd wodge of snot at waist height where some kid's slammed into a mirror. And according to my source, the cleaning supervisor's a real dragon lady and cleans the room herself. There's not been a smudge in there since the millennium.'

'Your source?'

'Security guard. Jason Murphy. Drinks in the Cross Keys.'

'OK,' she says. 'Thanks.'

'Talking of which, I'm going down there,' he says. 'Pub nearest Funnland. See if I can pick anything up. See you there?'

'Yeah, sure,' she says. 'I'm going to make a few phone calls first. Stacey Plummer?'

'Yup. Double "m", no "b".'

'Ta,' she says. 'I owe you.'

'Buy me a drink.'

He hangs up. She speed-dials through to the paper, to tell them to hold off on her copy.

Chapter Twenty-four

In for questioning. What does that mean, 'in for questioning'? Does it mean he's under suspicion? Is it the same as 'helping the police with their enquiries', or is it more definite, something that follows on from that? Amber racks her brain to remember what was said of herself and Jade all those years ago and realises that, shut away in the police station at Banbury, they had had no idea of what was going on in the outside world. Behind those walls, before the crowds saw the six o'clock bulletin and began to gather – shellsuits and placards and broken house-bricks, the good people of Oxfordshire showing their solidarity with the Francis family – it had just been them and the impassive police-men and the sincere social workers and Jade's mum bawling in the hall (her own, in transit to their Far East resort, took three days to be found and return) and Romina pacing and fiercely smoking and, later, solicitors. It had only been when her lawyer had suddenly stopped her and advised her to take care what she said that she had realised that they weren't getting out of there, that they weren't part of the routine; that the police had known all along that it was them, and were just waiting for their ver-sions to crack apart.

She prowls the house like a caged animal, afraid to go outside, afraid to show her face in case the news has got round the estate. Which it will have. They couldn't have been more public about how they went about it if they'd tried. And of course they probably *were* trying, she thinks. Five women are dead, and all they seem to have done is hold press conferences. It's no good just doing something; they need to be *seen* to be doing something. The frisson of murder always turns to outrage against the police if they are too slow to point the finger.

What does it mean, in for questioning? Do they know something I don't know? About Vic? Have I been blind?

Mary-Kate and Ashley trot up and down at her heels, shadowing her as she walks. He's been gone sixteen hours now. Sixteen hours. That's not a cup of tea and a quick chat, is it? Christ, what I would do for a cigarette. Five years without them, and the longing is just as ferocious. She wonders if Jackie has left any behind and finds herself turning over the kitchen drawer in search of a pack, though she knows he would long since have found and disposed of it if she had. Damn it, Vic. Day after day I've gone without sleep. What have you done to me?

He hasn't done anything. Amber, what are you like? There are a million reasons why his prints would be in there. He works there just like you do, for God's sake. He could have come in looking for you. He could have gone in to get out of the rain. They could have been there for years: maybe you're not as thorough a cleaner as you think you are.

It can't be him. Not Vic. Something like this can't happen more than once in a lifetime, can it? Not unless you're doing something to make it happen.

But she knows it can. A murderer has precisely the same chance of winning the lottery as any other ticket holder. Is just as likely to be struck by lightning, or be gunned down by terrorists, or succumb to swine flu. Defying the odds does not, in itself, confer protection against it happening again. And she's watched enough *Jeremy Kyle* and *Trisha* to know all about self-esteem, to know that people without it invite trouble into their lives without even realising they're doing so. No, she thinks. No, that's not me. It can't be. There's another explanation. There has to be.

Yes, but ... Amber, you don't know anything about him,

really. All these years you've lived together and really, you know no more about him than he knows about you. Not even what he gets up to while you're at work. He could be doing anything. He could be doing a doctorate in astrophysics, for all you share the detail of your lives.

The morning has come and gone. She has sat and paced and lain and listened to the sounds of the world outside: to the shouts and the bang of car doors and the bellowing of fighting dogs and the rev of engines. To the late-night cries of drunks and the yells of school-bound children. Sometimes she speaks to the dogs, simply to reassure herself that she still exists. They raise their heads, thump their tails, and for a moment she is comforted.

Amber's lying on the bed, half dozing with tiredness, when she hears a key in the front door. Sitting up, she swings her legs over the side of the bed, has to stop because the sudden movement has made her dizzy. She clutches the coverlet and closes her eyes until the moment passes, then calls out, 'Vic?'

He doesn't answer. She can hear him in the kitchen, opening and closing cupboard doors, filling the kettle.

'Vic?'

Still no answer. She finds her feet and goes downstairs.

In the kitchen, he has his back to the door, and is staring at his tea mug as though in a trance. 'You're home,' she says. 'Thank God.'

He doesn't answer for a moment, then says, 'Do you want a cuppa?'

She has to hold herself back from snapping. A bloody cuppa. 'No,' she says. 'I don't. I want to know what's just happened.'

Vic shrugs, muscles bulging beneath his T-shirt. She steps forward, goes to . . . she's not sure what. Hold him? Touch his shoulder? He shrugs her hand off as it approaches. 'Don't,' he says. 'I stink. I've not had a shower since yesterday.'

She snatches the hand back, stands uselessly in the middle of

190

the kitchen. His back is rigid, but she notices that he's tapping his foot restlessly as he waits for the kettle to boil. He's tense, she thinks. He knows he can't get away with just not talking about it. Even with me, the most unquestioning woman in history.

'Have you eaten?' she asks.

'Yeah,' he says. 'They order in from the Antalya. Whatever you want. I didn't know that. Did you know that?'

'No,' she says. 'Funnily enough, I didn't.'

He hurries on, the words rattling out with the random intensity that suggests a headful of cocaine. 'Yeah, well, that's where they go. 'Cause they're halal so they don't have to worry about that. Don't know what they do about kosher. Probably don't bother. I mean. Do you know what the difference is, anyway? Kosher and halal? Anyway. I had a lamb burger. It was OK. And a fry-up for breakfast. They get those in from the Koh-Z-Nook. They put chillies in the eggs, if you ask.'

She interrupts. 'Vic.'

He turns round at last. Glittering eyes, excited; like he's just had a big night out and hasn't come down yet. He looks like the man who's won the jackpot. 'What?'

'What happened?'

She expects something; some reaction. Discomfort, embarrassment, shame – a need to explain. Instead she sees white teeth, the upper lip drawn back in a way that suggests a snarl as much as a smile, and eyes that hold no life at all. It's the smile of a shark.

'You know what happened, Amber,' he says calmly. 'Why are you asking?'

She stays silent, breathless. She doesn't want to ask. Suspects that she knows the answer.

'Been up all night, have you?' He stares at her. His eyes flick up and down her body.

'Yes,' she says. 'I have.'

'And what have you been thinking?'

'What d'you think I've been thinking?'

Vic turns away, back to the kettle.

'I never know what you're thinking, Amber. Because you never tell me. You're the number-one secret keeper, aren't you? You should've joined MI5.'

No, she thinks. No, he's not going to get away with this. I'm not going to just ... there was a reason why they took him away, and I want to know.

'You owe me an explanation,' she says. 'Come on. I've been up all night and morning. I've been going out of my mind.'

He turns back and mocks her with his laugh. Props himself against the worktop, mug in hand, and crosses his legs at the ankles.

'How can you be so ... ?' she begins, falters, loses her thread. 'Why are you being like this?'

'You look like shit,' says Vic. 'It's no wonder, really.'

'No wonder what?' She hears an edge of panic in her voice. 'Vic, what have you done?'

He slams the mug down on the counter; hot tea splashes urgently into the air. She starts, then registers the momentary hiatus between the action and his face assuming a matching expression. He's playing me, she thinks. He's just pretending to be upset. He's not feeling anything at all.

'You're sure you want to know? You won't get to unknow it, Amber. Once you know, you'll know for ever.'

'Yes,' she says, 'I do. For God's sake ...'

He pauses for effect. Looks at her, gleefully. 'You actually think it,' he says. 'You think I've killed those girls, don't you?'

She feels it like a punch to the solar plexus. Feels the air hiss from her lungs, hears her back teeth clash together. It's what's been going through her head all night and all day since they fetched him away. How could it not be? Only a lunatic would refuse to countenance the idea, in the circumstances.

'I don't know,' she replies guardedly. 'Would you blame me if I did?'

A mirthless, bitter laugh: 'True love, eh, Amber?'

'Well, what would *you* think? If you were me?'

He smirks. Triumphant. Ready to pounce.

'Do you want to know then?' he says again.

'Yes,' says Amber, 'I do.'

'Go on, then. Ask.'

She fights for control. He's loving this game. I don't know why, but he's loving it.

'Right,' she says, slowly. 'Why did the police arrest you?'

The smirk again. 'They didn't arrest me.'

Deep breath. Count: one, two, three, four, five.

'OK. Why did the police want to question you?'

Vic picks up his cooling tea and slurps a mouthful off the top, his eyes never leaving her face. 'Why do you think they wanted to question me?'

'Because they found your fingerprints on the mirrors ...'

'Right,' says Vic. 'So if you knew, why did you ask?'

She can't stop a swearword leaking out. 'Shit,' she says. 'Don't be like this. I have a right to know.'

Vic laughs.

The tension is unbearable. She feels as though the tendons in her neck are going to snap in two. Again she breathes, again she counts. Vic really does seem high on something. Maybe it's just adrenalin.

'OK.' She starts again. 'Right, OK. Can I ask why they let you go, then?'

'Because I told them why I was in there,' he says.

'Looking for me?' she asks sardonically.

'Hah!' His laugh barks out. 'No. But I was looking for *something*.'

'Fuck sake, Vic,' she says. 'Stop talking in riddles.'

'You'd better sit down,' he says.

'Why?'

No one ever tells you to sit down when it's good news.

*

She leans her elbows on the tabletop and watches the tears drip on to the Formica. 'Why?' she asks, hopelessly. 'Why, Vic? You don't even *like* her.'

She's never known him so cruel. What would they think now, all those people who tell her what a gentleman he is, how lucky she is, what a catch she's got? Would Jackie be so keen to brace herself against the mirrors and hitch her skirt up if she could see him now, reclining against the cooker, smiling as she cries, as though he's won a victory?

'What's wrong with you?' she shouts. 'Are you some kind of fucking *psycho*?'

Vic shrugs. The smile hasn't wavered.

'Why?' she asks again. 'I don't understand.'

'Dunno, really,' he says. 'Because she was there? No, I'll tell you what it was. Because she wasn't you. That's why. It was because she wasn't *you*.'

She hears her own weeping as though it is coming from the far end of a tunnel. As though she's hearing it from underwater. The dogs jitter in the doorway, unsure whether to offer comfort or run away. 'But you don't even *like* her,' she says again.

'You don't have to like a woman to fuck 'er,' he says crudely. 'Surely you know that, by your age?'

'*Vic!*' she protests.

He shrugs again. 'I told you I didn't want her staying here,' he says.

'But you didn't *shag* her here.'

Silence. She looks up. He doesn't even have the grace to look discomfited.

'Oh *shit*,' she says. 'Not in my *bed*. Tell me you didn't . . . in my *bed*.'

'No,' he says. 'Not in your bed. Even *she* thought that was beyond the pale.'

Why am I crying? *Why am I fucking crying?* I should be roaring, I should be yelling and throwing things. Not behaving like some broken reed.

She heaves a breath into her lungs, feels it shudder through her body.

'So,' he says. 'Now you know. I told you I didn't want her here.'

'How long?' she asks.

He shakes his head. 'It doesn't matter.'

'It does to me.'

'It doesn't *matter*, Amber.'

'Fuck,' she says. Snatches up his tea mug and lobs it at his head.

The tears stop the moment the door closes. She's astonished at the speed at which they dry. She watches him walk down the path, then pulls the curtains. She doesn't want the world seeing in.

Amber collapses into the sofa. Lies full out and puts her feet, still in shoes, up on the arm. He hates that. Hates it. Well, who gives a fuck? She drags the blue fleece throw down from the backrest and pulls it over her. She lies there, dry-eyed and weary, and stares at the ceiling.

She's got an image in her head now, and it won't go away. Jackie Jacobs in the hall of mirrors, impaled against the wall by her common-law husband. For some reason her mind has dressed her in a red polka-dot halterneck dress, the sort of thing Marilyn Monroe would wear. She's got scarlet nails, and they're clutching on to the back of his strong, familiar neck. Her face is screwed up into a snarl as she bucks against him; a million howls of orgasm, a million pumping buttocks.

Fuck.

She closes her eyes, presses her palm and fingers across them.

Come on. It didn't look like that. She's rarely seen Jackie in anything other than trackies and a T-shirt. The night they all went out for Vic's birthday, she wore a short, tight denim skirt; meant to be white, but more like grey. She's not got a double life as a glamourpuss, a secret identity that seduced him with surprise.

Shit. Her mind's eye sees her now, with that skirt hitched up over her hips. She's not even bothered to take her knickers off properly; just kicked her pink stiletto heel through one leg for ease of access. And she's going unh-unh-unh-unh as he hammers away between her thighs.

Stop it. Stop torturing yourself. What are women like? Why do we have to dwell, when the facts are sufficient without the detail? She doesn't need these images, conjured up from the interior of her brain, getting in the way when she needs to think, needs to make decisions.

What am I going to do? Do I even care that much? When I strip away the humiliation, the outrage, the disgust that my good nature should have been abused this way, do I honestly, really care?

She's stunned by how indifferent she feels, in her core. Part of her simply watches herself, fascinated like a scientist watching a bug. Six years lost, and a part of her knows only too well that her tears earlier were as much to do with doing what would be expected as with actual pain.

Shit.

Mary-Kate comes in and stands by the sofa. Sniffs. 'Hey,' she says. 'Hey, honey.'

The dog stands up on her hind legs and scrabbles to get up beside her. Amber reaches out and puts a hand round her tiny, surprisingly round belly, and pulls her on to her chest. She stands there wagging, smiling her doggy grin; Amber moves her after a couple of seconds, because her paw is digging in to one of the bruises Vic left the other day, during his quickie.

I hate him.

Do you? Or are you just thinking that because you think you ought to? Seriously, do you care enough to hate him? Have you just been hanging on here for the sake of getting to stay in one place for a while? God. Maybe he's right. Maybe he's not just saying it to justify himself. Maybe I *have* brought this on myself.

A voice from the past – her mother's: *What do you expect,*

Annabel? All the things he's done for you, and this is how you repay us. You're such an ungrateful, nasty child ...

Amber closes her eyes and scratches behind the dog's ears. 'At least,' she says, 'now I can sack *her* without feeling shitty about it, eh, Mary-Kate?'

Mary-Kate wriggles forward and covers Amber's cheeks with wet doggy kisses.

'Fucking bitch,' says Amber, though she's not sure, really, who she's talking about.

Chapter Twenty-five

Although he thinks he might have a talent for it, Martin decides against a career as a private detective, because he quickly discovers that following people is seriously expensive. The bottom's dropped out of the private detective market anyway, since the Milly Dowler scandal.

Kirsty Lindsay is a very busy woman. Since he located her outside the daily police briefing, he has followed her all over town, and laid out what would usually be a week's living money on entrance fees and related expenses. He has followed her into the amusement park, ridden the train on the pier three carriages behind her, bought five cups of tea, two glasses of cola, a bacon sandwich, a chicken burger, three pounds' worth of tokens for the machines in the arcade, two newspapers and four bus tickets and now, after a trip to the cash dispenser, has spent fifteen pounds on the entrance fee to DanceAttack. But he still hasn't worked up the courage to talk to her and, to his astonishment, she's acted like she's not noticed him at all.

He waits by the dance floor and watches as she works the room.

She stands out like a nun in a brewery in a crowd whose average age barely brushes the legal drinking limit. He nods with approval as she buys fizzy water at the bar. Anyone weaker than her, or himself, would have to get slammed to bear the relentless thump-thump-thump, the sweat-haze hanging beneath the too-low ceiling, the flashing dance floor, the jangling earrings, the blue alcopops, the pinprick irises, the jerking pelvises and faint sense of menace that characterise Dance-Attack or any of its clones around the country. The noise and the crowded isolation would normally fill him with despair, but tonight he is not alone.

Though she, it would seem, is. Her colleagues have left her to it. It's been four days since the last murder, and now that Vic Cantrell – Vic Cantrell, who'd've thought it? – has been released, the nation is drifting back to Britney and Katie and how-dare-they spending cuts and inner-city looting. Now it's a quarter to midnight and she's standing on the edge of the dance floor, opposite him, and glancing at her watch. It looks like she'll be joining the other journalists any minute now. He needs to act, or lose her.

He walks across the dance floor towards her, sees her clock him and a look – recognition, speculation – cross her features. He doesn't turn his eyes away, as a stranger would do; holds her gaze until a group of teenage girls totters across his path and obscures his view. When he catches sight of her again, he sees that she is dripping, her plastic water glass on the floor, and two yobs are lurching unsteadily, propping each other up in trainers that must be sizes too large for their feet as they gesticulate apologetically. Kirsty waves, shrugs, dismisses them. Nice, pleasant; far nicer than he would have managed.

This is his opportunity, though, to be her knight in shining armour. He hurries forward as she gets a Kleenex from her bag and dabs ineffectually at her damp thigh. Positions himself in front of her close enough that, when she straightens up, the only thing she will see is him.

She comes upright, jerks back slightly as she sees his smiling face. Recovers her composure and looks at him seriously.

'Hello, Kirsty,' he yells.

Kirsty takes a step back, and he follows.

She takes her time to reply. Polite if chilly interest, no fear. 'Hello,' she says carefully.

'Let me get you another of those,' he says, his best suave voice.

'No,' she says, 'thank you. I was only drinking it out of ... politeness.'

She waits for him to say something; they stare at each other while the ceaseless bim-ba-bim-ba-bim-bim-bim-bim of the iden-tikit techno track shakes the air.

'What can I do for you?' she asks eventually. Cool and in control. He'd expected, somehow, more pleasure at his presence.

He can't hide his surprise. 'Don't you remember me?' he asks. It's unthinkable that their encounter on the beach would have no significance for her. Not after the way she made it so clear she wanted to talk.

A flicker of something. If he didn't know better, he'd have thought it was a flicker of incomprehension. 'We've met before ...' she ventures.

'On the beach,' he says, the subtext of the statement so clear that she can't fail to remember.

'Ah, right,' she says. Glances over her shoulder as though she's expecting someone, then looks back at him again, with seeming indifference. Playing her cards close to her chest. Fair enough. 'I remember. And you were down at the town hall earlier.'

He feels satisfied. He knew she'd remember. 'That's right. That's me.'

Kirsty feels increasingly vulnerable. It's not that often you find yourself face to face with a green-inker, especially one who seems to have been following you. 'Mmm,' she says, and tries to edge backwards again. She glances over her shoulder once more, vainly hoping that someone will have noticed her plight, but, lost in the crowd, she and her unwanted companion don't exactly stand out. The bouncers have drifted to the other side of the dance floor and are watching, cross-armed, a couple of lads square up to each other. The bar staff, sweating, never raise their eyes from the beer pumps, except to register the features of their current customer in case they try to do a runner.

She turns back. Takes in that he has the eyes of Simon Cowell and the mouth of a beaver. 'OO-K,' she says. 'Well, great to meet you again.'

'Let me buy you a drink. We've got so much to talk about,' he pleads, and accompanies the question with one of those expansive gestures you see in soap-opera pubs. In the crowded circumstances, it's an error; the remains of his own pale-brown drink slop on to the naked back of a young woman, elicit a shriek of protest. He glances at her, looks amused. Turns back to Kirsty and cranes in towards her recoiling face. 'Silly slag,' he says.

For a moment she think he's referring to herself, then realises that he is expecting her to agree. He can't tell the difference between newspaper comment and real life. She pulls herself together and plasters her smile back on. 'Thanks, but you're all right,' she tells him. 'I'm not drinking tonight. And I'm off in a minute. Deadlines. You know.'

'Oh.' He looks affronted. Kirsty switches the headlight beam of her smile to full. 'Thanks, though. I appreciate the offer.'

This is going well. She tries once again to step back, and runs up against a solid wall of bodies. He is frowning, confused. 'But we were going to talk,' he says.

She's surprised. 'Were we?'

'I was going to show you around.' He clearly thinks he's reminding her, that she should know what he's talking about.

'Oh,' she says, and tries to sound familiar with the inside of his brain, to construct a convincing lie. 'I know. It's just ... I'm on a deadline. Maybe another time? If I give you the office number ...' I won't be there, she doesn't add. Because I work from home.

He knows he's being fobbed off. 'No,' he says. 'Now. I've been waiting to talk to you all day.'

Shit. So he *has* been following me. He didn't see me with Bel, did he? There's no way he can put the two of us together. Surely?

'You can't go back to London. Not yet.'

'Farnham,' she says. 'We don't all live in London. Journalists. It's not all Docklands penthouses.'

'Farnham, whatever,' he says, and his tone is changing. 'I thought you were different.'

'I ...' says Kirsty.

'You're all the same. You don't care what the rest of us think at all, do you?'

'It's just a job,' she says. 'It's a living.'

'You think you're famous 'cause you're in the papers,' he says.

'No,' she corrects. 'I make other people famous by putting them in the papers.'

She knows she's made a terrible mistake as his head jerks back in offence. God, Kirsty, you should know by now not to get smart with the punters without a few other hacks around as back-up. Look at him. He's bonkers. A creepy little bonkers man, and he's not going to go away.

'Oh,' he bellows over the music. 'So you *do* think you're important then?'

'Look,' she protests, carelessly. 'I'm sorry. I didn't mean to insult you, and if I have, I'm sorry. That's all I can say—'

He pulls a wad of crumpled paper from his pocket, waves it in her face. He has a blood-blister under his thumbnail; must've shut it in a door or something. She glimpses the headline on her piece from last weekend: TWELVE ALCOPOPS, A KEBAB AND A MURDER: AN AVERAGE NIGHT IN WHITMOUTH'S SEEDY UNDERBELLY: he's printed it off the internet. It's a rubbish headline and she knows it, but she doesn't write headlines and she doesn't choose pictures. 'This is my home!' he squeals, and flecks of spittle land on her face. 'How *dare* you? If you won't talk to the real people who live here, then you don't have any right to judge!'

She reels. Knows that what he says is at least partially true. If anyone would agree with what he's saying, it would be Jade Walker, the wicked girl, the child with no conscience. But Kirsty's as prone to journalistic double-think as the next hack; can remember only her good works, will always deny her bad, pass the buck, avoid personal responsibility. Just like everybody in every office everywhere. 'That's not my fault!'

'You *know* it's your fault!' he cries. 'This whole place needs clearing up. I thought you got that. It looked like you got that. From what you said here. And you don't at all, do you? You're just – taking the piss, and—'

A voice – deep, confident – speaks from behind Martin's left shoulder, and her face melts with relief. 'Is he giving you trouble?'

Martin looks behind him and feels a wave of emotions. Victor Cantrell. Amber Gordon's bloke. You're kidding. She knows Victor Cantrell? How can she know Vic Cantrell?

He turns back and sees her drinking in the chiselled features, the thick dark hair, the Elvis cowboy shirt, the neat-cropped facial hair, with something that looks like gratitude.

'I think you need to leave the lady alone, Martin,' says Vic.

It isn't possible. How's it possible? It's some sort of – conspiracy. Some sort of ... plot to fuck me up.

'What are *you* doing here?'

'It doesn't matter what I'm doing here,' says Vic calmly. 'What matters is that I'm telling you to leave the lady alone.'

'Fuck off,' says Martin. 'You don't know anything about it.'

'I know enough, Martin. You need to stop making a nuisance of yourself.'

'I'll do what I want.'

Vic does something that frightens him. A tiny backward jerk of the elbow combined with a half-pace forward: too small to attract the bouncers, clear enough to make his intent plain. Martin hops back, feels a rush of fear and frustration. 'But I *know* her!' he shouts. He really feels like he does. After following her the last two days, after reading everything she's ever written deep into the night, he knows her as well as anybody.

'No you don't,' says Vic. 'You're just being a nuisance.'

Shit, Vic knows her, he must do, or he wouldn't be saying that. Martin's mind flashes back to yesterday afternoon, to looking in through the window of the Kaz-bar to see what she was up to.

With a leap of understanding, he realises who her companion was – though he couldn't see her clearly, what with the candlelit gloom and the pair of huge dark glasses she was hiding her face with. Amber Gordon. Oh my God. They've known each other all along. They're all ... in it together.

'Look,' says Vic, 'we've had to see you off once. I don't want to have to do it again. You're a bloody nuisance and you need to stop.'

Suddenly, Martin finds himself in tears. He turns away, swiping at his face with a sleeve. It's not fair. Everyone, always ganging up on him, setting him up, screwing with his head. It's this town. It's the people. They're all ... sick. Conspiring to keep him out, to keep him down, to refuse to recognise that he is Someone. She's been one of them all along.

He turns back and screams impotently at Kirsty Lindsay. She's stepped back, can probably barely hear him over the music, but his self-control is gone. 'You ... you bloody bitch! I'll get you! You'll see! You'll fucking see!'

Victor Cantrell repeats his elbow move, laughs in Martin's face as he recoils. Martin ducks back into the crowd. He knows when there's no point fighting. But someone's going to pay. Someone. He can feel sweat on his forehead, feels himself tremble. Wants to grab a glass and ram it into one of the laughing faces around him.

He contents himself, for now, with shoving at a couple of backs as he strides for the exit. For now.

She watches the man leave and realises that she is shaking. Looks up at her rescuer's face. 'Thank you,' she says.

''S'OK,' he replies. 'He's trouble, that one. Proper little stalker.'

'Well – thanks. I thought I might be in trouble there.'

The man shrugs. 'You shouldn't be here,' he says.

Kirsty sighs. 'Yeah, I know. I'm going to call it a night, I think.'

'You don't *look* like a slag, anyway,' he says. 'But then again, there's no other reason you'd be here. Are you a slag? You can't tell, these days. Maybe you are.'

She's shocked. Sees a glittering half-smile on his face and doesn't like it. She can't bear DanceAttack for one minute longer; wants out of Whitmouth. Blushing, she pushes away from him without another word.

Chapter Twenty-six

I'm going to enjoy this. I'm actually going to enjoy this.

Amber sits in her office, slowly and carefully applying her make-up. She's been locked in here since soon after her shift began. She showed her face briefly in the shadows of the main concourse as her staff arrived, then half sprinted to the administration block to put a layer of MDF between herself and the world.

Now she's covering up: the way she does every day. Foundation and blusher and highlighter, wiping away the lines and the shadows, as her fictions wipe away her past. They will not know. Her hands no longer shake and her eyes, soaked for hours with teabags, betray no tell-tale puffiness.

It's nearly two o'clock; the tea-break ritual approaches. Amber draws lines of black on to her eyelids and waits to take her revenge.

The cafeteria is full when she enters. Steam and food smells, and the rumble of weary mundanity. Another night, like any other.

But no. Tonight, she's New Amber: no bullshit, no advantage taken. The cleaners think she's a pushover, the lenient boss who'll overlook most infractions in pursuit of a quiet life. Well, not any more. She's been a yes-woman all her adulthood, rolling over and going with the flow, but not any more. Vic, the staff at Blackdown Hills, Suzanne Oddie, her mother and stepfather, every shitty man she's followed till he was done with her, every landlord, every employer, every woman who's deigned to be her friend, and it's got her nowhere. Taken her further down the road to nothing. Christ, if she hadn't obeyed Deborah Francis and Darren Walker unquestioningly one summer day twenty-five years ago, none of this would have happened. But not any more. After today, she's done.

'Moses,' she says. He looks up, smirking, expecting the usual timid word of reproof, and his face falls as he sees her expression.

'Yuh?'

'It's no-smoking in here.'

'I wasn't …' he begins, and trails off as he sees that she's deadly serious. 'Sorry,' he mutters.

Amber folds her arms. Counts one, two, three beats. 'It's time you stopped,' she tells him. 'I don't care what you do to your lungs, but doing it indoors is against the law. You're not to do it. There's a whole park to smoke in. Do it outside, or I'm going to have to give you a written warning. Do you understand?'

He glares at her from beneath heavy eyebrows. Then, saying nothing, he gets to his feet and, making an exaggerated show of picking up his Gold Leaf and his brimming Styrofoam cup, he stalks from the café.

She realises that the tables within earshot have fallen quiet. People are exaggeratedly not looking at her. Right, she thinks. This is what it feels like to be boss. They don't like you. Big fucking whoop. None of them liked you in the first place, not really. Not in any genuine, remembering-you-when-you're-out-of-the-room sense. Not in a calling-to-see-you're-OK-when-you're-in-trouble sense, like yesterday. You've been brown-nosing all your adult life in the hope that people will like you, and all it does is make them despise you. Make them think they can take advantage. Make them think they can take your hospitality and—

Clutching her clipboard like a shield, she walks forward. She hears an outbreak of whispered comment behind her back and smiles grimly. Just wait, she thinks. If you don't like that, wait till you see what's coming next.

Jackie is at her usual table, holding forth to Blessed. There she sits in her leather jacket, her sugar-pink trackies (the ones that proclaim her shrivelled backside JUICY), her Nike knock-offs, dangling gold hoops in her ears and a Diamonesque J dangling between her breasts. She's talking about men. Isn't she always? Amber stares at this woman and hates and hates.

' ... so Tania got talking to him and asked him what sort of girls he liked, and he said slim ones with olive skin, so I thought, you know, Ooh, I'm in with a chance ... '

Amber feels loathing pump through her veins, wonders at the way pity can turn to contempt at the press of a button. She keeps her expression steady: neutral but serious. She's not going to let her emotions get in the way of her revenge. The pleasure will be so much greater if the news comes out of the blue.

' ... and as it turned out, he had a cock like a baby's arm,' finishes Jackie.

Blessed starts back from the table as though Jackie has thrown a bucket of ice in her face.

'Jacqueline! Please!' she protests. 'I don't want to hear things like that.'

Jackie feigns innocence, grins at her. 'What?' she asks.

Blessed's eyes flash white, then she looks down, pursing her lips.

Jackie ploughs on contemptuously. 'So I took him back to mine, and I'll tell you what, he went like the Duracell bunny. All bloody night, it was, and then I couldn't get rid of him in the morning. I've got bruises on my bruises ... '

Amber doesn't want to hear any more. She clears her throat.

Jackie looks up. Plasters a false welcome on to her face. Now that Amber knows, the dissimulation is obvious; the tiny gloat that hovers round the edge of the lips, the almost imperceptible up-and-down flick of the eyes. Jackie's the sort of woman whose sex life is as much about scoring points as simple pleasure.

Amber should have guessed that she herself would not be immune.

'Hi,' says Jackie.

'Would you like some cheesecake?' offers Blessed.

'No, thank you, Blessed,' she says. 'Actually, I wanted a word with Jackie, if that's OK.'

Again the little flicker. Jackie knows she knows. 'Sure,' she says.

'In private, maybe?'

'No, that's fine,' says Jackie: a challenge. You know you're never going to expose yourself to ridicule, Amber Gordon. Go on. I dare you. 'I'm sure you've got nothing to say that can't be said here.'

Amber doesn't hesitate; sits straight down and puts her clipboard on the table, face-down. Jackie's P45 is clipped to the underside, but she doesn't want her to see it yet.

'OK, well,' she says. 'I'm afraid I've got some bad news.'

Jackie tenses. 'What?'

Blessed sits forward.

'Well ...' She's been rehearsing for hours, locked in her office, studying her face for inappropriate expressions. 'I had a meeting with Suzanne Oddie a couple of days ago.'

Jackie looks at her suspiciously.

'And I'm going to give it to you straight. The management are worried about costs.'

'Oh, right,' says Jackie. A flush creeps up her neck. She knows where this is going.

'There's a *recession* on, you know,' says Amber. She raises her voice, so she can be heard beyond their little huddle. 'Anyway, there's no point beating about the bush. I'm afraid that she wants me to make cuts, and they're big ones. I've been going over and over the books, but there's no alternative.'

Jackie is silent. Blessed shifts in her seat. Amber notices with pleasure that the tables around them have fallen silent; that everyone is listening. Some of the listeners will be feeling sick with concern for their own positions, she knows. Well, fuck 'em. It's not like they're friends. I know that now.

She continues, sticking to the communication plan she's scraped together from the internet. 'So I'm afraid that I have no alternative other than to cut back on staff,' she says. Waits a couple of beats for the words to sink in. Waits for the gulp and the tightening of the lips. Turns over the clipboard and looks down at it.

'Jacqueline,' she says, enjoying the feel of the name rolling over her tongue, 'I'm afraid I'm going to have to let you go.'

'What?' says Jackie.

Amber looks up and smiles – an expression that only Jackie can read for what it is. 'I'm sorry. I've tried every other avenue, and I can't find another solution.'

'Why me?' asks Jackie. The flush has gone all the way into her face.

Amber keeps the smile steady. Reaches out and pats the hand that fiddles with the old black Nokia on the table. Jackie snatches it away as though Amber's got the plague.

'I'm sorry,' says Amber. The fact that a drama is unfolding has spread through the room. It's fallen silent, breath held all around. 'It's nothing personal. I've got your P45 here, and we'll pay you to the end of the week.'

'You can't do this,' says Jackie.

Amber pretends to get the wrong end of the stick. 'Well, of course, we don't *have* to pay you, if you'd prefer. After all, you're casual staff. You don't actually qualify for anything at all. But I wouldn't want you to go short.'

Even the thick layer of fake tan on her face can't disguise the fact that Jackie has gone deathly pale. She is beginning to shake. 'Why me?' she asks again.

'Do you really want to do this here?' asks Amber. 'In front of all these people?'

'Yes,' says Jackie. 'Yes, I do.'

Amber shrugs. 'OK, then. As you like. I've chosen you because you're the person who pulls her weight the least. I've looked at what everybody does, and you do the smallest amount of work in the hours you're paid for. And you're the first, Jackie, but I'm afraid you won't be the only one.'

A frisson runs round the room. Right, thinks Amber. Bet you won't be lingering quite so long over your buttered scones for the next few weeks.

'I thought we were friends,' says Jackie.

She almost cracks. Almost says what she wants to say: Some bloody friend, Jackie Jacobs. Instead she blinks, channels Suzanne Oddie and says, 'I'm sorry. You can't let your personal feelings get in the way of business.'

She unclips the P45 and the cash-filled envelope and pushes them across the table. 'Of course, I'll understand if you don't want to finish your shift.'

My God, she thinks. This being-a-bitch is easy. And it's taken me all these years to find out.

As if she can hear her thoughts, Jackie pushes her chair back from the table and says, quietly: 'You bitch.'

Amber shrugs. 'I understand,' she says, in the HR style she's been rehearsing all evening in her office, 'that you're upset.' She's had plenty of experience of job loss from the other side in her life, but had never noticed how calculated to cause offence a lot of human-resources-speak actually is. 'It's a stressful event for anyone.'

'You fucking bitch,' says Jackie, raising her voice. The faint buzz of talk that had begun in the further reaches of the room stops dead. All eyes are on them. 'We both know why you're doing this.'

She wouldn't. Not in front of all these people, surely?

'You're getting rid of me because I fucked your boyfriend,' says Jackie.

A hiss of indrawn breath behind her. Tadeusz and Blessed sit rigid in their chairs. Amber blinks. Holds her ground, says nothing.

'Don't try and pretend you didn't know,' says Jackie.

Amber allows herself a spiteful imitation of Jackie's own words. 'But *Jackie*. I thought we were *friends*.'

There's not a movement in the room.

'You found out, and now you're getting your own back,' says Jackie.

Well what did you expect? A bunch of flowers?

'Trust me, Jackie,' she says with a lilt of humour in her voice that would infuriate a saint, 'if, as you put it, you … *fucked* … my boyfriend, all it means is that you're not just lazy. It means you're a lazy *slag*.'

Jackie looks like she's been slapped. Amber is tempted to reach out and push her jaw closed with a finger. Instead, she picks up the form and the envelope and tosses them across the table.

'Either way, you're unemployed,' she says.

12.30 p.m.

'Oh my God,' says Jade, 'you're, like, so posh.'

Bel hasn't thought all that much about the drive, or the house, or the effect they'll have on her companion. They're not hers, after all: they're Michael's, and her life's been hostage to Michael and Lucinda's choices since before she remembers.

'No I'm not,' she says. 'What makes you think I'm posh?'

Jade laughs out loud, scornfully. 'Are you mad?' she asks, eyeing the two-hundred-year-old beech trees, the way they're planted in a perfect line, a precise distance apart, along the length of the drive, masking the house at the end. Her own home is also set back from the road, also hidden from the glance of passing vehicles, but the approach is a muddy track where brambles, elder and blackthorn fight for primacy. To her, posh is having a shower attachment on the bath taps instead of having to use a mug to rinse your hair with. It's eating things you actually recognise from the adverts on the telly. It's scrapping your car when it can no longer be nursed through the MoT, rather than leaving it to feed the stinging nettles in the field. To Jade, the kids on the modern estate on the other side of the village are posh.

Where Jade comes from, 'posh' is an insult. To Bel's people, it's an expression of aspiration.

'So have you got a swimming pool?' she asks.

'No.'

'Pony?'

'Miranda's got a pony. Michael says there's no point in me getting one, as you need to start at Miranda's age to be any good.'

Even to Jade, this sounds like an excuse for unfairness. She squints sideways at Bel, but her face is impassive. Now there's

213

posh, she thinks. That face – the one where you don't show any feelings, ever – is something only posh people are good at. She finds a fallen stick on the gravel of the drive, and swipes at the heads of the cow parsley on the verge. 'I'm bloody starving,' she says.

'Nearly there,' says Bel.

'Who's Miranda anyway?'

'She's my half-sister. She's six. She's Michael's,' says Bel, and doesn't notice the purse of the lips that greets this statement. Every family has its moral code, and multiple parenthood is a violation of Jade's. Her father may be free with his fists, but he's never played away. It's never occurred to her to wonder who would want to play away with a pig farmer who holds his coat together with binder twine.

They pass through the high wall, bathed in the baleful glare of stone lions, and see the house before them.

'How many of you are there?' asks Jade.

'Four. And Romina. She lives in the flat,' says Bel, and gestures at the stable-block to the right; a red-brick mini-me of the big house, right down to the tall, fluted, non-functional vanity chimneys. She feels a twinge of embarrassment as she speaks. Hopes Jade won't judge her on her stepfather's shameless display of superfluity. She's glad the cars have been put away in the garage. Deduces that Jade doesn't have a Range Rover, a Porsche and a Golf GTI lined up on her own gravel sweep.

'Posh,' says Jade, and starts towards the front door.

'This way.' Bel turns round the side of the house.

'You don't use the front?'

'Nobody does, in the country,' says Bel grandly, parroting her adults, then blushes. 'N-no. I always use the back.'

Jade shrugs and follows. She doesn't like the look of the front much anyway: the shutters are closed across the whole façade, the dead eyes of the house staring sightless into the empty courtyard. She follows Bel up a dank side path. After what feels like

*ten minutes of damp and foliage, they emerge at the servants'
entrance.*

*Bel puts her hand on the large brass door handle and pushes.
The door doesn't move.*

'Bugger,' she says.

'What's up?'

'Locked.'

*'We never lock our doors,' announces Jade. They have nothing
to steal. And anyway, the dogs would see any interloper off
before they got within a hundred yards of the house. And if they
didn't, the sound of them would bring Ben Walker and his
twelve-bore round from the pig sheds before they got past the
washing lines.*

*Bel tries the door fruitlessly one more time, then starts off in
the direction of the stableyard. Jade plods patiently in the rear.
'Who's Romina?'*

*'Miranda's nanny. She's meant to be keeping an eye on me.
Come on. She's probably in the flat.'*

*She leads the way back up the alley and beneath the grand
arched entrance to the stableyard. It's quiet here, and shady: two
wise, curious heads, one bay, one chestnut, appear at stable
doors and watch them as they cross the flagstones. Bel greets
them and receives a friendly whicker in response from the bay.
'Trigger and Missy,' she says.*

*Jade walks over and holds a hand out to be sniffed. Feels
gentle velvet lips brush her skin, the snuff of warm damp breath
on her fingers.*

'That one's Trigger,' says Bel.

*'Hi, Trigger,' says Jade, and continues to rub the horse's nose
as she looks around. It's a big-face stableyard, the sort that was
originally built to house carriages. An elegant arched door, echo-
ing the lines of the belltower arch under which they've just
passed, leads to a barn. Funny, she thinks. I'd always heard it was
really old, this house, but it looks brand new. There's nothing out
of place here.*

Every door, apart from those of the two inhabited loose-boxes, is closed and latched; a burglar alarm is conspicuous in its turquoise livery on the wall of the tack room. It's weird, thinks Jade. I mean, you'd expect a wheelbarrow or a couple of hay-nets or some mucking-out tools or something. But the whole place looks disinfected, as though nothing ever happens to mess it up. It looks like someone's come along with a bottle of Domestos and scrubbed it with a toothbrush.

Trigger, finding that Jade has no titbits, chaws down on her knuckles with his teeth. She snatches her hand away, then pushes his nose softly away from her with a clenched fist. 'So which one's Miranda's?' she asks, though both look to be sixteen hands high.

'Neither. Trigger's Michael's and Missy's Lucinda's. They've just been brought in to be fittened up for hunting. Miranda's pony's in the bottom field.'

'Mmm,' says Jade. 'Better not go over my dad's land. He'd have your guts for garters.'

'I don't think anyone would want to hunt over your dad's land,' says Bel. 'They'd lose the scent among all the pig shit.'

She glances sideways at Jade as she says this, to check what the reaction will be. She's testing the waters, seeing how far she can go with teasing. Jade laughs. 'Too right,' she says, 'and I don't s'pose as the barbed wire'd be too popular neither. So where's this flat then?'

'Over here.' Bel leads the way to a neat white-painted tongue-and-groove door by the side of the barn, its ornaments the same twisted black iron that decorates every other door and window in the complex. 'Her car's not here,' she says. 'She wouldn't have parked it in the barn. She never puts it indoors when Michael and Lucinda are away.'

She rings the doorbell and they stand back as the sound echoes up the stairs. There is no response. Somewhere out in the cornfields a skylark gets up, twinkles its way into the blue, blue sky.

'Bugger,' says Bel.

'What? She gone out?'

'Dunno. Looks like it.'

'I'm bloody starving,' says Jade.

'Yeah, sorry. Me too.'

'Isn't there a key somewhere?'

Bel eyes her.

'Yeah,' says Jade, 'I'm not going to come back and burgle you.'

'You have to promise,' says Bel.

'Whatever,' says Jade, insulted. 'I'll go home if you like.'

'No,' says Bel hurriedly. 'No, don't do that. I didn't mean …
It's just, you know, if I told anyone I'd be in, you know, doo-doo.'

'"Doo-doo"?' asks Jade. 'Doo-doo?'

'Shut up,' says Bel. 'Come on then. But if anything happens,
I'm telling. I don't care how much trouble I get into.'

Bel opens the barn door and leads her inside. Through the
gloom, Jade can see that the same pristine tidiness prevails here:
a collection of lean, chromey cars that gleam, rustless and smear-
less, in rows so neat they might have been measured with a ruler.
Walls and rafters are whitewashed and cobweb-free. Not a drop
of oil or a tyre mark besmirches the swept golden concrete of the
floor.

'Bloody hell,' says Jade. 'How many cars has he got?'

'Ten,' says Bel. 'Michael's a collector.'

'And they all work?' asks Jade, thinking of her father's own
collection.

'I think so. He doesn't drive them. Except for car shows. He
takes them to car shows, but only on a transporter. The Range
Rover's at the airport. And yeah, Romina's car's gone. She has to
park it over there.' She gestures to a dark corner.

'Jesus, she must work hard.'

'What?'

'Keeping all this lot clean.'

'Don't be silly,' says Bel. 'Romina's a nanny. Ramón and
Delicious do the house stuff.'

'Delicious?' Jade starts to laugh. 'What sort of name is Delicious?'

'A Philippines name,' replies Bel loftily. 'They're all called things like that.'

'Where's Philippine?'

'The. The Philippines. They're near Hong Kong. That's where Michael picked them up. Hong Kong. That's where he used to live. That's where he made his money.'

Jade shrugs. Hong Kong means no more to her than France; both, she knows, are abroad, and she's only ever been as far as Oxford twice. London is as strange and as foreign – and as uninteresting – to her as either of the countries Bel has named. 'Well, why don't you get them to let you in?'

'They've gone home for their holidays. While the house is empty.'

'But it's not!'

'You know what I mean,' says Bel, and goes over to where a pile of tyres, clean and unmarked as though they have never seen a road, is stacked neatly in a corner.

'Who looks after the horses?'

'Suzi Booker,' she says.

'Can't she let us in?'

Bel tuts. 'She's outdoor staff. The gardeners don't have keys either.'

She puts a hand over the top of the topmost tyre, and feels around inside the rim. 'If you tell anyone,' she says, 'I swear I will come and get you.'

'I won't,' says Jade. Her tummy is rumbling. She's beginning to feel slightly faint. All she can think about is the huge collection of luxury foods she imagines to be sitting in the fridge indoors. They've probably got real ham, on the bone, she thinks. And Coca-Cola; not Co-op.

Bel rummages about, then looks surprised. Brings her hand back, clutching a piece of folded paper. 'Hunh,' she says. She unfolds it and reads Romina's scrawl, frowning. 'Oh no.'

'What?' asks Jade.

Bel shoves the letter at her. Jade pushes it back. 'I can't read that,' she says.

'Why not?' Bel looks at her for a moment, then a look of not-so-nice comprehension crosses her face. 'Can't you read?'

'Course I can read,' blusters Jade. 'I just can't read that sort of joined-up writing. You read it.'

Bel looks down at the capitalised words on the page. Romina's not so literate herself, especially in a language that is not her own. '"You say you back eleven o'clock,"' she reads out loud, '"and you not back. I go Bicester. Take key. You know you not allowed in house without me. You are bad girl. Now you wait I come back. You see how is feel."

'Bugger,' she says.

Chapter Twenty-seven

The noise level halves when Kirsty turns the corner from Mare Street. By the time she's reached Fore Street, it's as though the world has come to an end and she is the sole survivor. She's in the pedestrian arcade: chain stores and pound shops and discount chemists – all of them closed by six o'clock – and office suites on the floors above. A zoning desert, created by idealists from an era in love with the internal combustion engine and the garden suburb.

Not a light shows in a window. The shops are protected by grilles and shutters, as though awaiting a globalisation protest. Whitmouth got off lightly in the riots, mostly because it's not the sort of town that can support a Foot Locker. The only illumination comes from sodium arc lights which shine weakly through the foliage of weedy, salt-stunted saplings. She checks her watch. Half-past twelve, and cold enough to be autumn.

She hurries forward, uncomfortable with her solitude and keen to reach the station and the safety of her car. Her encounters in DanceAttack have left her buzzing, jumping at her own shadow. It's been a long time since she last attracted that sort of random hate, and the memory is as disturbing as the experience. Her heels scrape over the paving stones, the sound bouncing off the blank façades above. A couple of times, the echo sounds like there are two of her. She stops, twice, and glances sharply over her shoulder to check that that isn't the case.

Stupid, she thinks. What kind of idiot walks by herself at night in the base of the Seaside Strangler? I should have waited at the taxi rank. I had plenty of time, really. It's not like I've got a deadline to get home. There were only twenty people in front of me, for God's sake.

She can hear the rush of sea on cobbles half a town away, but she's not heard a voice in three minutes. How can this happen? In a town so full it takes ten minutes to walk a hundred yards, where a parking space is as rare as diamonds, how can the crowds simply vanish?

The same way those women vanished. Everyone's been speculating about morals and stupidity and how this man, whoever he is, can be so plausible that all these girls have ended up alone with him, and in the end it's a matter of town planning. You take an old town, its higgledy-piggledy people-on-people centre, and you zone it and control it and pedestrianise it, and you move the people out and up and away, and suddenly, when night falls, you're on the set of *I Am Legend*. How can anyone be safe when there's no one around to hear you scream?

She has another half-mile to cover. As she hurries along, she digs in her bag, looking for her key chain and her purse. She'll tuck them into her bra: make sure that, whatever else, she can get into the car and buy the petrol to get home. It's an old habit from early adulthood, living anonymously on the Stockwell Park Estate, filing housing applications for Lambeth Council by day and doing her Open University course at night. She didn't go out much at night back then, but if she did she always made sure that she, and not some lurking junkie, had the means to get back into the flat.

She wonders about the creepy little man. They're always the ones who attract the attention of the police. Neighbourhood pests, hanging about in the shadows, bothering women, playing with replica guns and, now, finding 'communities' to share their rotten little fantasies with on the internet. They don't necessarily act them out, but they make other people uncomfortable, and often that's enough. You can't change human nature.

Outsiders have always had a hard time of it. They disturb people.

She finds her purse, tucked where it is supposed to be, in the interior zip pocket of the bag. The keys have found their way out of the compartment into the general jumble. Her frustration mounts as she scrabbles in the depths; touches, loses, touches, loses again. Who is he? What did he want? Would I have found out, even if that other man hadn't got between us? I don't suppose he knows, himself. He's just one of those lone nutters who thought he had something to say to me.

Shit. I don't suppose he followed me again, did he?

She reaches the market cross halfway along Fore Street. She can go the short way – carry on up the hill through another half-mile of this wasteland to the station at the end. Or she could turn left, up Tailor's Lane, and work her way through to the lights and population of Brighton Road. It's a longer route, with a nasty little detour, but there will be people at the end of it. And right now people are what she craves.

She peers into the ill-lit depths of Tailor's Lane, trying to recall her daytime impressions. It's hardly a street – more an upgraded alleyway: narrow, and with a turn in the middle. A hundred yards to the corner, then another hundred to the main road. Behind her, the street is so silent, she feels as though it's listening.

She doesn't want to go up there. Doesn't like the thought of plunging into the dark. A couple of mews – if the rubbish storage for a bunch of shops can really be called a mews – lead off to left and right: pools of the unknown, lit only when the shops themselves are open. Because it's mainly blank walls and refuse containers, the road is perfunctorily lit: she can see the lamp that marks the corner, and the small pool of light cast by the one in between, but they are old Victorian lanterns that don't look as though they have been updated since they were converted to electricity. And, in between, deep, malodorous shadow.

There could be anything up there, Kirsty. Anyone.

Yes, but … at least you know what's at the other end. Fore

Street is half a mile of the unknown, no turnings off after this; just the choice of forward or back and a hell of a long way to run either way. It's two hundred yards, Kirsty. A two-minute walk. Just go confidently; don't look left or right, don't peer into the shadows. Don't think about what's in those alleyways. Just walk and look certain. Why would anyone hide on a road no one goes up? Just two minutes and you'll be out where the people are again.

She starts to walk.

The going is rough underfoot, the tarmac deteriorated by bin lorries and neglected because it's not a popular cut-through. She nearly turns her ankle twice before she reaches the mews. They keys still evade her grasp, distracting her from her surroundings; the chain is wrapped round something and the fob keeps slipping from her fingers when she pulls on it. She's loath to go further into the dark without at least the comfort of these sharp metal objects protruding from between her knuckles.

'Shit,' she says out loud, and stops.

Somewhere in the dark behind her, a single footfall sounds out into the silence.

A jagged shard of fear strokes its way down the back of her neck. She is all muscle, all tendon, her back pressed to the wall before she is aware that she has moved. She stands rigid, wide-eyed, and listens; strains to see the path she has already covered.

Nothing.

Against the lights of Fore Street, the silhouetted dumpsters crouch like dragons. She has no way of knowing what is hidden in the shadows. But she knows, too, that she must go forward. Further into the dark.

She forces herself to wheel and walk on deliberately, steadily, though her legs are liquid and her hands shaking. She slots the keys between her fingers, palm gripping on the ring that holds them together. They'll be little use as a weapon, but they might be enough to shock. Leave marks on a face. DNA on their jagged edges …

Jesus. Stop it. Don't make plans for how you'll help the police from beyond the grave.

External sound is blocked out by the swoosh of her circulation, the hiss of her breath. Her heart feels like an angry feral animal; threatens to punch its way through her sternum. Breathe. Breathe. Keep walking.

She counts her footsteps, concentrates on keeping them even, on maintaining her balance, on projecting a sense of calm control. If he doesn't know she's heard him, she might buy herself a few extra feet of head-start. Breathe. Breathe. One footstep, then another. The light on the corner dancing before her eyes, nothing but black around it.

Someone's foot catches a can in the road behind her. Sends it scuttering emptily along the pavement, closer than she had imagined.

Kirsty runs. Hears a sound – half moan, half shriek – burst from her throat, catches a heel in a pothole, staggers, bangs her shoulder against the wall, belts on. Heavy footfalls, no need for subterfuge, barrelling towards her, a splash as he stamps in a puddle, damp frogman tread as he slaps his way out the other side.

He grows, in her mind's eye, as he gains on her. Has transformed from a little rat-man into an ogre eight feet tall, with teeth of razors. Her bag weighs her down, slap-slap-slapping against her buttocks. She thinks about simply shedding it, decides, no, if it's the first thing he can reach, it'll be the first thing he grabs, and that will buy me one more precious second.

Help, begs her brain. Help me.

Her momentum carries her past the corner, bouncing off the far wall as she makes the turn. The man behind gains more ground as she recovers. She can hear his breath now: heavy, but not laboured. Not frayed like her own. More garbage hoppers here; piles of cardboard boxes, stacked wooden pallets and the lights of Brighton Road a million miles away. If he gets me behind one of those, no one on the street will ever see ...

Fingers brush against the bag; a promise of things to come. Kirsty lets out a gasp, finds a reserve of speed and hurls herself forward. Godjesus help me. Should I scream? Shout for help? She can hear the cacophony of Brighton Road – howls and laughs and cackling hens – and knows that any breath she wastes will go unnoticed.

'FUCK!' she shrieks, despite herself, and feels a hand clamp down on her bag strap. Feels it tighten and yank her body back.

Her response is rage. Fear, yes, but overwhelming it fierce, animal rage. She lets out a yell, whirls round with full-stretch arm and slaps the keys through the air. They connect with scalp; thick coarse hair under her fingers. She hears a grunt, then feels his other hand snatch at her head.

She slips her shoulder out from the bag strap, shakes her hair like a pony. She has never been so grateful for her practical haircut; there's not enough for him to clutch a forceful handful. Strong, hard fingers dig through, slither, snag in a knot and then, ripping a hank out by the roots, slip free. She pushes the bag towards his face and runs. Hurtles up the road, sees the tarmac fall into relief as the light begins to penetrate the gloom.

Still full-tilt now, though she knows already that he is no longer behind, that that last grab was his swansong. But she runs and runs, leaps a hole the size of a lorry wheel, surprises herself with the cat-like grace with which she lands. She doesn't slow until she has tumbled – crashing into the middle of a stag party – into the light.

Chapter Twenty-eight

Amber is shocked by how easy it is to make the change, now she's started. She's been so afraid of her anger, of being unable to control it if she ever gave it rein, that she's amazed by how restrained she can be as she lets it play out.

Instead of the frenzied stuffing of bin liners, the shower of clothes from upstairs windows, the bonfire-of-the-vanity products that the weak indulge in, she has quietly come home, waited for Vic to wake up, and told him it's time for him to leave. No screaming, no shouting, no tears: just a calm statement of fact. The mortgage is in her name, and for once, instead of running when things get difficult, she has stood her ground and stated her case. She's not flung him on to the street with a suitcase, not changed the locks – though she thinks she probably will, once he's cleared his stuff – or emptied the bank accounts. She's just told him that he needs to make other arrangements, and that then he must be gone. And then, quite calmly, she's gone to bed.

It's gone lunchtime when she wakes. She's only had a few hours' sleep, but they've been deep, dreamless and restorative in a way she can barely remember. She feels awake and alive; strong and decisive. The house is silent. Mary-Kate and Ashley curl round each other on the bedspread, chins on paws, gazing. A tail thumps as she sits up, and they jump down to follow as she goes downstairs.

He's still sitting at the kitchen table where she left him, staring into space, his face blank as though he's rebooting, his hands flat, palms-down on the table. She has an eerie feeling that he's been here all this time, switched off and waiting for stimulus. He doesn't acknowledge her as she enters; doesn't, as far as she can see, even blink as she crosses the room and puts on the kettle. The dogs skirt wide, eyes fixed on his rigid shoulders as though they expect him to spring suddenly to life like a big cat. She opens the back door to let them out, goes to the fridge to get the milk.

He leaps to his feet as though an invisible hand has thrown the On switch. 'Let me get that,' he says.

'Nope, you're OK,' she replies; tries to put herself between him and the fridge door. But he keeps on coming. Snatches the milk from her hand – she cedes her grip on it to avoid having a mess to mop up – and takes it to the countertop. Goes into the cupboard and gets down the mugs. 'Earl Grey?'

Behind his back, she shrugs. 'Earl Grey,' she says. She's never learned to like PG, not really. 'Thanks,' she adds. No point in dropping the façade of civility when it's all going to be done and dusted sooner or later anyway.

Vic drops the bags in the mugs, pours in the water. 'Do you want something to eat? You must be hungry.'

'No thanks. I'll get myself something in a bit.'

He adds milk, spoons in the sugar. 'Come on. I can make you a bacon sandwich.'

She shakes her head. 'Thanks.'

'Amber, you should eat,' he says in that reasonable voice of his.

She can't stop herself snapping. 'No, Vic! I said no!'

He does that infuriating shrug that indicates that all women are mad. Takes his tea and sits down at the table. 'How did you sleep?'

Her mood is deteriorating rapidly. She grunts and takes her tea over to the door and looks out at the dogs. They are sniffing and wagging around the gap at the bottom of the gate. I must take them for a walk, she thinks. Poor little sods don't get nearly enough exercise.

'I was thinking,' he says, 'about maybe building a proper barbecue. You know. Bricks and that. Then we could have people over. Not have to go out all the time.'

Shit. He's pretending it never happened.

'What do you reckon?' he asks. 'We don't do enough entertaining, do we? Wouldn't you like that?'

Amber sighs and turns back to the room. 'No, I wouldn't, Vic. I don't want you to do any DIY or make me meals or try to be nice. Thank you, but there's no point.'

Vic raises his eyebrows. 'Wow.'

'I've said my piece,' she says. 'I don't want you thinking I didn't mean it.'

'And I don't get a right of reply?'

She tips her tea down the sink. She doesn't want it any more. 'No. You forfeited that when you fucked my friend.'

'One mistake,' he says.

She feels like screaming. Wishes she hadn't tipped the tea away because the satisfaction of dashing hot liquid in his eyes would be exquisite. Instead she puts the mug down hard in the sink and snatches the dogs' leads from the hook by the door. 'I'm going for a walk.'

She goes out and crouches down by the dogs. It's hard to clip the leads on: her hands are shaking and the dogs are dancing with anticipation. She feels him behind her, in the doorway, watching; shakes Mary-Kate by the collar to make her stand still.

'God, you can really bear a grudge,' he says.

'I'm not talking about it. I'm not!'

'You at least owe me that,' he says.

She flings herself to her feet and dashes for the gate. 'No I don't!' she snarls back. She struggles with the bolt. It's hardly ever used because they always go in and out through the front, but she doesn't want to have to push past him, doesn't want to be confined within those walls, until she's regained control of herself.

'Here, let me help you,' he offers.

'No!' She's barely aware that she's shouting. 'Just fuck off, will you?'

'Amber!' His voice is calculatedly reasonable; designed to make her angrier. 'Come on, love. Calm down.'

The bolt gives suddenly. Shoots back and gouges a great runnel of skin out of her thumb. 'Shit!' she screams. 'Shit, shit, shit!'

'Oh my God,' he says. 'Let me look.'

He steps forward, his voice all concern, his face all enjoyment. She doesn't understand what he's doing. All she knows is that she wants him nowhere near. She hauls the gate open and steps backwards on to the road, screaming into his face. 'Just keep away from me! Fuck off! Don't fucking touch me!'

She wheels on her heel and finds that Shaunagh Next Door is standing on the weedy verge with her baby buggy and the gimlet-eyed biddy, Janelle Boxer, from number ten. They look thrilled. She doesn't care.

'I want you out of this house, Victor Cantrell,' she shouts. 'You just get out of my house!'

She turns to the women. 'What are you looking at?' she snarls.

Chapter Twenty-nine

'Luke, please. Just turn the sound off.'

'I need the sound,' says Luke. 'I can't tell if there's a troll coming if I haven't got sound.'

'You've played this game at least a thousand times,' Kirsty says. 'You must be able to remember by now.'

The noise is driving her mad. The beeps and boops assail her ears like tiny flaming arrows. With the tinny tinkle of JLS from Sophie's earphones and Jim's throat-clearing, she feels as though she is under assault from all sides. Her shoulder is stiff where she wrenched it, and a bruise on the back of her thigh makes sitting uncomfortable, moving more so, even without the wriggling fear of a deadline to hit and a forgotten car-insurance bill.

Luke doesn't raise his eyes from the screen. 'Just let me get to the end of this ...' he says, and swoops his arms out as a dwarf leaps out from behind a pillar and lobs a vial of poison. 'Awww, *Mum*,' he says. 'Now look what you've done!'

'Go and play upstairs,' she orders. Wishes for the millionth time that she was the kind of parent who made her kids share a bedroom to make room for an office. She feels like a teenager doing prep. You'd never think I was this family's main bread-winner. I'm the only person here who doesn't have a space of her own. Even Jim's got his shed, goddammit.

'In a minute,' says Luke.

'*Now*. I'm working.'

'It's not *my* fault you didn't do your work in time,' says Luke. Hammers at the Fire button repeatedly. Leaps out of his seat, punching the air. 'Yessssssss!'

Kirsty slams down the lid of the laptop. 'Luke!' she shouts.

'OK, OK,' he says, and presses the volume button, ostentatiously, for her benefit. 'No need to get your knickers in a twist.'

He sits back down again and hunches over his screen. Kirsty takes a deep breath, counts to ten, lets it out. Opens the computer and stares at the pitiful collection of sentences she's achieved since nine this morning. She can't remember words being so hard to find before; but then she can't remember having to write under such duress.

Jim's been quiet and humble all day, staying pointedly out of her way and bringing her cups of coffee on the hour, and all it's done is make her worse. I mustn't resent him. It's not his fault. He's trying, God knows he is. But can't he go and sit in that damn shed and give me some *space*?

The stuff I do for this family, and they don't have the first idea. But why the hell did I stay? I didn't *need* to go to that stupid club. I've seen enough of them to know what it would be like. I could've come home a whole day earlier and used my imagination instead of getting scared half to death for the sake of a bloody kill fee.

She's got away lightly from her experience, she knows, but that doesn't help her settle. The stags on Brighton Road piled down the alleyway, but her assailant was long gone, her bag and its contents strewn along the tarmac. So she's got her phone and her notebooks and her MP3 player and all the accoutrements of her daily life still with her. That the guy's motivation was clearly not robbery, she can't afford to think about right now. She's not told Jim. Not told anyone. She's damned if she's going to miss her deadline for the sake of being given an incident number and told to get in line.

She reads back what she's written, fiddles with the cursor key as though doing so will magically conjure words on to the screen. Even by the standards of the *Tribune*, it's pants. Repetitive pants. There's not a phrase, an observation, an adjective she hasn't already used last week. This is the bit of journalism she hates: the Groundhog Day of unresolved stories. She doesn't want to think about Whitmouth again, doesn't want to revisit it, even in her mind. And yet now, by default, because a staffer prefers the ongoing drama in Sleaford, she is the expert, and has to churn out holding copy until something happens.

I hate that place, she thinks. I can't believe I actually liked it when I first went there. And it's not just last night – it's all of it. The fact that going there has brought back a past I thought I'd overcome, my unpayable debt. The fact that the people remind me of the family I'll never see again, the fact that I feel my arse expand with every unspeakable meal in its grease-spattered outlets. The horizontal rain that soaks your pores with salt, the things that slide underfoot on Marine Parade. The blistering, blustering half-mile trudge to the end of the pier, the plastic seats in the pubs. The overwhelming smell of cooking oil. What can I say that's new? I said it all last week. The place hasn't changed.

She reads, again:

Despite it all, the crowds still come to Whitmouth. The council vans that ply the seafront remove five tons of rubbish from its bins alone each day: rubbish that includes 8,000 soft-drinks cans, 5,000 polystyrene food holders, 30 discarded shoes and 220 soiled nappies. No local business wants to discuss the specifics of their income, but it's clear that business is good. Funnland, the theme park where suspected fifth victim Hannah Hardy's body was found three weeks ago, claims gates of roughly 3,000 a day. 1,250 tickets are sold for the tiny electric train that goes to the end of the pier, half of them one-way, and The Old-Fashioned Sweet Emporium sells over 10kg of Whitmouth rock . . .

Blah, blah, blah. She highlights, deletes. Presses Control+Z to reinstate. It's 116 words, and she needs 1,500; she can't just waste it. Pulls up the STUFF file on her desktop, cuts and pastes into it, saves. Tries again.

In 2007, the most recent year for which there are statistics, 1.37 million people visited Whitmouth, spending, on average, £46 a head a day. Of those, 236,000 stayed a night, a weekend, a week – averaging four nights a head – in the town's four sprawling caravan parks, its 17 hotels and 87 B&Bs. All in all, that's an income, for the town, of £95m and change. Tourism is big business in Whitmouth – it's the only industry of any real significance. Half the working-age element of the 67,000-person population is employed – mostly on minimum wage and mostly seasonally – by the tourist trade. So the impact of the Seaside Strangler's reign of terror would be expected to be greatly more far-reaching than the devastation of the victims' families and friends. The Strangler, one would have thought, would be threatening the livelihood of the whole community.
Apparently not.

She shifts in her seat, feels the shriek of broken blood vessels. Suppresses a groan. Does a word count: 160. This is bollocks. Why am I bothering? It's taken me twenty minutes to turn that lot out, and that was the easy bit. And all for what? I *know* this is going to get pulled; that something more interesting will happen somewhere else in the country between now and Friday, when they finalise the news features. Unless the Strangler strikes again, Whitmouth will be old news, not even fit for Monday's fish-and-chip wrappings.

'Bollocks,' she says out loud. Jim looks up from the City pages of *Private Eye*. 'Sorry,' she says. They have an agreement that salty hack language will not leak into family life.

'Having trouble?'

She nods. 'I'm tired. And knowing it's probably not even going to run doesn't help much.'

'Shall I get you a coffee?'

'I've got coffee leaking out of my pores.'

'What can I do?'

'Take this lot out and throw sticks for them,' she says. She hasn't got the will for tact any more.

Luke huffs and throws his Nintendo on to the table.

'Luke!' bellows Jim. Kirsty slaps her hands over her ears, chokes back a matching howl. 'Don't you *dare* treat your toys like that! Have you any idea how much that cost?'

'Well, it's not *my* fault!' Luke shouts back. 'She *made* me do it!'

'We're not buying you another if you break that one!'

Sophie unplugs an earphone, looks imperiously at her family. 'Hello? *Listening*,' she says. Kirsty feels a vein in her forehead begin to pulse. That's all I need. I'll have a stroke right here at this table, *then* see where your Nintendo money comes from.

'We're going for a walk,' Jim tells her.

The phone rings. God save us from children. No wonder people have chihuahuas instead. 'I can't answer that,' she tells her husband. 'If it's work, tell them I'm stuck in traffic.'

Jim picks up. 'Walk?' whines Sophie. 'Who said anything about a *walk*?'

'Hello?' says Jim. Kirsty's brain begins to throb. 'Oh, hello, Lionel. Thanks for calling me back. No, no problem. It's always hard to get much work done in the summer holidays. I guess that's why we have offices. No, hang on. I'll just take this somewhere quiet.'

He leaves the room. 'I don't see why I should have to go out just because you can't do your work in time,' says Luke, and glares at her.

Kirsty slams the computer shut and stamps upstairs to her bedroom, slamming the door pointedly.

She gets into bed and starts to write again.

Apparently not. In a bizarre triumph of human nature over survival instinct, Whitmouth is enjoying a boom year of a sort it hasn't seen since the invention of the package holiday. A phenomenon that proves, once again, the old adage that there's no such thing as bad publicity.

Becca Stokes, 23 and down from Coventry with a group of friends, sums it up: 'I used to come here with my mum and dad when I was a kid and I loved it then. And then there's been all this stuff in the papers, and me and my mates all thought, you know: look at that. I had no idea they had so many nightclubs, and the caravans are dirt cheap. So we thought we'd come down for the weekend, you know? Check it out . . .

I can't, she thinks. I can't encourage people to go there. I'm the hypocrite of hypocrites: writing disapprovingly about a phenomenon I'm helping to foster. It's not safe. Every time they read statistics like this, see how many people are there, calculate the odds in their heads, they'll think it's safe. But he's still out there. Still mingling in amongst them, and they've no idea who he is.

She checks her watch. She can string the features desk along for another hour, and after that every ten minutes is another year off her career. But, she thinks, I can't do this 'balance' thing. They're all so obsessed with balance that they forget that, sometimes, there is such a thing as simple, black-and-white truth. Whitmouth's a horrible place. It's dangerous and seedy and people should know. I can't let them fool themselves that they can wander around it half-cut. I've got a story here.

And a small voice says: yeah, and if I tell it properly, they won't spike it and I'll earn actual wordage. And I've *got* to find the cash for that car insurance. *Got* to. There's two days left to run, and after that I won't be able to earn a bloody penny. Sod

Whitmouth. Sod balance. I got scared to stupidity last night, and I'm bloody well letting people know. And if that weasel-man reads about himself and doesn't like it, then maybe he'll learn a lesson he needs to understand.

She highlights again, cuts until the page is blank. Then she begins:

Women have died in Whitmouth. And on Monday night, I almost became one of them . . .

Chapter Thirty

The lower half of Ashok's face is smeared with mayonnaise. He speaks as he chews, and bits of lettuce spray into the night air. 'I can't believe they went in without us.'

'Course they did,' says Tony. 'Couldn't wait to get away from you, you wanker.'

Rav and Jez laugh while Ash flicks him a V. None of them is steady on his feet, and Rav slips off the pavement into Brighton Road, narrowly missing a passing car. It blasts its horn and carries on as they bawl and shake their fists at its receding tail-lights.

'God, it's bloody dead around here,' says Jez.

'It's two in the morning,' says Tony. 'What did you expect?'

Ash picks the last of the chicken out of his kebab, balls up the paper and drops it on the pavement. 'Bloody no bloody trainers,' he says. 'These cost over a hundred quid.'

'What?' says Rav. 'You got ripped off, mate.'

''Koff,' says Ash, and cuffs him round the back of the head. They stumble on. It's another mile to the B&B. Other knots of stragglers wander past: people who've blown all their money and can't afford a taxi, people who've been turned away from the clubs or got bored in the queues, and others, heading in the opposite direction, who are still hoping that they'll get in. Tony finishes off the last of his falafel and balls up the bag. Puts it in his pocket. 'That's what you're meant to do with rubbish,' he tells Ashok.

'Bollocks,' says Ash. 'If they hadn't got rid of all the waste-bins I'd've thrown it away.'

'Hah,' says Jez. 'If your lot didn't keep blowing things up, they wouldn't have got rid of them in the first place.'

'Yeah,' says Rav around a lager burp. 'Those Diwali bombings were a bugger, weren't they?'

The familiar press of booze on bladder is getting beyond a joke. Ashok wishes he'd made use of the filthy bog in the amusement arcade, but the lure of getting those 10ps to drop on the cascade machine had been too great at the time. He glances at Tony and Jez, feels a twinge of jealousy that their heathen upbringing has left them free of inhibitions about letting fly by the empty cashpoint a few hundred yards back. He's going to need to relieve himself before they get to the B&B. Lager doesn't agree with him, but you don't drink vodka-tonic on a stag night if you want to get out unscathed.

They start to pass the boarded-up frontage of a bankrupt ironmonger's, and he remembers noticing on the way into town that the next lot, before the job centre, is derelict: a mass of builders' rubble, elder and stinging nettles behind a loose wire fence. That'll do, he thinks. They can just bloody wait for me.

'I need a wazz,' he announces as they reach the fence. Grabs at the wire and gives it a shake. It's come free of the concrete post to which it was once moored, at this end. He's obviously not the first home-bound reveller to have this idea. 'Keep a look-out,' he says.

'What for?' asks Tony. He's already lighting a Marlboro, smoke hanging in the air above his head. 'Ladyboy to send in after you?'

Ashok ducks down and squeezes through the gap. The wasteground is dark, and stinks. It's clearly functioned as a makeshift toilet for the clubbers of Whitmouth for years. I'm going to have to give my trainers a wash when we get in, he thinks. Just hope I don't tread in anything solid.

Five yards in, a large elder bush blocks off the light from the street. This'll do. He picks his way carefully over piles of bricks and broken glass – the last thing he wants to do is lose his footing in this foetid jungle – and steps in behind it. Feels relief simply from unbuttoning his jeans, lets out a groan of pleasure when the beer-scented stream steams out into the night air.

'Thought you were having a wazz, not a wank!' shouts Rav. 'Can't you wait till we get home?'

The piss seems to last for ever. Ashok shifts his balance, waits as his bladder pumps and pumps. Now the initial stress has gone, he wishes he could stop and hold on to the rest until he's back in the bathroom at Seaview. He doesn't like standing with his back to the dark like this, can't shake the feeling that he's not alone. He tries clenching his internal muscles, but it's no good. The stream slows but doesn't stop and it'll just take him longer to get done, if he tries.

Street-side, he hears the sound of the fence shifting, then the slide and rattle of careless feet on the rubble he's just crossed.

'Where are you?' Tony's voice, slurred and overloud.

'In here,' he says.

'Right,' says Tony. Ashok sees him against the light, then he is standing beside him. 'Shift over,' he says.

'I can't,' says Ash.

'All right then. Don't complain if your feet get splashed.'

'Didn't you just go in the street?' asks Ashok.

'Lager,' says Tony.

The sound of Tony's zip going down, then suddenly, behind them, something thrashes in the dark, among the bushes against the blank wall of the ironmongery.

Ashok and Tony peer at each other in the dark, sobriety immediate and shocking.

'What was that?' asks Tony. His eyes are huge in the shadows.

'Dunno,' says Ashok.

'Just a fox or summat,' says Tony.

'Dunno,' repeats Ashok. 'Sounded bigger, didn't it?'

Tony nods, his bladder forgotten. They can hear the others out on the street, laughing and joking about. 'Come on, you two!' Rav's voice drifts through the foliage.

'Shhh!' hisses Tony redundantly. They turn, peer into the wasteland. 'Hello?' he calls tentatively.

Silence. They stand side by side, straining their ears for a sound. It feels weird, thinks Ashok. Like it did before, when I was alone: like someone's out there, listening.

Tony shakes his head. 'Badger.'

'Badger?' asks Ashok, incredulously. 'Do you *get* badgers in towns?'

'Well *I* dunno, do I?' says Tony. Looks down at his trousers, hoicks his zip. 'C'mon.' He turns away, starts back towards the fence.

Ash waits a couple of seconds, listens some more. There's nothing out there now: just the sound of shuffling on the pavement and the rustle of the leaves by his shoulder. It's nothing, he thinks. Just the sounds you hear sometimes. Things moving and settling, stuff slipping off roofs.

A cry, from the darkness: frightened, gurgling, cut off. That wasn't a badger. A girl. That was a woman's voice. Out there somewhere.

He hears Tony swear; hears the others, their voices suddenly alert. In the bushes something thrashes, bucks, falls still.

'Shit,' says Tony again. 'Fuck. That was … Jesus.'

Rav and Jez crash through the fence, shove the last bolt from its mooring. 'What was that?' asks Jez.

'I don't …' says Ash. 'I think it was a …'

Tony's running clumsily over the piled-up bricks in the middle of the yard, always the leader. 'Hello?' he shouts. 'Where are you?'

In the far corner, they hear a struggle, another gasp cut short. The three laggards set off in pursuit of their friend, spread out, run towards the noise. I'm scared, thinks Ash. I'm not a hero. I don't do this sort of thing. He catches a trainer on the corner of something sharp, stumbles, bangs his shoulder into Jez's arm. Feels a hand shoot out and push him upright.

Tony scrambles up the slope towards the bushes. He can see something behind now: something unnaturally white, something that doesn't fit. It moves. Christ. It's a man. There's a man in there.

'Over here!' he shouts. Isn't thinking now, is just doing: pushes aside the branches as he hears the others' footsteps veer towards him.

A body plunges outward, catches him round the knees, sends him tumbling. Tony screams, with shock, then with anger as he hits the ground and feels the sharp crack and slice of glass entering his skin. The guy's on top, but he's not staying there. He's struggling to disentangle himself, using Tony's crotch as traction as he prepares to make another run.

'Fuck!' howls Tony. This hurts. The fucker's got his knee on his hip, is sliding about. Tony grabs at his white shirt, pitches and rolls. Gets on top as the others arrive, pins the man down. He sees a flash of dark hair, a gold earring. Then Jez is there, pushing the man over, pinning him down.

The woman struggles for air behind the bushes. Ash and Rav push past. Tony can hear their voices: aggressive with alarm, trying to sound calm, self-assured. 'It's OK. It's all right. We've got you. It's all right.'

She's pale and plump and barely conscious; huddles with her dress rucked up over her hips and her hands in front of her face. 'It's OK,' says Ash, and tries to reach out to her. She sees his hands and starts to scream – a hoarse, shattered sound, as though her throat is damaged – as she swipes at them with broken fingernails. He has to grab her wrists to stop her, kneels in front of her, his knee between her naked thighs.

'Aaah,' she yelps. 'Aaah no, aaah!'

Pale light casts through the shadow and he sees her face, a

Chapter Thirty-one

Martin knows he needs to do something, but he doesn't know what. The shock was too great last night: the discovery of the links within links, the awful plots he doesn't understand, left him reeling helplessly, whirling in rage and impotence. His anger was so fierce, so near-erotic, that he almost went up Mare Street again to see if anyone had taken over Tina's patch, but at the last moment self-preservation held him back. He got lucky last Saturday. Can't expect for a moment that such dumb luck will hold again. If he's going to repeat the experience, he needs to be a lot more careful.

So he plans and he thinks, and in the meantime he sticks to his usual routine. Which, on a Sunday morning, is to treat himself to a sausage roll and a bar of chocolate while he does his washing.

Sunday morning is a good time to go to the launderette. The usual trade – holidaymakers and families whose washing machines have broken down – don't make it down there on a Sunday morning, and he usually gets a machine straight away. And the warm, steamy benches make for a cosy, intimate atmosphere. Once, he struck up a friendship with a young woman called Carly, who worked as a cashier at the amusement arcade on the pier. They talked three Sundays in a row, but just as he was about to invite her to dinner her shift changed and her laundry routine with it. He dropped in to the arcade a few times, hoping to find her working, but he never saw her again.

It's a beautiful morning. Weak sunshine breaks through last night's clearing clouds and a million hanging raindrops glitter on the promenade balustrade. It's one of those days when Whitmouth, washed clean by the rain, looks its sparkling best. Martin hoicks his bag of bedclothes over his shoulder and hurries through the sharp air. The street is surprisingly busy. There's a knot of people outside the police station, just staring at the door as though they expect it to burst into flames. He doesn't think anything of it. The station has had a magnetic effect on the press at start and close of play every day this summer. He brushes past and turns up Canal Street, skirts round a pile of uncollected cardboard boxes outside the gift shop on the corner.

The launderette is empty. A couple of machines churn in the middle of the row, but no one is about. Through the bubbled window of the office door he can see the pixellated version of the overalled Romanian woman who runs the place. She's talking on the phone and he sees her throw her head back and laugh. Martin chooses a machine, puts the open mouth of his bin bag into it and tips. He never has to sort: you only have to sort if you don't plan ahead. Everything he owns has been deliberately chosen to fit within the narrow spectrum of dark blue, grey and black. He adds the measured-out freezer-bagful of powder from his anorak pocket, dials it up to sixty. He's about to slam the door when he catches a whiff of his anorak and realises that it must be a year since he bought it. He turns out the pockets on to the bench – coins, a couple of sticks of chewing-gum he remembers buying before his first date with Jackie Jacobs and a spare chip fork – and throws the coat in on top of the rest. Then he goes to the shop to buy his treats for the day. The wash cycle will take an hour. Martin would never waste money on a service wash, but he'd never waste time either.

As he steps out into Canal Street, he almost collides with someone hurrying along the pavement. It's Amber Gordon – but not as he knows her. She's a strange shade of pale grey, and hasn't brushed her hair. She's walking so fast she barely avoids him; lurches as she passes. For a moment he thinks that her backwards jump is a personal slight, but then he sees that she hasn't clocked his face at all. He waits for her to acknowledge him, feels piqued when she doesn't. Her eyes are rimmed red, and she looks as though she's got dressed in the dark.

'Sorry,' she mutters absently, and hurries on down the road.

Shaking his head, he walks on. Doesn't really care what's going on in the woman's life, but feels a tweak of pleasure at having witnessed her distress. *I hope something's happened. It would serve you right. Bring you down to earth.*

The newsagent is almost out of papers, unusually for this time of day. There's only a couple of *Mail on Sunday*s and a *Tribune* left. He can't see why: the front-page headline on one is something to do with immigrants and house prices, and the other, faintly more left-wing, has led on a minor Tory spanking scandal. He snatches up the *Tribune* just before another customer. Is dying to know what Kirsty Lindsay has to say for herself this week.

He takes a sausage roll and a small bottle of Sunny Delight from the chiller cabinet. Then he lingers for a full five minutes over the chocolate bars and eventually chooses a Snickers. There's twenty per cent extra free on the Snickers bar, and it will fill more time as he waits for his wash to be done.

He has to wait while one of those tedious local-shop transactions wends its way to a close. A stout woman is counting up the change to pay for a two-litre bottle of full-fat Coke while Mrs Todiwallah waits impassively behind the counter.

'Have you heard who it is yet?' asks the stout woman. Finds a fiver in the corner of her purse. 'Ooh. And a pack of Amber Leaf and some menthol filters while you're there.'

'No,' says Mrs Todiwallah, turning to the shelves and picking up the tobacco. 'There is a difference between a newsagent's and a news agency, you know. We sell newspapers. They gather news.'

'And the filters?' says the stout woman. Mrs T bends creakily down in her plus-size shalwar kameez and collects the box. This, thinks Martin, is why people shop in supermarkets. You don't have to do chit-chat in supermarkets. You just buy your stuff and get out.

'No.' She straightens up slowly, slaps the goods down on the counter. 'There's been nothing on the radio. Just that a man's being questioned and will be charged maybe later today.'

'And no one's been in that knows anything?'

'I daresay,' says Mrs Todiwallah, 'they'd go to the newspapers before they came to the corner shop if they did. I don't pay for news, you see. I just sell it.'

Martin wonders vaguely what they're talking about. He's not the sort to intrude into someone else's conversation. He shifts from foot to foot, wishing that, if they insist on gossiping, the shopkeeper would carry on serving while she did it.

'Well, it's good news anyway,' says the stout woman.

'Yes, indeed it is,' says Mrs T. 'That's five pounds twenty-three, please.'

The stout woman starts counting out her change again, penny by penny.

Martin glances down at his paper and sees, tucked down on the bottom right, a small headline that might explain what they're talking about: HOLS RESORT MURDERS BREAKTHROUGH. Breaking news, 3 a.m., says the text below: Whitmouth police arrest Seaside Strangler suspect. More details: page 2.

He burns to open it and read it right now, but waits patiently to pay and get out. He has plenty of time. The printed word won't change if it takes him five minutes longer to start reading it. Nonetheless he finds himself hurrying along Canal Street, eager to fill himself in.

He sits on a bench, unwraps his sausage roll and takes a bite. Opens the page and sees, to his disappointment, that the details are very sketchy indeed. **Police arrested a man suspected of the Seaside Strangler murders at 1 a.m.**, says the report, written by someone called Staff Reporter.

Officers were called to the scene of a disturbance on waste ground off Whitmouth's main road, and arrested a man being held by passers-by. A young woman was taken to a nearby hospital and treated for cuts, bruises and shock. The man, after treatment in the same hospital, was taken to Whitmouth Police Station and charged with assault, GBH and threatening behaviour, and is expected to be remanded in the next 48 hours. No names have been released.

Is that it?

I must get down the station. See what I can find out. That's why all those people were there. He's actually being held inside, whoever he is.

He reads the piece again, takes another bite of roll and washes it down with a gulp of drink. At the bottom, in bold, a teaser catches his eye: **My night of terror in Whitmouth's sleazy back streets, page 27.**

Yes, he thinks, there she is. He leafs through showbiz stories to find the page, and feels a rush of blood to his cheeks. Here she is again, smirking in the postage-stamp picture beside the headline; there's a picture of the back of some other woman's head, looking down an alleyway, clutching her handbag, as illustration. It's not even Whitmouth – or not any Whitmouth he's seen; it looks like one of those bin-lanes you find up north. He starts to read, feels the flush spread across his cheeks as he sees himself – his unflattering portrait – spill out before his eyes.

Women have died in Whitmouth. And on Monday night, I almost became one of them.

247

Chapter Thirty-two

'Nice piece yesterday,' says Stan.

Kirsty blushes. 'Thanks,' she replies. 'I'm in deep shit now, of course.'

'Yeah,' says Stan. 'Thoughtless bastard, getting himself arrested after Features went to bed. He could've bloody waited till today so it wasn't so obvious. Still. They can't be *that* pissed off. You wouldn't be here otherwise.'

'Don't you believe it. I'm only here because the daily and the Sunday don't cross over. I don't suppose I'll ever write for the Sunday again. And Dave Park doesn't work Mondays. I'll be right back on the phew-what-a-scorcher circuit after today.'

Stan shoves the strap of his man-bag back up his shoulder. 'Hardly your fault, K. And apart from the fingering-an-innocent-bystander issue, it was a good piece. Good drama.'

'Yeah.' She shrugs miserably. 'And now I look like a hysterical dick.'

Stan laughs. They shuffle up as Nick from the *Mirror* pushes through the crowd to stand beside them.

'Kirsty Lindsay,' he says. 'I'd've worn my anorak if I'd known.'

'Fuck off,' she grunts. To be fair to my peers, she thinks, we're just as gleeful about each other's misfortunes as we are about the civilians'.

'Don't sweat it,' says Stan. 'We've all cocked up in our time. Jesus. Remind me to tell you about how I libelled the chief of the

Humberside Police one day. Lost a bit of sleep over that, I'll tell you. You just need to put a dozen pieces between yourself and this, and they'll forget all about it.'

'I hope so,' says Kirsty. 'Because I'm screwed otherwise.'

Nick pats her shoulder. 'It was a good piece, if it's any consolation. Made my hair stand on end, that's the main thing. And you can always work the was-he-working-alone angle for a bit, till they've all forgotten.'

'Thanks, Nick.'

'Don't be too grateful,' he says, 'I don't want you stalking me' – and she punches him on the upper arm.

'So what's the scoop, anyway?' he asks.

They're outside the police station. Nobody really knows why, as it's obvious that no one will be coming out to talk to them for a good while. But the pubs won't open till noon, so they might as well be here as anywhere else.

'Bugger-all, at the moment,' says Stan. 'Now he's been charged for Saturday night's shenanigans, they can stay quiet for as long as they want, basically. I reckon it's going to be speculation and hearsay till tomorrow now.'

A BBC outside-broadcast van pulls up on the other side of the road. 'Uh-oh,' says Stan. 'Here come the Royals.'

'Don't let the bastards through,' says Nick. 'If they can't be arsed to show up on time, they can stand at the back.'

'Don't tell them anything,' says Stan.

'They never ask me anyway,' says Kirsty. 'So c'mon, Stan. What rumour and speculation have you been privy to?' Stan knows everybody. And anybody he doesn't know knows someone he does. If anyone's going to be up on the rumour and speculation, it's going to be him.

He lowers his voice. He's not handing his gleanings over to the whole world. Especially not the BBC. 'Don't quote me on this, but I heard it's the same guy they had in for questioning last week.'

'Seriously? But I thought he had an alibi.'

'Less of an alibi than an explanation,' says Stan. 'Just because he had a reason to be there some other time doesn't mean he wasn't there at the time in question.'

'There's a few political writers who could do with remembering that,' says Nick.

'Huh,' says Stan, and laughs.

'How's the girl?' asks Kirsty.

'Still in ICU. Pretty beaten up. Her windpipe's swollen up from the bruising, so they're keeping a tube in it till it goes down. They reckon she's lost an eye, too. He's been getting more violent as he's gone along, hasn't he?'

'Well, I suppose if you *can* escalate beyond murder ... Poor kid,' says Kirsty.

'Lucky kid,' corrects Stan. 'If it weren't for the pissed-up youth of today, she'd be a dead kid.'

'Got any rescuers' names?'

He checks his pad. 'Ashok Kumar, twenty-three, Anthony Langrish, twenty-two, Ravinder Doal, twenty-four, and another one. Barred from Stardust for wearing trainers, God bless the doormen of the south coast.'

'So, Victor Cantrell,' says Kirsty. 'That was the name, wasn't it? Of the guy they were questioning before?'

'Yes,' says Stan, 'but I'd keep it out of your copy for now. Don't want a libel suit on our hands.'

''Specially not you,' says Nick.

She rolls her eyes. 'Settle down. OK, but ... Funnland employee, lives in town, drinks at the Cross Keys, popular, nobody would ever have guessed, right? Did you get the address before he was released?'

'Yup,' says Stan. 'I'll pop up there again later. Best way to verify is to see if he's at home, I'd say.'

'And how the little lady responds,' says Nick.

'Well, she's not answering the door at the moment,' says Stan. 'Curtains shut tight.'

'Poor cow,' says Kirsty. 'I wonder how she's feeling today.'

'Guilty, I should think,' says Nick. 'Wouldn't you?'

'Why?'

'Well, c'mon. She must've had her suspicions.'

'Why?' she asks again. 'That's a bit harsh, isn't it?'

She remembers the look of blank incomprehension on her mother's face as she saw the squad car bumping up their lane. Remembers the dawning horror as she turned and looked at her daughter and understood why they were there. Thinks about Jim and the kids, and feels sick. 'A lot of partners don't have the first idea.'

'Well, they *would* say that, wouldn't they?' he replies.

'Thanks, Miss Rice-Davies,' says Stan. 'Whatever, she's in for some fun anyway. I don't suppose people round here are much of the empathetic persuasion.'

A stir on the street side of the crowd. The hacks instinctively close ranks; don't want any newcomers thinking they can steal their pitches. Kirsty cranes, and sees the top of a blond head weaving a stilted route through the rows behind. Sees the edges of a pair of oversized sunglasses and thinks: Oh God, I know those.

'Someone coming,' she says. 'Not one of us.'

'Ah, right,' says Stan. Starts to edge aside; knows that being remembered for being helpful can swing the odds in his favour later on. 'C'mon, guys!' he shouts. 'Let the lady through!'

Grudgingly the crowd edges apart and the blond head starts to progress. A couple of flashbulbs go off: opportunity photos, the sort that, in the digital age when no one has to worry about wasting film, everybody takes by the thousand just in case they turn out relevant later.

'Christ,' says Stan, who's taller and can see better.

'What?'

'Bang on the nail, as ever,' he boasts. 'That's Victor Cantrell's missus. For definite.'

And Kirsty guesses, with plummeting dread – before the grey-white, tear-streaked face comes fully into her field of vision – that Victor Cantrell's missus is also Amber Gordon.

1.30 p.m.

'I'm hungry.'

Debbie Francis shoots her sister a look so filled with venom it almost burns. 'Shut up, Chloe,' she says.

Chloe squats, troll-like, on the verge on the other side of the road, sucking on a Chupa-Chups lolly. 'Mum said you was to look after me,' she says.

'Oh for God's sake,' says Debbie, and climbs off Darren Walker's lap. She pulls her T-shirt down under her leather jacket – it's too hot for leather, but this black, studded blouson is the coolest item of clothing she's ever owned, and she'll take the discomfort for the sake of style. She stalks across the tarmac in her four-inch heels and towers over her sister.

'If you don't shut up, I'll pinch you,' she says. 'Mum left me in charge and that means you have to do what I tell you. All right?'

'But—' begins Chloe.

Debbie sticks out two hard red-nailed fingers and pinches the skin above her elbow. Chloe yelps, then begins to cry. Debbie made her take her anorak off an hour ago, and her skin is already lobster-pink; stings hard enough where the pinch was to make her eyes dazzle.

'Now shut up,' she hears Debbie's voice through the haze of pain, 'or there'll be more where that came from.'

'But she said. She said!'

She sees the fingers come up again and feint towards her, and shrinks back into the grass. 'And. I'm. Bloody. Busy,' snaps Debbie. 'Just sit there and eat your lolly and I'll get you some dinner when I'm good and ready, OK?'

She turns her back on the weeping child, and her stalk becomes a sashay as she sees her Romeo, legs apart on the *bench, his arm laid out along the length of its back. With his crotch thrust forward, she can see the outline of his erection and feels a rush of teenage pride. Not everyone can get Darren Walker. He may be rough, but he's choosy. She reaches the bench, glimpses his self-satisfied smile as she climbs on board. I shouldn't like him, she thinks. No girl should like a boy who look at her like that. But I do, I can't help it. There's something about him that does something to me.*

There are no subtleties, no niceties, with Darren. The boys she's known before are fumblers; apologetic and tentative. They'd never simply return to where they were before an inter- ruption. Within ten seconds his hand is back up inside her shirt, inside her bra, stroking her nipple with his thumb. She's used to the squeezing, probing, poky fingers of her peers. The sensation makes her melt, makes her shift her purchase on his lap the better to feel his tumescence. She hears a surprising, delicate sound – half sigh, half moan – escape from somewhere deep inside her, and wonders: where did that come from? Sees the smile – that look of triumph – return to his face and feels him bury his free hand in the hair at the back of her neck. He smells of cigarette smoke and chewing-gum.

Thighs astride his, she presses herself crotch to crotch with him, feels that familiar twitch deep inside. 'Nice,' says Darren Walker. 'Now, where were we?'

'What are you doing?' asks Chloe. Gives a huge snotty sniff as emphasis.

'Never you mind,' says Darren, and shifts beneath Debbie on the bench. He moves his hand round to attempt to unsnag her bra at the back, and she slaps it away.

'Someone'll see,' she says.

Darren laughs at her nastily. 'Bit late to worry about that now. And besides, they're all down at the river, ennit?' Most of the population of the village has taken off to a stretch of the Even- lode by the railway tracks a couple of miles away: a chunk of broomy watermeadow that's gradually turned into a communal

swimming-hole since the embankment rendered it unfit for graz-
ing anything but sheep.

'Not all,' says Debbie.

'Yeah,' he says, and throws her sister a look of disgust. He's
finished with trying to impress Debs by getting the kid rides on
the swings and tuppenny chews; she's served her purpose and
now she's nothing more than an annoyance. 'We can go up
Chapman's barn, if you like,' he offers.

Debbie sneaks a look around her to hide her excitement.
Chapman's barn is one of the village teens' most fabled places,
somewhere the grown-ups rarely go. She knows that Chapman's
barn has been the venue of many of Darren Walker's conquests;
that girls older and more experienced than she is have been pinioned by him on its dusty straw bales. And because she knows it,
the very mention of the place is enough to produce a musky,
salty taste in her mouth. She knows this will be a brief and feral
coupling; that it will be accompanied by no protestations of
affection or even much effort to ensure any satisfaction for herself, but the thought of Darren Walker's thick, stubby cock inside
her, of the scratch of straw on her buttocks and the breathless-
ness as he crushes her carelessly beneath him makes her weak
with lust, impatient of anything that will get between her and its
satisfaction. She's sixteen years old, been on the pill for a year,
and it's about time she started living.

As if reading her mind, he bucks sharply against her pelvis,
making her yelp.

'What are you doing?'

Now they both speak together. 'Shut up!'

'That boy's called Darren Walker,' announces Chloe. 'Mum
said you wasn't to go near him.'

They break apart, sit angrily side by side on the bench and
glare at her.

'You don't know nothing about it, Chloe Francis,' says
Debbie. 'You best keep your mouth shut or you'll be sorry.'

'Take me home,' says Chloe. 'I'm hungry.'

Darren groans. 'Fuck sake,' he says. 'Can't you get rid of her?'

'You know I can't.'

'How old is she anyway?'

'I'm four,' says Chloe.

'Well, fuck sake,' he says again.

'I'm thirsty,' says Chloe. 'I want my dinner.'

Darren reaches into the inside pocket of his jacket and produces a single cigarette. He lights it with an Army Surplus Zippo and sits there looking up at the sun, flipping the lid open and closed. 'Don't give me one then,' says Debbie.

'You're not old enough to smoke,' he replies.

'Am too,' says Debbie. 'Have been since April.'

Darren takes a long, long drag, holds it deep in his lungs, joint-style, and exhales a thick stream of smoke into the air. 'Sixteen, huh? Not jailbait no more then.'

Debbie doesn't know whether to laugh or snarl, so she settles for something in between. Chloe glares at them from her perch on the verge, digging the heels of her sandals over and over into the turf to expose a pair of brown earth runnels. She's a pretty child – fair in a pink, formless fashion, dimples in her cheeks – but she looks like a grubby hobgoblin right now, glowering under the hedge. 'I'm telling Mum on you,' she says.

'Telling her what?' says Debbie. 'Who d'you think she'll believe, anyway?'

Christ, she thinks. I'm sixteen. I'm starting work in two months. This should be the best summer ever, and instead I'm stuck being a babysitter because Mum couldn't be bothered to take her on the bus to Chipping Norton. Shouldn't have had another kid if she couldn't be bothered to look after it.

Darren takes a small curl from behind her ear and twists it round his finger. She feels that small rush of liquid lust once more.

'I want a drink,' says Chloe. 'Take me home.'

'Why don't you just go home?' asks Darren nastily. 'Go on. Shoo.'

Chloe looks stubborn.

'Bloody hell,' says Debbie. 'I'll give you ten p.'

'You haven't got ten p,' says Chloe doubtfully.

'Yeah, but I do,' says Darren grandly. His erection is painful in his drainpipes and he's afraid they might cut off his circulation altogether. 'Here. You can buy a Mars Bar.'

'Don't like Mars Bars.'

'I don't care,' he says, and throws the coin at her. 'Just bugger off, will you?'

Chloe is torn between crying and collecting the money, so she does both. 'I'm telling Mum,' she assures her sister again. 'You said bugger.'

'Didn't,' says Debbie. 'He did. Now, you go straight home after the shop, yeah?'

Chloe unbundles her anorak from under the hedge and starts to slowly put it on. 'Come on,' says Debbie. 'Seriously. I'm going to have to start throwing stones in a minute.' Darren's hand has slipped under her skirt and a single finger is working its way inside her knicker elastic.

Chloe starts to plod up the road. Gets about twenty yards, then stops uncertainly. 'I don't know the way,' she says.

'Gaaaah!' Debbie's eyes roll back into her head with frustration. 'Chloe! We come up this way every day! Just go, will ya?'

Chloe's eyes fill with tears. 'I don't want to! Mum said you was to look after me!'

'Oh Christ,' says Debbie, defeated. 'Well, you can't keep the ten p.'

'Chrissake,' says Darren, and slings himself across the bench temperamentally to change the pressure on his 'nads. 'We've got to get rid of her,' he says. 'I'm not taking her with us.'

'Yes, but, Darren,' says Debbie, torn. 'Mum'll rip me to shreds if anything happens to her.'

'Oh yeah – Mummy,' says Darren, and turns his back on her.

Silence. They can hear how summer-sleepy the village is; can hear the cattle lowing all the way down at the home farm.

'You're just a kid anyway,' he says sulkily. 'Don't know what I was thinking.'

Debbie heaves a sigh. She hates her sister, hates her mother. *This is meant to be* my *summer. They're all so selfish.*

She gazes up the road despairingly, feeling the moment slip away. *He's the sexiest boy I'll ever go with,* she thinks. *And bloody Chloe . . .*

Two small figures round the corner from the war memorial. One sturdy, brown-haired and wearing red, the other willowy in comparison, and blond.

'Oi, Darren,' she says. 'Isn't that your sister?'

Chapter Thirty-three

She's crying before she sits down. Humiliating, gopping, over-whelming tears that stream from her eyes and her nose and the corners of her wide-open mouth and fill her with shame. She searches in her pockets – they've taken her bag off her at the front desk – for a snot-rag, but finds nothing. Turns in appeal to the constable-chaperon who stands impassively by the door and realises that she'll get no help there.

They've broken his nose. His face is a mass of purple-yellow bruises, but it's still him, staring at her unblinking across the table. It's all still there: the fine, noble bone structure, the rich dark hair and the lock that curls down over his high, intelligent forehead, the strong hands with their long artist's fingers. His face suddenly breaks into that wide blue social smile with which he keeps people at arm's length.

'Hey, babe,' he says. 'I was beginning to think you'd forgotten all about me.'

She's so stunned that the tears stop dead. She stares at him open-mouthed – partly because of the surprise and partly because she has been unable to breathe through her nose for the past thirty hours. She didn't believe it while he was still in custody, while she wasn't allowed to see him; could still persuade herself that there had been some terrible mistake, that she'd wake up and find it had all been a dream. But now that she's here, and he's charged – with, they say, more to come –

and she can see that sunny smile, she believes it all, every word of it.

'*What?*' she asks.

The smile again, the hand reaching across the table top for hers.

'Did you bring my shirts?' he asks. 'Like I asked?'

'I ...' She's lost for words. It's as though she's visiting him at a day-spa. 'Yes,' she says. 'They're outside. I left them at the desk. They wouldn't let me bring them in.'

'That's my girl,' he says. 'I knew I could rely on you. Did you put the Elvis in there? With the embroidery?'

'Yes,' she says. Finds herself adding, as though this were a normal situation, 'And the green one. You know. The cord. You always thought that suited you.'

'You're a gem,' he says. 'A good girl.'

My God, she thinks. I don't know you at all.

'So how are you keeping?' he asks, as though she's a maiden aunt come in from Sevenoaks. 'What have you been up to? How's work?'

She wants to shout, to punch him. *What do you think I've been up to, you arsehole?* Throwing cocktail parties? I've not *been* to work. How do you think I'm going to go to work? I can't get out of the *front door*, for God's sake.

'Seen anyone? Anyone been round?'

'I ...' she blurts. 'I don't know you. I don't know who you are. I thought I knew you, but I don't.'

Vic sits back, presses his hands palms-down on the tabletop and raises his eyebrows. 'What do you want me to say?'

She feels another fit of weeping sweep over her. It's like a hurricane – destructive, unstoppable. 'You – oh my *God*, Vic. What have you *done*?'

'I dunno,' he says calmly. 'What have *you* done, Amber?'

She wants to slap him, add her marks to those of his assailants. But she knows she'll get halfway across the table before their minder pulls her back. Now he's safely locked up,

Vic is protected. Amber's got the curtains closed; she's got the phone pulled out from the wall and the mobile on mute; she's living on tins and pulses because the trip to the car, let alone the supermarket, is already a terrifying rat-run of accusation and flash photography – and he's still, in theory at least, only a suspect.

He is studying her the way a scientist studies a bug, fascinated by her display of emotion as though it were some unusual mating ritual. It's like being stabbed with an icicle. He isn't bothered at all; doesn't look as though any of this – the crowd, the charges, the trouble he's in – is affecting him. Is this the way I looked? she wonders. I was frozen with fear. Maybe I was like this too; maybe that was why they hated me so much. If I'd cried, or struggled, or had hysterics ... would that have made them see me differently?

'My God, Vic. Those poor women.'

Vic tuts and rolls his eyes, as though she's sentimentalising insects.

'Don't you feel anything at all? My God. Five of them. Or seven? Don't you feel *anything* about what you've done?'

The eye-roll again. 'Fuck sake,' he says. 'I can't believe they're still counting that old bag on Fore Street in with the rest. It's a fucking insult. Did you ever see me covered in blood? Did you?'

She gulps, hauls air down her frozen throat. Realises it's the first breath she's taken since he started talking.

'Fucking cheek,' he says. 'As if.'

She stares for a moment.

'They're saying I must have known. I can't get out of the house.'

'Well you're here now, aren't you?'

She drinks in the look of mild entertainment on his face, understands that this – this flaw in his character, this inability to empathise, to put himself in someone else's shoes – is, in fact, one of the things that made their relationship work, after its own

260

fashion: that she never had to deal with viscous, frightening, dangerous emotion. Emotion has signified pain her whole life; and Vic, with his distanced, empty soul, seemed like an oasis in the desert when she stumbled across him. I am empty myself, she thinks. A killer too. No wonder I thought he was a kindred spirit.

'Why me?' she asks suddenly. 'Why did you choose me?'

The smile again. Playful. Candid. 'Oh, I think you know.'

'I don't. I really don't.'

'Oh, Annabel,' he says, reprovingly. 'I think you do.'

For a second she thinks she's misheard him; that her distress and the similarity of the two names has made her ears play tricks on her. Then she sees his open smile and knows that he knows. That's he's always known. That he's waiting for the gloating pleasure of seeing the knowledge dawn that the lie she's been living is not the lie she'd thought.

The room swims. 'How long have you known?' she asks. No point denying it. Not when he's looking at her like that.

His smile widens now he's extracted his confession. 'I thought you were familiar before,' he says. 'I used to see you about, and think, I know that woman. Like attracting like, I guess. But I'll tell you when I knew for sure. It was when I saw you with the kid. Bending over that kid. It all became blindingly clear when I saw that.'

'The kid?'

He nods, prompting. 'You know. The kid.'

She knows what he's talking about. Knows exactly, because it was the first time she noticed Vic – really noticed him, not simply enjoyed his good looks. The first day that something passed between them – the first day, she realises now, that she read him wrong. It was back when she worked the day shift, and some kid who'd ignored the rollercoaster's height restriction had slid free of the safety bars, flown off on a bend and plummeted head-first into the side of the shooting gallery. She was standing nearby with her trash bag full of discarded drinks cartons, heard the sound of splintering wood and the rising screams for what felt like an age before she took in what had happened. The kid's head had split open like a watermelon. It was obvious that he was dead, or soon going to be.

'Oh my God,' she says. Glances over her shoulder at the copper to see if he's noticed. But though she knows he must be listening, he shows no sign that he has any clue as to what they're talking about, or that he has any interest. Why would he?

'You were great,' says Vic. 'You were so great. So calm. Like nothing could get through to you. That was when I knew for sure.'

Someone's turned the air-conditioning on full-blast. The cold crawls over her skin like leeches.

'Was that what it was like the first time, Annabel?' he asks. 'I always wanted to know. I was just waiting till you wanted to ...' he rakes his fingers through the air to look like inverted commas, 'share.'

The child lay like a broken doll, half propped against a broken wall whose garish red and green stripes were smirched with blood, his jaw opening and closing automatically as though he were being operated by strings. Amber dropped her bin bag and started towards him through the crowd, the old familiar feeling of icy calm washing over her. Even from here, and above the screams of the crowd around her, she could hear the rising wail of the kid's mother, the feckless bint who'd finally learned that sometimes rules are there for a reason, still strapped into her seat on the coaster, forced to sit out the corkscrew, the loop-the-loop, the whole of the rest of her ride, while her offspring leaked white matter from what was once his head. His eyes stared straight ahead. He seemed to see Amber as she approached; seemed, strangely, to recognise her.

Her hearing changed focus. Distantly she registered someone throwing up, sparking a chain reaction. Walked, unaffected, through a morass of gagging, sobbing, screaming people, and heard it all as background. All she could hear clearly was the kid's voice: the nonsense syllables that spilled from his tongue as his mangled brain struggled to function. She dropped to her knees beside him: the two of them in a pool of quiet, his eyes fixed on hers.

She was wearing an oversized belted cardie that came down to her knees; it was the beginning of the season and the weather had yet to warm up. She gazed into his rapidly darkening eyes as she sat back and stripped it off. Shaved head, puffy arms, grey cheeks as full as a hamster's. He was wearing a Liverpool strip: she remembers the horrid blue and yellow nylon, the Carlsberg logo, the dark damp patch that grew and grew as cerebrospinal fluid dribbled down his neck.

'Oh look,' she said, as kindly as she could, 'you've got cold.'

She draped the cardie over him – she never saw it again once the ambulance had taken him away – and took his hand; felt the weakening pulse, knew that he was dying. 'It's OK,' she said. 'I'm here. I'm with you.'

'Ak-haaaaaaaaaa,' said the boy. He couldn't have been more than eight. What a way to go. Rides and candyfloss and – death. She wondered, randomly, what he had had for breakfast that morning. A last meal of Coco Pops and milk, eggs and soldiers, half a pack of Hob Nobs?

She tore her eyes away for a moment, looked over her shoulder. A couple of hundred gawpers now: the sort of people who slow down to look at car crashes. Faces wide-eyed and full of speculation as they formed the words to make the anecdotes. Poor little mite. Blood everywhere, people screaming, and there was nothing we could do.

'Ambulance,' she cried out hoarsely. 'Has anyone called an ambulance?'

*

Vic suddenly bursts out laughing. 'Oh my God,' he says, imitating her. She gapes, recoils.

'You didn't know,' he says. 'All this time you didn't know. Oh my God, you thought *you* were keeping a secret from *me*!'

She can feel a scalpel-edge of panic slice at her skin. They're not alone. He can't – he *mustn't* – carry on like this. 'Don't,' she pleads. 'Vic, don't—'

He's tickled pink. 'Oh, don't worry, *Ambel*,' he says, the mispronunciation deliberate and obvious only to her, 'your secret's safe with me. It's just – hah! – all this time I've been thinking we didn't talk about it because we didn't need to. Because we understood. And those presents I've been leaving you ...'

'Presents?'

'Oh, come on,' he says. 'You know.'

And she does. She should have seen it before. Two of those bodies were left where she would find them, and it was only pure chance that prevented her being the first upon the second. And his questions. Those little probing, gloating, prurient enquiries as to how she'd felt, what she'd seen.

'No,' she says. 'No, no, no. *No.*'

Vic stepped forward, his face a portrait of calm under pressure. 'Done,' he said. 'It's on its way.'

The kid began to flap his hand in hers, dragging her eyes back. Drool pooling at the corner of his mouth. Some pointless urge to preserve his dignity drove her to dab at it with the sleeve of the cardigan. The syllables had deteriorated, now, to formless gurgles. A woman sobbed hysterically in the crowd. She noticed it; thought, with irritation: If you can't handle it, just *go away*. Do something useful, or fuck off. Even in a situation like this, there are people who think that it's all about *them*. Who parade their distress for others' benefit to demonstrate their greater sensitivity.

As if he could read her thoughts, Vic turned and spoke over his shoulder. 'Can someone take that woman away please? She's not helping.'

A stir. A ripple of comprehension. Someone led the woman away and a straggle of gawpers, chastened, followed. Vic knelt down beside her. 'How is he?' he asked.

Amber shook her head, because words wouldn't come. Held the child's hand and felt the pulse flutter, weaken.

He came closer, put his face next to the child's. 'Hello, mate,' he said. 'You've had an accident. Don't worry. The ambulance is on its way.'

Then he stared into his eyes, as though drinking in the last of his life.

'You thought I was your hero?' asks Vic. 'Oh, Amber. I'd thought better of you than that.'

She feels sick. Sweaty. Afraid.

'I noticed you noticing me, you know,' he says. 'That day. It wasn't just me recognising you. You recognised me back. I saw it. That was the start of everything, wasn't it? When you noticed me.'

The smile flicks back on like a searchlight.

'Yeah,' he says. 'That was a good one. I was a bit late to the party, but it was fun.'

Chapter Thirty-four

Despite the fact that they lead down to the seafront, the botanical gardens are almost always empty, mostly because big signs at the gates forbid alcohol, barbecues and ball games. The only people other than Martin himself who ever come here are pensioners with foil-wrapped sandwiches and the odd mother with toddlers, though the formal flowerbeds and lack of swings don't make it particularly attractive to them. He likes to come here to think – and, after what he's read in the *Tribune*, he has a lot of thinking to do today.

He takes his usual seat, on a bench on a hummock of earth that raises him high enough to see over the hedges that surround the garden and watch the comings and goings without being forced to participate.

And the first thing he sees is Kirsty Lindsay, hurrying from the direction of town, her head bowed. He almost jumps out of his skin. The bloody cheek of it. She's the last person he expected to see. She shouldn't come here ever again. Not after what she's done to his town; what she's done to him. Then he thinks: If I can see her, she can see me, and ducks down on his seat to take himself out of her line of vision. An old couple, toddling along below him, look up at the sudden movement and cross to the other side of the path, as though the extra five feet will act as a barrier against lunacy.

He gives them a big wide smile to assure them that they're

safe. It seems instead to make them more afraid. The woman clutches the man's wool-wrapped arm and they march purposefully towards the nearest exit.

He waits until they've passed, then pops his head up to see where she's got to. Registers with amazement that she's covered a couple of hundred yards in the twenty seconds he's been down, and is very nearly at the fence. She's not looking around her. Seems to be buried in thought. She crosses Park Road, reaches the fence and swings left towards the entrance. My God, she's coming in here, he thinks. Stoops down once more and scuttles for the cover of the hydrangea bushes behind him.

Through his screen of heavy foliage, he watches as she turns in through the gate and starts to walk along the path. She slows her pace a little now she's off the road, but still seems blind to her surroundings. She seems to be having trouble breathing. Certainly, her chest is heaving like a character in a Victorian melodrama. Intrigued, he creeps round as she circles his mound, and watches her progress. She does a full circuit of the park – it doesn't take long, as it's barely bigger than one of those London residential squares – then flings herself down on a bench as though she's simply run out of puff.

She does some strange things. Holds her hands out in front of her and stares at them. They seem to be shaking. Then she puts them up to either side of her forehead and rocks back and forth like a child's toy. Something's upset her, he thinks. Good. See how she likes it. Gingerly, he comes down the mound on the far side and works his way along behind the gardener's hut to where a big clump of rhododendrons looms darkly, covering him until he's within hearing distance.

She's already on the phone. Her voice sounds high and weak; different from when he last heard it. As though she's had a shock. As though she's filled with panic and doing her ineffective best to control it.

'Hi, Minty,' she says. 'It's Kirsty Lindsay. Is there any chance Jack's out of conference yet? Damn. OK. Can you get him to call me the minute he is? Yes, my mobile. I'm down in Whitmouth. Yup, OK. Thanks.'

She puts the phone on the seat and resumes her rocking. Wraps her arms round her body as though she's cold, though the sun is bright enough to show up the peeling paint on the façades in vivid detail. She gets up and moves to another bench – Martin has to shadow her movements, as quietly as he can, to keep himself behind his cover – in the shade of a stately beech tree. Sits back and closes her eyes, covers them with her palm as though she has a headache.

The sound of her ringtone shatters the quiet. She snatches it up. 'Hello? Oh, hi, Jack. Thanks for calling back. Yes, not yet, but I think it'll definitely happen today. He's still only charged with the stuff from Saturday right now, but I'd say it was ninety-nine per cent they're going to do him for the murders. Name? Yes. Victor Cantrell. Yup. Same guy as last week. Works the dodgems at the theme park. No, not officially, yet. They're holding off till they do the other charges. But half the town seems to know it's him, and the wife just turned up to visit. So yes, I'm pretty sure. I'll write it so you can drop the name in later if they announce it. Yeah. Look, the thing is, I've got to go home. Sorry. I don't think I'll be late filing, but I ... can't stay here ...'

He hears her pause. She's rethinking what she's just said, he thinks. Didn't mean it to come out like that. 'I mean, I've got to get home. Childcare, I'm afraid. Yeah, sorry. Jim's working in town this week and Soph's gone down with something. Looks like flu. She's really ill. Yuh, her school just called. No. Like I said, he's in town. It's got to be me. I'm sorry.'

She's lying through her teeth. He can tell because she wrings her hands, the phone tucked between her shoulder and her ear, as she speaks. 'Yeah, I know. But it's not even noon yet. It won't take me more than an hour to file once I'm back. But I don't have any alternative. I'm sorry. And Dave's on the case tomorrow anyway.'

She goes quiet, and listens. When she speaks, it's in a small voice. 'I know. Yes, I know, Jack. I've got a couple of contacts down at the scene and I know they'll call me if anything happens. And it'll turn up on AP in seconds anyway. I know it's not ideal, but it's the best I can do. I can't just leave her in the sick bay. And Jack? I don't think I'm going to be able to get out for the rest of the week. If you've got any pieces I can do on the phone, maybe …? No, OK. I understand. I'll call Features. Hopefully they'll have something. Yes, I know. But you've got kids yourself, haven't you?'

Another silence as Jack speaks. Martin sees her blush, sees a look of exquisite pain cross her face. 'Yes,' she says, 'I understand. No later than four. And I'll give you a call next week when—'

She pulls the phone away from her head and looks at it. Jack has clearly hung up. She opens her bag to put it away, then sits up, alert, and looks towards town.

Martin looks too. He's been so engrossed in Kirsty's conversation that he's not noticed an approaching hubbub. But it's unmistakable now. Voices, calling, and many scuffling feet. He turns within his cover and looks towards the top gate. Hears a name separate itself from the cacophony, then hears it over and over. 'Amber! Amber! This way, Amber!'

She's half walking, half running as she enters the park, preceded by a dozen men in waxed jackets who run backwards, bump into each other and shout her name. Every now and then one breaks loose and scurries a few yards forwards, stops and holds his camera high in the air above his head, pointing down at the approaching mob. Behind, another knot of followers, all calling her name. 'Amber! Amber! Amber!'

Amber Gordon is white and shaking, and holds her handbag up in front of her face like a shield. Stumbles forward like someone who has suddenly lost her sight. She doesn't speak. Just staggers on, moving the bag from side to side in a futile attempt to block the cameras. She too has a phone clamped to her ear, though Martin can't make out who she might be talking to.

They come nearer. He can make out more of the words now. 'How are you feeling, Amber?' 'Do you have anything to say to the families?' 'How was Victor when you saw him? What did he say to you?' 'What does this mean to you, Amber? Did you have any idea?' 'Has it come as a shock? What are you going to do now?'

So it *is*. It's Vic Cantrell. He's heard the name half a dozen times, in the shops, on the Corniche, in the café where he bought his breakfast, as well as from Lindsay's lips just now. And if ever there was proof, the sight of Amber Gordon and her sea of followers is it. He thrills at the sight. How are the mighty fallen, he thinks. That's all you have to do, isn't it? Wait for long enough and they all come tumbling down, one by one by one.

He glances over at Kirsty Lindsay and sees that she's left the bench. But she's not done what he would have expected. She should be running up to join her colleagues, but instead she's doing something very strange. She's clambering into the earthy flowerbed, over the roots of the beech tree, crushing the leaves of left-to-rest bluebells as she goes. She reaches the trunk of the tree and puts her hands on it. Works her way round it and hides herself behind, in the shadow of the hedge. Martin frowns. What the hell is she up to?

The front-running photographers are almost parallel with him now, their faces lit up with the thrill of the chase. It's like watching a fox at bay. Amber's hair is wild and her lips are pulled back in a snarl – rage? Fear? – that shows her teeth all the way to the molars. For a second he almost feels sorry for her, but then he remembers the humiliation, the cold way she saw him off when he called Jackie, the shock when he uncovered her link with Kirsty Lindsay, and the pity vanishes. She's getting what she deserves.

She stops stock-still and tries to appeal to their better natures. 'Please!' she cries. 'Please! Leave me alone! I don't know anything! I don't have anything to say!'

Silence hangs in the air for one, two, three seconds, then the baying begins anew. 'Where are you off to, Amber?' 'How did you find out?' 'Tell us how you're feeling!' 'Are you standing by him?'

Amber takes a deep breath and lets out a scream. 'Leave me alone!'

She breaks into a faltering run. Looks like there is little strength left in her legs. The chase continues, past Martin's hiding place, past Kirsty Lindsay concealed in the shadows, past benches and bins and flowerbeds. She comes to the side gate and shoves her way through, staggers up Park Road towards the seafront. I'll bet she's going to Funnland, thinks Martin. That's where I'd go. At least they've got security of sorts there.

Kirsty steps back out on to the path and stands for a moment staring after her bloodhound colleagues, her mouth taut, her face unreadable. Then she wheels on her heel and starts to walk, quickly, in the direction of the town gate. She's up to something, thinks Martin. Anybody would think she's trying to keep away from Amber. That she's scared of something.

He waits till he's sure she's not going to look back, then comes out from behind the rhododendrons to follow her.

Chapter Thirty-five

Home. Sanctuary. Walls that enfold and protect. A barrier against the world outside, the place you long for in the storm. Kirsty sits in her quiet dining room, the *Sun* spread out on the table before her and sunlight falling through the window to her right. Wonders about Amber. Wonders if she's home too, or if she's been driven out to some anonymous motel room, some friend's spare bedroom, some safe-house for the relatives of the loathed.

The *Sun*'s gone front-page with Whitmouth. A huge, grainy colour photo – in the absence of a court appearance by the man himself – of Amber in the park, dark glasses covering the upper half of her face, a cream mac tightly belted. A phone clamped to her ear and her teeth bared in the age-old primate expression of distress. But that's not how the paper interprets it. Or chooses to, anyway. There's not an editor in the world too green to tell the difference, but that doesn't mean they'll go with the truth when there's righteous outrage to be drummed up. NOT A CARE IN THE WORLD, says the headline.

Kirsty scans on. Heartless Amber Gordon takes a seaside stroll, chatting and laughing on her mobile phone, mindless of the pain of victims' families.

Shit, she thinks. They've turned her into Sonia Sutcliffe.

She reads on.

The cleaner, wife of Seaside Strangler suspect Victor Cantrell, dropped off a bag of treats for her husband at Whitmouth Police Station yesterday morning and spent some time closeted away with him before emerging. Amazingly, she then walked on through the town to spend the day at the Funnland theme park on the beach. Families riding the famous rollercoaster unawares would have been shocked to know that they had such a notorious figure in their midst.

Works there, thinks Kirsty. She works there, for God's sake. And you know it. You all know it. You were all making up quotes from her ten days ago when she found that body.

Cantrell is awaiting charges over a series of murders in the town. For Gordon, though, it's business as usual. **See page 5**.

Kirsty opens the paper, finds the rest of the story, accompanied by a smaller, older picture of Amber and Victor together on the beach. 'Said a neighbour, Shaunagh Betts, 21,' it continues:

'It's amazing. You'd have thought she'd have some shame. She's always been weird – a snob, always interfering in other people's business as though she was better than the rest of us – but the way she goes on, you would have thought she was completely innocent.' Holding her daughter, Tiffany, 2, tightly, she continued: 'If it was me, I'd be on my knees apologising to the people round here, but she behaves like she's done nothing wrong. I can't believe I've been bringing my kids up next door to people like that all this time. What if something had happened? I would never have forgiven myself.'

Another neighbour, Janelle Boxer, 67, said: 'She always treated him really badly. They kept themselves to themselves most of the time, but sometimes you'd hear her having a go at him, really belittling him. I heard her doing it only the other day, right out in the garden where anyone could hear. It's hard to believe she didn't know anything. She must have noticed something. Some of those girls fought back, and there must have been marks on him. I know no one wants to believe they're living with a monster, but there must have been more to it than that.'

Cantrell is expected in front of Whitmouth magistrates tomorrow, charged with the murders of Nicole Ponsonby, Keisha Brown, Hannah Hardy and Stacey Plummer, and the attempted murder of a young woman, whose identity we are protecting out of concern for her recovery, on Friday night. The women's bodies were found dumped heartlessly in spots around the south-coast resort after being attacked and violated. More charges, related to unsolved murders in the town in previous seasons, are expected later in the week.

Gordon (pictured with Cantrell, above, at a seaside barbecue earlier this year), meanwhile, is unrepentant. 'I've not done anything,' she told our reporter yesterday. 'Why can't you just leave me alone?'

In bold type beneath the story, a puff for another: **My nights in strangler's lair: centre pages.**

Kirsty stares at the picture and recognises Victor Cantrell as the man who rescued, then abused, her that night in DanceAttack. God, she thinks. Was it him all along? Did I finger Rat Man in the *Trib* when I really *was* being followed by the genuine article?

She feels sick: ashamed of her colleagues and their ability to use words to throw any light they choose to on a situation. Innuendo, allusion and false connection: the staples of a media that's still awaiting facts. She feels ashamed of herself for having indulged the same faults in her own piece on Sunday. It's hardly the first time she's done it – you can't avoid it when an editor's had an idea and is paying you to establish it as fact – but she doesn't think she's done it by mistake before.

God, we're all such liars, she thinks. Is that what made me decide to do this for a living, because I'm the biggest liar of all?

I lie to my husband, lie to my children, every single day, and it's only going to get worse. Even after a quarter of a century, Bel and I are linked by an unbreakable thread, and I can no more forget about it than I can tell the truth.

She looks down at the paper. Wonders what other delights it has in store.

Blessed turns up with food and a copy of the paper, her face solemn with sympathy. Amber almost doesn't let her in, but she knocks and shouts for so long that eventually she peeps through the curtains and sees her there among the crowd. She opens the door and a photographer immediately slips a foot into the gap, hoping to prise it open long enough to get an interior shot. Maybe a picture of Amber looking dishevelled: the woman who spent so much time in her dressing gown she drove her man to murder.

There's a scuffle, and Blessed starts haranguing the man in ringing evangelical tones. And then she's inside, and stabbing at the foot with an umbrella, shouting, 'You will not pass! You will not *pass*!' Mary-Kate and Ashley yap furiously by her ankles as she slams the door and turns to Amber, brushing herself off as though she's just emerged from a sandstorm. 'There,' she says. 'That was easy.'

Amber bursts into tears.

Blessed puts down her shopping bags and gives her a hug. The first hug Amber can remember receiving in years. Vic was never a hugger: too keen, she understands now, on carrying his embraces through to death. It makes her cry harder.

'I'm sorry,' says Blessed. 'I would have come before, but you weren't answering your telephone and I thought maybe you'd gone away. Until I heard you'd been at Funnland.'

'No,' says Amber. 'No, I've been here all the time.'

'I brought you some food,' says Blessed. 'I didn't know what you liked, so I got a bit of everything. You must tell me what you need, and I'll bring it.'

Amber sniffs and wipes her eyes. 'Maybe some ... I've run out of dog food. They're living on tuna and toast.' She'd really like a bottle of whisky, but knows it's too much to ask of a woman who thinks that drinkers go to hell.

'OK,' says Blessed. They carry the bags through to the kitchen. Baked beans. A cauliflower. Some plantains. A bacon joint. Chocolate mousse. Wonderloaf. Peanut butter. Cheddar. Some tomatoes. Some chicken nuggets, which Blessed makes haste to put in the freezer compartment. Full-fat milk.

'This is ... you're so generous,' says Amber. 'Can I give you some money?'

Blessed shakes her head vehemently. 'Absolutely no. It is my duty. I cannot take money from someone who is in trouble. You must tell me what you need, and I will bring it for you, maybe tomorrow, maybe the next day. Can I make you a cup of tea?'

'No,' says Amber, 'I'll make it.'

Blessed lowers herself into a chair as Amber fills the kettle. 'How's work? What are they all saying?'

She tuts. 'The things you would expect, Amber.'

'Who's supervising?'

Blessed looks slightly uncomfortable. 'They have asked me to do it, in the hiatus. I hope that this is all right with you.'

The kettle clicks off. 'Yes. Of course. I should think you'd be good at it. You've always had an organised mind.'

A flash of teeth. 'Thank you,' says Blessed. 'Your confidence means a great deal to me.'

'Milk and sugar?'

'Yes please. Two, please. Amber?'

'Yes?'

'I have something I must show you. I was unwilling to do so, but then I thought, Perhaps she should know.'

Amber feels weak. Steadies herself against the kitchen counter. 'OK. What is it?'

*

Kirsty comes back to the table with another cup of coffee, and turns to the centre pages. A young-middle-aged blonde, plastered in make-up – thick blusher, scarlet lips – and sporting an obviously new haircut sits on a studio floor on a sheet of white background paper, weight thrown back on one hand, in high heels and a wrap dress. Her legs are crossed at the ankles.

THE LUCKIEST WOMAN ALIVE, says the headline. *Blonde tells of bizarre life inside Strangler's home*, says the strap.

A woman told of her incredible escape from the clutches of alleged Seaside Strangler Victor Cantrell yesterday. Attractive blonde Jackie Jacobs, 38, was ensnared by the womaniser's charm and spent four months secretly dating him earlier this year.

If that woman's thirty-eight, thinks Kirsty, I'm Kate Moss. And, wow: if they're only describing her as 'attractive', that stylist must be one skilled worker. There's only one step down from 'attractive' on the tabloid beauty scale, and it's the simple description of hair colour. Under the slap, Jackie Jacobs must look like a bulldog.

'I'm in shock,' said Jackie yesterday. 'I never thought, when I got involved with him, that Vic would turn out to be a cold-blooded killer. He was the most charming man I've ever met. And good-looking too. I couldn't help fancying him. He really knew how to look after himself!'

Jackie met Vic when they both worked together at the Funnland theme park on Whitmouth's seafront – Jackie as a hygiene consultant and Vic as a jack-of-all-trades working the rides. 'He was a bit rougher than what I'm used to,' says Jackie. 'I usually date men in the professions – my last partner was an IT consultant – but there was something about him that just drew me like a moth to a flame.'

Jackie knew that Vic was living with a woman who at the time she thought of as a friend – Myra Hindley lookalike Amber Gordon, a cleaner at the same park – but she was unable to stop herself from getting involved. 'It's not something I'm proud of,' she says, 'but I couldn't stop myself. Vic was so charismatic I was helpless around him. And besides, later on I realised that there was a lot more to the situation than I had thought.

'I keep thinking,' she says, 'that I should have realised at the time. It wasn't like I didn't notice that things were weird in that house. No one could fail to notice it. They hardly ever talked, and he was always out in Whitmouth's famous bars while she worked the night shift. And Vic wasn't exactly a gentle lover. You wouldn't call it romantic. Sometimes he'd just come and find me at the park and get me to perform a sex act on him in one of the rides that was closed for maintenance, or in an area that was closed to the public. He liked that: the sex acts. He'd put his hands round my neck, sometimes, and it makes me shake to think about what he must have been thinking about.'

Things took a turn for the weirder, though, when Cantrell's common-law wife began to take an interest in Jackie herself. 'I didn't think anything of it at the time,' says Jackie. 'I just thought she was being friendly. I didn't think she knew that anything was going on between me and Vic. But now I look back on it, I think there must have been more to it. But she was weird anyway. Always sticking her nose into other people's business. Controlling. Always coming up to other people at work and asking them how they *were*, like she had something on them.

'I felt uncomfortable around her, of course, because I thought I was sleeping with her man behind her back, but now I wonder if she didn't know all along. And not just about us, either.'

The piece is illustrated with more photographs. Amber and Vic at a pub table, and Jackie – a far less glamorous Jackie, she notes – standing at the entrance to the helter-skelter on the pier. The captions are gems of innuendo and twisted information. *Weird: Cantrell and Gordon enjoy a drink at the seafront*; *Innocent: Jackie in happier times with lover Cantrell. She had no idea of the secret he was hiding.*

Kirsty doesn't really understand why the paper seems to have cast Amber in the role of villain's sidekick. Probably the fact that she's given no interviews, that she's not made a PR company her first stop *en route* to Cantrell's holding cell. The reasoning of the papers, in their invention of villains and innocents, has always been a mystery to her. It's often, she suspects, something as simple as the baddie involved reminding an editor of their school bully or an unpopular politician: the 'lookalike' tag they often earn gives the game away a bit. Or there's another agenda, like the *Sun*'s fawning attempts to get the city of Liverpool to drop its fatwa twenty years after the Hillsborough disaster. Or something as basic as a story happening on a slow news day when no one wealthy has poked a prostitute. But she knows all too well what it's like to be a Celebrity of Evil.

A few months into her secret relationship with Cantrell, Jackie started having relationship problems with a man she had also been dating publicly. Gordon, however, took it upon herself to make the situation untenable. 'It wasn't anything, really. Silly stuff. I'm sure I could've handled it, but she insisted on getting involved. She took over completely.'

Gordon even insisted that Jackie move into their two-bedroomed ex-council house so she could 'keep an eye on her'. Jackie's suitor was keen to patch things up, but Gordon was having none of it. 'It was as though she didn't want me to have a boyfriend,' says Jackie. 'Now I look back on it, the whole thing was bizarre. She used to follow me everywhere.'

Jackie soon found that she wasn't allowed a moment to herself, in the house or out of it. Gordon escorted her to and from work, and even insisted on going along when she went out in the evening. 'I guess she didn't want me bumping into him,' she says. 'She wanted me all to herself. Or maybe she'd guessed about me and Vic, and wanted to keep an eye on me.'

Cantrell, meanwhile, had withdrawn and become distant. He seemed as keen to get Jackie out of his house as Gordon appeared to be to make her stay. 'I don't know what was going on between them. Maybe he was getting jealous,' says Jackie. 'There was something not right about Amber's behaviour. I think she thought I'd see it as protective, but it felt like there was more to it than that. I think she wanted control over me. I think maybe she fancied me. She certainly didn't fancy her boyfriend, from what I saw.'

There it is. The old lesbian accusation. There's not a female villain in the land who can't be made more villainous by hints of Sapphism. We've a long way to go still, thinks Kirsty.

Jackie had experienced a similar situation before, continues the piece.

When she was a teenager, an older couple seduced her into taking part in a threesome. 'I don't know what it is about me,' she laughs, 'but I've obviously got something. But after I turned Amber down and moved out of the house, she turned against me big-time. Suddenly she was always finding fault with my work, picking arguments with me, making trouble for me with management. Eventually it got so bad I had to leave. She drove me out of my job, and I'd worked there for years.'

The news of Cantrell's arrest came as a surprise. 'It was a terrible shock,' she says. 'I remember standing there in the newsagent's, shaking and shaking. I kept thinking: What if it had been me? I'd been alone with him so many times, and he'd had so many opportunities.

'I don't know why he didn't choose to kill me, but what I do know is that I'm the luckiest girl alive.'

Amber had thought there were no tears left, but they pour from her as she reads; choke her, drip on to the page. Blessed sits quietly and watches, her hands folded on the tabletop. She's not touching me, thinks Amber, because she knows I couldn't bear it. I feel dirty, betrayed and totally alone.

She opens her mouth to speak, and all that comes out is a low moan of misery.

'Oh, Amber,' says Blessed. 'I'm so sorry. I wasn't sure whether I should show you.'

'No, no,' she says. 'I was going to find out anyway. I needed to know.'

'You need to get away from this place,' says Blessed. 'Those people outside – this will kill you. Don't you have anywhere you can go?'

She shakes her head. Hopes against hope that Blessed will open her own door to her, but knows it's impossible. I don't have friends, she thinks. Thirty-seven years old, and the number of friends – real, brave, damn-the-rest-of-them friends – I've amassed is literally zero. A few friendly colleagues, like Blessed, good people who hate to see others in distress, but not one person who would go beyond the call of decency, or who will miss me when I'm gone. No friends, no family. I am still alone, after all these years.

'But surely the police …?' Blessed asks. 'This cannot be … there must be a …' she pauses as she considers the phrase, 'safe-house?'

Amber shakes her head again. Feels misery break over her like a wave. 'They sent a uniform down to stand on the door for a couple of days, but mostly because the neighbours couldn't get into their houses.'

'But Victim Support ... ?'

'Victim Support's for victims. Anyway, I've got to stay put. I have to be available for questioning.'

And because the terms of my probationary licence say I have to. I can't just go – I have to register the fact of my going. And it's the same old story every time I ring, month on month: the last officer I dealt with has left – it's department policy to keep them moving – and the person who's replaced them has no idea who I am, until they pull up my file and I hear their voice change as they realise, and then they don't know what to do and have to call me back. I may still be a high priority in the eyes of the world, but I got lost in the system years ago. Even if I tried, nothing would happen before this time next week. People like me stay put, because we don't have much choice about it. Probation aren't there to help you if you get into trouble. They're there to punish you if the trouble's your fault. A lifetime licence: it's not about supporting you, it's about keeping an eye.

Blessed looks shocked again. 'For questioning?' Amber can see the thought forming in the back of her mind. She blurts it out. 'Surely they can't think you're ... that you were involved in this?'

And now you're wondering too, thinks Amber. Before, you were on my side, all righteous indignation, but now I'm under a cloud of suspicion, even from you. She feels the cold come over her. The old, old coping mechanism.

'No,' she says. 'And Blessed? I'm not.' She pushes herself back from the table, goes to the sink to start washing up. Dishes have piled up on the draining board. I don't know how, she thinks. I don't remember eating.

'No!' stumbles Blessed. 'No, that wasn't what I meant at all. No, I—'

'Don't worry, Blessed,' she says. 'It's only natural. I lived with the man, after all. I could be Rose West for all you know.'

'No,' protests Blessed. 'No, I wasn't thinking that.'

'Everybody's thinking that,' says Amber, and the tears come again. Rage more than sadness.

Her phone vibrates. Holding tightly to the edge of the sink for support while she struggles to regain her composure, she ignores it.

'Are you going to answer?' asks Blessed.

She shakes her head. 'It'll be another journalist. That's all it's been since Saturday.'

'Not always,' corrects Blessed.

'No,' she says. 'No, I'm sorry.'

'Would you like me to answer it?'

Amber shrugs. Blessed picks up the phone on the final ring.

Kirsty doesn't really know what to say, just that she has to say it. She's expecting the answerphone, and is surprised when a real person picks up. A low, rich voice; the careful, enunciated grammar of central Africa. 'Amber Gordon's telephone?'

'Oh, hi,' she croaks, self-conscious and afraid of letting out too much information. 'Is she there?'

'Can I ask who is calling, please?' asks the woman.

'Um ...' She is momentarily flummoxed. Will she remember my now-name? Which should I use? 'Kirsty Lindsay,' she says eventually.

'Kirsty Lindsay,' repeats the woman, and pauses. Then: 'And what is it about?'

'I – I just wanted to see if she was OK,' she says, half honestly.

'Yes, she's fine,' says the woman. 'Would you like me to take a message?'

'I – can't I speak to her?'

'No,' says the woman. 'I'm sorry, but she can't come to the phone at the moment. If you would like to leave a message, I will ...'

A rustle, then the sound of the handset changing ears. Amber's voice, unfriendly, defensive. 'What? I suppose you thought you'd be able to get a story?'

'No!' she protests. 'No, Amber! I—'

'I saw you, you know,' says Amber. 'Outside the police station. Out there with your *buddies*.'

'I was ... yes. It's my job. I wasn't exactly expecting it to be you who turned up.'

'Some job. Nice. So now what? I suppose you want an *exclusive*?' The emphasis of the word is sarcastic, resentful, the cynicism acidic.

'I ... no. Of course not. I'm gone. I've packed up and come home. I went the moment I saw you.'

'Good. Hooray. Bully for you.'

'I'm sorry, Bel.' She uses the name unthinkingly as she tries to back away from the conversation. 'This was a mistake. I thought maybe I could ... I don't know ...'

'Fuck off,' says Amber. 'I've got enough of your kind camped outside my door right now to last a bloody lifetime. Christ, Jade. What on earth made you think it would be *nice* to be a journalist?'

'I ...' says Kirsty, shocked back to her senses by the careless use of her old name, 'I'm not being a journalist right now, Amber. I'm not calling as a journalist, I'm calling as a—'

The voice cuts across her, full of contempt. 'As a friend? Was that what you were going to say? A friend?'

'Y-yes.' She feels small, contemptible.

A sound of derision. 'Do me a favour,' says Amber. 'We're not friends. We only knew each other for one solitary day, you silly bitch. One day. And see where that got me.'

1.45 p.m.

The shop is closed, the roller-blinds pulled down. It's Wednesday, so it's early closing.

Chloe starts up a childish wail when she realises that she's getting no sweets, no drink, and rubs at her eyes as though they are full of smoke.

'Shhh,' says Bel. The sound sets her teeth on edge, for it's the same tone with which her sister Miranda attracts attention – attention that usually, one way or another, results in Bel being punished.

'There's no point in doing that,' says Jade, more pragmatically. 'It's not going to make any difference, is it?'

'Want to go home,' wails Chloe. 'I want my mummy!'

'Come on,' says Jade. 'We'll take you back to your sister.'

Chloe, as puce as the hood that wraps her head, hangs behind as they silently retrace their steps.

They've both sort of known, of course, that Debbie and Darren won't be there when they return to the bench, but it doesn't stop Jade from swearing out loud when she finds it empty. 'Bloody fucking Norah,' she shouts. 'That bloody Darren!'

'Where've they gone?' asks Bel.

'I don't bloody know, do I?' snaps Jade.

Chloe bursts into tears again. 'Waaaah!' she bellows. 'I want my mummy!'

'Shut up!' shouts Jade. 'It's not my bloody fault, is it?'

'What are we going to do?' asks Bel.

Jade frowns, thinking. 'Well we can't leave her here, can we?'

'I don't know ...' says Bel. 'It's not our fault, is it?' she repeats hopefully.

'Yes, but,' says Jade, 'it will be *our* fault, won't it?'

'Uh,' agrees Bel, 'I suppose it will. Should we ask a grown-up?'

Jade imitates her, nastily. She's hot and hungry and thirsty herself, and doesn't want to hear any more rubbish. 'Should we ask a grown-up?'

Bel colours and shuts up. Chloe sits down on the tarmac, feet in front of her like a plastic dolly. 'We can't leave her here,' says Jade decisively. 'Anybody could come along. You never heard of stranger danger?'

'Well, what do we do with her?'

'Take her home, I suppose,' says Jade.

'D'you know where she lives?'

'Yeah,' says Jade. 'Down Bourne End.'

'But that's the other end of the village!'

'Have you got any better suggestions?'

Bel is silent. Of course she hasn't. She just wishes she'd not got mixed up in this in the first place.

Jade crouches by the crying child and tries to look into her face. 'Come on, Chloe,' she says. 'Up you get.'

Chloe just cries louder; adds a slap to Jade's face to punctuate her howls. 'OW!' shouts Jade. Loses her temper and starts to drag at the kid's arms. 'We're bloody taking you home, you little cow! Come on! Get bloody UP! Come on, Bel. Help me, will you?'

Between the two of them, they get Chloe to her feet. She dangles between them by her armpits, but refuses to put the soles of her shoes on the ground. 'Oh, for God's sake,' says Jade.

They drag her along the road. The sun beats down, and even though there are two of them, she's made a dead weight of herself and seems to weigh as much as a small bullock. The three hundred yards to the gates of the school take ten minutes to cover, and all three, by the time they get there, are wringing with sweat.

'Come on, you selfish little cow,' pants Jade. Her heart is

pounding and she feels like steam is about to burst from her eye-balls.

'Leave me alone!' screams Chloe. 'Put me down.'

Jade loses her temper. Hurls the child on to the ground and shouts: 'Bugger it! All right, I bloody well will then!'

'Help!' shouts Chloe. 'Help!'

A voice, behind them. 'What are you doing?'

The two girls look up, surprised to find themselves in any sort of company. The Good Woman of the Flower Committee stands there, holding her basket, hand on the door handle of a turquoise Toyota. 'None of your business,' says Jade.

'It certainly is my business,' says the woman, 'when I see two big girls like you bullying a child like that. I've a good mind to take you straight down to your mother,' she says to Bel.

'Can't,' pants Bel. 'She's not there.'

'We're taking her home, not bullying her,' says Jade, 'Mrs Nosy-Parker.' Then has a flash of inspiration. 'Don't you recog-nise her sister?' she asks. She knows that Bel's half-sister is close to Chloe's age; and the furious beetroot face, half-hidden by the hood, is unrecognisable really. 'She's having a tantrum, 'cause the shop was shut.'

The woman looks doubtful.

'She's not my sister!' bawls Chloe.

'Half-sister,' says Bel, picking up the theme and riffing on it. 'Everybody knows that.'

'Get off me!'

Jade turns away from the woman and glares at Chloe. 'Well, bloody walk then,' she snaps. 'Then we won't have to carry you, will we?'

'And why don't you have a grown-up with you?' asks Mrs Nosy-Parker.

'We do,' says Bel. 'Romina's at the garage. She'll be along in a minute.'

'What's she done to her knees?' says the woman.

Both girls look down, surprised. Somewhere along the way,

Chloe's knees have dangled along the roadway. They are a mess of oil and blood and grass stains. 'She's bleeding, look,' says the woman.

The girls shrug and start to bat at the cuts, as though they'll just brush off if they use enough force. Chloe shrieks and bats back with clenched fists.

Mrs Nosy-Parker checks her watch. 'I'm meant to be over at Great Barrow in five minutes,' she says.

'It's OK,' says Bel. 'We'll get her home.'

'And clean her up,' adds Jade. 'She's just having a tantrum.'

'Well, I'm not surprised,' says Mrs Nosy-Parker. Checks her watch again and decides to settle for a lecture. 'You can't treat smaller people like this,' she says. 'I don't care who's dragged you up, Jade Walker. Even you know better than that.'

'Yes, Mrs Tonge,' says Jade.

'I'm going to ring your mother tonight and tell her what you've been up to,' she tells Bel. 'It's disgraceful. I suppose I wouldn't expect anything else from a Walker, but you ought to know better.'

'No, Mrs Tonge,' says Bel. The woman's eyes flick suspiciously over to her, but she's fixed a look of unctuous respect on her face. Tilts her head to one side like Shirley Temple.

'Right,' she says, opening the car door. 'Well. Personally, I think the pair of you would benefit from a good spanking, but there you go.'

She slams the door, starts the engine and winds down the window. 'And get some Dettol on those cuts,' she orders. 'They'll go septic. Honestly. You should be taking care of your little sister, not treating her like a doll or something.'

She puts the car into gear and drives away. The three girls – two standing, one glowering on the verge between them – watch her leave, silently.

'Three bags full, Mrs Tonge,' says Jade. She aims a sly kick at Chloe's thigh. 'That's for getting us into trouble. Come on. Get up. Any more noise from you and we'll just leave you here.'

Chapter Thirty-six

Everyone who still reads a newspaper has their ritual for doing so: the place and time and posture they reserve for only this activity. Lunch hours, commutes, those snatched moments when the baby's gone down for her nap; a ritual more personal than anything the television can offer. On a normal day, Kirsty and Stan and their peers skim them all online while the kettle's boiling and the twenty-four-hour news channels play in the background. While they wait for conference to be over and commissions to come in, they fish through the Reuters and AP news feeds to give them a chance to get ahead of the game; then, mostly, they settle down with their favourite read, though they'd all pretend to the outside world that their favourite read is the paper that mainly employs them.

Martin Bagshawe usually does his reading at the library, but today he buys a bottle of chocolate milk, a Scotch egg, some cheese-and-onion crisps and a copy of the *Sun*, and reads it while he waits for Kirsty Lindsay to show her face so he can tell which of the five houses he's looking at is hers. He's rented a white van with his emergency credit card and bought navy-blue overalls from Millets, because no one ever, in his experience, questions someone in overalls snoozing in a van. He has no idea how long he's going to be waiting; he just hopes he can spin out the sudoku.

*

Deborah Prentiss works the early shift at Asda, and reads the paper at two o'clock when she gets home, before she scoots through the housework and goes to pick the kids up from school. She has the same ritual every day: comes in, puts the kettle on and goes upstairs to change out of her hated polyester uniform. Deb takes pride in her appearance; always has, since she was a teenager. She never stays in that uniform for a moment longer than she has to. She reapplies her make-up, brushes out the hair that's been squashed by the net hat she has to wear in the bakery and, once she's in a skirt and a decent jumper, comes down and makes a pot of tea. Then she sits at the kitchen table and takes a precious half-hour out to scan the *Mirror* for scandal and disaster. Despite having been the subject of tabloid speculation herself in her time, she loves it; loves the window on a grim and ugly world from her nice quiet house, and believes every word. She calls it her 'me-time'.

Millions of people, same blank expression. Soaking up the words and believing that, having done so, they are In the Know. Kirsty, still digesting her phone conversation, catches sight of herself in the mantelpiece mirror and observes that her own face betrays none of the emotions she feels. I've done what I can, she thinks. I'm mad to have even involved myself this far. I need to get a grip and call Features before all the assignments have been handed out for the rest of the week. I need to forget about Amber Gordon. It's the past. She needs to mean nothing to me now.

Martin finds Jackie spread across the centre pages and feels his upper lip curl as he reads her account of herself. He winds the window down and spits on to the tarmac. The road is empty, not a sign of activity behind the neat suburban nets, but the self-employed don't keep the same hours as the rest of the world. Kirsty Lindsay could come – or go – at any time, and he'll be here to see it when she does.

Jackie looks old and slutty beneath the make-up. He finds it hard to believe that this woman can ever have excited such intense emotion in him; he feels nothing now, other than a faint contempt and an amused interest in what she has to say. He doesn't want her back now, and as he reads and sees what a weak woman she is, how easily influenced, he wants her even less – but it feels good to have his suspicions confirmed. He wasn't dumped because of himself, he was dumped because of other people. The story of his life. He's been tripped up and blocked all his life, and Amber Gordon is just one in a long line of teachers, officials, bosses and so-called 'friends' who've stopped him ever, ever catching a break. And now this Kirsty Lindsay, accusing him of something he never did, on the smug assumption that her position would protect her. And all along she's clearly been protecting Vic Cantrell, which means she's been protecting Amber Gordon too. In collusion with him. In his opinion, she's as guilty of his crimes as if she'd done them herself.

Except that she's not reckoned with Martin. Amber Gordon can wait. For now there's not a hope of finding her alone; though he hopes fervently that the company she's in is giving her hell. The world is full of women with no morals. Jackie Jacobs, skirt hitched up to show her legs, is just the tip of the iceberg. You can only do one thing at a time. You have to prioritise. And right now Kirsty Lindsay is his priority. His anger has been building ever since his humiliation in DanceAttack; has become, once again, a gnawing, living thing. And now he's had a taste of relief, he also knows the best way to get it.

It won't be long now, he thinks. She'll have to come out from behind one of these smug suburban front doors, and then I'll know for certain where she lives.

He takes a bite of Scotch egg and reclines the seat so that only the top of his head, baseball cap and celebrity sunglasses can be seen from the road. He's enjoyed his preparations, the crafty plans he's made so that he will not be recognised. Feels like 007, like MI5 and Andy McNab, adrenalin coursing through his veins every time someone turns the corner. It may take a while, watching these houses till he identifies which one is his target's home, but he's in no hurry. He's got it down to a postcode by the surprisingly simple expedient of calling the *Tribune* and asking for Minty (he remembers the name from overhearing it in the park) on the news desk, and pretending to be a PR with a goodie bag and only half an address. The fact that he knew she lived in Farnham seemed to be enough to satisfy the girl.

He polishes off his egg and smoothes out the page.

Deborah looks down on people who read the *Sun* with all the righteous scorn of someone who identifies herself as belonging to the left. She doesn't know it, but the *Mirror* has gone as big on Whitmouth as its red-top rival, and in the same manner. Speculation, retrospective wisdom from the neighbours (the same big-gob neighbours they're reading about in the *Sun*, if only she knew it) and the small amount of information that can be dug up about such anonymous figures as the Seaside Strangler and his harpy girlfriend. There's only one thing the country loves better than a nice juicy serial killer, and that's a serial killer's wife. Deborah assumes the frown all right-thinking people have worn all day while wallowing in the sketchy, blown-up detail, and bites into a custard cream.

Her paper has much the same photo as the one adorning the *Sun*'s front page: dry, straw-like blond hair, dark glasses and a cheesy grin. In this one, though, she's halfway through raising her hand to cover her face, so it looks like she's waving. Who does she think she is? thinks Deborah, and polishes off her biscuit. Sharon bloody Osbourne?

Weird, she thinks. She looks familiar. Like I know her from somewhere. Not like I've seen her picture, though God knows it's been smeared across the papers enough in the past couple of days, but like I've seen her in real life. There's something about the way she's holding herself, something about the nose and the jawline, and that bloody great mole on her face. I wonder if I've met her? It feels like it. Where was it? Certainly not Whitmouth. Absent-mindedly, she takes another biscuit from the pack and dunks it in her tea.

I know what it is, she thinks. It's that bloody mole. I can't help it. I see a mole like that on a woman and I just immediately dislike them. Because of Annabel Oldacre, I think of everyone with a mole like that as a killer in disguise. I remember staring at that mole for hours on end during the trial, watching that little bitch who killed my baby sister get her punishment. It's obviously stuck. All the feelings I had are concentrated on that one facial flaw.

But it is *very* like, she thinks, sucking tea through the softened biscuit. It's even in the same place as hers was.

Martin turns back to the front page. Gordon is all over that one as well. He chews his lip as he looks at her, grinning away as she walks down the street like she's going to a party; he's edited from his interpretation the fact that he was watching when the pictures were taken. I suppose she likes the attention, he thinks. She's got her fifteen minutes and she's making the most of it. But she's not like Kirsty. At least she's not dedicated her life to making sure her lies make their way into everyone's homes.

Jim calls in to divert himself from his nerves before his meeting with Lionel Baker. He's been reading the papers on the train and Kirsty can practically hear him shaking his head as he tuts over the Whitmouth coverage. 'That poor woman,' he says. 'They're crucifying her.'

'I know,' she says. 'It's awful, isn't it?'

'You're the only person who seems to have been even remotely fair.'

'Yeah. God knows how *that* got past Back Bench.'

She hears the sound of folding paper. Jim always takes revenge on publications that have annoyed him by screwing them up and

293

dropping them in the bin. She stares out of the window, notices that that damned Russian vine that next door planted three years ago is sprouting from a hole in the foundations of their shed. Dammit, she thinks. Life's one long treadmill of fighting against nature, one way or another.

'I think I'm going to give up reading the papers,' he announces. 'It just seems so ... unnecessary. They're just making things up as they go along. They don't know anything, so they've just decided to turn this woman into a pantomime villain, to fill the space till they do. You see them doing it all the time. They just can't bear to admit they don't know any more than the rest of us.'

'Steady on,' says Kirsty. 'And if everyone stops reading them, what am I going to do for a living?'

No one has been able to find out much about the Alleged Strangler himself. There's maybe a page about him, but in the silly season a page is not enough. The *Mirror*'s photographer has followed Amber Gordon all the way to Funnland and then to the unremarkable ex-council house she lives in. There's a picture of her walking a pair of those yappy, snappy little dogs you usually see tucked under the arms of the likes of Liza Minnelli. The house is clearly neglected, a wooden board nailed over a window, the flowerbeds trampled and muddy. Deborah reads the screed below the pictures, and wonders.

Seaside Strangler's girlfriend, Amber Gordon, walks her dogs as though it's an ordinary day. Gordon, a cleaning supervisor, refused to speak to the *Mirror*'s journalist when he confronted her after dropping off a bag of goodies for her lover, currently undergoing questioning at Whitmouth Police Station. Back at their scruffy house on the outskirts of the town, she swore at photographers. 'Leave me alone!' she said, when we attempted to ask her about her partner's crimes. 'I've not done anything!'

The making of a murderer, page 13.

In the doorstep picture, the woman is clearly shouting. About my age, thinks Deborah. Maybe a bit younger. I wonder what it's like to be her? Did she know? She must have known. You can't live with someone and not know something like that, surely?

She turns to the 'making of a murderer' feature and starts to read.

Martin looks up the road as he scans through the radio channels in search of Radio 2. Some classic pop, that's what I need. Classic pop for the classic suburbs.

He's surprised by the road she chooses to live on. He'd imagined something more modernist, more minimalist, the sort of thing favoured by Channel 4. A warehouse conversion, all naked brickwork and stark white plaster, or something whose walls are made of glass. What he hadn't expected was an ordinary four-up-four-down in a medium-sized garden full of clematis and concrete dolphins. A series of near-identical 1930s semis, brave little flourishes – a garage, a brickwork turning-circle, a pergola, a porch – attesting to their owners' individuality. If she lives somewhere like this, he thinks, she's probably got a family. Two girls called something like Jacintha and Phoebe. A Weimaraner.

A dignified Burmese cat stalks out of a drive, sits on the pavement to survey his territory. Yeah, thinks Martin. Too normal. She'll have one of those hairless sphinxes, or a Dalmatian. Something stupid and useless, designed to impress fashion victims.

He glances in the rear-view, sees the front door a couple of doors back open and Kirsty Lindsay emerge. She goes over to the dusty little Renault that sits on the drive and unlocks the door. She looks unguarded, innocent, filled with thought. Martin slides down in his seat, though there's not a chance that she will recognise him like this, from behind, and watches as she scrabbles around in the glove compartment and comes back out brandishing a satnav and its lead. Of course she's got a satnav, he thinks. Nice work if you can get it.

Funny, though. It's the dullest house on the street, covered in wisteria, and that Renault's eight years old if it's a day. He would have bet his weekly budget that she lived in the one with the Jag.

There are more photos of Amber Gordon in the 'making of a murderer' feature: the implication clear that her contribution has been bigger than any other, even though she's only known him for six of his forty-two years. It seems that there are very few photos of Victor Cantrell before he met her, just a couple taken in a caravan park in Cornwall where he worked before he came to Whitmouth. Deborah feels another twinge of visceral dislike as she eyes the woman. It's that bloody mole, she thinks. It really is identical: same place, same shape, same colour. What are the odds? How many people can have that same blemish, in just the same place …

She feels a jerk of realisation … And be the same age?

Deborah hears the breath hiss from her body. She grips the sides of the paper in fisted hands, presses her face close to the image on the page. Oh. My. God. Under the bleach, the twenty-five years, the tense defiance, the celebrity sunglasses. She still has the same jawline, that same upper lip half the width of its lower twin, the eyebrows heavy and dark and at odds with the shade of the skin.

It can't be.

She feels freezing cold. She went to the trial every day, with her mother: the bereaved, the living victims. She stared at Annabel Oldacre and Jade Walker as she sat on the witness stand on the first day and gave her testimony. They stole my little sister. I only asked them to take her to the shops, and they kidnapped her. Bitches. Those little bloody bitches. And later, when she was done, she stared at the backs of their necks, at their profiles as they looked up at their lawyers (they never looked at each other, not once through the whole four days); glaring into their faces, willing them to look at her as they passed in and out of the courtroom, willing them to see what they'd done. She memorised everything about Annabel Oldacre, but she never expected to see her again, with or without the changes of a quarter-century disguising the child within.

'Fuck,' says Deborah, and reaches out for the telephone. 'Fuck.'

Chapter Thirty-seven

They're heckling the politicians on *Question Time* when her phone starts to ring in her bag. She considers not answering. Jim's had a good day. He's come home full of hope and *grand cru* Chablis consumed at the Paternoster Square Corney & Barrow, and it's raised her own mood for the first time in days. She doesn't want the world intruding any more. Wants to pretend, for this night at least, that life is sweet, and calm, and hopeful. Then she answers anyway.

Crackling, then shouting, down the line. 'Hello? Hello?'

'Stan?'

'Hello?' he yells again, then swears. 'Hang on.'

She waits. His voice comes on, quieter, clearer. 'Bloody hands-free,' he says. 'How are you?'

'OK,' she says. 'You?'

He doesn't bother to answer. 'Where are you?'

'Home,' she says.

'I'd've thought you'd've been down at Whitmouth.'

'No. Dave Park's taken over there now. I'm home.'

'Shit,' he says. 'Dave bloody Park.'

'It's OK,' she says. 'I think I've had my fill of Whitmouth, truth be told.'

'Sod it,' he says. 'Don't suppose you've got his phone number, have you? No, don't worry. It doesn't matter.'

'OK,' she says. Shrugs pointlessly.

'Anyway, it was you I wanted,' he says.

Jim is frowning, and fiddling with the remote. He hates people talking on the phone while the telly's on. Any second now, he'll turn the volume up to make his point. She gets off the sofa and takes the call through to the hall. Plonks herself at the foot of the stairs, by the pile of laundry that always sits there, and starts sorting socks.

'I was hoping,' continues Stan, 'we could do an information swap.'

'Uh-huh?' she asks.

'I'm on my way down there now. For the *Mirror*.'

'The *Mirror*? For real?'

'Yeah, well,' he says, 'all they've got down there at the moment is some twelve-year-old on work experience. The rest are all chasing Jodie Marsh or something. They thought they might need someone with a bit more experience for this.'

'This?'

'Shit,' he says. 'Are you not checking the wires?'

'Not since teatime. I'm off duty.'

She hears a twitch of astonishment. Stan's never off duty. He'd be seeking out the broadband in intensive care. 'Right. Well, there's something come up,' he says. 'The *Mirror*'s got it as an exclusive, in that they've got the dobber on retainer 'cause that's where she saw the photos and made the connection, but it's been up on PA for an hour or so now. It'll be everywhere tomorrow.'

Get to the point, Stan. 'Uh-huh?'

'Someone's rung in and the whole Cantrell story's gone a lot bigger. I need ... you know. Her number, if you've got it. You know, 'cause you ...'

'Stan,' she interrupts, 'what are you on about?'

'I'm going down to doorstep Amber Gordon,' he says. 'I'm giving you the heads-up. I thought you might want to come too. Being as ... you know, you're a mate. And freelancers have to stick together, sometimes, and I owe you a couple. And because

299

I think I might need a chick. They all seem to think that doorstepping's just a question of sticking it out for longer than anyone else, but sometimes, you know, you just need a woman, not a man, and ...'

'I don't suppose,' she says, 'if she hasn't wanted to say anything so far ... if she's going to talk it'll have been negotiated.'

'No,' he says, 'you're not getting it. It's not about her bloke. Well, it is, of course it is, 'cause no one would have spotted it otherwise, but ...'

She knows what's coming immediately. Feels fear wash through her like Arctic ice. Drops the socks she's rolling into a ball and clutches the phone tightly because she's afraid she'll drop it too.

'Turns out our Mrs Cantrell is actually Annabel Oldacre,' he says.

A 'no' falls from her mouth. Not the 'no' he takes it for.

'Yes,' he replies. 'Can you believe it?'

'No,' she says again.

'It's a pretty definite ID,' he says. 'Victim's sister, apparently.'

'But she barely knew her,' she blurts. 'They only met when—'

She pulls herself up short before she lets any more out. She barely remembers Debbie Francis herself, she's more of a blur of piercings and nickel-studded leather than she is a face. She feels her skin crawl at the thought of how close she's come to exposing herself; feels iced water trickle down her back. In the other room, a burst of applause.

Stan continues as though he's not noticed. 'Well, yeah, but she went to every day of the court case, apparently. I guess they must've thought it would be some sort of closure, or something. But she certainly got a good chance to study their faces while she was there, didn't she? Anyway, what are the odds?'

'Not as long as you'd think,' she says. 'Surprisingly short, if anything. They're the same odds it would be for anyone, actually, with her social status and where she lives factored in. The fact that she ... has a history ... makes no difference to the odds. There's the odd violent death in Whitmouth every year, even without a serial killer. Someone's got to be married to the people who do them.'

'Mmm,' says Stan. 'You're right, I suppose. Anyway. It's a story, isn't it? Thing is, once it's pointed out to you, it's obvious. You'd've thought they'd've got that bloody great mole taken off her face when they changed her name, wouldn't you? It's sort of like they *wanted* her to be recognised. And "Amber". They didn't exactly fish about for a name, did they?'

'I . . .' She catches sight of her reflection in the window by the front door. Stares into it, studying her face for signs of the child that once lived there. She sees little that she recognises: her face was always less individual, more common-or-garden, than Bel's, even without that mole; the sort of face you see streaming from school gates by the score. And besides, I was fat then, she thinks. My features were blurred by years of chips and ketchup.

'You coming, then?' asks Stan.

Are you fucking kidding me? she thinks. I've got to be as far away from Annabel Oldacre as I can get. I should be on the next plane to Australia. Tell Jim I've been sacked, leave journalism, get a job selling pizza in Queensland or somewhere, except that no country worth living in would accept a residency application from the likes of me, and anyway that's just the sort of job the papers have been spotting me in for years. Getting a career, getting a degree, being a social-services success story – that's been the best cover I could have found. Hiding in among the jackals who seek me, the greatest camouflage. The only thing better would have been to find some way of joining the police.

'I – shit, Stan.' She scrabbles for excuses. 'No. I'm sorry. I can't. Even if it wasn't Dave Park's territory, now. We're going up to Jim's mum's tomorrow. In Herefordshire. I've got to pack the kids' stuff, get the house closed up . . .'

'Jesus Christ,' says Stan. 'Priorities?'

'Yeah, it's called a family,' she says, knowing how much it'll annoy him, hoping it'll make him hang up in disgust.

She hears him splutter. 'Oh, come *on*, woman. What are you

on about? You've been trying to get a regular gig on News for *years*. If you can get her to talk, it's a picture byline. Good God, it's probably a *staff* job, if you can scoop the *Mirror*.'

She stays silent. Doesn't trust her voice not to betray her fear. Hears him light a cigarette, prepare to have one more go at persuading her. 'Fish-and-chip wrappings, Kirsty,' he says. 'It'll make fish-and-chip wrappings of that cock-up you made last week. They'll forget all about it.'

She pretends to consider.

'God, look. No, Stan. Thank you. I can't tell you how grateful I am, but I'm sorry. I'll give you Dave's number, look. I'll call him for you. And anyway, he'll have it in for me for ever if he thinks I've stolen his glory. You know what he's like.'

'Well. OK. Don't say I never did you a favour.'

'I won't,' she says. She can barely breathe. Wants him gone, so she can think. 'I'm sorry, Stan. I'm dead grateful. Really grateful. But I can't do it. Gotta go. I'm sorry.'

'Hang on—' he starts, but she cuts him off. Sinks back against the step behind her. Sophie's shed a sweatshirt, unwashed, in among the clean laundry. She picks it up, buries her face in its musky pre-teen scent and breathes deeply. Oh God, the kids, she thinks. What would it do to them?

She is frightened. A different fear from the fear she felt that night in Whitmouth, though the sense of something following, something approaching from behind, is similar: an ancient, long-suppressed fear that creeps through her viscera, leaves her hot and weak. You never know who's watching, who's waiting. You can never let your guard down, never feel safe. You can go a year, three years, without an incident, then one day you open your inbox to find that someone you've always thought of as reasonable, as civilised and thoughtful, has forwarded a round-robin email saying you're about to be paroled and must never, ever get out. Or someone goes to the papers claiming to have been drinking with you in a theme bar on the Costa del Crime, or to have bought a house from you in Wythenshawe, or to have been the object of your predatory lesbianism in some random prison, and you're terrified all over again: waiting for your husband to study those old photos one more time, and this time to look up with dawning recognition on his face. Waiting to wake up one morning with the mob on your doorstep.

They're already there on Amber's, primed and ready for action. Dear God, she's already been thrown to the lions. Those pictures of her house – it was obvious they've been out there with their flaming torches and their pitchforks for days. It's going to be a bloodbath.

She hears the *Question Time* music start up in the living room. Struggles to compose herself before Jim comes out to find her.

Chapter Thirty-eight

Amber wakes to the sound of breaking glass. She hadn't realised she'd fallen asleep; had only lain down on the bed to rest for a few minutes at eight o'clock. She sits upright, fully dressed as she has been for the past few days, and ready to run. Wonders whether to turn the light on and decides against. Light will show that she's home, and at-home is more provocative than away. Some irrational part of her has clung to the hope that, if she keeps a low profile, refuses to talk, refuses to cooperate, the watchers outside will give up and go away. And even as she was hoping, she knew she was fooling herself. This is the third window that's been broken in the past twenty-four hours.

The clock tells her it's gone eleven. She's been out for the count for three hours. She feels for the table-leg she's been carrying around for comfort – wishes dearly that she lived in a country where baseball was commonplace – and gets carefully out of bed. Her shoes – easy slip-ons for speedy exits – are on the bedside rug; she finds them, in the dark, in seconds.

She creeps through to the spare room. Even from the landing, she can hear the sound of movement out in the front garden: feet shifting and the rasp of a throat being cleared. She can see the curtains wafting in the tiny breeze, a brick lying in a mess of glass in the middle of the bed. They're back. The neighbours, the drunks, the people who want her to know their Values: they like to come down when the pub closes and share their feelings once the press have gone to bed. The teenage policeman who occasionally stands outside is obviously gone, again. No one to take pictures, so no need to be there. No one throws stones when the police are around.

She retreats to the bedroom, sits against the door and turns on her phone. Thirty-three missed calls, twelve messages. My God, it's got worse, she thinks. That's more than yesterday. Has something happened? Something new? Or is it just that my number's getting passed around, from person to person, until by Thursday the whole country will have it? She ignores them; scrolls through the address book to find the police station. No point dialling 999. It'll come through to the same people in the end, anyway.

She hunches against the door, listens to the empty ring. Registers, puzzlingly, that the dogs aren't with her. They've been reliable as the sunrise, since Vic was arrested. They follow her upstairs at bedtime to settle, comforting and thoughtful, at the foot of the duvet, and are there to greet her in the morning: the we-have-survived-the-night awakening that gives her the strength to go on. I must be sleeping more deeply than I'd thought, she thinks idly as she counts the rings. I've never noticed that they get up in the night and do their own thing.

On the twelfth ring, a voice comes on the line: casual and unconcerned, for someone whose job it is to answer the phone in the middle of the night. 'Whitmouth Police?'

'It's Amber Gordon,' she says, keeping her voice low, as though the people outside might be able to hear her through wood and stone.

He doesn't seem to recognise the name. 'Victor Cantrell's . . .' she prompts.

'Ah. Hello,' he says, but his voice doesn't sound friendly.

'There's someone outside my house. They've broken a window.'

'OK,' he says, but he doesn't sound unduly concerned. 'Give me a moment.'

Amber goes back to the corridor and listens. There are definitely people outside. They're being quiet, deliberately so – she hears a voice stage-whisper and another shush it quiet – but she can feel the presence, not just of people, but of a crowd. Thinks she hears the metallic chink of someone trying the garden gate, tenses as she wonders if the bolts will hold. It's a feeble protection, she knows. The gate and fence would give under a couple of kicks. She just has to hope they know that there's a line that can't be stepped over, a line where protest becomes trespass.

Though that's not stopped them when it comes to criminal damage. It can't be long now before someone decides that, with the breaking already done, the entering is the next logical step. She can't stay here.

'Ms Gordon?'

Her heart jolts. She'd almost forgotten what she'd been waiting for.

'We're sending a patrol car round. They should be there in twenty minutes or so.'

Twenty minutes? I could be dead by then. 'Can't they get here sooner? What's happened to the lad who was on my door?'

'Limited resources,' he replies. 'Maybe you'd like to take it up with the Home Secretary. I don't know if you've noticed, but half the forces in the country have been providing backup to the Met this summer.'

How much am I supposed to bear? She feels her eyes fill with tears.

'If you like,' he says, 'they could bring you down here.'

'What for?'

'We've been calling you all evening. You might want to consider protective custody. For the time being. It's up to you.'

Cells and locks and corridors; the echo of painted concrete, the long, empty waits before the brief highlights of bland meals. Solitary confinement without the human rights. The crushing memory of guilt, and Vic three rooms down. She jerks, like a dreamer who's found themselves falling. His 'n' hers jail cells: partners in everything.

'Why?' she asks. 'There must be some other ... somewhere else. It can't be a choice between here and a cell ...'

'Like I say. It's up to you. But it might be best,' he says, and adds again, significantly: 'Under the *circumstances*.'

'The circumstances'. What a lovely way to put it. 'Can't I ... isn't there somewhere else? I ... you can't really expect me to ... can't you take me to a hotel or something?'

'Well, Ms *Gordon*,' he says, drawing out the name so it's no longer a simple address but some insult she doesn't understand, 'it's the only way we can guarantee your safety, *under the circumstances*. We've been calling. You didn't answer. And anyway, I very much doubt there's a hotel that'll be prepared to take you.'

'You couldn't guarantee my safety yesterday either,' she protests. 'Why are you suddenly so ... ?'

'Oh,' he says. 'You don't know.'

Creeping disquiet. 'Know what?'

'They know who you are, Ms Gordon. The papers.'

Her mouth goes dry. 'Who I am ... ?'

'Annabel Oldacre,' he says. Then adds, spitefully: 'But of course, *you* know that already.'

Amber hangs up.

She crawls, hands and knees, across the spare room and cracks a curtain aside. Peers into the darkened road, the glass-strewn front garden. Jumps back, gasping for air. There must be thirty of them out there: standing, hands in pockets, staring at the house like extras in a zombie movie. Oh God. I'm dead. By morning there will be hundreds.

She has to accept the policeman's offer. The moment the squad car turns up, she's got to be out of here, and damn what happens next. If they come in, she will never survive.

She creeps downstairs, gets a hooded fleece and pulls it on. Calls, in a whisper, for the dogs. They have to come with her, there's no way she can leave them. Once the crowd has seen her the house is done for, and its contents with it. She knows they won't let her keep the dogs in the station, but once she's brought them in, they will become someone's responsibility: they can't just chuck them on to the steps to fend for themselves. They'll have to find something to do with them. The RSPCA. Something. Anything is better than being left to the tender mercies of the mob.

They don't respond. No patter of paws, no claws clicking on the kitchen floor. They must be outside. They've gone out through the cat-flap for some night-time dog life. She is afraid to follow. Wants to shelter in the safety of locked doors and a boarded-up living room until the police come. But she has to find them, and now. There won't be time after. Once she's answered the door, and the crowd is certain they have her, there will be time for nothing other than flight. She'll need to scoop them up, grab the bag she's been keeping ready-packed in the hall, and run for the patrol car before outrage turns to action.

She snatches the back-door keys from the hook in the hall and creeps into the kitchen. Dark and still; familiar objects crouched shadowy on countertops as though waiting to pounce. She stops halfway across the room, and scans the garden; wants to be sure there are no unseen visitors before she lets the outside in.

And then she sees them.

They're only little. Little and defenceless, and never did harm to anyone. Oh, my darlings.

Amber steps into the garden and realises that tears are pouring down her face. I can't bear it. I can't bear it. This is beyond bearing. They've come and they've taken them and they've used their trusting natures, and they've punished them to punish me.

She stands helpless and gazes at the tiny corpses. They've been strangled; had their souls squeezed out the way Vic did to those girls. And they've left them dangling from the washing line by their collars, the breeze catching their feathery coats and turning them, round and round, like gibbeted vermin. Dark saucer-eyes, bulging as they gasped for life.

An animal keening escapes her open mouth. Mary-Kate and Ashley, my friends. My poor friends. Oh, my darlings. They didn't have to do that to you. You never did a thing.

She drops the keys in her shock, falls to her knees to feel around in the shadows. Gazes up at the strangled faces, and weeps and weeps.

The gate rattles on its hinges. Someone outside has heard her.

Amber freezes. Crouched below the bodies in the moonlight, she watches the gate bounce. They won't bother to climb over, this time; this time they're coming straight through.

'Annabel!' shouts a voice: male, high, excited. 'Zat you, Annabel?'

Amber jumps to her feet. No hope of help from the police now. They know she's here. She's given herself away.

The gate rattles again, and she hears something crack. Doesn't wait, doesn't really think. She runs to the neighbour's fence on the far side, and scrambles over. Lands hard in a flowerbed, feels the snap of brave perennials beneath her feet. Races across the garden, towards the next fence. There's no way she's getting away through Tennyson Way. Her only way out is if she can make it to Coleridge Close.

2.30 p.m.

Bel flops down on the doorstep. She wants to cry, but Jade looks like she might explode and she doesn't want to rile her any more than she's riled already. Chloe plays with the toggles on her anorak and sticks out her lower lip. She's got mud on her face, somehow, and looks like she's come down a chimney. Bel is soaked in sweat. The hunger has started to translate into faintness. I don't know how much more of this I can take, she thinks. I just want to lie down and sleep.

'Well, *why didn't you say there wasn't nobody here?' asks Jade.*

'My *mum's gone to Chippy,' says Chloe, as though this is an answer. 'To the shops.'*

'Well, *fuck's sake,' says Jade.*

'*I thought Debbie was here,' says Chloe.*

'*Of course she isn't here,' says Jade crushingly.*

'*Where's she gone?' asks Bel. She knows she's slow on the uptake, but even she had managed to work out that Debbie was getting off with Darren Walker when they came across them on the bench. It seems logical to her that they would have come here to have sex in her bedroom, because everybody knows that that's where sex is done. 'She's not gone to* your *house, has she?' she asks doubtfully.*

Jade bursts into sardonic laughter. '*No, she's gone to Buckingham bleeding Palace for a garden party.'*

'*In a leather jacket?' asks Bel doubtfully.*

Jade catches the look on her face and laughs again. She's beginning to think that Bel is simple. She's missed three of her jokes now. 'Joke,' she says. 'But I can guarantee you she's not at ours.'

Chloe starts to whimper again. Both the older girls roll their eyes. 'Don't start that again,' says Jade. 'There's nothing we can do about it, is there?'

As fast as Chloe started, she stops again, and sniffs. She's had an idea. 'The river,' she says. Her mum never takes her down the river. She's only been twice. The river, to Chloe, is as magical and magnetic as Disneyland. If she's not going to get her lunch, she's going to get to paddle, at least.

'The river?' Jade is suspicious.

'She went down the river.'

'What's she gone down there for?'

'Swim.'

'Why din't she take you?'

Chloe starts to well up again.

'All right. All right. We'll take you down the river,' says Jade, rolling her eyes. 'I'll kill Darren. I'll bloody kill him.'

'You're kidding,' says Bel.

'What?'

'It's got to be three miles.'

'All right then. Have you got any better ideas?'

'I ...' Bel looks hopelessly round the deserted close. 'When's your mum coming home?'

Chloe shrugs. She has no idea; has very little concept of time. 'Hours and hours and hours,' she says. Her mother is, in fact, standing at the bus stop in Chipping Norton right now and will be home in thirty-five minutes. But Chloe has no idea what the time is; couldn't read a clock even if they passed one. All she knows is that, when her mum comes home on the bus, it's always long gone lunchtime. And as she's not had her lunch yet, it must be hours and hours. And the river is calling: its plashy depths and weedy paddling, and the picnics and the lollies and the drinks people bring down in cool-boxes and sometimes share. She's only ever gone by car. Has no more idea how far three miles is by foot than how long it is till lunchtime. 'Hours,' she repeats, and waits.

311

'And your sister's definitely down there?'

'Yeah,' says Chloe confidently.

'We'll go over the fields,' says Jade decisively.

'The fields?' asks Bel. 'But there isn't a footpath, is there?'

'Oh, it'll be fine,' says Jade. 'Get a life.'

Chapter Thirty-nine

The last barrier before Coleridge Close is a yellow-brick wall topped by a trellis through which climbing roses twine. Amber is panting with the effort of her flight, of climbing and running and stooping to stay out of the light; of throwing herself backwards as number seventeen's Rottweiler bellowed and hurled itself against its chain as she passed. The dog has alerted her pursuers to the path of her flight. As she stares at the obstacle before her, she hears a crack and a stream of swearing as a fence gives way beneath a muscled body, and the lights four doors down blaze into life.

'Where's she gone?' A voice drifts over the night air, alarmingly close. She'd thought she'd put the best part of a road's distance between herself and them, but this one's nearer than that. Maybe two plots away. 'Where the fuck is she?'

'Coleridge,' shouts another. 'She must be heading for Coleridge.'

'Fuck,' says the first voice. Takes two deep breaths. 'Come on. Fuck.'

He raises his voice to a theatrical bellow. Lights are coming on in every house now. The people in this one must be away, or she'd be a sitting duck. 'Oi! She's heading for Coleridge!'

In the distance, in her own garden, a yell of understanding.

Shit. Her pulse hammers in her ears. Amber takes a run-up at the wall and vaults, throwing herself bodily into the mat of thorns. It'll take them no time at all, if they come by the road. She can't afford to be careful. Needs to be out of sight by the time they turn the corner. She hears the trellis crack beneath her weight and draws blood on an exposed wrist. Feels her shirt snag and catch. Doesn't stop to think; just forces her way through the debris and hurls herself at the other side.

The shirt holds for a moment, leaving her dangling in dark air, face in the foliage, then it rips and lets go, dropping her on an awkward foot-arch. She feels a sharp pain, something ripping deep within, and stifles a cry as the bones grind together. Then she's free, and hop-running, adrenalin killing the hurt as it propels her forward.

She glances over her shoulder as she runs, losing precious moments as she slips on the scrappy verge. They'll be halfway up Tennyson by now. She needs to get off this road; needs to drop out of sight. She limps to the corner of Marvell Street and dives into its temporary sanctuary.

She knows this road well. It's the route she walks to Blessed's flat; an empty stretch of garages and feeder roads. Halfway up, a kids' playground, between the turns leading back to Browning and Tennyson, long since abandoned by families as the tidal wave of crack washed over the south-east. The junkies have moved on, but the playground – and what remains of its slides and swings and its crumbling jungle gym – has never been reclaimed.

The slap-slap-slap of boots on tarmac back in Coleridge, chillingly close behind. She can't go on much longer on this foot. She hesitates for a second, then dives through the playground gate and ducks below the hedge.

Litter, blown in and dropped; she crawls gingerly among the bricks and ragwort. She hears the footsteps turn the corner, hears them slow as their owners find an empty road. Amber inches forward. Over beyond the sandpit there's an old plywood climbing frame in the shape of a train, water-warped and splintered and four feet high, buried in a clump of smutty nettles. She knows they'll look over the hedge, that they might even venture into the park. But they'd never think her fool enough to trap herself like that. She hopes. Has to hope. She has nowhere else to go.

She reaches the train and squeezes through a circular hole designed for a six-year old. Snags, sticks, heaves herself through and into the dark. Portholes throw light on the wall above her head, but down here on the floor, as she closes her mind to the objects she's sharing the space with, is reassuring darkness.

They come along the road with the swaggering stride of numbers, swipe at foliage as they pass. She hears them pause by the gate, hears the click of a lighter igniting, smells the drift of cigarette smoke across the night air.

'Fuck,' says a voice. The man who tried the gate. 'Where's she gone? She can't have doubled back, can she?'

A woman replies, the sound of the feminine more frightening because so unexpected. It's Janelle Boxer, Shaunagh's friend from a few doors up. Amber can see her in her mind's eye: squat, thick-set, a face to match her surname. 'No time. She's gone down here. Down one of them two, there. She won't have had time to get to the end.'

Someone swings the gate. The crunch of boots on gravel. She knows that eyes are scanning her hiding place, holds her breath as though it will cloud the midsummer air. The concrete on which she lies is damp and piled with musty earth and leaves. It smells of body fluids.

'We could get the dog.'

'Naah. She'll be well gone by the time we do that.'

A swish of some long object – baseball bat? Scaffolding pole? – across the undergrowth an arm's length from her head. Amber stiffens, presses herself deeper into the dark.

'Fuck,' says the first man, and something hits the wooden wall. She shrinks away, bites her lip.

'You think she's gone home?' His voice slightly quieter now; he's moving away. 'It's up this way, innit?'

The others fall into step. She hears the gate drag across the gravel, the clang of the broken latch. 'Naah,' replies someone. 'You know where she's gone? Pig farm.'

'Well, let's hope they keep her.'

Someone raises his voice. 'Annabel!' A chorus of laughs. 'Come out, come out, wherever you are!'

They laugh again, their voices fading as they walk away. 'Can't believe it. Can you believe it? Fucking right in the middle of us all this time. I remember it. Poor little kid. D'you remember? All cut up. Covered in bruises. Broken bones. Fucking little sadist.'

'Someone should show her what it's like.'

'Can you believe it? It's Rose bloody West all over again. I've got kids, for fuck's sake. She could've ...'

'Let's go down the police. She mightn't've got there yet ... maybe if we split up ...'

'C'mon then. If we get the cars we can beat her down there.'

'Don't be a div. There'll be Plod all over the shop.'

A laugh. 'I wouldn't be so sure about that. My cousin Ray's on duty tonight. They're fucking furious. Trust me. If anyone's going to turn a blind eye ...'

The voices fade into the distance. Amber sits up, leans against the spongy wall, feels the shriek of pain in her foot. In the darkness the image of Mary-Kate and Ashley, her darlings, her sweet friends, swims back into her mind and winds her. She wraps her arms round her body and weeps.

She doesn't know what to do. She can't let daylight overtake her. The darkness is her only protection. She waits for what feels like an interminable time before she dares to use her phone, afraid that someone will hear her voice, that the light from the display will give away her location. Then she calls Blessed, because it's the only thing she can think to do.

She counts the rings. Six, then Blessed's voice, blurred with sleep, answers. She must have fallen asleep over the order books. It happens to Amber all the time.

316

'Blessed, it's me.'

'Who?'

'Me. It's Amber. It's Amber, Blessed.'

'No,' says Blessed. The line goes dead, and she is alone in the dark.

She can't stay here. She wipes her eyes, crawls out into the night. The road is empty. In the distance she can hear the monotonous thump-thump-thump of the nightclub strip, hear the shrieks of Whitmouth's holidaymakers, unaware of the fear in their midst, celebrating their liberation from the threat of death. Her foot throbs, but takes her weight. She starts down the road towards town, dodging round the pools of light beneath streetlamps, pausing at corners to scope the road ahead. There's only one place she can think of to go.

It takes her an hour. In daylight, in safety, without injury, it takes half that, though the walk along the A-road is so unappealing that she only normally does it when the buses aren't running. She pulls up her hoodie and dips her head, looks at her feet as she limps and hopes that passing headlights will not illuminate her features for long enough to make her recognisable. On the seafront, her progress slows to a crawl. She shelters in doorways whenever a figure approaches, feigns fascination with window displays and advertising cards. The town is crowded, but she feels naked, exposed: the only person fully dressed, the only one sober, the only one alone. A group of lads surrounds her, drunk and laughing, gurning with slack lips into her shrinking face.

'ALLLL *RIIIGHT*, Grandma!'

She recoils, heart thudding, but they don't recognise her. Of course they don't. They're not locals; come from Yorkshire or Lancashire if their accents are anything to go by, and they've been drinking all night, not scouring the internet for breaking news. She's probably as safe here as she would be anywhere, among the young and careless. And yet ...

They must be somewhere. Her neighbours have not gone home, she knows it. Too worked up, too excited, too full of righteous anger. They're stalking the town, staking out the police station, waiting for her to make her move. Nowhere is safe; not really. But at least she knows somewhere with gates, and locks, and security, even though they are designed to protect valuable assets and safeguard ticket sales, rather than people.

She sees the sign ahead: the garish lights turned off for the night, but the staff entrance still bright and welcoming. Funnland. The closest thing to a home she has left. The turnstiles are long since locked down, the ticket offices plunged in darkness. She feels as though the waters have closed over her head. She's been off sick for a week and the only one who's shown any interest in her welfare is Blessed, but even though Blessed is clearly done with her now, it's the only sanctuary she can think of. Surely Blessed can't turn her away if she's actually there.

A hundred yards to cover. The crowds on the pavement have thinned, for there's little to entertain a teenager on this strip once the park is closed. Amber instinctively tugs at the string of her hood, pulls it up over her chin. Shows nothing to the world but huge, frightened eyes.

She reaches the staff gate. Feels in her pocket for her swipe card, feels a rush of relief as her fingers close easily over it. Jason Murphy sits in the security-office window, reading. Not looking up. Good.

She runs the card through the reader. It emits a hollow, dead boop. She pushes the gate and finds it still locked. She swears under her breath, and tries the card again. Same sound. No cheery beep of ingress, no comforting clunk of lock, no grind of opening hinges. The card has been disabled. She is locked out.

She feels eyes burning her back, and looks up. She's got Jason's attention now all right. He sits with his chin in his hand, a faint smile twisting his mouth, and watches her discomfort. She raises a hand, points at the gate. Jason doesn't move. Just watches. Amber shows him her card, shrugs out a signal of confusion and mimes pressing a button to get him to let her in.

Jason's smile turns into a nasty grin; triumphant, gleeful. He shakes his head. Then she sees him reach over and pick up the telephone. Their eyes meet.

Still looking at her, he begins to speak. She sees his lips form the syllables of her name. Amber Gordon. Annabel Oldacre.

She turns away and hobbles down the road, towards the beach.

Chapter Forty

Jim falls asleep quickly – wine and tiredness and the stress that comes with hope – and Kirsty lies awake, staring dry-eyed at the streetlight on the ceiling. Somewhere out there in the night, the drama is playing out and she has no idea how it is unfolding. Knows only that she is afraid, that she wants to pack up and run, to distance herself from any evidence that she has ever been to Whitmouth.

I am such a fool, she thinks. Such a fool. The first time I saw her, I should have run. Should have called the probation people and got what had happened on record: put myself in the clear, established myself as a victim of extraordinary coincidence. If they ever find out now, if anyone ever puts the two of us together in that café, I'm screwed. And Jim's screwed and Sophie's screwed, and Luke, and their worlds will crash to the ground and they will never, ever trust anything – no situation, no story, no appeal to kindness – again. Everything I have done, every attempt at reparation, every moment of following rules and obeying instructions and being good and penitent and kind, wiped out in an instant by one stupid, crazy impulse of curiosity.

Tomorrow, she thinks. When we go up to Jim's mum. I'll call in to work and sign off till it's over, whatever 'over' will mean. Bird flu. Typhoid. Hepatitis B, meningitis, doesn't matter what, as long as it's catching and no one will want me near them. I'll keep away from Whitmouth, pretend I've never seen the place. I'm good at that: at dissembling. I've been doing it all my life.

On the bedside table, the phone springs to life. Bright light and the rattle as it starts to dance across the polished surface. Jim stirs, grumbles, turns over. Kirsty seizes hold of it, looks at the display. A number, no name. She doesn't need a name. It's Amber.

She sends her to voicemail. Seconds later, the phone rings again. She's not even paused to leave a message. Oh God, thinks Kirsty, how do I get that number off my call history? They'll check her phone records; they're bound to, aren't they? No, why should they? She's not done anything wrong in twenty years. Apart from telephoning me. She presses the Reject button again, goes hot as, without delay, the ringtone restarts.

'God's sake answer that,' mutters Jim. 'Trying to sleep.'

Kirsty gets out of bed, slips into the *en suite*. Doesn't turn the light on, as the sound of the extractor fan will wake him further. Sits on the lavatory in the windowless pitch-black and, when the phone starts to vibrate again, answers in a whisper.

Amber's voice – panicked, whispering too – over the drag of waves on pebbles. She's on the beach. Must be. 'You've got to help me.'

'Where are you?'

'Please. They're looking for me.'

'Where are you?' she repeats. She has some idea that she'll block her number and call the police, call Stan, call Dave Park, and send them down to collect her.

'You've got to get me out of here.'

'No!' The word bursts from her mouth like a bomb. 'I can't, Amber. You know I can't,' she adds. 'It's crazy. A crazy idea.'

'I'm not – Jesus, you don't understand. There's – there's a *mob* out there. They broke my windows. They killed my *dogs*. Jade, they're going to kill *me*.'

'Please,' says Kirsty, 'you're not thinking straight. Tell me where you are and I'll send someone. I'll get the police to come and pick you up.'

'Don't be stupid,' says Amber. 'The police are Whitmouth people too. You tell them, and ... You've got to get me out of here. I have no one else to ask.'

'I can't. You know I can't. Amber, if I come down there now, if I'm anywhere near you, they—'

'I'm not fucking asking you to ... throw a party, you silly bitch. Just ... for Chrissake, you've got a car, haven't you? Just come and get me. Take me somewhere else. It doesn't matter where. Take me up the motorway to a Travelodge and book a room and leave me. It doesn't matter. I'll work out what to do after that. But I have to get away from here. Don't you understand? The minute it's daylight, I'm dead.'

'No,' says Kirsty. 'No, I can't. You know I can't. Tell me where you are. I'll send someone.'

She hears a tiny, tinny scream at the other end of the line. Thinks for a moment that it's already too late, then realises that it's a sound of frustration. 'NO!'

'I'll do what I can,' she says, 'but I can't do that. I won't. It'll all be over for both of us, you know that.'

'Kirsty,' says Amber, 'you can't leave me here. I'm begging you. You have to help me.'

She struggles to stay firm. I can't do this. It's too much. She's asking too much. They'll know. They'll know it was me, and they'll know who I am. I can't. It's not my fault. I wasn't the one who chose to ... it's not *my* husband who ... 'No,' she says. 'No.'

Silence. Breathing. Three waves roll up the shore, suck away again. 'You have to,' Amber says again, and her tone has changed.

Kirsty is enraged. Who is she, this woman, to tell me what to do? She's not my boss. She's not my friend. She's the cause of everything, the reason I've had to live a lie my whole life. I owe her nothing. Nothing at all. 'No,' she says firmly.

Amber's voice has gone hard; emotionless. When she speaks

again, it's with cold authority, the authority Kirsty remembers so well from the day they killed Chloe, when she took over and started issuing orders. 'No, but you do,' she tells her. 'Because you're involved, whether you like it or not.'

The implicit threat makes her angry, defensive. 'What do you mean by that?' she snaps.

'Fuck you, Kirsty Lindsay. If you don't help me, I'm calling them all. Every single one of them. All of them, do you get it? Every newspaper, every TV station, everybody I can bloody think of. And then it won't be just me any more. Do you understand? Do you understand what I'm saying? They know who I am already. I have nothing to lose. If you won't help me, then I swear to God they're going to know every single thing about who you are too.'

Chapter Forty-one

Martin is woken by the sound of an argument. Forgets, in his discomfort – he's been sleeping sitting up in the van's cramped driving seat for hours – where he is for a moment until the sight of the neat suburban road, neat suburban cars parked in neat suburban driveways, restores his sense of place. He raises the peak of his cap and cranes round, to see Kirsty Lindsay standing beside the little Renault, bag over her shoulder and keys in her hand, deep in disagreement with her husband. Gingerly, not wanting to make them aware of his presence, he cracks open the window and listens.

'I don't believe this,' says Jim. He's not put anything on his feet, and clutches his dressing gown over the boxer shorts he's worn to sleep in since Soph hit the toddling stage.

She opens the car door, throwing her overnight bag on the back seat. She's no idea whether she'll need it, but the habit is so ingrained after years of news-driven changes of plan that she is barely able to go to the supermarket without loading it for luck. 'I'm sorry,' she says. 'I have to.'

'No you don't,' he says. 'You *don't*. They *know* you're on holiday. Why did you even answer the phone?'

She takes the lazy option and throws the blame back in his lap. 'You *told me* to answer the phone. And anyway, *you* always answer the phone.'

'Well, that's different,' he begins. 'My mum—'

He catches the look on her face and stops. In the course of a marriage, you learn that there are subjects it is unwise to broach. Kirsty's untethered status is one of them. She feels keenly the habit that people from loving backgrounds have of assuming that those from bad ones have no emotional attachment to them. He remembers the ferocity of her reaction the first time he pulled the 'It's all right for you' line, and knows it's a potential deal breaker. He gulps back the words when he hears her sharp intake of breath.

'Sorry,' he says.

'That's OK,' she says eventually. He wonders if she'll use his carelessness as a weapon. Feels he'll probably deserve it if she does. 'I'm sorry that I don't *have* a mother of my own to worry about,' she adds, 'but funnily enough, I *do* worry about yours.'

The ball's back in his court. 'So much so that you're bailing on going to see her tomorrow,' he says. 'She's been looking forward to this for ages. You know that.'

'And I told you. I'll catch up with you as soon as I can. I've just got one job, Jim. I don't have set hours and holidays and a pension. All I've got is my willingness to adapt. It's really, really tough out there at the moment. People are giving up all over the shop, you know that. We need the money. I can't turn stuff down.'

Christ, I'm even convincing myself, she thinks. 'You've not got a job in the bag yet,' she adds sharply, and sees him recoil as though she's slapped him. God, oh God, she thinks. All that work, all that care I've taken not to mention the elephant in the room, not to undermine his confidence, not to make him feel unmanned in unemployment, and I've blown it all apart with one simple sentence. It'll take us months to get over this. Months. And he'll never know I did it to protect him.

He's silent for a moment. Then: 'I can't do much more of this,' he says.

Kirsty slams the car door and rounds on him. 'More of what, Jim? More of *what*? You don't seem too upset when people tell you they've been reading my stuff in the papers. You don't mind showing off your insider knowledge at dinner parties, do you?'

A light goes on in a window next door. 'Shh!' hisses Jim. 'Keep your voice down!'

She's been inflaming the argument as a means of leaving without telling him too much. Persists. Jim can't bear the neighbours knowing their business. He'd sooner bleed to death in the kitchen than make a spectacle of himself by going outside with a knife in his guts.

'*What?*' she replies aggressively.

'The neighbours,' he says.

'Well *go inside*, then!'

He knows it's hopeless. She's not going to be talked out of anything. He still can't believe she's taken a phone call at two in the morning and simply got dressed and headed for the car, but he's known her long enough that he can tell when there's no point arguing. He knows, too, that she's not telling him the whole story. Has known it over and over again through the course of their relationship, the way her eyes glaze and her jaw sets when certain subjects come up. She's a fucking oyster, he thinks. And she can be such a bitch when she wants to head a subject off. And I'm so soft that I just let it pass because I don't want to distress her, even though everyone knows that sometimes you have to lance a wound to let it heal. I've got to change. Once I've found a job and the balance is restored, I've got to toughen up, or we'll be skating round stuff in our eighties. I love her so much, but sometimes I think we've only got half a relationship.

He shakes his head. Turns back to the house. 'OK. Well, there's no point arguing. Just so you know. I'm not happy. I'm pissed off, actually. You promised you'd be here, and I'm not happy.'

She almost relents. Remembers Amber's threat and finds herself torn in half. 'Jim,' she says.

'Whatever,' he says.

'Come on. Don't let's ...'

'I'll see you in Hereford, *eventually*. Keep me posted. If that's not too much trouble.'

'I'm sorry,' says Kirsty. 'I'm sorry.'

'Sure,' he says, before he closes the door. 'Sure you are.'

Kirsty waits in the drive until the hall light goes off. If I carry on lying like this, she thinks, we're going to be in trouble soon. He's not stupid. Tolerant, but not stupid. I see him, sometimes, wondering, when he looks at me. It's only because he's such a gentle soul, because he doesn't want to push me, that we've survived this far. I'm so lucky I found him. I can't think of another man who'd leave me alone like this.

She gets into the car, pulls out the phone. It takes a few rings for Amber to answer, and when she does, it's in a low voice, as though she's afraid of being overheard.

'It's me,' Kirsty says. 'I'm on my way.'

She hears Amber inhale heavily, hears tears in her voice when she answers. 'Oh, thank you,' she says. 'Thank you.'

'Are you safe?'

'Sort of ... I think so. I'm on the pier. At the end.'

Kirsty sees her in her mind's eye, huddled on the benches in the bullring of faded Edwardian amusements beyond the train terminus, her face periodically lit by the orange warning light on top of the shabby helter-skelter. Maybe I *should* call someone, she thinks, do her a favour by betraying her. But no: there's no way she can call anonymously, not in a world where phone calls are routinely traced. And just because it would be the better thing to do doesn't mean that Amber will see it that way and keep quiet about her.

'It's going to be an hour and a half. Will you be OK?'

'I hope so,' says Amber. 'No one ever comes here at night. The gates are locked. I used my Funnland ID card to break through the lock on the staff entrance. It's only a Yale.'

'OK,' says Kirsty. 'I'll be there as soon as I can.'

She hangs up and turns the key in the ignition. She has no idea what she's going to do once she gets to Whitmouth. Hopes she'll drown her rage and resentment long enough to formulate a plan on the long drive over. Otherwise, God knows, the chances are that Jim's wish that she'd open up more might come appallingly true.

Martin watches the Renault back out of the drive and start down the road. He puts his seat upright and starts his engine, but leaves the lights off as he pulls out of his parking space, to avoid alerting her to his presence. Waits till she's turned the first corner before he pulls out and flicks on his beams. The roads are empty enough at this time of night that he will have little trouble finding her again, and he figures that the most powerful weapon he will have when they reach their destination is the element of surprise.

4.15 p.m.

The gate is locked and an electric fence runs through the hedge. The farmer's keeping sheep on the field this year, and everyone knows that sheep are a bugger to keep in. The gate, meanwhile, is rickety: half off its hinges, all splinters and creosote, the cross-bars too close together to allow even their undersized bodies to slide between.

'Right, well,' says Jade, 'we'll have to climb over.'

She eyes Chloe appraisingly. The kid seems to have gone wobbly in the last fifteen minutes, as though her legs are losing the ability to hold her up. Has fallen down every hundred yards, and takes longer, each time, to get up.

'You should take that thing off,' she says, tweaking at the strings on the anorak. 'You must be boiling.'

Chloe is sluggish, unresponsive. She seems to have lost the will even to cry. Even when she caught her shin on the barbed wire two fields back, she let out little more than a dull moan of pain. Only another four fields till we reach the river, thinks Jade. A good thing. I don't know what to do with her. I think she's getting ill.

She has severe doubts that they will find Debbie at their destination, but they've come this far and the shrieking, splashing party that takes place on the Evenlode every afternoon of the summer is the nearest source of help she can think of. She and Bel unzip the anorak, peel the passive child out of it. Her thin white arms are covered in bruises, her skinny-rib top stained with sweat. For the first time they see that her hair is a bright, golden blond, curls plastered to her scalp like astrakhan. She staggers slightly; her eyes seem to have gone blank. She snatches the jacket from Jade and clutches it to her chest like a teddy bear.

'Come on,' says Jade, in a tone more gentle than she's used all afternoon. 'See over there?'

She points to a line in the grass that emerges from the woods to their right and slashes across the heat-scorched meadow. 'See it? That's the stream. When we get there, we can have a paddle and a drink. Cool you off a bit. And then we just have to go along it till we get to the river.'

Chloe looks ahead without interest. 'Come on,' says Jade again. She puts a foot on the bottom rung of the gate, grabs the top to show how it's done.

'I'm not sure ...' says Bel.

'Don't be stupid,' says Jade. 'I've been climbing gates since I was three.'

She's not sure how much truth there is in this statement, but she knows she's been doing it for years, and anyway, it's not as if climbing gates is a highly rated skill. Besides, there's no other way through she can think of, short of breaking it down. She scales the gate like a ladder, swings her leg over as though she were mounting a horse. Sits astride it, looks down at the others. 'Easy-peasy,' she says. Swings her other leg over and drops to the ground. Chloe stares, her mouth half open.

'Go on,' prompts Jade. 'Give her a hand.'

Bel shuffles the kid forward. Her feet seem to be made of concrete. They drag and catch on the ground as though they're too heavy for her legs. Bel gets to her knees and lifts one of Chloe's feet on to the bottom bar. Tries to clamp the child's hands on three bars up, but Chloe refuses to let go of the anorak. After several goes, Bel unpeels a single arm and hooks it through the rungs. 'See?' she says. 'It's like a ladder.'

Chloe just stands there. Presses her face into the anorak and inhales, deeply, for comfort. Stares at Jade like she's visiting the zoo.

Eventually Bel puts her hands under Chloe's bum and heaves. Unwillingly, the leg on the bar straightens up. The other just hangs in the air. The kid wobbles. Looks scared. Says nothing.

She's been silent since they waded through the dock leaves on the edge of the Hundred-Acre.

'It's OK. Go on. Put the other one on the next bar. You can do it.'

Bel stands up and leans her body against Chloe's, takes the weight against herself. Wow, she thinks again. I thought she was heavy before, but now she feels like a bag of sand. She unpeels Chloe's anorak hand and puts it on the top of the gate. It's a weak grip, for the child is pressing her elbow into her side so as not to lose the sacred garment. 'There you go,' says Bel. 'Almost there.'

It takes for ever to manoeuvre Chloe to the top. But eventually her crotch is on a level with the bar and she's wibble-wobbling at the hips. 'Lift your leg up,' says Jade. 'Go on. Just swing it over.'

Chloe looks down, as though she's noticed the ground for the first time, then she bends at the waist and lies the length of her body along the top bar. The anorak slips between her torso and the gate; a sheer, slippery base to take her weight.

'Come on,' says Jade. Chloe stares at her, frozen. Grips her perch with chunky thighs.

'Oh, come on, Chloe!'

Bel has a rush of rage. Doesn't know where it comes from, just knows that she wants this afternoon over. She's sick of being patient, sick of the way her day's turned out, sick of thistles and cowpats and nobbles of hardened earth that get into shoes, and can't bear the sight of the kid any more. She wants her off the gate. She jumps forward and shoves, with all the strength she has left.

Chloe slithers round the bar and pitches forward, head-first, through the air.

It seems like a very long time until she lands.

Chapter Forty-two

He guesses almost as soon as they set off that she is heading for Whitmouth and, with the radio rolling news out constantly as he drives, he's got a pretty good guess as to what is bringing her there. By the time they arrive, at half-past three, he almost feels cheated. Every journalist in the country must be converging on the town right now; there's not a hope of getting her alone, and it's clear to him that, whatever it is he plans to do – and he's not entirely clear in his mind what he *does* plan, just that she won't enjoy a moment of it – he needs to be alone with her to do it. He's tempted to throw the towel in for the night, to go and get some sleep, because after all she'll still be here in the morning, but then she does something that surprises him. Instead of leaving her car in her usual slot at the station, or checking herself in at the Voyagers Rest, she continues straight on down Brighton Road and into the town centre. Intrigued, he follows her.

It's slow going. A fine drizzle hangs in the air and the bars are closed, but the town is full of people. And not the usual young crowd, but middle-aged men and women with determined faces and cricket bats. Even through tightly closed windows, he can feel that the atmosphere is as thick as soup. He smiles as he understands that the whole town has heard the news about Amber Gordon. Couldn't have happened to a nicer person, he thinks.

They seem to be concentrated around the police station, though someone stands on virtually every street corner they pass. T-shirted, muscle-bound men with necks like tree trunks and arms that bulge their seams; women whose default expression, from early youth, has been disapproval. They stand, still and watchful, glaring into the dark as though expecting a squadron of Daleks to materialise from thin air. Outside the police station there's a gloomy, angry party going on beneath the blank gaze of shuttered doors. Press, of course, in search of the morning scoop – but more, far more, ordinary people. His neighbours, roused from their dens by the scent of the hunt.

He expects Kirsty to pull up somewhere near by, but she carries on driving, crawling past the massing bodies, winding her window up as she goes, as though she expects to be robbed. Martin frowns and drops back a few yards. They're the only vehicles on the road, and he doesn't want to have come this far for her to spot him now.

Kirsty drives slowly, wonders if she has something – a scarf, a stole, a hood – in her overnight bag with which she can hide Amber's face, if she finds her. There's no way they'll make it back through town without it, with all these eyes staring suspiciously through her windows as she passes. As she approaches the sea, the crowds thin out. A few stragglers from the bars lurch through the escalating rain, but down here they're not looking at anything other than their own feet. The Corniche itself is an empty sea of fast-food wrappers and cigarette butts. Even the death-burger van has moved up to Brighton Road to make the most of the unexpected glut of customers. Maybe, she thinks. Maybe we just might get away with it. If I put her in the boot, or lying down on the back seat.

She pulls in to the loading bay at the foot of the pier and kills the engine. Cracks her door and realises that, for the first time since she came to Whitmouth, she can actually hear the sea more than she can hear anything else. It sounds huge as it thunders on to the beach, dragging great cobblestones one over the other with its suck. To disguise the sound of a sea as wild as this, the daily cacophony must be more deafening than she had realised. She scans the road as she feels for her bag. A couple snog against the window of WHSmith, but otherwise the Corniche is empty. As she pulls on her jacket, a white van cruises slowly past and pulls in to the space vacated by the burger van. She peers through the distortion of rain on windscreen, but sees no one get out.

She grabs the phone off the passenger seat, slides it open and hits redial. It thinks for a moment, flashes up the number, goes blank.

'Shit,' says Kirsty, out loud. Presses the Call key again. Nothing. She's made the most basic of schoolgirl errors: forgot to plug it in to charge before she got into bed, despite the fact that she's been melting the battery all day.

'Shit,' she says again, and slams her hand down on the steering wheel. Fights back tears. Closes the window and allows herself a moment of release by screaming at the top of her lungs. 'Shit! Shit! Shit! Shit! *Shit!*' She can't call, can't tell Amber she's here, can't verify her whereabouts, can't organise a rendezvous. The pier gates are closed, high, forbidding, the rain beginning to step up, and Amber, if they've not found her yet, is counting down to Kirsty's destruction.

I don't want to go out there, she thinks. I'm afraid.

Then she opens the door and steps out into the night.

Martin watches in his rear-view as she gets out of the Renault. She stands beside it and stares up towards town. And then, as if she's satisfied that she's unobserved, she wheels on her heel and hurries past the foot of the pier on to the beach.

He's caught off-guard. He'd been expecting her to go up to where the people are. Can't believe she's cut him an easy break like this. He rushes to get out of the van, closes the door as quietly as he can behind him. If she's really down on the beach, the noise of the sea and her feet sliding on weedy pebbles will drown out most sounds, but there's no sense in being careless. He jogs up the road, stays in the shadow of the Funnland fence and, pressing himself against the corner strut, peeps round the corner.

Her ears are pricked for sounds of company, but all is quiet, just the roar and rag of sand on shingle and the moan of wind in the wires of the switched-off fairy lights along the front. Twenty feet along the pier, small and inconspicuous, there's a gate, let into the metal slats of the fence, which cleaning teams and maintenance workers use to get on and off the structure out of hours. Kirsty jumps on to the shingle, feels a stone slip over another beneath her foot and goes down on her knees. 'Fuck,' she mutters; looks over her shoulder with wild fear that she will have been heard. Stupid trainers: not made for any surface less steady than a tread-mill. She steps carefully the rest of the way, holding on to the fence as she goes.

It looks locked. Is locked. But closer inspection shows that the lock is a Yale, more there for show than blow. She digs her Oyster card – she learned not to use her debit card for this sort of thing years ago – from her bag, slips her hand through the bars and has it open in seconds.

She looks behind her once more, checks that the coast is clear and steps through, pulling the gate to behind her, then limp-runs up the short flight of stairs to the pier top. Squinting through the gloom at the long walkway in front of her, she sets off to walk to the end.

Once again he feels the tug of an erection. The blood pumps as he watches her fall on the shingle, struggle to her feet and feel her way into the shadows under the pier. He's really on to something. Whatever the outcome, it's a win-win. Either Amber Gordon is hidden away somewhere out there in the dark and Kirsty Lindsay is walking up to find her, or she's not there, and then Lindsay will be up there alone.

He hears the sound of a gate opening and footsteps mounting metal stairs. She's found the service entrance and is going up to the boardwalk. Martin smiles. Perfect, he thinks. I can't lose her now. There's only one way on to the pier, and only one way off.

The little faux-steam train that plods its way up to the pier's end and back from eight in the morning until the last patrons of the amusement arcade run out of fifty ps has been parked up in its shed, the doors secured with a chain-and-padlock extravaganza. It's a quarter of a mile to the end. An easy walk under normal circumstances, less so when the boards are slippery with mounting drizzle and you don't know what you'll find when you reach your destination. She might not even be there. She might have fled already, found some other hiding place and be waiting for your call.

Come on, Kirsty, she tells herself. Get a grip. It's a quick in-and-out and once you've got her somewhere safe you'll be safe as well. Never have to see her, speak to her, think of her again.

She starts to plod, wraps her scarf tightly round her head. Only August and the air, as she heads out to sea, is as dank as a cellar.

She hears her own footfalls, thick on the night air. Her nose is running. What am I doing? she wonders. This is the stupidest thing I've ever done. Corrects herself. Second most stupid. But in this case, I don't have a choice. Because it's not just me, is it? I fucking hate her now. I pitied her before, thought we shared some understanding, but now I hate her. Maybe I should just go back up into town and tell those zombie-people on the corners where she is. She can't talk if she's dead, after all. If I let her die, my problems are over ...

She shakes her head, dismisses the thought. This is not who I am. I'm not like that, however much I'd like to be.

The railway line is punctuated by tiny, pointless stations,

all white-painted iron and panes of greenhouse glass. Like everything here the pier is a relic of more elegant times, when travel abroad was only for the rich and their servants, and lawyers and doctors would come here and take their pleasures among the grocers and butchers. Now, the elegant lines of its railings are hidden by garish advertising hoardings. The moon filters weakly through a gap in the clouds, showing up the fact that half the windows of the station-stops are broken. A gust of wind drives raindrops against her cheek. The weather is getting worse.

She hears a sound behind her: metal hitting metal. The gate?

He waits five minutes – times it by his watch – before he follows her through the gate. No need to stay close. He knows where she's going, after all. He crouches below the wall and sees her head, silhouetted above the railings at the top of the steps, turn left and walk out to sea. Then she's gone, all sound buried by the crash of the waves.

He takes a chance and scuttles, crabwise, into the shelter of the pier. Now there's no way she'll glimpse him. He's safe and hidden and she has no idea he is behind her. He has a sudden urge to laugh out loud. Slips and slides to the gate and gives it a push. She's left it on the latch and slipped a torn-off piece of the cardboard backing of a spiral-bound notebook between latch and frame. He hasn't expected it to give, and fails to stop the gate from swinging back against the fence behind. Grabs it just as it hits, but not in time to prevent the clank of metal ringing out into the air.

Martin stoops down and waits, statue-still, at the bottom of the steps.

Kirsty ducks in behind the building. Waits, breathing shallow, and watches. Nothing. No one emerges from the staircase. Just the flutter of a poster advertising the magician whose matinées are the council's contribution to calling the shack at the end of the structure a theatre. You're jumping at shadows, she tells herself. Because you know what you're doing is stupid. Because you got yourself scared out of your wits the other night in Tailor's Lane, and now you're expecting to be followed.

She crosses over the railway line and carries on along the other side of the tracks, as though doing so will somehow cover her progress.

I hate you, Amber Gordon. When I see you, it will be hard to be civil, however frightened you are, however much you need my help. Because of you, I too am afraid. Because of you, the corrosive, acid terror of discovery is eating away at my mind, eating away at my marriage. I love him. Oh, God, I love him, and you don't care. It wasn't me who killed her, Amber, it was you.

A blustery gust snatches at her scarf, leaving her gasping at the sudden bitterness of the sea-wind. How this town ever managed to be somewhere people came for pleasure is beyond her imagination. The boards are slippery, and there are tools and materials lying around where the walkway is being mended. Bloody great hammers and crowbars, lying about for anyone to find.

Over halfway now. She can't shake the feeling that she is being watched. CCTV? She hasn't noticed any cameras, but it's practically compulsory to have them these days. But Amber's been up here for a couple of hours now, though; if she's still here, then no one's turned out to turf her off. Either there aren't any cameras, they're not working or not manned.

Of course you think you're being watched, she thinks. Because being watched would mean the end of the world. Stop it, Kirsty. It's a situational fear, not a real one.

But she stops and looks behind her again anyway. An empty walkway, the steps to the gate barely visible in the distance. Stupid, she thinks. I've never been any good at telling the difference between imagined dangers and real ones. Perhaps if I had, we wouldn't be in this situation.

*

He crawls on hands and knees to the top of the steps and looks out on to the boardwalk. She's not come back. Stupid woman's walking on, has crossed to the other side of the railway track to make his own progress easier. All he has to do now is duck-run ten feet to the cover of the station, and he can follow her as closely as he likes.

The moon breaks through the cloud for a second and makes a river across the sea. For a brief moment, Whitmouth looks beautiful, bathed in mournful light, the starkness of the Sixties blocks behind the seafront softened by the encroaching haar. Then, as quickly, another gust of wind slaps pinprick raindrops into her face, sends her scuttling for the shelter of the penny arcade's stingy awning.

Deep darkness inside; machines hunched and lurking, the floors damp and sticky, awaiting the arrival of the dawn cleaning team. Two huge pillar ashtrays overflow on either side of the double door. As she huddles below the five-inch overhang, the heavens open like someone's turned a tap on, and rain starts to sluice through the gutters. The sea changes mood; the dull roll and suck becomes a growl of annoyance. She feels the ground tremble beneath her feet.

Kirsty dashes the last fifty feet and hits the central square. It's empty. No sign of Amber, just full bins and empty benches. She splashes to a halt, looks wildly around. No one. Only herself and the beating rain, and the flashing light on the helter-skelter. The theatre looms, Edwardian-grand, in front of her, box-office windows like black eyes, Marvo the Magnificent sneering, twenty feet tall, from a poster. She half expects to see Amber sheltering beneath the canopy, but the area is empty.

'Shit,' says Kirsty out loud, rain running off her face. Knew I should've stayed at the car. Knew I shouldn't have come. She could be bloody anywhere. For all I know the police have taken her in and there's no need to be here at all ...

She opens her mouth and yells at the top of her lungs. Yells to be heard over storm and sea and the flapping canvas of the tarot tents among the flowerbeds, the clatter of something caught by the wind behind the arcade. 'BEL! BEEEELLLLL!'

Movement, out of the corner of her eye. She whirls, ready to defend herself, sees that the front door of the cruddy little wax-works has come open. Amber's head appears: frightened, hopeful.

'Fuck!' shouts Kirsty and splashes over the boardwalk, into the dry.

Chapter Forty-three

It's called Dr Wax's House of Horror, and it is well named. The place has a musty smell of damp cloth and hopelessness, and the sight that greets her as she plunges through the door is a tableau of an execution at the guillotine. It's dark, lit by emergency lighting, and faceless forms loom from murky niches in the side walls.

The rain drums on the tar-paper roof and the floor shifts with the surge of the sea. Like being on a boat, she thinks, in a harbour, midwinter. 'Where did this come from?' she asks, peering through the gloom. 'It was just drizzling when I got here.'

'It happens all the time. It's called the Whitmouth Wilding. Something to do with the Thames Estuary and the North Sea.'

'We can't go out in this.'

'No,' says Amber. 'But it'll die down in a bit. It never lasts long. Come on.'

She leads her between the heavy velvet curtains that divide the lobby from the main hall. The hall is cramped and crowded, lit eerie red; faces familiar-but-not-familiar stare frozenly into a mysterious otherworld, eyes blank and mouths forever frozen on the edge of words. More tableaux, more savage now they've passed the entrance hall: a man stretched on a rack, his face a screaming rictus; a Cambodian peasant holding a plastic bag – the striped kind, the kind you get from corner shops every-where – over the face of a man in a suit; First World War soldiers wallowing in mud and barbed wire. MAN'S INHUMANITY TO MAN, reads the banner stretched from wall to wall. And all for an entrance fee of £9.95 inc. VAT, thinks Kirsty. A bargain.

'Good God,' she says, 'it's a cocktail party in hell. I'd've been crapping myself if I'd had to wait in here.'

Amber laughs humourlessly. 'Strangely enough, I was crapping myself *before* I got here. To be honest, they're the best company I've had in days.'

She slumps on to a cushioned seating platform in the middle of the room. 'Thank you for coming,' she says. 'I don't know what I would have done.'

Kirsty's anger returns. 'Well, you didn't give me much choice, did you?'

Amber looks away, ashamed. 'I'm sorry.'

Kirsty glares at her. Amber looks back, and meets her eyes. 'I *am*,' she assures her. 'I'm sorry. I didn't know what to do. There are people looking for me, everywhere, and no one to help me. I *needed* you.'

Kirsty remembers the crowds in town, the home-made weaponry and the absent police. Walks to a bench a few feet away and sits down. She knows that what Amber has said is true, but she doesn't want to be near the woman. Doesn't want to have to look at her.

'How was your drive?' Amber asks suddenly, in a bright social voice, as though Kirsty has simply turned up for brunch.

'It was fine.' Kirsty is amazed at the teatime voice she uses in return. 'The roads are good at this time of night, of course.'

'Yes,' says Amber. 'We – Vic and I – we always left at this time of night, when we went to Wales. Took about half the time, he reckoned.'

'Right,' responds Kirsty. It takes a couple of seconds for her to register that the Vic Amber refers to so casually is the same man that she and her colleagues are already automatically referring to by his formal title, the Alleged Seaside Strangler, Victor Cantrell (the 'Alleged' to be dropped after conviction, of course). She sees

Amber's face fall as she remembers her reality. She's behaving like my mother-in-law, thinks Kirsty, after Jim's father died and it hadn't sunk in completely yet. She'd talk about things they would do together, opinions he would hold, things he'd said, and then her face would fall in the same way, and awkwardness would grip the room. It was a good couple of years before she, or anyone in her presence, could mention his name without the grief closing over their heads.

This must be how it is for Amber, she thinks. The same bereavement, without the sympathy. A widow's state is essentially a noble one; there is no such solace for the intimates of the notorious. I was so busy crying for myself, all those years in Exmouth, that it never occurred to me to think about my family. It's only since I had Soph and Luke that I've thought about what it really must have been like for them.

'What was in Wales?' she asks.

Amber sighs. 'Oh, nothing, really,' she says. 'We just used to go there, sometimes. In the off-season. The Pembrokeshire coast. He – Vic – went there once with some needy kids' scheme. He liked it there. Liked to go back.'

'Yeah, it's beautiful down there,' says Kirsty.

'You've been?'

They're making conversation out of discomfort, the small-talk essential to fill the chasm between them. This is beyond abnormal, thinks Kirsty. We're talking like strangers on a bus. Come on, rain, stop, God damn you. I don't want to be here, doing this.

'Jim's grandparents retired to Saundersfoot. He's got a lot of good memories.'

'Jim . . . ? Oh, yes. Your husband,' says Amber distractedly.

Kirsty remembers again the circumstances that have brought her here. 'Yes,' she says pointedly. 'My husband.'

'What did you say he does again?' Kirsty hears echoes of Bel's silly, social mother in the question. Talking constantly to keep intimacy at bay, training her daughter but never loving her.

'It doesn't matter what he does,' she replies impatiently. 'It has

343

nothing to do with you. But if you're going to ask questions, I'm going to ask one back. Did you mean it?'

'What?'

Amber sees the look in her eyes and understands her meaning. 'Oh. My threat. Do you want an honest answer?'

'Yes. If you can give me one.'

'OK. Then – I don't know. I'm sorry. Probably not. I don't think I'd've got anything from carrying it through, do you?'

Kirsty isn't really listening; is more intent on sharing her feelings than on hearing what her blackmailer has to say. 'Jim doesn't deserve that. I can't believe you'd do it. Nor my kids. What have they ever done to you?'

Amber breathes deep. 'Nothing,' she says.

'So, what? It was revenge against me? Because of what your husband's done, you'd destroy mine?'

'I'm sorry,' says Bel again. 'I'm sorry, I really am. I'm sorry I did that to you, but I was—'

'Oh, I don't care about *me*,' Kirsty interrupts.

Amber looks sceptical. 'Sure.'

Kirsty subsides. They eye each other suspiciously and listen to the wind. 'Well, I'm here now,' says Kirsty eventually. 'What do you want me to do with you?'

Save my life? thinks Amber. It's just a small thing, but—

Somewhere in the back, a door bangs; keeps banging. Kirsty jumps, stares at Amber, eyes wide in the gloom. Amber looks calm. This is weird, thinks Kirsty. This isn't how I'd be, if I were her. It's as though the fight's gone; as though she can't be bothered any more.

Amber shakes her head, as though she's forcing thought back into it. 'It's OK. I sort of – had to break in. I thought it was better to do it round the back. The latch is probably a bit kaput now. That's all it is.'

Kirsty raises her eyebrows.

'What?' Amber looks irritated. 'Kirsty, I was *cold*. What did you want me to do?'

'It's OK,' says Kirsty hastily. 'It's all right. Sorry.'

'I guess we should shut it.' Amber gets to her feet.

'Yes. We should.'

Beyond the main hall, where Hitler jostles Stalin and Kim Jong Il jostles Mao, the museum splits into a series of rooms off a narrow, red-painted corridor, the signage above their doors denoting themes like MASS MURDERERS, PLAGUES and TORTURE. Amber leads the way with surprising confidence, Kirsty following timidly behind, glancing as she goes into the dark spaces beyond the doorways. Anyone could be in here. Anything.

The corridor ends with a fire door. Through it, the drumming of the rain and the roar of the sea comes louder, like a distant crowd. On the floor to their side of the door, a small puddle of water. The open exterior door bangs monotonously behind.

'Wow,' says Amber, clocking the water at her feet, 'serious rain.'

She pushes the fire door open and wet wind bursts through, buffets their faces. Beyond, a storeroom-cum-rec-room: a shabby modular settee, a coffee table, discarded mannequin body parts piled in corners like the aftermath of battle, a coffee machine (switched off), polystyrene cups flying through restless air. On the far wall, the door flaps uselessly back and forth, knocks against a Formica-topped table pushed against the wall. Amber strides forward, catching a faceful of salt spray, and forces it shut.

The sudden quiet is almost deafening. 'Well,' she says. 'Nothing wrong with the lock, anyway. Phew. I was worried I might have damaged it.'

Kirsty laughs nervously. 'We've already broken in, Amber.'

Amber gives her a look. 'There's a big difference between breaking and entering and trespass, Jade. How did you get to be so wet behind the ears?'

She leads the way back into the corridor. The water seems to have spread. There's a trail of it leading all the way back up to the main hall. I must still be dripping, thinks Kirsty. Jesus, it's wet out there.

'Oh, by the way,' says Amber, suddenly, 'we're in here. Did you know?'

Kirsty quails. 'Really?'

'Yuh.'

'Where?'

'We've got a category all of our own.' She gestures at a doorway to her left. It's labelled TOO YOUNG TO KILL.

'No,' says Kirsty.

'Yes. Fortunately they've not actually put us in with the kiddie-murderers. Though I'm surprised they didn't.'

Kirsty doesn't really want to look, but she is drawn inescapably to the doorway, hovers in it with sinking heart. Amber flips on the light. It's a poky little room, and contains few figures, which somehow makes it worse. Despite the fact that there are over a dozen murders by children each year, only five are represented here among the deliberately emotive trappings of youth – rocking horses and record players and party dresses on the backs of chairs – none of which she ever had. The same old five: John Venables, Robert Thompson, Mary Bell and, huddled conspiratorially by a five-bar gate, herself and Bel.

Kirsty walks over and studies her mannequin, feels her skin crawl as she sees herself again through the eyes of national condemnation. Five feet tall, it's been based on her school photo – the only photo anyone ever got hold of other than her police mugshot, mostly because there weren't really any others – but they've replaced the school uniform with a shapeless, childish dress designed to make the figure look even younger than her real years. The face is puffy, the hair cut in a pudding-basin bob, the lips turned down at the corners like an old woman's; an old woman who's lived a life of ill-humour and small-time cruelty. It's a crude facsimile, like those medieval lion sculptures you see in museums, made by someone who had never seen a lion, had just heard them described by sailors. And yet it's undoubtedly herself, most easily recognised by her proximity to the haughty, imperious blonde who stands beside her with a rock in her hand.

Jade Walker and Annabel Oldacre, reads the label. It is faded, the edges worn shiny by fingers over the years it has stood there.

Both aged 11, Walker and Oldacre shocked the world with the brutal murder of Chloe Francis, aged 4, in fields near the village of Long Barrow, Oxfordshire, on 17 July 1986. The girls had abducted the child by the village sweet shop and taken her to a number of locations, eventually bludgeoning and drowning her in a stream in the late afternoon. Chloe's body was covered in cuts, grazes and bruises, and three broken ribs and a dislocated elbow showed that they had subjected her to a day of brutal torture. Her head wounds alone were so ferocious she would have been unlikely to have survived them. To cover up their crime, the girls then callously buried little Chloe's body in woodland, where it was mutilated by wildlife – her family were forced to bury her in a closed casket – and feigned ignorance of their crime for days. Walker came from a deprived background, but Oldacre, seen by many as the dominant one of the pair, was the daughter of a prominent businessman and attended one of Britain's top boarding schools, leading the detective in charge of the investigation to describe her as 'the coldest creature he had ever encountered in all his years of police work'.

'Is that how we looked?' Kirsty asks, in a small voice. She still has difficulty associating herself with this long-ago child, the one who killed Chloe. 'Did I really look like that?'

'Christ,' says Amber, disgust in her voice. 'Does it matter?'

'Well, yes, I – no. It's just I … do you recognise yourself? From the things they say about us?'

'Every fucking day,' says Amber bitterly, and steps back out into the corridor. 'Don't you?'

'I ...' Kirsty turns away from the statues, finds them too painful to look at. Switches off the lights as though doing so will make the image leave her mind. 'We're never going to get away from this, are we?' she asks miserably. Hears a gasp that sounds like outrage from halfway down the hall.

'This?' cries Amber. '*This?* What do you mean, "*this*"?'

She steps out and sees anger and despair in her old conspirator's eyes.

'How come they ever let you out, Jade?'

'What do you mean?'

'You're in denial. That's what they always said to me. If I kept on denying it, if I didn't face up to my crime, they'd never let me out.'

'Well, yes,' protests Kirsty. 'Of course! God, I don't pretend for a minute that—'

Amber storms up the remainder of the hall, stamps back to her red velvet seat. 'Oh yes you do. Every day you pretend. Same as I do. Go on, then. Tell me who you don't pretend to? Tell me one person, apart from whatever trainee's been assigned to supervise your licence compliance this month? Go on.'

Kirsty can't answer. Amber has coloured up; spits the words out like they've been building for years.

'Your husband – what's he called, Jim? Ever shared it in your pillow talk? When you're strolling hand-in-hand on the beach at Saundersfoot? When he takes you out to dinner on your anniversary? How about then? Over the candles and the bruschetta? The oh-go-on-let's-have-a-glass-of-champagne? Well? Have you?'

'Don't, Bel. Please.'

'"By the way, darling, did I ever tell you about the time I killed a little kid?"'

'Shut up!'

'You think ... you think 'cause you've made something of yourself that it'll all go away? You think 'cause you've got a husband and kids and you go to Christmas services and drink mulled wine and no one knows about you, that that means it never happened? You can't wipe out history, Jade!'

'No!' she protests. 'No, I never … but, Bel! I'm not *her*! I'm not that girl any more! I'm not, and nor are you!'

'Bollocks,' says Amber. 'You'll be her for the rest of your life. That filthy little shit who killed a kid is right inside you. Better get used to it.'

Kirsty stands in the doorway and takes a deep, shaky breath. She's so angry, she thinks. I'm not sure I know how to cope with this. I find it hard to remember the child I was. What we did – it's like a dream to me. A horrible, ugly, remembered nightmare.

Amber lies down and throws an arm over her eyes. Kirsty checks her watch. Gone four o'clock. They'll need to get moving soon, storm or no storm. They can't rely on the weather to keep the cleaners away. She walks over, sits down and lays a hand on Amber's arm, a futile gesture of womanly comfort.

'I think about it every single day,' says Amber. 'You know? All of it. How it happened. All the stupid … oh, God. I remember her face every single day. That stupid fucking anorak, the way she looked. The mud in her eyes. Jesus.'

Kirsty has a flashback: Chloe's face vanishing beneath a double-handful of earth and leaves hoisted from the edge of the hole. She remembers an earthworm, surprised by sudden exposure to the evening light, squirming away, digging itself a speedy haven down beside where the child's ear was hidden. She's not forgotten. Has never forgotten. Sometimes, she has fantasies of violating the terms of her licence, of seeking out the Francis family, of trying to make amends. But how do you make amends? What possible payback could there be?

'We were kids,' she says.

'It's not an excuse,' says Amber. 'Adulthood is just more layers on top. Don't you wish that there was some sort of time machine? Some way to turn the clock back? Just … if we'd left her, at the bench. That's all. If we'd gone, "No, she's not our responsibility, let's just leave her." D'you remember?'

'Yeah,' says Kirsty, and smiles ironically. 'I said we couldn't leave her, 'cause someone might come along and kill her.'

On the edge of her field of vision, Kirsty thinks she sees a statue move. She sits upright and gasps; peers into the gloom, expecting the comfort of hallucination. She's exhausted; she's starting to see things. It's fine.

But no, it moves again. A slight, male figure steps out from among the murderous autocrats. At first she thinks he's a ghost; still clings to the hope that he's simply stepping out of her imagination. But when he comes into the light and she recognises the weird little man from the nightclub, she knows that he is real. And that he has heard every word they've said.

Chapter Forty-four

He's not hanging around. He makes a dash for the door. Catches his sleeve on Josef Stalin as he goes, bringing him crashing to the floor. Amber opens her eyes and sits up.

'Shit!' shouts Kirsty. '*Shit*, no! No!'

She doesn't think. Leaps to her feet and runs after him. Lunges at the back of his anorak and feels it slip, nylon-smooth, through her fingers as he throws himself out into the howling night. Amber still sits on the bench, stunned, uncomprehending.

'Shit!' Kirsty screams again, as the door bangs to.

'Who *was* that?' Amber sounds like she's emerging from a dream. She's not taken in the gravity of the situation. She's sleep-walking.

'It doesn't matter!' The door resists her attempts to reopen it, the wood is swollen and it sticks; and he's closed it with the force of flight. She struggles, heaves against it. 'I don't know! I don't know who he is! Bel, he *heard* us!'

The door gives and she bursts out into the rain. She doesn't wait for Amber to take her words on board; just hurls herself after him. My kids, she thinks. Oh God, my kids. I don't care about *me* any more. I don't. But oh, God, they're so young. They won't know what to do, their whole world crashing down around them. I'd do anything, God. Anything. I'd fucking *die* for them, God. I'd fucking *kill* ...

She sees the hem of his coat fly past the corner of the gift shop and takes off in pursuit. Horizontal rain and salt spray: it's going to be hell out there on the walkway, beyond the shelter of the buildings. But she goes anyway, her trainers sliding on oil-slick rainwater.

She rounds the corner and sees him twenty feet away, hunched against the rain as he runs. Eight paces away, just eight paces. But he pulls ahead as she approaches, and her feet won't give her traction on the boardwalk. 'Wait!' she screams. 'Stop! Please!'

He glances over his shoulder and Kirsty sees him fizz with fear and triumph. He hates me. I don't know who he is, but he's hated me since long before tonight, I can see it in his eyes. I remember him, in that shitty club. He's the man I thought was chasing me. I'd forgotten him, because what happened with Vic Cantrell had changed my mind, but I remember now. And he hated me then, he told me so. How long has he been following me? How long?

Over the sound of the wind, she hears the door bang open behind her. Amber must be following. Into the storm.

She steps up her pace and tries to catch up.

As she emerges, Amber skids on the greasy boards and feels her damaged ankle go out from under her. Lands on her back, slides across the square and fetches up against a bench, the wind taken from her. She squints against the driving rain, wipes the salt spray from her eyes with her sleeve and looks around. There's no one in sight. She is confused, panicked; it took her several seconds to register what Kirsty had seen immediately, and now she doesn't know what to do. After her fugitive night, her instinct is to run away, as far and as fast as she can. But there's only one way off this structure, and it's the way she knows Kirsty and the man have gone. She has no option but to follow. He's going to be running; he's not going to stop and chat, not with what he's found out. Not now he knows they know. Maybe they can get to Kirsty's car before he raises the alarm. She has to try. Has to keep hoping.

She pushes herself upright and looks down the walkway beside the chip shop. She can see nothing. Everything more than thirty feet away is a blur of wind and water.

She gets to her feet, brushes the wet off her legs. Tries, experimentally, putting her weight on her ankle, hisses with pain. She's never going to keep up. But she must follow. Limp after them.

And what then? she thinks. Even if we do get away, it's all over. Even if this man doesn't know who Kirsty Lindsay is, he knows we've seen each other and my licence is breached, and so is hers. I could deny and deny, I suppose, but where's the use? Maybe we can catch him up, persuade him he's mistaken. Maybe. Or maybe we can appeal to his good nature; convince him that Kirsty's kids' lives are worth more than his finder's fee from the *Mail on Sunday*. It's a slim chance, but it's the only chance we've got.

No chance at all. Amber knows her life is essentially done with; has known it since Vic was arrested, has wondered why instinct still drove her to fool herself that she had a chance. There's nothing, now: no freedom, no safety, no peace. The whole country has seen her adult face; shouting from their TV screens, snarling over their morning cuppa. She belongs to them now: the bogey-woman made flesh; public property once more. She knows she'll never walk in anonymity again.

Nonetheless, she sets off after them. Maybe there's a chance for Kirsty still. A chance for her children.

Martin is a buzzing mass of joy. He can hear her voice drifting over the sound of the sea, hear her desperation as she begs him to stop. This is the best thing that has ever happened to me. Tomorrow I'll be visible. Tomorrow they'll all know who I am. The man who uncovered the truth.

Excitement makes his body fleet. Normally, running, even a quarter of a mile of it, renders him weak and self-hating. Tonight, with the stirring sea-surge and the thrill of his discovery to spur him on, he covers the ground like a young gazelle; jumps the builders' detritus by the side of the railway stop without breaking his stride, races on towards fame and freedom.

He feels wild with power. His two worst enemies. Life drops a gift like this in your lap once and once only. Kirsty Lindsay: I *knew* there was something about you. I knew you were hiding something. But this? I never would have imagined it. There you've been, hiding in plain sight, probably been keeping up with *her* all this time, laughing in the face of the world. But you're going to get yours now. Oh my God, you're going to get yours.

He hears her bleat again over the wind. 'Wait! Oh, please! Please wait!'

He hears a scuffle, a clank, behind him, and hazards a glance over his shoulder. She's reached the building site, has hit something and fallen. Martin stops for a moment to watch her flounder. Throws his head back and laughs.

They're halfway down the pier now, and Kirsty continues to run, pushing herself through pain, feeling the tightening in her chest, the panic pounding blood through her jugular. Stop. Please stop. We can talk. We can work something out.

But bit by bit, she's gaining ground. She's never been a runner, but desperation lends her speed. I have to stop him. *Have* to. He reaches the building works at the station, skims over the top of them as though his shoes have wings. Her knee hurts where she banged it. She knows she's not going to be able to keep up the pace, that she's pushed beyond her capacity; but he's only six paces ahead now. If she could just slow him down. Make him stumble.

She reaches the pile of builders' rubbish, tries to vault it as he has. But her foot catches on something – some metal thing, half hidden in the dark – and suddenly she is falling, hands out to catch herself. Lands on a pile of timber, her hand slipping down the side and landing on something with rough metal edges. She feels a stab of pain, then her hand closes, instinctively, over it. It's heavy and curved: two short lengths of tube, set at right-angles to each other, with bolts protruding from their ends. She knows, without seeing, exactly what it is: a coupler, the heavy metal joint that links the struts of scaffolding, makes the structure strong. She knows all about scaffolding. She and Jim spent eight hard months with it cladding the house when they first moved in and discovered that they'd bought a home with subsidence.

The thought of Jim makes her jerk her head up, makes her stare down the walkway, expecting to see Rat Man's retreating back a hundred, two hundred yards ahead. To her surprise, he's still there, standing just the other side of the works, his arms folded pugnaciously, laughing. 'Jade!' he shouts. 'Jade Walker!'

She feels a surge of rage. The memory – ingrained, festering – of being that girl. Of being singled out in the schoolyard over ancient slights by long-gone siblings; of adults chasing her off wherever she settled; of barred doors and hungry nights; of the father with the brutal hands; of the vicars-teachers-case-workers who turned their faces to the wall. It all slow-burns inside her, ready always to ignite. Being Kirsty is her control, her safety; the one thing that stands between her and the savagery of her past.

'No!' she shouts, buffeted by the wind, struggling to her feet. She is barely aware that she still has the coupler in her hand, that she's gripping it tight enough to bruise, her fingers full-stretched to hold its bulk. 'No! I'm not! I'm Kirsty Lindsay! Kirsty Lindsay! I'm not *her*! I'm *not*!'

'Jade!' he repeats, and points at her; the priming gesture of the schoolyard bully.

'Don't say that!' she shrieks. Her legs carry her towards him through the tempest. She no longer harbours hopes of reasoning with him; no longer thinks of anything other than the gloat on his face, the triumphalistic bray of his laugh. 'Stop it! I don't know her! I'm Kirsty. I'm not her. I'm not *her*!'

'Yeah,' shouts Martin Bagshawe, flushed with victory, mouth wide with hilarity. He's never felt so alive, so electrified by his own power. 'But you will be tomorrow, won't you?'

She swings her arm at the gaping mouth, to shut him up.

Chapter Forty-five

The rain begins to weaken as quickly as it picked up. Shuffle-jogging up the boardwalk, Amber almost trips over them before she sees them. And then they're there, beyond the heap of scaffolding poles, in the shelter of a pile of boards. She sees Kirsty's back first, hunched over as though she's crying. She thinks initially that he has got away: that she's given up in despair and resigned herself to mourning. And then she sees the legs, the white sneakers, the toes pointing up at the racing clouds above.

'Oh God,' she says, and stops, dead. Kirsty doesn't notice her at first; she's bent over him, staring at his face. Sick and weak, Amber gets into eyeshot and sees that the man on the floor is Martin Bagshawe.

She gasps. Kirsty hears, whirls round, white-faced. 'I didn't mean to,' she says. 'I didn't ... '

Amber covers the last few steps, and stands behind her. 'Oh Jesus. What's *he* doing here?'

Martin is snoring. Though she recognised him from a distance, she sees now that the whole of the left side of his face – the side that was away from her as she approached – is stove in like it's hollow, broken teeth scattered in the pooling blood beneath his ear.

'You know him?' asks Kirsty.

She shrugs the question off. Immaterial. 'Jesus,' she says. 'What did you hit him with?'

'I don't . . . I . . .' Kirsty looks down at her right hand. Sees the coupler still gripped in her palm and flings it away as though it has turned red-hot in her hand. It clatters across the boards, comes to a rest in the gutter. 'I didn't . . . Oh God,' she says. 'He's OK, right?'

'No,' says Amber. 'He's not OK.'

She drops to her knees beside Martin and feels for his pulse. It's slow, but it's there.

'I didn't mean to,' begins Kirsty. 'I didn't realise I . . . Oh God, what are we going to do?'

Martin draws a blubbery, wet sigh through his mangled mouth. He's not breathing through his nose, because his nose is smashed sideways like plywood. She must have hit him with the full force of her arm.

'What are we going to do?' she asks again.

'I don't know. I don't know.' Amber's trying to think, trying to brush away the memories of how her mind worked all those years ago. We've not got any woods to bury him in, that's for sure.

'Where's your phone?' asks Kirsty.

She looks up, startled. 'Why, Jade?'

'Kirsty,' she protests. 'I'm *Kirsty*. We need to call an ambulance. He . . .'

'And then what?'

'I can't just . . . We can't just . . .'

She is wringing her hands like a little kid, hair plastered down over her forehead, middle-class-mum jeans-and-jersey uniform clinging to her body.

The decision goes *snap* in Amber's head like the gears of a machine meshing into place.

'You're not thinking straight, Kirsty,' she tells her. Imbues her voice with all the authority she can muster. 'You need to leave.'

Kirsty reels as though she's been slapped. 'What?'

'Go on. Go.'

Kirsty is dazed. Looks at Amber with empty eyes.

'I can't. I can't. Look what I've done. *Look!* Look at him!'

Amber is surprised by how calm she feels, now her decision is made. 'It's not too late,' she says. 'If you go now, nobody need ever know. If I say it was me, they won't even bother to ask.'

Kirsty's mouth is open. She looks from Amber to Martin Bagshawe, his snores wetter and thicker and slower as the blood spreads across the weathered gloss paint. The first glimmers of sullen dawn are creeping through the clouds. The early shift will be up, soon, making their way to town with their mops and buckets and casks of bleach. 'I—'

'Don't,' says Amber. 'Just go.'

They face each other in the silver light. Beneath their feet, the suck-and-drag of a turning tide, above their heads, the shriek of seagulls getting up to seek out the remnants of the night. Go, thinks Amber. Just go. If you wait much longer, I won't be able to go through with this.

Kirsty looks like she's going to cry. Takes three long breaths and wraps her arms around her body, as though her ribcage hurts. And then she turns on her heel and runs away along the boardwalk.

4.30 p.m.

There's a crunch as Chloe's head hits the hardened mud. Jade and Bel brace themselves for the howl to come. Instead, silence drills into their ears. Hot-day country silence, filled with larksong, the shush of the breeze that stirs the treetops, the lackadaisical trickle of the stream across the meadow and, in the far distance, the laughter of their neighbours as they duck each other in the smooth-running Evenlode.

Each has the same thought: Oh God, I'm in trouble now.

Chloe lies still like a discarded doll, her head thrown back, her right hand at an impossible angle against her shoulderblade. She's bleeding: from the nose, and from the split in her scalp: a slow brown ooze filled with lumpy snot and viscous, transparent matter. Her mouth is open. So are her big blue eyes.

'Chloe?' Bel is the first to speak. Her voice wavers, like she's short of breath.

Chloe gives no reply. Just lies there and oozes.

'She's unconscious,' announces Jade, though she's only ever seen the state as a result of alcohol before, and the two look quite different.

Bel rushes to the gate, hurdles it and drops to the earth beside the body. 'I don't even know if she's breathing,' she says. 'Oh God, Jade, I think she's really hurt.'

Jade just stands there. Bel glares up at her and swipes at her leg with a dusty hand. 'Jade!' she shouts. 'Help me!'

Jade becomes suddenly animated and throws herself down beside them, grabbing Chloe's hand – the one on the ground, not the one that lies beneath her back – and presses a thumb over the inside of her wrist like she's seen the medics do on General Hospital. She feels nothing, but she doesn't know what she's feeling for, and anyway the beating of her own heart drowns everything else out. 'Chloe?' she says. Then repeats the name in a louder voice, as though this will somehow make a difference. 'Chloe?'

She searches her mind for other things she's seen people do with the unconscious on the telly. 'Cold water,' she says.

'What?'

'If we throw water in her face, it'll wake her up.'

Bel has no experience of unconsciousness. But the assertion has the ring of sense. Certainly, a faceful of cold water would wake her up if someone threw it at her.

'We've nothing to carry it in,' she says, looking over at the stream. It's a couple of hundred yards; there will be no chance that a running child could bring more than a few damp drops in their cupped hands.

'Well, we'll take her to it, then' says Jade. 'Come on.'

Bel eyes the silent rag doll doubtfully. 'I don't want to touch her. Look. She's all over blood.'

Jade surprises herself with how practical her responses are, how matter-of-fact. 'All right,' she says. 'You take her legs. I'll take the top.'

Bel still looks queasy. 'Her arm. That arm looks … please don't hurt her arm.'

'I think the damage is already done,' says Jade.

The field is full of thistles. Jade has Chloe under the shoulders, her head flopping groundwards; sees body fluids smear themselves on her skirt and thighs, feels the scratch as she walks backwards through the plants. I won't forget this, she thinks. This is a day I will remember all my life. She catches her heel on a tussock, staggers and almost goes down. Chloe's head bounces, rebounds off the ground. Jade shivers as she feels the horrid scalp bash itself against the front of her knickers.

'Oh God, let her be all right,' pants Bel. 'D'you think she's all right? We need to get a grown-up. A grown-up will know what to do.'

Jade almost drops her end of their burden. 'Are you mad?'

'What do you mean?'

'Look at her, Bel. Look at the state of her! They'll put us in prison.'

Bel's red face gets redder as she grasps the gravity of their situation. 'But ...' she protests, 'it was an accident. We'll tell them. It was an accident.'

'Yer, right,' jeers Jade. 'And they'll believe us, yeah?'

'Why wouldn't they?'

'Because my name's Jade Walker, for a start.'

'But I—' begins Bel.

'But you nothing. You're with me. Everybody in this village's been saying it's a wonder a Walker hasn't killed anybody yet. No. We need to get her woken up, and then we need to work out what to do next.'

Chloe emits a sort of gurgling exhalation. The girls looks down, each filled with a surge of sudden optimism; see the blue lips, the rolling eyes, and feel it drain away. 'C'mon,' says Jade. 'We can wake her up. I know we can.'

She lifts the shoulders once more, and Bel takes hold of the ankles. Now they are trying to jog with their burden, tussocks impeding their way, the sun harsh in Bel's eyes. They reach the edge of the stream. Low, cliff-like banks and a gritty, shallow bottom. A few feet to their left a cattle-wallow; the bank broken down on either side and, in between, a wide pool deep enough for large wet noses to drink their fill without having to strain out mouthfuls of mud. Jade nods towards it and the girls turn up the bank.

The field has been stocked recently. The slope is slippery, the floor six inches deep with grey-brown mud, the air thick with flies and cow-pats. They lurch down the slide with their burden, and find themselves having to drag their feet from the mud as it sticks to their soles. Jade loses a shoe, mutters a curse beneath her heaving breath. Wrenches backwards and lands on her arse, up to her neck in the water.

361

Chloe slips from her grasp, lands side-down. Bel, stuck in the mud herself, wobbles, lets go, flails and, coming abruptly free, falls forward on top of the others. She feels Chloe's slimy face against her own, panics, thrashes in the murk, comes up gasping. Jade is down there, somewhere, forced underwater by the weight on top. Bel can see her feet kick, sees a starfish hand break the surface, grabs the wrist and hauls. Puts her weighted foot on a lichen-slippy rock and feels her feet go out from under her again. She lets go of Jade's wrist and tries to find the bottom with her hands, to push back to the air. Under the surface, it's particles and brown and bits of weed, the whoosh of bubbles stirred up by her struggling limbs.

She breaks the surface. Jade is on the other side of the pool, sliding backwards on her elbows, coughing and spitting, hair black with twigs and earth, a single mallow stem wound round her ear, the flower dangling, showy like a pirate's piercing, by her left cheek. She feels it, swipes at it, panicked, and flings it out into the middle of the water.

It lands on Chloe's half-submerged body. She is not moving. Her face is below the surface.

'Oh Jesus,' says Jade, and lunges back out into the pool. She grabs the back of Chloe's top and flounders back to the bank. Bel throws herself after them. Together they manoeuvre the child on to stable ground, look desperately into her face for signs of life.

There's duckweed hanging from her mouth, snagged on her gappy incisors.

'She's not breathing. She's not breathing!' Bel flops a lifeless wrist about; pats at lax white cheeks.

'CPR,' says Jade. She's seen it time and time again, on General Hospital. The dead springing, coughing and weeping, back to life under the pumping fists of paramedics. She pushes Bel away, leans both palms on Chloe's chest and pounds up and down from the hips. Keeps doing it, over and over, until, after five minutes, she hears something go crack inside and an oily bubble rises up from the child's parted lips.

Chapter Forty-six

She finds the crumpled remains of a packet of cigarettes in her pocket: three Camel soft-top, a miniature lighter tucked beneath the foil: Jackie's brand. She must have left them in here one of the many times she borrowed the fleece to go and stand in the garden. She looks at them for a moment, then thinks, Oh, what the hell. There's no one to tell me not to any more, and it's not as if I'm riding high on the longevity list.

She puts one in her mouth, lights it and inhales deeply, filtering out the ugly optimism of the dawn. It's stale and harsh, and makes her out-of-practice brain stagger under the force of the nicotine. She has to lean one hand against the station wall for a few seconds, to stop herself falling down. Goddamn, she thinks. You hardly notice the effects if you do it all the time, but tobacco is powerful stuff.

Martin stirs and utters a gurgle of mindless humanity. Amber looks down, sees that his blood has almost reached her feet. She steps back, repelled, and takes another drag on the cigarette. If he's still bleeding, his heart's still beating, she thinks. I have to wait till it stops. I need to be certain he's dead before I call.

On the seafront, she hears a car engine start up, the crunch of tyres as it pulls out of its parking place. That'll be her, she thinks. Please don't let her change her mind. There's been enough waste already. Our lives, this shrivelled, bitter existence, it has to stop at some point. The cycle of revenge and punishment and passing it on to the next generation, it has to stop. I won't let it spread out, destroy her nice husband, those clean, safe little kids. What good would it do? Who would it help? Society. I know. Society. But let's face it: society doesn't really care who it blames, as long as it blames someone.

She takes another drag and walks over to where the coupler lies, blood and skin and hair entwined among the bolts and the butterfly nuts. The iron has been painted red against rusting, flakes chipped off where it's seen impact. She picks it up, two-fingered, and dangles it in front of her face, strangely fascinated. Bet this won't go down so well with Health and Safety, she thinks. Bet someone will lose their job over this.

She leans her arm out over the guardrail, and heaves the weight of the coupler out into the air. Watches as it spirals downward, is caught by a wave and sucked beneath. She can see it sink for a foot or so after it enters the water; is impressed that the Whitmouth brine is clean enough to allow any visibility at all. The sea will do its work. Nothing remains unscoured for long in those endless, restless depths. Even if they look, if they find it, if Kirsty's fingerprints are still on it, there won't be anything else to link her to the crime.

A sound attracts her attention. Martin has started to fit, there on the floor. His heels drum like pistons on the wood, fingers bone-straight and brittle. It won't be long now. Even if she does call an ambulance, the chances that he will survive, she thinks, remembering the deaths she has seen before, are slim; his skin is blue and what remains of his lips are drawn back to show his wisdom teeth. But she's not going to. There will be no one to bewail his passing, she's sure of that, and if she's going to make this sacrifice, she wants to ensure that it is not in vain.

She finishes the cigarette and drops it after the coupler. A gull swoops down in hope of a tasty titbit, sweeps on with a shriek of disgust. To her surprise she finds herself smiling. I should make the most of these last few minutes, she thinks. I suppose this is the last time I shall ever see the sea.

There's a bench beside the station: white-painted wrought iron, a lovely view of Funnland. Beyond the walls, her friends – her erstwhile friends – will be finishing up: wiping down the final surfaces, packing away their gear with a yawn and a sigh of relief. She sits, and surveys the view: flags and bunting, the blue-and-white of striped canvas awnings, the shine of rain-soaked stones catching early-morning rays. Three tiny figures pick a slow route along the top of the rollercoaster: a maintenance crew, or some teenagers who got past Jason Murphy and are celebrating their sense of immortality. You're not much of a place, Whitmouth. But you're my place. The only place I've ever thought of, even if only for a while, as home. I shall miss you.

She lights another cigarette.

Another parting, a quarter-century ago. Amber remembers her mother, visiting her in the remand centre. Coming empty-handed, wrapped in cashmere, looking older. Bel attempts to throw herself into her mother's arms, and finds a hand extended, blocking her approach. 'Don't,' says Lucinda. 'Just don't.'

They're not allowed to be alone – Bel is slowly understanding that she will never, to all intents and purposes, be alone again – but the crop-haired weightlifter in charge affords them what privacy she can by sitting on the far side of the rec room. Bel sits on a stained, armless, tweed chair with tubular steel legs. Lucinda, after scanning her options, picks a moulded grey-plastic chair beside a table four feet away and perches on it gingerly, as though she is afraid of infection. Both seats are fixed to the floor: a precaution against fighting. She puts her bag on the table, leans an elbow watchfully on the strap, even though they are the only people there. Crosses one knee elegantly over the other. She wears graceful wedge-heeled boots in green leather.

'How are you?' She doesn't sound more than politely concerned.

Bel responds as she's been trained to from earliest childhood. She fixes a bright smile on her face and says, 'I'm very well, thank

365

you. How are you?', as she has said to everyone who has asked her since the day of the murder. Lucinda is her first visitor – or the first one she knows personally, anyway – since the trial.

'Well, I'm glad to hear it,' says Lucinda. 'I'm glad to hear *you're* very well.'

Bel's eyes fill with tears.

Lucinda pulls a face. 'Oh, stop being such a baby,' she says.

Bel hangs her head and seeks composure. Her mother has never liked displays of emotion; not from Bel, anyway.

'How is everyone?' she asks eventually.

'How do you expect them to be?' replies Lucinda.

'I don't ...' says Bel.

'Michael almost divorced me,' says Lucinda. 'But, thank God, he's changed his mind. He understands, you see. That I can't be blamed for what you've done.'

'I'm sorry,' says Bel, humbly. Looks down at the worn cuffs of her sweater, wonders how much longer this visit will last.

'Anyway,' says Lucinda, after a pause. 'I just came to let you know we're leaving. Going to Singapore.'

Bel doesn't answer. It's already clear to her that it's all over, on the outside, that the house is locked up and the family fled. No one has made much effort to hide the press coverage from her; she's seen the boards over the windows, the steel grille on the door, like the burnt-out wastes of Broadwater Farm. The Walkers have been rehoused, their names changed, the younger children taken into care and the eldest scattered to the winds. Her own people – there's less help from the state if you've got bank accounts. Less interference, too.

'The bank's transferred him,' continues Lucinda. 'Kind of them, really. But then again, he's good at what he does. Popular, too, though I don't suppose you'll appreciate that. Anyway, that's it. I dare say we won't come back. So that's us, condemned to life as international gypsies, thanks to you. I thought I'd tell you. Let you know.'

'OK,' says Bel passively. In a way she feels relieved, knowing more clearly what the future holds. They're not going to fight for her. She's on her own.

'Right, well.' Lucinda starts to root in her bag. For a moment, Bel has a wild thought that she might have brought a gift. A keepsake for the years ahead, some small token that will remind her that she did indeed once have a family. Her mother's hair, usually immaculate, is unruly, tied back in a ponytail, roots showing among the candystripe blond. She's developed lines, she notices, around her mouth, in the six months since Bel last saw her. I did that, thinks Bel. It's all my fault.

Lucinda finds what she is looking for, brings it out: a handkerchief, embroidered: her initials in one corner. She blows her nose delicately; brings her oversized sunglasses down from their perch on her head and covers her eyes.

'At least your sister'll get some chance of a normal life,' says Lucinda. 'Without people knowing. People looking at her. Wondering.'

'Yes,' says Bel.

'How could you do it, Annabel?' she asks.

'I don't know,' she says. 'It wasn't meant. We didn't mean to – it just *happened* ...'

'Oh, for God's sake.' Lucinda dismisses the crime as though it were some petty gossip, some vandalism, some schoolyard scrap. 'Not *that*. For Christ's sake. I mean those lies. All those lies about Michael.'

'They weren't lies,' she says defiantly. 'I told you. I told, but you wouldn't listen. They weren't lies.'

Lucinda doesn't want to hear it. Has never wanted to hear it: not about the cellar, or the stables, or the late-night visits when her mother is deep in Valium dreams.

'I tried to tell you, Mummy,' she says, 'but you wouldn't listen.'

And she won't listen now. 'Oh, for God's sake. He *paid for your lawyer*, for God's sake. How could you do something like that to him?'

'Mummy—' she tries one more time.

'Oh, shut up. I just wanted to tell you, that's all. What I think of you. That man's brought you up since you were a toddler. He took you on out of the goodness of his heart. He's given us everything. I can't *believe* you'd repay us like that. How did you get to be like this, Annabel?'

You taught me, she thinks. I learned that lying was the best chance I had. She stares and shakes her head. There is nothing to say. Nothing that will be heard, anyway.

In the corner, the corrections officer turns a page of *Woman's Own* pointedly. Lucinda glances at her, then gets briskly to her feet. 'I'm done,' she commands. 'I'm ready to go now.'

The woman slowly puts the magazine down and starts to pull her keychain from the pocket of her navy trousers. Her expression is inscrutable; the expression of someone who's storing every detail for later dissection. Lucinda turns back to Bel, gives her the Look again.

'Dear God,' she says. 'You always were a little liar. From the minute you could talk.'

She wheels on her elegant green heel and marches towards the door. The officer points at Bel's chair. 'Stay there,' she says.

The door bangs to behind them.

A cigarette is at its most delicious in damp sea air. She rests against the station wall and savours every last lungful. Waits as the lights on the front fade to insignificance and Martin releases a final, surrendered sigh. He's gone, thinks Amber, and Jade is safe. No one to tell, no one to see.

She takes her phone from her pocket, dials 999. Looks at the watery sun as it leaps over the horizon, gets out the last of the cigarettes, crumples the pack and puts it, tidily, in her pocket. 'Hello,' she says, calmly, when the operator answers. 'I need help. I think I've killed someone.'

She lights the last of the cigarettes, sits back and waits.

Epilogue

Jim's mother goes up to bed and they do the washing-up. She's aged noticeably since their last visit, and seems relieved to hand over the chores, though she has always been one of those old-fashioned women for whom late rising, public displays of emotion and leaving the washing-up are all, if not mortal ones, sins nonetheless. She'll be eighty in a couple of years, thinks Jim. I wonder how long she can keep this house going for. Maybe we should be talking to her about her plans, before she gets too frail to make them.

Kirsty washes and he, still knowing his way round the kitchen of his childhood, dries and puts away. Kirsty is quiet. Has been all day. She must be exhausted, he thinks. Apart from her nap in the car while I drove us over here, she's barely slept since the night before last. She stands on one foot as she scrubs; dangles her sandalled other to take the weight off it.

'How's the knee?' he asks.

'OK,' she says. 'A bit hurty.'

'I'll get you some ibuprofen,' he says. 'I'm sure Mum's got some in the bathroom.'

'That would be nice,' says Kirsty. 'Thanks, sweetie.'

Jim puts down the dishcloth and makes his way as quietly as he can to the bathroom. It's all so familiar. Same old Flower Fairies on the hall wall, same old umbrella stand by the front door. At what point in life do you stop buying things? he wonders. He loves the stability of his mother's domain: the memories in every chair, the china picked out with his father before their wedding and cared for and husbanded so that the service is still intact nearly fifty years later. But he doesn't remember them ever doing the acquisitive thing that seems to be expected of you these days. By the time he was aware of his surroundings, they'd reached a point where they only went to the shops to replace things when they actively wore out. They never spent their time combing country-house sales looking to upgrade, or threw out curtains simply because they'd tired of the pattern, the way he and Kirsty do.

He tiptoes past his mother's room and lets himself into the bathroom. White tiles, cautiously chosen to not reflect the vagaries of fashion, dark green lino, sink and bath and toilet plain white and still good a hundred years after they were first installed. The room smells of lavender and talcum; old-lady smells, he would think, except that it's how his parents' bathroom always smelled, one of the earliest scent memories he possesses. He is suddenly filled with nostalgia; a strange nostalgia for something that still, after all, *is*. What if she has to move out? he thinks. If she has to move down to something smaller, has to choose which belongings to take with her? I think it would slay me. I think I'd want to cry myself to death.

He opens the mirrored door of the medicine cabinet and shuffles through its contents, feeling, as he always does when he goes through other people's stuff, a bit like a burglar, like a snoop. His mother is taking statins, he notices. He must remember to ask her about them tomorrow. And how her arthritis is. The first night is always such a rush of news and greetings and suitcases tucked beneath beds. They rarely get on to the family stuff until all the details of his schoolfriends' parents' funerals are out of the way. He finds the ibuprofen, tucked in with the Rennies and the Night Nurse and the Sudafed; tips a couple into his hand and takes them back to the kitchen.

Kirsty has finished the crockery and is on to the casserole dish; scrubs with a level of concentration that he knows from experience is a sign of tension. We've not talked yet, he thinks. Another piece of talking that's been sidelined by the necessity of action. I hate parting on a quarrel. The 'sorry's need to be said. He comes over and holds the pills out in his hand. Kirsty takes off the rubber gloves, wipes a strand of hair out of her eyes and takes them.

'Thanks,' she says.

'You didn't say how you did it.'

There are shadows under her eyes and her expression is faintly haunted. Jesus, she's tired, he thinks. I must make her stay in bed tomorrow morning, even though she gets embarrassed about doing it here. 'Oh, stupid,' she says. 'That bloody shingle beach. I don't know how anybody gets up it without breaking a leg.'

'The beach? You were on the beach?'

A touch of colour crosses her complexion. 'Oh, don't worry, Jim,' she says. 'There were loads of people. I'm not going anywhere by myself in Whitmouth ever again.'

'Well, thanks for coming home,' he says, and touches her shoulder. 'It means a lot to me.'

For a moment she looks like she's going to cry. 'Yes,' she says. 'I'm sorry. I'm sorry, Jim. I'm a bad wife.'

'No.' He gazes into her eyes, wills her to believe him. 'You're a wonderful wife. I'm just sorry I shouted.'

'I'll be better,' she promises. 'I won't do it again.'

'Shh,' says Jim, and puts his arms round her, there at the kitchen sink. 'Shh, Kirsty, it's OK. I'll be better too.'

'It's all of you,' she says. 'Nothing is more important than all of you. You must know that. I would never hurt you on purpose. You have to know that.'

He strokes her hair, shushes into her scalp. 'You're the best thing that's ever happened to me,' he says. 'You make me whole.'

The grandfather clock in the hall whirrs in preparation for a strike. He glances over her shoulder at the clock on the stove, sees that it is nearly ten o'clock. She always watches the news at ten; it's part of her emotional make-up, as essential to her routine as the news wires on the internet in the morning. 'C'mon,' he says. 'I'll make you a cuppa and we'll watch the news.'

She stiffens slightly in his arms. As he breaks away, he sees a strange look on her face, almost an unwillingness. He laughs, runs his palm down her cheek. 'It's OK, sweetheart,' he assures her. 'Once a hack, always a hack. I don't *really* want you to change. It was a— I was cross. I didn't mean it. You wouldn't be the woman I married then, would you? Go on. I'll be through in a minute.'

She goes off to the living room and he hears the sound of the adverts, blasting loud, at his mother's volume, for a moment, before she finds the remote and zaps them down. He puts on the kettle and hunts in the cupboard for a biscuit. He knows his mother always keeps digestives in the house. There's usually a cake, too, but even as an adult he still feels bound by the rules in place in his childhood. Cake is something you eat at teatime. Fruit's expensive; you have one piece after lunch, and cherries are counted out in batches of ten. Sweets are things you get after lunch on Sunday, if you've been good. If you're hungry, have a piece of toast. But don't eat too much, mind; you don't want to spoil your dinner. He smiles at the memories, feels comforted, as he always does, by the everlasting presence of his childhood. I can't imagine what it must be like to be Kirsty, he thinks; there's so very much to be made up for.

He finds the biscuits and puts four on a plate, puts the plate and the tea mugs on a tin tray with the Guinness toucan on it. His father must've half-inched it from a pub at some time, though he still finds it impossible to imagine that his parents could ever have had moments where scrupulous morals weren't observed. He makes two mugs of tea, sugars it up, nice and sweet, the way Kirsty likes it but rarely allows herself to have.

Really, this is what the big stuff of life is made of. It's not the holidays and the dinners out and the wish for more, it's about the cups of tea and the curling up together after a long day. It's about forgiving and forgetting and making allowances. It's about honesty and truth and trust, it's about making a place of safety and keeping the ones you love warm within it.

He takes the tray through. The room is dark: just the standard lamp in the corner, dust and old-fashioned tassels on the shade, and the flickering light from the television to light her serious face. She's on the sofa, knees pulled up and feet tucked underneath her, her arms wrapped around a cushion in her lap, watching. He puts the tray on the coffee table and hands her her tea; settles down beside her, thigh touching her toes, companionable. Some people in grey suits are shaking hands outside a white concrete building with flags.

'So what's the news?' he asks.

'United Nations. Pakistan. Security Council not doing its stuff. The usual.'

She wraps her hands round the mug as though they are cold; blows on it like a child. 'D'you want a biscuit?' he asks.

'Yeah,' she says. 'Go on.'

He smiles as he watches her almost dunk, then remember and stop. Though most New Year's resolutions fall by the wayside, she's stuck with this one, has a theory that you eat more of the things if you don't have to chew them. 'I'm glad you're here,' he tells her again. 'This is nice. Just ... you know.'

Kirsty unfolds a hand from her mug and puts it in his. Squeezes. They turn their attention back to the television just in time to see stock shots of Whitmouth seafront, some footage of police cars and jostling crowds, and a picture of that woman Amber Gordon, the one from last week whose plight made Kirsty so angry, while the voiceover intones. An arrest, this morning. A murder in the night, the suspect in custody, charges expected tomorrow.

'Jesus,' he says. 'What's gone on there, then?'

Kirsty is silent, her face a mask as she watches the scenes unfold.

'Oh my God,' says Jim. 'I don't believe it. I felt really sorry for her last week. Good God, I even felt sorry for her *yesterday*. Didn't I say so? God, Kirsty, didn't I?'

Still she doesn't speak, but nods robotically in agreement.

Jim puts down his mug. He feels as though every belief he's ever held – all his liberal pieties, his loosely Christian belief in redemption, his adamant conviction that a child cannot be labelled evil, however monstrous their acts – has been smashed with a sledgehammer. How could she? he thinks. How could she?

'Oh my God,' he says, surprised at the strength of his feelings. He feels as though he personally has been betrayed; as though Amber Gordon has come up and physically slapped him in the face. 'I don't know what to think any more. I really don't. How are we supposed to argue for the innate goodness of the human spirit when people like this ... How *could* she?'

He watches as police manhandle a female figure beneath a blanket up the steps of Whitmouth Police Station. They're not gentle, and the crowd is ill-controlled. He sees her trip on the first step, then she is hauled upright and practically thrown through the doors.

'Well, if it's true,' he says, 'bang goes everything I ever believed in. I guess I'm going to have to accept that it's true. That some people just are born evil, like they say. I suppose it's possible. I didn't want to believe it. But, God – like attracts like, I suppose. Hindley and Brady. Fred and Rose. Her and Cantrell – God.'

He glances over at his wife, surprised that she's so quiet. Normally she would be talking as much and as quickly as he is, watching a story like this. He's shocked to see that her face is wet with tears. They stream unstoppably down her cheeks, but her mouth is closed and her eyes, still wide, continue to stare at the screen.

'Oh, Jeez, babe,' he says, and enfolds her unresponsive body into a hug. 'I'm sorry. I know you've been fighting her corner. But it's not that bad. You're knackered. It's OK, Kirsty. I shouldn't have kept you up. Come on. Up you get. Let's go to bed. You need to get some sleep.

'Trust me,' he says. 'It'll all look better in the morning.'

Acknowledgements

Books never come into being in the solitary confinement of an ivory tower. I owe debts of gratitude to many people; I only hope I don't cause offence by failing to mention any of them.

Laetitia Rutherford and her colleagues at Mulcahy Conway Associates. A good agent is much more than the superficial job description. Laetitia's sharp brain, unerring ear, sound advice, dogged approach and, frankly, at some points, patient nurse-maiding, have honestly revolutionised my existence. I can't express my gratitude enough.

There are so many people at Sphere for whose knowledge, inventiveness and enthusiasm I have reason to be grateful. But particularly, of course, Catherine Burke and Thalia Proctor. Such a relief to find one's work in safe hands!

My dear friend John Amaechi, whose professional wisdom in matters of both child psychology and identity have been invaluable, as have his always-entertaining from-the-spotlight tales of media interpretation over the years.

Alastair Swinnerton, for a late-night flippancy that turned into a solution.

Mum and Bunny. No need to explain.

Dad and Patricia. Ditto.

William and Ali Mackesy, whose support and love have carried me a long way.

Cathy and David Fleming, for the same reasons.

In no particular order: Chris Manby, Antonia Willis, Brian Donaghey, Charlie Standing, Stella Duffy, Shelley Silas, Lauren Milne Henderson, Jo Johnston Stewart, Venetia Phillips, Claire Gervat, Diana Pepper, Chloe Saxby, Jonathan Longhurst. And the Board, of course. What's said there, stays there ;)